WATCHER IN THE FALL
Connections

Ronald Townsen

authorHOUSE®

AuthorHouse™
1663 Liberty Drive
Bloomington, IN 47403
www.authorhouse.com
Phone: 1-800-839-8640

First published by AuthorHouse   10/17/2011

ISBN: 978-1-4670-3807-2 (sc)
ISBN: 978-1-4670-3806-5 (hc)
ISBN: 978-1-4670-3805-8 (e)

Printed in the United States of America

Any people depicted in stock imagery provided by Thinkstock are models,
and such images are being used for illustrative purposes only.
Certain stock imagery © Thinkstock.
Library of Congress Control Number: 2011917217
This book is printed on acid-free paper.

Art for this book cover is provided by Ina. S. Townsen. www.ina-artwerks.net
Visit our web sites at www.WatcherInTheFall.com and www.TooBooks.com

All characters and events depicted in this story are purely fiction
and have no relation to actual people or events.

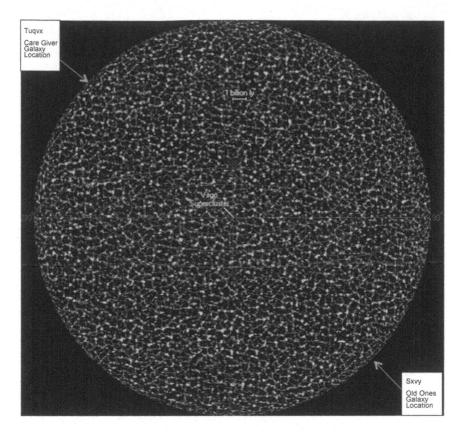

About the map. This map attempts to show the entire visible universe within 14 billion light years as found at *www.atlasoftheuniverse.com*. The Virgo Super Cluster is a cluster of galaxies that includes the Milky Way galaxy. For Reference purposes of this story, the galaxy of the Old Ones would be located in the lower right edge of this map and the galaxy of the Care Givers/Tern civilization would be located in the upper left edge of this map.

Dedicated
To my parents
Their love and support provided me the understanding of how to work
hard, be dedicated and to dream.

PROLOG

The pattern has existed before, an unknown number of copies exist now; it will exist into eternity.

It was born in the beginning of the universe; it is a child of other universes; it is the mother bringing forth a new universe.

It could not be seen, it could only be sensed. It is partly an invisible point but at the same time, a definer of the universe's structure and space.

It was a mother, but like its connected siblings, was simply a portal to gather and transfer energy for the next birthing of a new universe.

It is a fundamental pattern of every universe.

The pattern is a mix of connections across the many dimensions which define the foundation of the universe. Within one of the massive species of life, the pattern was known as a black hole although it is much more that the singularity and encompasses the complete definition of the basic structure of the universe and is part and parcel of dark matter.

Looking from what we perceive as the normal, to the molecule, to the atom, to the fundamental particle, to the foundation of bubbling energy of the mass of patterns that is the building base of all space, time and all other dimensions (called by some the quantum foam), is the lifeblood of existence, the very definition of existence, the essence, the blood of God. Quantum foam is a misnomer used to convey an image. It actually is much more of a continuous, complex dance of energy bridging between different points within the multiple dimensions. The energy flow is like the blood and the connection patterns, along which the energy flows. The links are like the blood vessels connecting points within the multiple dimensions of a universe. The points which support the energy flow and make up the patterns of the universe, defines the extent of the universe.

The black hole pattern that forms the basis of a universe's evolution, even if it could be measured, was formed in a location in our view of space and at a time that makes finding it almost impossible. It comes into existence and is the very foundation of a black hole/dark matter (BHDM) pattern and not just any black hole/dark matter pattern, but the first and every BHDM pattern as it grows and expands our known universe.

*The pattern is not unique; it was the same pattern definition that had funneled energy to form our universe. It holds an additional ability that evades most other transient patterns in our complex universe, it is connected. It isn't just connected to other patterns within our universe (that's normal across a number of patterns); it is **the** connection that across the universe links all the singularities known as black holes and dark matter to all other universes.*

The BHDM pattern formed and evolved throughout the life of the universe, the pattern is the connection. As patterns we define as basic matter are absorbed into a black hole, the actual pure energy which makes up the matter merges with the BHDM pattern, driving this unique pattern to its ultimate destiny.

The BHDM pattern is only a part of the mosaic that forms the Master Pattern. The Master Pattern extends across all universes and all patterns in every universe. The Master Pattern directs the birth and death of universes and everything contained in all the universes. It controls the birth, life and death of every atom, living creature, star and galaxy in every universe.

Each and every pattern is part of the ultimate mosaic that makes the Master Pattern. Each contributes to its evolution, its purpose. Each sub atomic particle that lives for only a fraction of a second, each galaxy that lives for billions of years, each leaf that falls from a tree and each civilization on each planet; all are just as important and all play a key part in the Master Pattern. Each can enjoy the discovery of its path in the life and each can wonder at the glory of the immensity and complexity of the design.

The Master Pattern is the manager of all, the master of all and it has a purpose.

CONTENTS

INTRODUCTION

With the explosion of energy that forms the universe, patterns evolve from the swirling and expanding formations. Patterns are the basis of the design and they exist from particles to volcanoes, stars to atoms. Some patterns are simple while others are complex building blocks that are the foundation of life itself. Patterns related to life extend from DNA to advanced animals; from foundations of the planets to the winds that blow through the leaves; from the seasons of the year to the colors of life. Some are the patterns of life itself, from the simple virus to the higher life forms.

Hidden in the complex patterns of life, exists a rare pattern. Rarer than diamonds, rarer than any mineral, the Watcher pattern is found perhaps once or twice in the life forms of most galaxies. The pattern builds from the intermix of DNA with the quantum foam in a dance that creates a unique ability that even the life form is not truly aware of. It drives their very actions and creates a unique path in their life setting them apart but giving them an ability that is one of the rarest in the universe.

Being a Watcher is one of the many patterns that's been defined by the path of the universe. The Watcher pattern evolves from the billions of years of mixing particles formed from the blast of energy that brought the universe into existence. Particles blended by the birth and death of stars are blown across the cold and seemingly desolate void of space by the beacon flash of radiation from the powerful and unknown forces of the singular points in space called black holes. The partical blends are spread by the intense explosions of dying stars or blown by solar winds from the billions of stars sending their very existence across known time and space.

The interaction of the particles defined by the dance of the bubbling foam across the multitude of changes of the complex dimensional structure we view as space-time, all came together with the formation of your genetic code and drove to shape the events of your life that made you a Watcher.

While the wind blows the fire from the trees and flashes the colors past the road, the trees shake in the thought of the winter which is on its way. The bright leaves mix with the proud stars and stripes as they are held at attention on the flag pole by the warning of winter soon to be blowing across the land. You watch as the summer fades to the fall that rushes to winter and the pattern of life evolves.

You watch as the thought of winter comes, the warm thoughts of cuddling up by a fire with someone special burst as flashes through the mind. Hopeful warmth in the heart keeps the cold at bay as you walk down the street. The wind tries to cut through the thin sweater as fall tries its best at identifying the loneliness of the past and tries to steal the thoughts of hope for a winter of love to remember as the pattern evolves.

You watch, but you are aware and constantly being reminded that you are different. While you are confident of the love of your family, a few people you call friends and the co-workers that respect you, you are not a person which the path of the universe has deemed to be like most. You are the Watcher; a fundamental pattern of the universe. Others are the people who enjoy life and know how to find someone that wants to be a part of their life.

You are a Watcher. Watchers like yourself are taught by life that you will not find the soul mate to share a laugh, understand your life, to allow you to be part of theirs and allow you to get to a close intimate point and want or need to be close to you. You feel you are not to have a soul mate that will be deeply connected to you. While you may find someone that could meet the needs, there will be barriers that will not allow it to happen. As your life fades back to the universe which has formed you for its own secret purpose, you are on the sidelines watching, always quietly watching and analyzing.

You are a Watcher. You are destined to see the emotions of others, but not allowed to share them.

You are a Watcher and a fundamental pattern of the universe; you are there to watch, support and help where possible. You are not destined to be like others. You will be alone with your thoughts, never having someone to listen to your fears and desires and give you the support that others gain from their close connections.

Being a Watcher, you are aware of the forces in your life. You see the connection from the very beginning of the known universe to the foundation of known time and space. You can connect the flow of time and particles to form the very life that you now live and the environment you watch. You can feel and understand from the perspective of a young child watching an ant farm, the dimensions that we view as space and time along with others we don't even normally sense, have formed to create the unique ability that allows you to be aware of your own existence. You are not able to comprehend all the fine details, you can watch and absorb as others attempt to fill in the details of the play, but you know through instinct the connections and see the intricate pattern that forms the ever evolving universe.

And the pattern continues to evolve, instant to instant as you watch.

CHAPTER 1: THE UNDERCOVER SECRET

It was another sad day.

The math team members began to wake up; take a quick shower and after dressing they trudge from the barracks to the mess hall, through the cold wind hailing the coming snow of winter. They were not old men. Most were in the late twentys or early thirtys, but they looked much older and moved slowly due to the hard conditions of their existance and stress of the knowledge about their future. The breakfast was the typical dark heavy bread and tea only interrupted by the gun shots of an execution being held. With each sound, the team members shook with the thought of their "non productive" ex-teammates lives coming to an end. The men finished their meal before heading to their team area and desks.

The team went back to work arguing over the symbol transformations, each trying to give their insight, working their hardest to find a breakthrough in the equations. Each variation was tested against actual measurements to validate or invalidate the transformations. The work was long, constantly back tracking and little progress was being made.

New team members had been brought to the army base in the Ural Mountains of Russia to replace members who had recently been *excused*. The men were aware that they would never go home alive without success and even then, seeing their loved ones was questionable. Most had been pulled from Moscow or St. Petersburg, but a few were grabbed from cities farther east.

While they had officially worked for the Russian government, they were not given an option other than death and each was well aware that this operation was run by the Russian mob. After the fall of the Soviet Union, the mob which had been closely affiliated with the Soviet KGB took advantage of the turmoil to take control of the new Russian government through murder, blackmail, intimidation and general corruption. The puppet government heads were in place and acted as if they were in control, but with the exception of those who were part of the mob power structure, the power behind them was actually the mob and its internal management.

While the math team continued their work in the old wooden buildings, voices could be heard across an old thin wall. A conversation could be heard from the security people on the other side of the wall about plans to disrupt the American team. The rumor about the Americans making a breakthrough meant they had to be attacked to slow them down. Failure would put the Russian effort further behind and leave their country at a greater risk along with their ability to gain profit from weapons development and foreign sales. Instructions had been passed down from Moscow to exercise maximum force to delay and distract the American team.

Vladimir, at 35, was one of the older members of the team. While the debate on the equations continued, he was taking notes on the math conversation but quickly excused himself. As he headed down the hallway headed for the bathroom Macao, a soldier known to Vladimir, was walking toward him. He closed his eyes and sighed as a private signal. He continued on and upon leaving the bathroom, saw his friend, Tanya, a lovely young woman, with a pile of papers in the hallway. She had dropped the pile and was trying to collect them. Vladimir stopped and bent down helping her to collect the paperwork. As they quietly collected papers, he added a small sliver of paper to the pile. Without any words being passed but with their eyes watching for anyone appearing, they finished collecting the papers and went on their separate ways.

Tanya continued back to her desk and while reorganizing the stacks of files, she pulled out the small piece of paper and without anyone seeing, quickly slid it into her bra hiding it from view and avoiding detection upon leaving the office if she was searched.

That evening she had received her usual order to be the escort of the base commander Alexia Kotlyarevsky, to a local party. This was an event that was held bi-weekly and she had been the commander's escort to the party many times. Alexia had a wife and children, but his wife was older and rotund. Alexia preferred the company of a young sexy woman where he could use his position to "enjoy" her tight body.

The car arrived at the party with the commander and Tanya. She was dressed in the low cut tight fitting white gown, off one shoulder and reaching to her knees that Alexia had bought her for his pleasure with her raven hair cascading down to her back. As their car pulled up to the local hotel, the army driver came around and opened the door for Alexia dressed in his commander's uniform that was tight around his expanding belly, and then moved around to open the door for Tanya.

Alexia came around to take Tanya's arm with her forced smile and, like the trophy that he saw her as; he wore her on his arm as they climbed the five steps to the entrance of the hotel. To their left was a small restaurant and to their right, the hotel desk. As they continued forward, they came to a small staircase that led to the first floor rooms. The elevator on their right took them to the top floor where the large suite was located for the party being held. As they went up in the elevator, Alexia looked down at this young trophy woman and the exposed tops of her breasts. She reminded him of his service in the past to train a young beautiful agent for the mafia.

While Tanya was not quite as beautiful or as sexually hungry, being in this area of the country, his choices were somewhat limited, but she did satisfy. Maybe he was getting older, but his stamina was not what it used to be. Tanya on the other hand pulled from the depths her strength to get through the evening by recalling images of her parents and brother in Moscow whose lives were hostage to this pig through her willingness to give him what he wanted.

Exiting the elevator, they turned to the right to the double doors that were the entrance to the party suite. As the doors opened, a young woman with deference in her manner stepped up to take their coats and they continued into the party. The room was decorated in a 1940's semi-bland design with a simple chandelier and simple lamps spread around the room for lighting. There were approximately twenty couples mingling in the large suite with waiters roaming with food and drinks. To their left was a small bar with a bartender pouring wine, beer and making mixed drinks. The younger women were surrounded by the men as they bantered for favors and kept the liquor flowing in hopes for a quick fling in the reserved rooms adjacent to the suite. The sofa, chairs, and coffee table had been moved out of the center of the room and against the walls with the main window presenting a view of the mountain range with the soon to be snow capped peaks.

Waiters moved around the room offering food and drink, other couples

3

arrived and the party grew to its normal size of sixty people. Over time the party progressed; some of the men and women would pair off and leave the suite only to return a little later with flushed faces and slight hints of disarray while others would not be returning. As a waiter approached the commander and his escort, Tanya took a glass of red wine from the tray and the waiter moved on around the room.

One of the older couples in the room approached the commander and his escort and began a conversation. The woman, Della and her husband Gregory had been acquaintances of the commander over the past few years. As the discussion continued, the men and women drifted slowly apart by a few feet pressing close to others in the crowded room as their discussions were focused on subjects of male verse female interest.

While men kept approaching Tanya, as soon as they saw the commander look at them with his icy stare, they quickly backed away. While the women were discussing their dresses, Tanya reached out to touch the fabric. She had a small piece of paper in her hand she had taken from her clutch purse when looking for lipstick and in a single motion, tucked the palmed paper inside Della's dress under the bra strap while they continued their conversation.

After a period of time, Della excused herself to use the bathroom off the main living room. In the bathroom she, quickly moved the paper from her bra strap to her clutch purse, spent a moment to straighten her cloth's and hair, and returned to the party.

The party continued and the commander's hands found their way to Tanya's firm breasts as he invited another couple to join them in the suite's bedroom for some "games". This was the part of the party that Tanya hated, but had come to accept in exchange for the life of her brother and parents. Failure to perform was also a forfeit of her life, while not specifically spoken, indications were given and she knew it. While death did not bother her so much anymore, the thought of her family's execution because of her failure was not something she could allow, so she knew she had no choice but to endure.

Late in the evening as the party broke up, the older couple, Della and her husband Gregory, with the slip of information hidden away, drove away from the hotel and discussed their preset plans to travel to Finland for a short weekend vacation. Sometimes they took the trip, other times they would cancel with apologies to their friends in Finland who worked as part of the Russian embassy and had been positioned there for many years.

As they arrived home, they went to their small office. Della took out the paper from her clutch purse. Gregory went to a book case and removed a group of books. Behind the books he disabled a security monitor and pushed on a special panel. The panel opened to a small space that held an even smaller camera. Using the camera, he took a picture of the statement on the piece of paper and went through a quick process to make a micro dot. Using a microscope on the office desk, they together examined the micro dot to ensure the information was captured, and then destroyed the original paper by burning it and flushing the ashes down the sink in the connected bathroom. The micro dot was transferred to a Thank You card, which was attached to a present destined for the couple in Finland.

After making sure all equipment was put away and security detectors were re-enabled, they headed to bed. As they layed together in an embrace, they thought about the news of the execution of part of the math team they read about. As they cuddled, Della and Gregory recognized again how their lives were fragile and their life together of love could be taken from them at a moment's notice, much as their son and daughter-in-law's life had been taken a few years before. Their son had made the mistake of calling on the police because of the murder and rape of his wife by a prominent Russian mafia member.

In the morning, they completed the packing for the long weekend trip and called for transportation to the local airport. As they took the trip to the airport, they talked about their pleasure of the new Russian system with casual enthusiasm, giving the politically correct image that would help allay in public any suspicion from their true beliefs and hatred of the Russian system of corruption.

Once they landed in Finland and the gift with the card attached in their hands passed through security, they were met by their friends at the airport and driven to their small house in the outer area of Jakobstad, an ancient city founded in1652. The couples enjoyed visiting a number of historical sites that provided a relief from their daily boredom and mundane activities. The present they brought with them was given to their friends and together they enjoyed a simple meal after opening the gift. Before handing it over, Della had slipped the thank you note into her purse. The two couples headed out to see the country side and take a walk in the town streets.

Chapter 2: George

George Scott was a Watcher. He could feel he was different in his bones, better yet, he knew it in his loneliness.

There was nothing grossly unusual about his life, one of the many kids that grew up as a bit of an outsider, but many kids had a hard time fitting into the "in crowd". He enjoyed music (classical symphonies were his favorite followed closely by folk music), but was only average as a trumpet player. He enjoyed astronomy, cosmology, science fiction and adventure books.

Growing up on a farm, George began at an early age to understand farming was not for him. He enjoyed math, but was only slightly better than average in his classes. He enjoyed science, but would never get his advanced degrees. He never attended parties and was seldom invited, which made it easy to not have to attend. He skipped his senior prom dance but instead spent the graduate night celebration at a bowling alley alone on a single lane since the other kids were playing either in groups or in the game room.

He was average in most senses of the word. Not quite six feet in height, he had lost his hair on the top of his head at the age of twenty one thanks to the genetic inheritance from his father's side. His earlier years in college produced a fairly lean body at 175 lbs, but over the years of meetings, sitting at computers, snacking, and not being able to put down any good food since all food was good to George, he was now at the age of 58 years old and found himself in the higher realm of 290lbs and closer to the look of Santa Claus than a body builder.

In college, he tried engineering, but decided he enjoyed physics, even though he knew that he would only be average and work in a lab somewhere. He was always intrigued by astrophysics and the birth, death and life of the universe. But his life had evolved to being a computer programmer supporting those elite scientists and engineers at government labs and running elite programs at large companies.

George was not a handsome man; he spent too many years sitting at a computer to be someone that would turn a woman's gaze. In an attempt to make up for the lack of hair on the top of his head, he had recently grown a beard. The beard was a losing effort to achieve some character in his looks. Try as he might, between extensive travel and long meetings, his sporadic workouts at the hotel gyms were not enough to give him the toned body. It didn't seem to want to change, although it did appear to have stabilized recently.

He personally prided himself on understanding patterns. He used his talent to earn a modest living, never enough to be comfortable, but enough to support his kids; some considered him just a pushover. He worked hard in an attempt to help others to whom life was not as giving and helpful.

George's ex wife was somewhere. She had been his hope to erase the loneliness through love, but in the end, she had only used him to escape and when the chance came, she moved on leaving George and their two daughters to their own destiny, not wanting to be involved but to follow her own dreams. George took her leaving as proof that he was destined to live alone as he trudged his path through life. Annually, he sent her the year's worth of alimony checks to an address she emailed him and that was all he knew. His daughters had found their own lives and while they made contact with their mother, they relied on their father when they needed help. He worked hard to make sure they had the essentials to keep them from the desperate straits others in life were forced to live. It wasn't so much that he wanted to give them an easy life, just a chance to make their own lives.

All George wished for, all he dreamed about was someone to love, someone who truly loved him for himself; not someone that only needed him for what he could do for them. He wanted the warmth of someone who wanted to snuggle in bed, someone with whom he did not have to prove his love. He dreamed of having a love that allowed him to know that no matter how bad the day's work was, they together were more important and they together would be okay. He wanted a love like in the movies or at least the happiness knowing someone just wanted to love him. He was a romantic, but to him, romance was only a dream.

George had met one or two women that he hoped would create a change in his life pattern. He tried to find someone, but with each failed attempt came a longer gap between tries. Each attempt resulted in his understanding he was only a casual friend to them and it reinforced the view that the universe had a plan of solitude for him.

George had grown to accept his lot in life. While not seeing himself as a victim, he did have an evolving sense that his life was not a matter of choice, rather a part of a greater plan that he was simply playing his part in. With that acceptance, came a type of peaceful calm. While not a joyful condition, he saw it more of being a trumpet in an orchestra; he had a part to play and can only learn to enjoy the sum of the parts, even if his part was not especially outstanding. In this acceptance, he did not have anger toward his ex wife, he saw it simply as her part of the music to perform, and a part she too had little control over. So with each fading failed attempt at finding a partner to ease the loneliness, grew the acceptance of his part of being one whose life was destined to not include a close companion, for George, there was no better half.

|||||

The fall day was nothing unusual, at least for the Washington D.C. area. It was cold, it was windy, the trees were on fire and the crunch of the dried leaves could be heard as George walked to the sports bar. It was close to a November election and the TV's were full of the political heads making useless statements based on claims that the world would be a glorious place if you just voted for them; statements that really meant nothing compared to reality, despite what every news station and commercial claimed. The football games were all weekend long and the bars were full of people cheering on their teams and enjoying the playful taunts with fans from the opposing sides.

George was on one of his long trips from home; he was normally on a long trip. Home was just a stop over to take care of the mail. The saying goes "home is where the heart is," for George there was no home, just an endless string of hotel rooms, meetings and take out dinners in his room while answering his email, working on documents and listening to his music or watching TV in an attempt to numb the mind. Actually, the apartment where he kept his meager possessions was less comfortable than the hotels. At least at the hotels, there was maid service. The TV could be seen from the bed and every night, chocolate was delivered to the room. All in all, not a bad deal for an old bachelor, but being away from co-workers just increased the feeling of separation and thus enhanced his loneliness.

For George, life was an endless shift of hotels, meetings, documents and negotiations. Even an occasional cycle through his home town was just a different room, and meetings with negotiations amongst the family.

He was reconsidering even holding an apartment. With all of his constant trips, he had only visited it four night|||nd him with his life, work and family that he observed on a daily basis. He watched the greater universe around him with awe and reverence as he flew and saw the stars at night or happened to find himself outside on a night with clear skies, through random visits to Mt. Palomar observatory, visits to the National Aerospace Museum or when watching a program on the creation and life of the earth.

CHAPTER 3: THE PASS

Della, Gregory and their friend's were wandering an old Finish town when they came upon a group of Russian singers. They were singing Russian folk music and selling CD's representing better days in their lives as members of Russia's Army lead choir. The couples dropped money in their coffer and the lead stepped forward to shake their hands. Della had pulled out the thank you note and as she shook the Russian singer's hand, she passed the thank you note to him unseen.

As the couples moved on, the Russian group continued for a short period of time, then collected their articles and headed out to catch a car ferry to Kiel Germany where they were scheduled to sing in the streets as part of their late fall/early Christmas festivities.

The Russian choir arrived in Kiel, Germany on Saturday morning and quickly moved down the streets to set up in front of the Meislehein department store. Their manager took their bags to the hotel while they got right to work and soon the street was filled with the soulful sounds of Russian folk songs adding to the sounds of the shopping crowds on the cobble stone street.

When the afternoon ferry docked at the Kiel Germany port, a tall, stately man slowly walked off the connecting exit bridge with a graceful woman on his arm as another apparent elderly tourist couple arrived for the pre-Christmas season. A gentle mist drove the people to the local shopping stands in the town center for warm spiced wine drinks and food. The couple browsed through the local stands as they meandered through the streets buying some food, hot spiced wine and a few small gifts for their grand children.

While the crowd mingled with laughter, smiles and handshakes; the couple slowly eased their way to the edge and broke away, continuing their slow stroll down the busy street filled with shoppers. It was heading towards early evening and stores were still open with the shoppers and their packages.

The couple walked down the street, spotting a Russian mens' choir singing folk songs with their accordion to the German shoppers in front of the Meislehein store with its sign about having been in Kiel since 1880. They stopped to listen to the music and drop money into the group's coffer. As they dropped in the coins, the leader of the group came forward to shake the man's hand and completed their part in the transfer.

While the elderly couple continued to meander down the street, they spotted the Antikrouariat Schrat book store on their right with its old books and maps in its display window. The couple headed into the store and started looking at the maps, old books on the shelves and picture hanging on the walls. As they were discussing a 17th century map of a castle and surrounding country side, the owner Gustafson, came forward and spoke in broken English, "This is very nice piece, and it has unique history. I could make very good deal on it."

The couple smiled and the man nodded: "Yes, we are interested. Do you have the papers on the pieces history?"

"Yes, wait moment and I will bring them out." He walked into the back room and a moment later emerged with a folder.

After examining the documents, the couple decided to purchase the piece and handed the debit card to the owner. After the paperwork was completed Gustafson wrapped the purchase. The couple shook hands with the store owner and left, turning toward the ferry dock and retracing the path that had previously led them to the store. As the couple strolled past the church, Gustafson changed the sign on the door to indicate that the shop was closed, locked the door and headed into the back room. Using his favorite magnifying glass with the sheep horn handle, he looked at the thank you note which the couple had given him during their final handshake. He examined it until he found an iniquitous dot above a small letter "i". With a small knife, he transferred the dot to a glass slide with a smile.

||||

It was a summer day's afternoon two years before when Tim and Judy Decant looked at each other and smiled. The paper was finally done.

The paper had a title that few would understand; "Multi-Dimensional M-Theory Effects on Electromagnetic Curvature in a Non Mass Related Field" and fewer still could understand the detailed math of it. It was the end report for the Decant's on a major funding grant from DARPA (Department of Advanced Research Program Administration) and it had caused the Department of Defense to increase their funding to insure that the office in their home had been raised to maximum security levels with 24 hour a day monitoring of their home, both electronically and with hidden, but positioned security guards.

Judy was expecting and the date for delivery was only a month away, so they were both eager to finish the work which could only be considered a crown jewel in Tim's short but quickly rising career.

Tim was by his nature very outgoing and happy with his life. Still showing his form from his younger days, Tim was a 6'4" athlete with a full head of dark brown hair. He had been a sports star in both in high school and in college, along with being a scientific wonder. His mental abilities easily competed with and surpassed his physical abilities. This combination had attracted many young women when he attended MIT, but Tim had been attracted to only one: the one he married. While in college he had played football and basketball, but physics and math were his second true love; his first was Judy and now his son Brady. That would never change.

Judy wasn't a cheerleader, but despite her focus on physics, had the look of a runway model; tall, thin, raven haired and with all the right curves in all the right places. Unfortunately for most young men that she ran into, few had a mental capacity to keep up with her keen mind and analytical capability. When she had her quantum physics class and Tim walked in, she was immediately drawn to him and Tim was quickly entranced by her.

After the class, they had gone to the cafeteria at MIT and within the hour, knew that their lives were meant to be shared together. As their schooling continued, they stayed engrossed and in love, each pushing the other in their studies and drawing each other together.

When Tim and Judy reached graduate school, Tim received a number of research grants to support work in the unique, small and very competitive field of cosmology. With Tim's early success and the ability to draw funding grants in the field, Tim and Judy were married and on their happy path into life.

Judy was also a physics student but unlike Tim, excellent at writing and often helped Tim on his paper publications. Over time, she became both a housewife and editor to Tim's papers.

Tim's fame had grown quickly as he continued to break ground in the dizzy realm of cosmology. With Judy at his side, they soon found thimselves traveling the world and working with other great minds of the time as Tim argued his points of view backed by the power of his mathematics to prove his point more often than not.

Tim and Judy reached the age of thirty and Brady was soon to be born. Tim's life was about to make another great leap forward. Based on Tim's paper their lives began to take a radical turn.

The latest paper was not to be widely distributed like most other papers they had produced, since it was under a security restricted grant for DARPA and would have had to go through Department of Defense review, with eyes only clearance. The public would never see this paper and Tim's new research team was about to be born from the results of the paper at about the same time as his son Brady

Tim was a unique soul. His math and physics abilities, combined with his intuitive understanding of the most advanced concepts in astrophysics and cosmology, held him in a rarified level of people on the planet. His was a strong leader personality and as such he was designated as a program lead for DARPA into possible applications from String Theory and as it evolved and merged into advanced "membrane" theory. While large parts of the scientific communities were skeptical about String or Membrane Theory (String theory that energy vibrations form strings that are the basis of all particles in the universe, Membrane Theory adds an extra dimension to the theory) being the great unification called by some as the "theory of everything", Tim was not one of those people.

Once Tim and Judy's paper was delivered to his contact at DARPA, events moved quickly. By the end of the week, Tim and Judy had an invitation to a private meeting with the President of the United States and within a week after the meeting, Tim was in charge of a highly black program to change the paper into reality while Judy settled at home to prepare for the coming of Brady.

The President had allocated space in the President's Black Budget that only a limited few knew about. There was a unclassified name that appeared in DoD's budget, but no links could be found between the unclassified names and the classified BELLOWS name. Only a very few cleared people understood the linkage.

The BELLOWS project team had been forming in expectation of the paper's delivery. The team was formed between the Washington D.C. area where Tim and Judy lived along with some of the DARPA staff assigned to the project and a group of DARPA engineers based in New York City.

Two weeks before Brady was to arrive, a party was given for all the current team members to come together with their families to get to know each other since the team members would be spending long days and weekends working together. The party was held at the Pentagon with all the wives and husbands from both Washington D.C. and New York. Because of the nature of the program, while the wives were not furnished any details of what the program was about, all had been screened, provided security clearances and had been briefed into the outer edges of the program to insure that if they heard or read any classified information, they knew they were responsible to protect it.

At the party was the new head of security Jack Bord and his wife Shelly. It was instant friendship between Tim, Judy, Jack and Shelly. Tim had meet Jack briefly in the weeks leading up to the party, but in the relaxed atmosphere as the two couples talked and enjoyed themselves over good food and punch, the bond became tighter. Their homes were separated by less than a mile, both living in the Alexandria Virginia area. Jack and Shelly having two young daughters and Judy expecting, there was an instant empathy between the two women.

Over the following months Shelly was able to help Judy through and after the birth of Brady since Tim and Judy had no family in the area and their parents were only able to come down to the D.C. area for a short period of time from Ohio. As time progressed, Shelly and Judy spent many weekends with the kids together around the Washington D.C. area shopping or visiting museums and historic sites. Jack and Tim spent many weekends and many long days working.

Time moved forward drawing the couples closer together. During Christmas and other key holidays, the two families often found ways to share time together. During normal weeks, the couples often babysat for each other and helped out in emergencies. The families were in many ways like parts of one larger family.

While Tim focused on the technical aspects of the program, Jack focused on security. It was a little unusual in that this was a Department of Defense program and Jack worked for the FBI. But with the changes in coordination after the attack on the New York Twin Towers, under Presidential directive, the FBI had offered one of their star agents to organize a multi-agency security program for this highly unusual program that transcended DoD and encompassed an "eyes only" security that had connections across all security agencies.

Jack had grown up in law enforcement being the younger of two brothers (his older brother Jim had decided to start a local Texas business). Jack's father was a town sheriff in Plainview Texas. As Jack grew up, he knew he wanted to be in law enforcement like his father. Between playing baseball and working in the cotton fields around Plainview to earn spending money, he much preferred his father's type of job. Upon entering college he decided to get his degree in accounting and given both his intelligence and physical capabilities, was easily able to enter the FBI academy after graduation. He also joined the Army reserves and had served a tour in Iraq as a prison guard for the army.

In an attack on the prison by Shiites while serving in Iraq, Jack had taken a bullet in the upper thigh but it had missed the fennel artery and beyond a scar, Jack had survived and recuperated with no side effects. After his injury, he had been transported back to the United States since his tour was about to be completed. Upon return state side, he met Shelly through a mutual friend. Shelly had grown up in the Fairfax Virginia area and it was love at first sight. A year later they were married, and a few years after after that they had their first of two daughters.

Jacks rise through the ranks of the FBI was attributed to his willingness to take on, coordinate and succeed with tough problems with other agencies. His leadership, interaction, and friendships across agencies provided key abilities to take on complex coordination jobs which, in turn, directly lead him to his current position.

Jack's father had died two years earlier and his brother took their mother into his home where he and his wife helped take care of her; their children were grown and their house being big, it was a natural decision. Not having to move out of the community also allowed her to stay close to her lifelong friends, so it was a good situation for her and relieved Jack and Shelly of worry. Jack and Shelly tried to visit as often as possible, but it never seemed enough with Jack's long and busy schedule.

Over time, the BELLOWS program work continued at a hectic pace as everyone on the team could see the success close at hand. The program began to expand, along with Jack's work load, as the funding expanded to add in computer and math team resources. With success of their initial project came new opportunities. With their success, DARPA was eager to find other potential avenues that might prove fruitful, all of which added complications to the problems of security.

Chapter 4: The Event

George had long recognized his life was just a moment in the life of the universe, no less important than the birth, death and life of a star or galaxy, just different.

Each galaxy within the universe has been built around a Black Hole and Dark Matter (BHDM) pattern. Each of the billions of galaxies are constantly absorbing matter/energy into their BHDM patterns. The patterns evolved early in the life of the universe, but continued their task of gathering energy from their galaxies from far in the past to the present and will continue far into the future.

One of the unique things about this quantum level BHDM pattern: the more energy that was absorbed by the universe's black holes; the more it was ready to fulfill its destiny. In the billions of years of its existence, the energy level continued growing.

Scientists across the universe had decided they knew a fact. The fact they had decided on independently (since few knew of each other) was that energy was never created or destroyed in their universe. The fact was, they were only partially right. From their perspectives, it was a law of their universe. What they didn't suspect was that it really was a law of the sum of all universes, and there were many more that they were just getting a glimpse of in the math which Tim's team was studying.

So the pattern continued over the billions of years in the local universe and increased in energy as stars and dust continued to fall into the growing number of black holes from the billions of galaxies and multitude of universe all feeding the unique pattern.

From the pattern's perspective, it had only existed for a moment. From the view of an observer in a universe, it had been a stable pattern for billions of years. Time was one of the key parameters that formed this family of patterns and each had a different balance of dimensional connection that made them different. Each was born the same way, each would evolve differently. The interaction was across dimensions where only symbols of concepts represented by mathematics could hope to describe existence.

This pattern's time had come and in a flash of the transfer of energy, a new universe was born. It was not a single point of eruption, but rather could be described as a non-symmetric area tear. As energy burst forth, energy absorbed from its parents across a multitude of interconnected universes was spread through the blast of radiation into this newest universe, creating space-time itself. There was no sound, but it fully fulfilled a name given it by many races across many universes: The big bang.

The trigger of the universe creation pattern was digital in nature. The energy storage in the BHDM connected patterns would reach a trigger level and upon reaching that level, a new universe was born. The definitions of the dimensional connections that define the very existence of a universe were preset in the Master Plan and are applied with its creation.

If an observer was watching any of the billions of black holes in the universe, they would never have seen anything unique because the minute ripple was far beyond even the oldest civilizations capability to detect. The black holes still existed and still provided the same effects on space/time in their respective universe. The absorption of mass into the black holes continued unabated. The observed size and strength of each black hole, based on how much matter it had absorbed since its inception, as seen in the universe, continued to grow along its normal path. The black holes had not lost anything; they just formed a new connection to a newly created universe.

The various civilizations across George's universe had varying degrees of understanding. None had reached the full truth of the parallel universes, their connection their births and deaths. The most advanced races had seen a hint of parallel universes in their most powerful mathematics. They could not even conceive of how to build a sensor or experiment to attempt to start to unravel the indication of this complex multiple dimensional set of parallel universes. The oldest had started to probe the quantum foam patterns, but only a few were beginning to understand. Their senses were tuned to their own universe and they dealt with life and known objects in their universe, not multiverse connections.

During the short period of time prior to George's current trip starting, the event of universal proportions happened. Most did not know that it had happened; certainly George was not aware of the event that would change the lives of everyone on Earth and across his universe. To George, there was just a minor moment in time that he felt disoriented, and then life moved on.

The eruption of energy creating a new universe was usually in a space-time location that was never observable from any of the other universes in existence. The constants that define a universe normally vary enough to ensure their separation and lack of any interaction. The eruption was normally outside of the space and time occupied by any one of the other universes such that there was no overlap or when overlap occurred, they existed orthogonally to each other. Normal universe creation was such that it created a unique universe outside of any of the other existing space/time points currently in existence.

In this case, it didn't totally fit the normal pattern; it was part of a larger pattern and purpose. Its constants of definition matched an existing universe and its eruption occurred beyond the outer edge of its older sibling existing universe, driving a collision that occurred between the old and the new. It was a rupture that allowed the life blood of the new universe to spill out and like an ocean breaking through a barrier, began to spill its life giving and destructive forces in direct collision with its older sibling.

The energy flowed outward from the large areas of eruption, at a tremendous rate in three dimensions within only an instant in the flow of time from the perspective of its sibling's universe. In the instant that the pattern erupted, energy appeared across tens of millions of light years of space, rushing outwards in all directions. A subtle unevenness of the energy in this early moment was developed from the interaction of the multiple dimensions that made up the pattern from which the eruption occurred and the spread of the eruption positions.

The uneven relationship of the many dimensions resulted in a small bias of the energy spread and would evolve to cause a clumping effect as the energy density was reduced and basic particles including electrons, neutrons, positrons and foundations of dark matter were formed from the dimensional interactive patterns of the subatomic energized quantum foam of the new universe as the energy would cool. The filament style distribution of the resulting dark matter in turn would eventually drive the formation of black holes creating new connections in the BHDM patter. The BHDM pattern in the new universe would eventually drive the clumping of visible mass that was the pattern forming the basis of the new stars and galaxies.

The interaction of the two universes created an effect on a massive scale with expansion rushing outwards at a speed multiples of the speed of light in the old universe. The high levels of energy flowing outward from the new universe interacted with the galaxy sized patterns speeding outwards from the old universe. The old galaxies on the outer edge of the sibling universe were consumed as leaves in a blast furnace but with an effect of altering the energy eruption in the new universe as it flowed outwards, much as the lava from a volcano slows and quickly cools as it flows into the ocean.

Life forms in the old galaxies disappeared as their matter added to the energy collision evolving towards a mixing of the two universes of a design similar to the collision of two galaxies, only on a much grander scale.

With the collision, the energy cooled much faster in the interaction with the old universe and the transformation from pure energy to new particles would occur more quickly. Basic element creation happened over a much smaller time frame than in other parts of the new universe.

The rush between the two universes happened at rates far beyond the speed of light. While observers deeper inside the old universe, would see the interaction over a period of time, the relativity effect on those being consumed were affected by a massive space-time dilatation, ripping large parts of galaxies apart far in front of the rushing energy wall. But only after the early burst of the new universe occurred and interacted with the older universe, did the energy flow cool and slow down to speed of light interactions. In the early phase, events appeared at speeds massively above the speed of light as the fabric of space was being altered and energy transferred through dimensions which included not only space and time, but also other dimensions.

Most Watchers across the old universe had an uncomfortable moment, but it was just a bad moment in time and they moved on with their lives. The energy spikes in the old universe occurred as noise compared to normal energy levels in the multi dimensional foam.

|||||

The Old Ones were an ancient race that lived in a galaxy on the edge of the universe they called Sxvy, where the collision was beginning to take place. The ancient race monitored the dimensional connections as part of their continual efforts pushing forward on the limits of science. During their normal monitoring, they did see a rise in energy, but at their point in space-time, it was only a minor step up and not of major concern. As they continued to watch and started receiving communications from their deep inter-galactic probes, they saw the multiple dimensional energy flow begin to rise in the direction of the new universe.

This rise was not quickly understood and the Old Ones injected this new information into their analysis of the Master Pattern. This was not a simple calculation and would take much time to understand how it would affect the future and how they needed to adjust.

Their major calculations were based on knowledge of their galaxy and observations from their remote position in the universe. The calculations included information on the massive numbers of life forms, the structures of the stars and their evolving locations. It did account for information they had developed from their inter-galactic probes, but that information was miniscule compared to the massive amounts of information from their own galaxy and watching the movements of other known galaxies in the universe.

While this news was disturbing and conjured much speculation on the communication net channel, it was not totally unexpected and to find the answer to what this meant would take very detailed and complex computing. Their systems were up to the task of the computation, but even with their newest and fastest systems, this computation would take time.

Time progressed and their distant sensors continued to register increasing energy flows, the Old Ones continued to add computing resources to the calculation and enlarge the computation team. The understanding of what this would mean to their galaxy continued to increase in priority and urgency, pushing deeper into their priority list of other needs supporting their work across the galaxy.

CHAPTER 5: A FAR EAST TEAM

Each race has a different history. In the galaxy known as the Milky Way, on a small yellow star system on a smaller blue planet known as earth, the races had diverged in multiple ways. The diversity of the human race blended with the diversity of opionion and desire for control resulted in a fracturing over the many years of existence.

Somewhere between the forced labor of the M-Theory scientist in Russia under the control of the Russian mob and the United States effort based on freedom of choice, the Chinese relied on their culture and national pride to organize their scientific team, combined with a hidden threat of death for defiance. Many of the team members had been trained in the West, but since there were freedom "issues" in China, were under constant surveillance to ensure they did not in any way contact their Western comrades. Work was established on a military base on the edges of the city of Guangzhou in southwest China, just up river from Hong Kong. While security in the area of a key transit way like the river created certain unique problems, the desire to keep the work in the south far away from the Russian border was a key driver.

The operation was overseen directly by top central committee members and funding was hidden in their military budgets from prying outsider eyes. Their international spy operations were directed by the military and had a working and financial relationship with the Chinese underworld triad for conducting "specialized" operations. Surveillance and information gathering (spying) operations were normally done by embassy or business related personnel under the control of the government, and under the guise of business and international cooperation. The triad offered unique resources for offensive based operations that a businessman was not suited for.

The U.S. spy operations focused on the Chinese were making use of operatives that had been in place since World War II and had progressed to the second and third generation trainees. The information flowed through Hong Kong and continued unabated with the return of Hong Kong to the Chinese from the British. The U.S. spy team in China watching the M-Theory work was organized from a larger team that had been in place for many years and had worked many different operations to support the CIA as well as British Intelligence.

Monitoring of Chinese operations in the U.S. by the FBI had increased in recent years as Chinese intelligence and military budgets increased. In Washington D.C. the number of Chinese known operatives had risen at a ten percent per year rate over the last decade, mostly directed out of New York City and the Chinese UN delegation and the FBI had increased its surveillance proportionately.

Triad connections posed a different problem for the FBI. While little constant activity was observable in Washington D.C., there was direct linkage to major activity in New York and San Francisco. Tracking gang operations and personnel was a nationwide focus for special task forces within the FBI.

|||||

Gustafson was the third generation in his family to own the store. It had been started by his grandfather in the late 1800's and had survived two great wars. Gustafson Antikrouariat had been recruited by the CIA in the mid 1900's while in college, exuberant to help in the effort against the Soviet Union during the cold war and help reunite Germany. Now he was older, but his fire to help the West against the Russians continued, partly because of his distrust of the Russians, partly because he remembered what had happened to many of his friends who had tried to stand up to the Soviets.

The microscope was old. He had owned it since he was a student at the university in Berlin. He was used to the image and while the new tools made the image better, he liked his old ways, they were comfortable.

Once he looked at the message from the micro dot, he frowned and knew that life was about to get more difficult. The message was short but very direct:

The math solution did not give the desired results. Some members of the team were terminated and a new team is being formed. Movement in the West spotted. Directions have been given to discover movement and slow down the Americans while ensuring no success for the Chinese. Agents are to continue to execute their attack on the Americans with prejudice.

He stared, he knew that the storm was here and the defenses had to be alerted.

Opening the desk drawer, he pushed a button mounted inside under the lip of the frame. He reached over and removed a book from the shelf to his right. The action caused the shelf to rotate outwards and inside was a phone with a key card slot. He took a key that looked like a normal business card from the drawer, inserted it into the phone and pressed a preset speed dial number.

A voice at the other end answered with "Red Message, please provide verification".

"S Mark; Blue, Green, Yellow" The code was unique to him. S Mark identified him and if the three colors were spoken in a different order or a different color was exchanged, there would be nothing obvious in the transmission, but it would be a sign that there was something wrong and this communications flow would be considered corrupt and immediately reconstituted.

Antiouariat read the message to the man at the other end of the phone. When he was done, he replaced the phone and key card, closing the panel. He went to the bathroom, burned his notes including the micro dot, and flushed the ashes. When he was done, he walked back into his small kitchen, sat down at the simple white wooden table, poured a glass of his favorite red wine and considered his next move.

While the store owner in Germany was pondering his next move, a beautiful young raven haired woman arrived at the Union train station in Washington D.C. She collected her baggage from the overhead, caught a cab and directed the cab to an apartment building in Crystal City, Virginia. Upon arrival, she took the elevator to the fifth floor.

The apartment was a block from one of the Department of Defense controlled buildings on the east end of the area, but that was just coincidence. Using the key card passed to her, and in her purse, she opened the door and rolled her bag inside.

The man sitting on the sofa turned his head "Did you have a good trip?"

"It was long, and I'm tired. You are not staying." She said in a matter of fact tone.

"No, just wanted to give you a quick rundown on your assignment."

She silently said to herself **that wasn't a question** as she left her bag against the entry wall and moved over to the chair across from the sofa. The package was laid out on the coffee table with pictures of a man, a rundown on his normal itinerary and his background along with a set of false documents for her.

"You should find this enjoyable; I hear he is quite the ladies man. His position is an aid to a high ranking senator on the Senate Intelligence Committee. You need to be in place quickly as our friends need to know what the Americans are planning for reaction to the operation that is being set up."

After quickly looking at the provided material she nodded, "I understand, I expect to be in position within the week. You can leave now." With that she got up, grabbed her bag and headed to the bedroom; closing the door behind her.

She had dealt with the operative before and he was a pig. She did not enjoy his glare constantly look at her perfect C cup breasts like she was a slut. She knew that if he could, he would force himself on her. While she had enjoyed many lovers and during her training had to suffer a number of animals who saw themselves as great bed partners, he would not be someone with which she would enjoy herself. But she need not worry about that, her position was secure and she was highly prized within the organization. Any move by him would quickly result in his termination, a fact he was well aware of.

Her new assignment on the other hand, may be an enjoyable time she thought as she unzipped her dress and let it fall to the floor. She quickly removed her bra and panties and after she turned around viewing herself in the full length mirror with a smile of satisfaction, she turned and walked to the shower.

She did not consider herself a whore; she was a first class operative to whom sex was a tool of her craft. While she did not pick her assignments, she also did not do this for the money; her enjoyment was the power of her position and control of her target, the excitement of the risk. Yes, the money was good. In fact it was very good. So much so that after this operation, she was looking forward to a fun vacation in Brazil with her sexiest bikini, sun, food, gambling and a few flings just to keep her talents in shape. **After all**, she thought with a smile, **perfection takes practice** as she turned on the warm water.

She stepped into the warm shower making the water even warmer with her sexual aura. She thought about her new name, Sonja Baker. She liked the name. The set of false documents indicated her original hometown was in Reno Nevada, but that she had lived in Moorestown, New Jersey for the past year and that she had no living relatives. What the documents did not show was that she had been an operative for the Russian mafia for over 10 years since her early age of 12 while living as an orphan on the streets in Moscow.

|||||

It had been a fun weekend in New York City. There had been parties and a private tour of the Statue of Liberty with everyone staying at the New York Regency hotel. The BELLOWS technical team leads and their wives had seen a Broadway play and a New York pre-season basketball game. They finished the weekend off with a dinner at one of the finest restaurants in New York City. The short flight back to Washington D.C. on a chartered jet was the end of a well deserved celebration of the completion of a major milestone in the project. The four men and their wives, along with the program lead Tim, his wife Judy and their son Brady had been treated like royalty as a culmination of their work and sacrifice on a project that would only be released to the rest of the world in some far off distant future.

Jack and Shelly had not attended; this was for the engineering and technical staff. Jack stayed in Washington D.C. and had been involved in his normal briefings to Congress and providing oversight support on classified security for a number of key programs. Security for the trip had been taken over by a team within DoD. While Tim and Judy had wished for Jack and Shelly to come, it was decided to keep this strictly to the technical team and they would celebrate with a quiet dinner at The Crystal City Steakhouse on the weekend after the team returned. Tim had already made reservations and ordered a table with a fantastic view of the Downtown D.C. and Reagan Airport area.

The success being enjoyed by the team was a direct result of extended work from Tim and Judy's highly classified paper. Those who understood the feat of science and engineering done by the team as lead by Tim knew they deserved something closer to the Nobel Prize, but would never see it in their lifetime. This project was black and release to the world any time in their lifetimes was highly improbable.

The group was leaving the party of New York behind, headed from the airport lounge toward the plane, as Tim's encrypted cell phone rang.

"This is Tim."

"Tim, this is Bobby in the New York engineering section."

"Yes Bobby, what can I do for you?" he asked with a bit of intrepidation.

"Well, the stability problem has appeared again and needs your attention before you head back."

"I understand. I will be back in an hour." Tim answered with a sigh of disappointment.

Tim turned to Judy and Brady He didn't have to say anything. Judy smiled and squeezed his hand to let him know she understood. As they moved toward the plane, they held hands and acted like they did during the early year of their courtship, kissing and laughing at small personal jokes as Tim carried Brady.

Tim escorted them to the plane and helped them get settled. "Sorry honey, I'll catch a flight back as soon as I can." He gave each of them a hug, kisses and rustled Brady's hair. Waving to the rest of the team while grabbing his bag, he left the plane and headed out to catch a cab.

Shortly after liftoff, the pilot came on the speakers;

"I want you to sit back and relax. The weather is good and the view should be clear all the way down to D.C. We don't expect any turbulence so I will be turning off the seatbelt sign, but if you are seated, please keep the seatbelt attached, we never know if there is some turbulence not expected. Enjoy the flight and we should have you to D.C. within the hour. Thank you for flying with us and the bar will be open in just a couple of minutes."

Once the plane lifted into the sky, a man dressed as part of the ground crew jumped into a cart and headed away from the terminal to a location where he had a car parked. He had performed his part of the operation and now needed to quickly disappear. He stripped off his overalls and threw them with his badge into a trash bin, got into his car and drove away.

The plane circled out over the ocean, ten minutes into its flight plan Brady was laughing as Judy tickled him. A quick and massive explosion ripped the plane into thousands of pieces in an instant. No one onboard had but the the blink of an eye to know what happened before they died. The pieces of the plane fell from the sky and scattered across a large path in the ocean. The explosive was located next to the fuel tanks to ensure maximum destruction.

The FAA quickly sprung into action as the air controller reported that the plane was lost from the radar. A Coast Guard cutter arrived on scene within the hour. As the Coast Guard helicopter circled overhead reporting on the spread of the debris field, the commander on the scene radioed in with a request for help. The area quickly filled with ships and boats of all types as the Coast Guard called in a flotilla to collect debris for analysis.

The site was gruesome, parts of bodies and the aircraft were scattered within the debris field. A few pieces still gave off smoke, but mostly the pieces were small parts and seats with bodies still strapped into them. The Coast Guard unit had trained multiple times, hoping never to have to actually do the work. Each piece was collected, marked for location and cataloged. As the night's work continued, two seats were pulled on-board, one a small boy strapped into his seat and another contained body parts of Judy.

A warehouse was cleared and as the pieces arrived, the officials were trying to organize the parts to understand what happened. Within hours of the arrival of parts of an engine mounting, it was evident after quick chemical tests. The plane had been destroyed by a bomb of C4 explosive located by the engine mount near the fuel bladder on the left wing. The parts were sent out for chemical analysis to try and track the explosive manufacture of origin.

The FBI was well aware of the importance of the people aboard this flight and with the loss of the plane, assumed the worst. They quickly focused on the ground crew to see if there was a penetration. As they contacted all the ground crew that had worked on the plane, they at once discovered that one of the ground crew had reported sick that day and a replacement was brought in by the company that leased the plane. The replacement had recently arrived from working in Philadelphia but was no longer at the airport. No one appeared to know where he was and had not seen him since the flight had departed.

The investigating FBI agents tried to contact the ground crew member that reported in sick. After no one answered the phone, agents were sent to his apartment in the Bronx. Upon arrival, they found the back door ajar. They pulled their weapons and entered the house to find the man dead in his kitchen apparently attacked and killed with a butcher knife from the kitchen.

An agent from the New York office of the FBI tried to contact the replacement ground crew member that the company indicated. After no one answered the phone, agents were sent to his apartment close to the airport. Upon arrival, they found no one answering and had the building supervisor open the door. They pulled their weapons and entered the apartment to find the man dead in his bed, shot through the head.

The onsite team of the FBI continued the search at the airport for the fake replacement; they found clothes and a badge stuffed in a trash can by an exit to the airfield. The ID appeared to have been altered with a picture inserted over the actual owner of the badge, the dead replacement. The FBI agent on the scene quickly relayed the picture on the ID to the New York office and after a twenty minute computer search the picture matched the photo to Nika Kerstaf, a suspected Russian mob member in the Philadelphia area who recently moved to New York.

An all points bulletin was issued for the suspect with the indication of armed and dangerous. The broadcast was sent out across FBI and police units from New York, Pennsylvania Connecticut and New Jersey. He was known to drive a Black 1988 Volvo license, Pennsylvania XXY3374.

In the early hours of the morning, Kerstaf's car was spotted by a New York state highway patrol car and the chase was on. As Nika headed south along I295, with the police pulling up behind him, he increased his speed reaching 100 mph in an attempt to outrun them and find a place to hide since his instructions were to not be taken alive. The FBI had helicopters in the air joining the ever growing chase headed into New Jersey. As the car speed along the freeway passing other cars by weaving across lanes, the Volvo swerved to avoid a slower car in front; the front right tire hit the edge of the freeway.

The Russian mob in New York City was run by a quiet but intense Russian immigrant nick-named Gorbi, a five foot eight inch stocky man built of muscle. He maintained a luxury apartment and workout room on the Lower East Side for entertaining and relaxation. His family lived in Connecticut away from his operational work in the city. As Gorbi relaxed in his Lower East Side apartment, he heard the cars pull up on the street. He sat down his wine glass and put out his Cuban cigar in the ash tray, then walked to the front door. With confidence, he opened the door; a man in a suit greeted him with his FBI identification held up. "We would like to talk with you downtown."

Nika had lost control and his car had launched into the air, rolling over in a flight path that hit a light standard along side of the freeway. Once the car hit the ground, it flipped and rolled. The gas tank ruptured and the electrical break in the light standard ignited the fuel causing the car to explode and burn. Nika died in the flames while locked in by his seat belt ending that evidence path for the FBI. The focus shifted back to Gorbi.

Gorbi had half expected that the FBI would be calling and previously told his lawyer to meet him at the FBI office *unless* he called him off. He, as always, had been careful to make sure there was no way they could trace the operation to him or his team so while they may know there was a connection, they couldn't prove anything.

The FBI agents led him out to the street after he locked up the apartment. Exiting the building, they approached the FBI SUV. One of the agents opened the back door of their car and pushed Gorbi into the back seat, making sure he didn't hit his head. After a short trip to the downtown federal building, they escorted him up to the FBI spaces and placed him in an interrogation room. This was almost a normal dance between him and the Fed's. Anytime a major event occurred, suspicion was focused on him. Although they could not prove any connections, it normally was somehow connected to him.

At the offices, the FBI attempted to get him to answer questions about Nika, but Gorbi denied any knowledge of Nika or anything he may have been doing. As his lawyer arrived shortly after Gorbi's arrival, he protested the harassment of his client. The back and forth slowly evolved to a stalemate and eventually Gorbi was released to go home.

Gorbi left the FBI offices laughing inside. He smiled thinking, just another night at the ballroom dance.

Gorbi was fully aware that the FBI would continue to probe and search for connections. He was also aware that his team needed to be careful about their current enterprises to not give the FBI any reason to continue to harass them and if possible to let the situation cool down. Given time, it would be another dead end that would go on a long list of suspicions never proven and be filed away. Unfortunately, orders that had led to the bombing were making Gorbi increase activity, not decrease it, so extra care needed to be taken.

A large investigation was underway into the bombing of the plane, security surrounding the protection of the team members and plane and security for Tim and his remaining team. The investigations and upgrade of security became the top priority to the U.S. government. Since Jack was in charge of leading the total team security in coordination with NSA, DoD, and CIA, he had to set his personal feelings aside and quickly reset security for the team.

Jack immediately had a discussion with the head of the Secret Service, the President, and the head of the FBI, and a decision was made to have Tim's complete team moved with all dispatch to a highly secret facility in the Washington D.C. area that was underground and provided heavy controlled egress.

The underground facility had initially been created secretly in the early 1960's as a location to protect the President and members of the Executive as part of the Cold War. Over time, nuclear tests had shown that being close to a fission or fusion explosion would create a shock wave that would destroy even people within a deep bunker. From that understanding, the flying command post was created for the President. Over time, the facility had gone largely unused and while kept clean and updated in its communications ability, few were aware of its existence and the number grew smaller with each new administration.

Jack now had a complex job in front of him. On one hand, Judy and Brady had died, Tim would need his and Shelly's emotional help; on the other hand, part of a team he had been assigned to protect had been killed by the Russian mafia and he needed to strike back. He was now in a war zone between the Chinese with their triad team and the Russians with the Russian mafia. Every member of the team and their families needed personal protection twenty four hours a day, seven days a week (seven agents per family would be needed) and all team members outside of D.C. had to be discretely moved to the D.C. area without raising any notice. In addition, he and Shelly needed time to grieve over the loss of their close friends.

Tim was a public figure and with the death of his family, now required help both professionally and as a friend. Jack assigned an agent to contact a well known psychiatrist from the D.C. area to work with Tim to help him to find his way through the grief and to cope. The agent assigned must also conduct a background investigation of the doctor as a precaution. Jack and Shelly took on the job to help Tim as close friends through the grief. At the same time, Jack had to allow Tim to keep his public face but protect him from the deadly threats which were trying to consume him. While Jack and Shelly had each other and their daughters to help them through the tragedy, Jack, Shelly and other team members had to pull together to help Tim.

|||||

It had been only months since Tim had lost his wife and son. His life had gone on even though he felt as if his soul had died. The pain of his loss was as real as having a knife in his heart. The fire of the work that had been the basis of his loss became his only remaining purpose in life and continued to drive him to a focus he had rarely seen in himself in his earlier days. Work drove him and sleep eluded him as he attempted to find a moment of peace from the pain.

The paper Tim and Judy had written for DARPA showed there was a possibility of developing a unique capability that could warp electrical and magnetic fields with only a small amount of energy, not as currently understood in the world, requiring massive bodies like stars. DARPA could not hide the fact that Tim worked for them; only the true work that had been undertaken with a very large budget was hidden from view.

The very fact that Tim was involved in research on M-Theory and was working for DARPA had triggered competitive research projects in Russia and China. Russia's work was controlled by the Russian mafia (using the resources controlled by the Russian government) since many of the key research scientists were no longer capable of gaining funding from the broke Russian government. The mafia saw both political and financial possibilities of a breakthrough should one ever happen. China, on the other hand, saw the project as part of its massive military buildup and a chance to control the world with a set of unique new weapons.

Prior to the bombing of the U.S. team plane, a rumor had emerged that Tim's group had discovered a unique capability through the equations. No guess had emerged about what the breakthrough was. No proof had emerged; but the idea of its very existence was enough to cause added pressure on the Russians and Chinese.

During the meeting held in New York that had forced Tim to miss the flight on the fateful night, Tim had received a phone call with the shattering news that sent his life in a new and sadder direction. The flight had disappeared from radar while south west of New York and a crash site had been located with no survivors.

The official word was "pilot error", but the key information was classified. The plane had been taken down by a bomb and the prime suspect was the Russian mafia with the Chinese military a close second.

The FBI increased an in-depth tracking of local agents and the CIA started looking for ways to increase their infiltration effort into the Russian and China research efforts. In addition, a Presidential order was given to "retaliate" once the evidence was documented.

While the BELLOWS program was designated as *black* before, it could now be considered a black hole. It was far deeper, far more restricted than even the rare *black* programs that existed. Key information was maintained outside the team as "President's eyes only" and not even the Vice President was briefed into this work. If anyone asked what happened, the word was to be passed that the program (whatever it was), had been disbanded and no longer existed.

Team members were not allowed at the different funerals of their co-workers, the connection of people could not be exposed. The funerals were given with only family and outside friends. A service was held for the team members and in recognition of those that had died secret Presidential medals that would be kept by the team in a display within the new location in honor of their service. Team members and their immediate family were placed under higher levels of monitoring. In addition, security check-ins were now required on a set schedule along with tracking devices.

Tim and a security team flew Judy and Brady home to Ohio where the family held a closed casket memorial and burial service. Tim spent the week with Judy's family before returning to the Washington Area to pick up the pieces of his life.

Tim now spent two evenings a week working with Dr. Bob Thomas, a doctor of psychiatry to get his soul in a position of simple ache from the intense pain. Through their sessions, they also became friends as Tim grew to admire his caring and gentle spirit and Bob grew to respect Tim's depth of love, intellect and determination. Tim was never able to truly give Bob the details of the incident, but with a new intense focus on his work and the support of his team and friends, Tim was able after a month to begin to step back into his lead position.

Jack made use of Tim's well known status to create diversions and deceptions for the rest of the team to keep their identity as hidden as possible. Word was passed quietly by the CIA to the Russians and Chinese that any further attempts against Tim or the team; would result in unspeakable effects; a threat that neither the Chinese nor the Russians felt would be backed up given the U.S. history of wimpy threats and being "caring" people.

While Tim was able to work at facilities outside the team's underground location through remote classified connections to the team, sometimes he had to just be there. For those occasions, special procedures were in place in an attempt to keep any agent from following him to the team's location.

Because of Tim's status across the world, Tim resumed his schedule to travel to conferences and report on innocuous research (done by others but delivered by Tim as a cover). While the work related to M-Theory, it showed little progress and often contained public hints that if the competition studied them, would waste their time and lead them to false conclusions.

While traveling to one of the conferences in England two months after the bombing, Tim had a normal complement of security agents protecting him. During the trip, word arrived to Tim that Jack had a situation. Bobby from the Engineering department was missing. He had left his home as normal in Manassas, Virginia; headed to the metro but had not made his normal contact point.

Within fifteen minutes of searching, they found Bobby's car where it had been run off the road just down the street from his driveway. A satellite was quickly positioned to monitor the area and NSA started reviewing any and all communications. As the FBI and police quickly attempted to put up road blocks, NSA was able to locate a telephone conversation with eighty percent probability that one of the voices was "Gorbi" in New York. "Yes, boss, we have him under sedation, removed his tracker and we're headed for the warehouse."

The "boss" responded "Get the information or don't bother to come back alive."

As the FBI quickly reviewed records of all known mafia locations and identified two possible places that fit a description of a warehouse in the adjacent area and units were dispatched to investigate both.

The FBI units approached the second of the two locations, a car was observed with two men positioned to defend the front entrance. An FBI SWAT team was called in and a warrant was quickly signed by a security judge to allow them to search the premises.

Once the swat team arrived, they quickly positioned themselves around all the possible exits to the compound and activated a block to all cell phones along with cutting the phone wires on the telephone pole. The agent in charge proceeded to announce to the men ourside that he was with the FBI and they had a warrant to search the premises and interior of the building. The agent continued that the men needed to put down their guns and allow the FBI agents to proceed.

The answer was a volley of gun shots that were quickly answered by sharp shooters taking the two gun men down. The swat team proceeded to drive their trucks up to the warehouse blocking all doors as they prepared an assault. Again, the agent in charge announced to all those inside to come out with their hands visible.

A man's voice from inside the warehouse yelled out "We have a hostage and if you enter, he will be killed. Stay back. We have rigged this place with explosives."

The agent tried to strike up a conversation to cool down the situation while distracting the man inside. "If you come out, we promise no harm will come to you. We don't want this to end with anyone else being hurt. Your two men are injured but will survive. Just drop your weapons and come out."

The men inside were under orders and knew that no one would be able to protect them if they failed. At this point they had failed. Their orders were to kidnap and interrogate Bobby and find out what secret the team had discovered, then get rid of the body. Bobby was just waking up from the drug they had given him, and they didn't have the information. If they didn't get the information to Gorbi, it wouldn't matter what happened here, they were as good as dead in jail.

The kidnapping lead had been working for Gorbi for a long time and knew that his life was pretty much over. He was trying to think his way out of the situation when a shot came from the window above taking out the man with a gun next to Bobby. At the same time, a series of flash bangs went off as the assault team rushed through the doors. As the lead grabbed his head too late to block the sound and light flash, he just reacted and dropped the dead man switch he was holding. A large explosion ripped through the building.

The first men from the assault team died from the blast along with the sharp shooter on the roof. Bobby died in the blast with all the mafia men. It was over in seconds.

The FBI agent in charge had lied; the two gunmen outside had died in the initial volley prior to the assault.

CHAPTER 6: ANCIENT KNOWLEDGE

They were a rich race. They measured their wealth, not in the old way of money or minerals, but rather in terms of access to, and use of, energy.

Their civilization was known by many names throughout the galaxy such as The Singers, the Old Ones, The Bringers of Knowledge, and The Mind. Some of the names were not so flattering, like "smart plants" because of their apparently unique hands and their genetic line tracing back to a mobile carnivore plant strain, and were a reflection of failures and earlier times when they were arrogant enough to think they were the purpose of The Master Pattern.

There had been nothing unique that they had identified about the rise of their civilization, except they had survived. Over time, this simple fact brought them humility and respect for others that struggled to survive. While in the beginning, their race survived by being a predator, they evolved to a point where they felt they were the reason for life itself. Over time, their race became mature and humbled by their evolving understanding of the "Master Plan" and grew from craving food, to craving knowledge. They now were true believers of the math of their future and spent their existence following the direction their computations derived from it, adding information to better predict the future and, in doing so; understand their path based on the predictions.

Their planet of origin was located within the habitable zone, the outer third of the galaxy where star density was lower, orbiting originally a yellow star of moderate size. Their galaxy existed on the outer edge of the universe. As life evolved, they had traced their early years to a water based plant that captured and ate larger and larger life forms. It slowly evolved over time to have a complex brain with a body capacity for both mobility and limbs to support manipulations of tools to keep up with the evolution of its prey. Over time, evolution created a mobile land based version of the plant that received part of its nutrients from the atmosphere. As the prey evolved, it also evolved into a pack hunter until a beginning civilization was formed that became basic herders. With the change came time to progress to the advanced creatures they now were.

The atmosphere on the planet of origin for the Old Ones was filled with hydrogen and with a strong mix of oxygen with traces of sodium. The water on The Old One's home planet that gave their race the ability to thrive showed traces of sulfur dioxide to which the race had biologically adapted.

In their early years, the Old Ones were similar to what on earth would look like a small tree with four legs where a tree's roots would be and a number of *branches* that ended in what could only be described as flexible vines allowing them to manipulate minute objects.

Over time, the Old Ones continued to evolve to something more like a bi-ped upright animal. The plant race reached a point where they were able to manipulate their genetics such that there were many different looks within their race. They found through science, the ability to change their body design to look closer to any given race that they needed to interact with. In early contact, this had the benefit of not looking too alien and having a better level of acceptance. As their connection with a race grew, they could introduce them to the wider design of their race without the impact of first contact shock.

Over a long period of time, their star had used up its fuel and had changed to a Red Giant. Prior to the time of transition, the Old Ones had advanced far enough that they were able to travel within their system and take on operations that allowed them to create a new planet in their system out of danger and in a location allowing them to survive based on the energy input from the modified star just as they had predicted. While their early world had been consumed by the expansion of the star as it grew from the yellow to red phase, they had not perished, but rather had transplanted themselves to the new world of their own making allowing them to continue to evolve with the Master Plan and eventually begin their movement throughout the galaxy.

Evolution does not stand still. The Old Ones were not able to stop evolution as much as they were able to understand its direction and funnel changes to those directions of observed benefit to their mission as they saw it. This allowed them to be able to adapt to new planets as they dealt with other life forms, and ensure that on contact with other environments and life forms, they did not bring in contaminations that would result in harm or be harmed by a new worlds contaminations.

The language of the Old Ones grew from simple tonal based communication of their early civilization to one that encompassed the mind and the imagery now needed. Their civilization grew increasingly complex. They dealt with a blending of their minds, so too grew the fundamental language that helped transmit knowledge between them and other civilizations. This included both the sound based communications and the written symbolism to express the complex ideas and information that had grown over their millennia of existence.

The symbol based language of the Old Ones grew from the basic symbols established long ago, but as with their tonal communications, adopted enhancements of subtle shading and line variations to express added complexity. By maintaining the initial symbolism, it was easier to establish communications with other civilizations and then as they grew in knowledge, they were able to evolve to the more complex symbols with minimal adaptation.

Almost all civilizations communicated with a sound based language based on the simple fact that without an atmosphere, advanced life is not possible. Their sound based communication was largely maintained to support communication with other civilizations since most of their communications between those having joined the galaxy community were now based on their mind transmissions, although even with these, imagery fit well with the complex tones and symbols as such normally communicated along with graphic imagery to ensure proper understanding of information. Like their written language, the tonal communication was based on a simple construct that projected simple ideas. As the construct was enhanced to project emotional and technical variations, the simple tones became a more complex design. A new race could easily be taught the simple patterns and through growth, evolve to understand the more complex intricacy of the language.

With progression of time, they found ways to use their technology and understanding to remove the individual mind isolated by physical communications of sound and visual images. They had been able to link their minds through the use of technology and their finding of a way to transfer information through a dimensional connection into a shared network. Each mind operated independently, but had access to all other minds and information storage systems throughout the galaxy. They had created millions of channels of information flow between the minds, each separated to deal with categories to allow them to monitor and sort the massive information flow.

The basis of the communications had evolved over the centuries, after they had discovered one of the many dimensions which allowed them to bypass physical space and send information across space and time without delays caused by the maximum speed-of-light limit. In effect, they had discovered a means for instant transmission of their very thoughts throughout the galaxy. They had discovered this by way of understanding the math of the universe, and how certain particles appeared to interact faster than the speed of light.

Given their inherent long life span and their developed ability, on needed occasions, to travel faster than the speed of light and bypass space-time curvature, they had traveled and contacted many stars in the galaxy. Their science allowed them to travel within the galaxy through a warping of space-time like folding a piece of paper, and then to tunnel across this warped condition. Due to the energy requirements and the need to draw upon gravitational fields, they had only recently understood how to engineer an equivalent ability to travel between galaxies, but they were working on a new design and were close to being able to deliver an intergalactic solution.

Not every race they encountered throughout the galaxy was invited to join, some were too young, and some too arrogant; some had evolved in directions which would be disruptive to the communitys chosen path of gaining knowledge. They shared where they felt it would benefit and helped when they decided it was the right thing to do. They were always guided by the predictive ability related to the pattern. One of the hardest problems they dealt with was the decision of when to assist. Sometimes assistance was decided as better not rendered, but it caused significant pain to them when they had to make such decisions, as a parent feels pain when their child has to suffer to learn.

The math and research of the Old Ones and the community of civilizations they had knitted together over time had many missions. The two fundamental areas of work in terms of research were in understanding of the basic physical structure of the Master Pattern along with an attempt to understand the evolution to provide a basis for prediction.

Much time and effort went into the attempt to predict the path of the existance and over time, with development of their most powerful mathematics, basic ability had been shown. The Old Ones used this predictive ability to help them understand what civilizations they should contact and in the recent times, actions they should consider.

Events from each civilization they encountered, the life and death of stars, changes in other galaxies they observed; all were inputs into their analysis. The advanced statistics that allowed them to predict evolutions of sub-groups in a civilization and thus be able to pull the patterns together to predict the probability of a civilization surviving and being an acceptable candidate to join the galactic community was a well understood set of math. Their predictive math reached to the ability to understand the ebb and flow of the galactic community and allowed them to understand the effect of decisions and events with growing precision.

Two findings had evolved from their recent research on the future; there was a 98% chance there would soon be a change in the Master Pattern and its results would drive them to other galaxies. In addition, there would be a major change in their galactic civilization that they should be ready for. The math showed that this was almost a certainty, but what was the driving force was less well understood. Just as the understanding of what happens to energy entering a BHDM pattern was hidden deep and shrouded in immense complexity, so too was the reason of why the design of everything evolved as it did. They had grown intelligent enough to understand they could only attempt to understand what, not why.

When these findings were first discovered, work was quickly started to evolve a new fleet of ships. Where their current fleet supported transport within their galaxy, this new design would support transport between galaxies and beyond. Their future was more than in the stars; their future was now in the universe.

Their most distant traveled system on the outer edge of the galaxy was being used to host their latest and greatest device. Their research station was developed on a shell built around a small red star on the outer edge of the galaxy. They had specifically chosen this location due to the need for a complete star for the necessary energy and also as a safety measure.

This was one key experiment along with many others. Most of the experiments at this new base could not be easily controlled if something were to go wrong. They were literally dealing with the essence, the foundation of the universe. While they felt they understood basic information about multiple dimensions and used the ability to transfer information around their galaxy, this was different. The machine being developed allowed them to interact with a specific pattern spread across all dimensions, something that they understood in concept; saw in the mathematics, but still had trouble understanding in all the details. Even with their great energy sources, the cost to develop such a powerful and precise machine with all the necessary monitoring, recording and experimental subsystems and to support the large research staff was enormous and extremely dangerous. The device to support multiple experiments was derived from an initially simple design using a small power source and small amount equipment, but they had a much grander plan and until they knew it would work, the new design was much more powerful and complex. Only upon success could they scale the scope of design back to the scale of the simpler initial designs.

The new key experiment had been under development for over 50 central star time reference years (STRY) and consisted of an attempt to interact with key patterns that they had been able to recognize. Through much work, the Old Ones had categorized and mapped the energy wave connections for five unique wave patterns. One they knew was tied to a specific intelligent life energy design which they had identified as "The Watcher", while the others related to physical entities and low life forms had names of "The Star", "The Planet", "The Virus" and "The Atom".

The Watcher pattern had a direct relationship to their work in the Master Pattern. Although they did not know what the path was that this would take them in, they knew that the path to their future was directly tied to this work and must be taken.

The Watcher pattern had actually been an unexpected discovery that came about during a planet monitoring session. The being called "The Watcher" had been brought to their attention during the monitoring of a young race located on the outer third of the galaxy in a young but stable star. While the being was not outwardly unique, their sensors had identified an unusual multi-dimensional connection and energy flow during their annual monitoring survey that was distinctly different from what they had seen before. It was this connection that their new sensor measurement had spotted that had led them to the discovery of how to map patterns of the universe.

The work of finding suitable pattern sets to map is a complex and slow process. The work had begun over four thousand years ago (Earth Time, 50 STRY time) and for the first five hundred years, only 2 patterns were mapped. Once the initial mapping was completed, the idea to probe the multi-dimensional interactions led to the experimental system.

Another race would consider their discovery of a basic universal pattern as a *lucky accident*. The Old Ones knew better, every event is part of The Master Pattern. The Old Ones knew that there was no such thing as luck, only a point of interaction in the planned future. Each instant in time was predetermined and their discovery was no different. What made it unexpected was that they had not seen the event in their predictive math due to their calculation imprecision at that stage of development.

The initial discovery of the Watcher pattern was on the world of humanoid creatures during a survey. The contact team was carrying a newly developed probe looking at Quantum Foam energy flow patterns. As they approached the system and eventually landed on the planet, an unusual reading on the probe began to appear and grow. After the initial survey of the population, the Old Ones were able to establish basic communications using their language translators and over a short period of time were able to focus on the unusual probe reading.

The probe reading was not an object as they initially had expected, but rather was related to a member of the humanoid population. Nothing special in the beings background or abilities was obvious, and the person held no special position within the society other than a relatively higher than average ability to deal with pattern recognition. But the probe showed unusual connection to many of the dimensional parts of the Quantum Foam in an unusual configuration. The very collective wave pattern of the particles that made up this being and their related positions within the structure created a greater than normal pathway supporting potential energy flows that were not seen before or in any of the other life forms on the planet.

The Old Ones continued their study of this unique person. They began to understand some of the basic features of the connection and because the being had a somewhat odd personality compared to others in his social group, his fellow beings, somewhat with a joke, decided to label the pattern as the *Watcher*. Over time, they discovered the same pattern on an additional world and they began to understand it was a universal pattern albeit somewhat uniquely so, within the Master Pattern of the universe.

The basic understanding of the universe that they held had long before convinced them that only information could be sent through the dimensional contacts. The fact that only energy flowed along the pattern connections, allowed them to encode basic information within the energy flow along basic threads of the patterns connection by modulation of the energy levels; in simple terms they sent information into the pattern and were able to listen to information coming from the pattern to make it work like a "two way radio". This was not something they knew would succeed, rather their theories predicted that some life forms who were children of this pattern they were interacting with, would be able to sense the information. They could only hope that it would succeed, but had seen early signs of success. In the early phases of the project, using much less sophisticated designs and lower energy levels, they had made quick broadcasts that the known Watchers had sensed, but now with the new design, the window of communications could be held open for large amounts of time allowing for immense amounts of information transfer and gain an interactive feedback.

|||||

Sxxty emerged from the protective enclosed area located on the station orbiting above the artificial shell's specially designed sulfur based atmosphere enclosure. The message had already been distributed that initial contact had been successfully made as reports from around the universe were starting to be cataloged. Once Sxxty removed the environmental mesh from the body, this creature of the Old Ones race knew that work had only begun. While the reports of successful contact with Watchers of advanced enough civilizations were being identified by the cataloging part of the system, the work to prioritize information to transfer while leaving enough transmission capability to have a respectable two way information exchange with a specific civilization was not yet completed.

Sxxty was scheduled to travel back to the research facility on the outer shell. The lab from which he had just emerged was a facility in orbit beyond the outer shell placed around the star. Sxxty proceeded to the shuttle for transport and settled in for the short ride. He looked out the window while waiting for the transport; he continued to enjoy the view of the outer shell, glowing with life. The design was not unique, the Old Ones had built many such designs around different stars, but still the wonder of the Master Pattern that allowed one such as Sxxty to reach such heights in evolution was truly an honor. Sxxty had done his required work with lower level civilizations and knew the difficult time that most civilizations must pass through to have a chance to survive and reach such heights.

Unlike the transports between stars, local transport units were simple rooms that one entered. The systems surrounding the room communicated with the receiving port location to ensure no contention, drew power from the inter-dimensional connection, opened a connecting wormhole and executed transport.

43

Longer trips used transports with many rooms including a nutrition refresh room (rejuvenation area), sleeping quarters and engineering controls. The ships were designed to support a wide range of life forms that worked with the Old Ones. Trips between star systems were not long, but consisted of multiple jumps so the systems could collect and focus power for each segment. Because they were in a less dense void where gravity fields were weaker, the collection took longer and the wormholes needed to cover larger distances. While time of movement between two stars was less than a normal refresh cycle, with older ships, some trips were much longer as they moved between stars far distant around the galaxy so minor comforts were accommodated for.

A new ship design was under construction that would enable direct jumps anywhere within the galaxy with expectations of working between Galaxies. The fleet was in assembly heading to completion and some ships would be delivered at any time capable of collecting and focusing energy to a level that was expected to finally give galaxy level jumps.

The ship had a functional design, not an asthetic design, but was of immense proportions. The look was that of a number of rectangular rooms stacked together like children's blocks, some of which were well over two hundred meters in height, width and length. There was no need to deal with atmosphere entry that requires a more sleek design. This was designed strictly for travel between planets, stars, and now, galaxies. The engine was more of a field generator spread throughout the ship that allowed for the creation of the warping of space-time and the ability to create a field that pushed the ship into the warped worm hole. The design was focused on strength to hold together given the great stresses.

Transport between ship and planet surface used the same ability built into a simple pin that could be attached to a covering as well as built into a suit that enabled a single person transport along with a number of other abilities to account for environment or invisibility needs. Other variations of the devices allowed transport of stacks of gear or supplies and in the larger forms, complete physical structures such as a building. On rare occasions, small shuttle craft were available to actually fly to the surface.

The Old Ones had no reason to add weapons to their ships that was a waste of time and energy. In those cases of attack as they dealt with a new civilization, their simple ability was to block and disrupt any energy beam weapon. For any explosive or kinetic based device, they trapped it in a warp field that shifted it to a region where there was no danger. In their experience, they trusted these abilities to quickly show the civilization that even their best weapons were of no threat to the Old Ones.

The ships of the Old Ones did more than just provide simple transportation; in key times, such as when a civilization's star transitioned, their ships were required for complete movement of a population. The ships could be brought together quickly to support this effort and had preformed this feat multiple times within recent history; some of which Sxxty had been involved in. This need lead to the large ship designs capable of carrying tens of thousands of life forms along with food supplies, complete physical structures and anything else of major importance. With the new galaxy class ships, the size would shift to more than one hundred-fold increase in size.

Sxxty blinked and the transport was over as a small worm hole had been opened and closed over the short distance. He was on the outer shell surrounding the enclosed star. He left the transport, walked down the hallway and entered the rejuvenation area for the Old Ones where it was warm. In the Old Ones section, a breeze blew and nutrients could be absorbed through Sxxty's skin similar to the atmosphere on their original home planet. After a quick stop to refresh, Sxxty moved on to his rest area and settled down for a rest period.

Sxxty had been assigned to the connection machine program as part of the standard rotation. The Old One's fate had been tied to the object of the communications; The Master Pattern had defined Sxxty to be the broadcaster. By the time he reached the shell and entered his research rest location, over ten thousand advanced civilizations' Watcher patterns had made contact and had been cataloged, indicating that they had received the contact calling card. Eventually, millions of contacts were expected but at this point they were only looking for the most advanced of the pattern.

Sxxty's life began as all Old Ones now begin, in a genetic lab. The cloning of new members of their race had been happening for millions of generations. The original race had been born through the production of seeds and germinated in warm, still mud until the new life came forth and evolved through the early stages of creation of appendages.

Now through the evolved techniques of cloning, new life was born in a small dish and within weeks evolved to a stage where connection to the communications net occurred. Once connected, the race took on the job of training the new ones. Training evolved as the body matured and within a period of two cycles around the home star, they were fully grown and fully integrated to the society.

New members were created only as needed. Sometimes a member would die through a physical accident. Sometimes the society would decide that growth needed to occur as they added new races that needed support and sometimes individuals just wanted to reach the end of their very long lives naturally.

With each member of their civilization being brought to life, a study was undertaken to see the new life impact on The Master Pattern. In Sxxty's case, it was soon discovered the key point in the pattern he would play. It wasn't so much that he didn't have a choice in what his path was, it was more of a case of discovery of a key point in Sxxty's life. He still had the excitement of discovery of the path forward and only was given the probability of this major event happening (78%) within the life path and how it crossed with the research work on the connection machine.

Given all the systems and work, the amount and control rate of information transfer was not yet totally solved. The initial broadcast was one way and intended strictly as an attempt to make first contact for a brief period to see if there was any response. After the contact with races advanced enough to understand was made, more advanced information could be transmitted in what they hoped would be a complex two way communication.

There were risks, the biggest of which was to possibly alter the path of a civilization in such a way that could cause danger. Not all civilizations were fundamentally good; some had not been able to overcome a self centered nature and as such were deemed a danger to all others. Their prediction from the Master Pattern showed a ninty three percent chance that over the next thousand generations of the Old Ones, nothing bad would happen from contact and basic information release. That still left a risk that needed to be watched, but the community considered it manageable and, given the scope of the effort, acceptable.

While risks existed, it was evident in their detailed study of the Master Plan that this risk needed to be taken. However precautions were built into place to ensure that while advanced technology would be broadcast, key advanced capabilities and knowledge of the study of math study projecting the future would not be revealed until such time as they could ensure the receivers were not of a type to disrupt. This decision too was just a part of the future analysis.

Sxxty settled into his rest unit. One part of his mind drifted to his last civilization assignment prior to transferring to the connection machine. The planet was beautiful, but would soon be destroyed by the transition of its yellow star to a red giant. The people were a kind and gentle bi-ped race known as the Txxan's. Sxxty had become friends with the son of a scientist. His friend Tia was very young, playful, and enjoyed learning. Sxxty would take young Tia on walks beside their green seas to watch the dance of the three moons and set of rings around the planet that were clearly visible in the sky. Tia was able to pick up the Old Ones language rapidly even though he was only 12 cycles old and their friendship became a unique pleasure to Sxxty.

The Old Ones had looked at this race in the master plan and had determined that even though they were still a young race, their kind gentle nature would allow them to evolve into a benefit to the galaxy and that early contact would not be disruptive to them. So Sxxty and three others were sent to prepare them for a move to a new home to protect them from the coming destruction of their planet.

Tia and his friends taught Sxxty how to play the game of ynot, where a round object was kicked around as the children tried to get it into a hole in the center of a large ring. Since Sxxty had played no games in his young training, this was quite different and the joy and laughter on the childrens' faces was a wonderful experience to this focused and controlled emotional being.

The Old Ones had found a suitable place for the Txxans to move to in a star system close by. Over the cycle of movement around their star, Sxxty and the others worked with Txxans to teach them about the coming death of their planet. Sxxty grew to understand the simple yet enriching lives that these kind people lived. The race was not large in numbers, only being five million soles due to the limited land space on the planet (mostly water) and while there were other creatures on the planet, none had reached any significant level of mental ability. The Old Ones as part of their standard review process had studied the genetics of all the creatures on the planet and determined that none would progress to a state of advanced mental capability other than the Txxan's.

Unlike most races that the Old Ones worked with, the decision was made to not integrate the complete race into the galactic communications network, but rather to start by taking in only a few that desired to be their representatives. As discussions with the older and generally acclaimed leaders of their race, it was decided to connect two from the leadership council and train them in the communications of the galactic race. The two leaders were chosen by the people and provided the communication link that consisted of a simple attachment of what looked like a patch of skin to them, although this was their form of attachment designed by the Old Ones. The device was placed as a small dot on their head and was capable of reading and communicating thoughts between their mind and the Galactic community. At first, Sxxty's companions worked with the new members to slowly ease them into the flood of potential information so as to not over whelm their minds. But slowly over time, they adapted and were able to share and mix with the galactic community.

When the end of the first cycle approached, one of the attached leaders was taken by transport to see the new planet that the Old Ones were preparing for their new life. The planet was different, but the basic environment needed to sustain life and provide them with food, water and shelter had been engineered and was ready. To assist in making the transition easier, a new moon and a set of rings had been added to the planet with protection capability to ensure that debris from the rings would not affect the planet.

After the leader declared it suitable, the transport of the Txxan race and some other life forms from their home planet began. At that time Sxxty was shifted to the communications project as others took on the heavy lifting of moving a race. The final goodbye of Sxxty with Tia was an experience that this Old One would long remember. They had grown close over the year and to know that he may never see Tia again or at least not for a long time, had broken through the controlled emotion state of this Old One. Sxxty last saw Tia on the sparkling beach with his friends kicking the round object while Tia wept at the goodbye of his friend.

Sxxty had continued to monitor the movement of the Txxan race to their new home and was provided updates by the leader of Tia and Tia's family. The move had gone as planned and the race had started to settle on the new planet. The Old Ones had planted their crops for them so when they arrived, they were able to harvest food. The main city had been positioned along the water side as it had been on their home planet and all seemed to be settling well into their new planet.

Under the watching eyes of the Old Ones, the Txxan population appeared to be doing well. As they continued to adapt to the new planet and its slightly different chemical mix, a report by a survey team indicated that the Txxans appeared to be changing and one of them was showing signs of taking on the traits of a Watcher pattern. This created excitement on the communication net since never before had they seen a new pattern arise in an existing life form. It had always been assumed it was determined at the point of creation.

The connection team waited for results to see if any of the Txxans responded to the Watcher communications; the Txxan that had been identified was Tia. So if Sxxty and the team could communicate with Watchers, perhaps, just perhaps, Tia would be in the mix.

Chapter 7: Contact

While George was sitting in the local sports bar snacking on chips, drinking his iced tea and waiting for the political commercial to end, there was a moment. No one else noticed, but George was a Watcher and it was as obvious to him as was the couple across the table in a deep, lip locked embrace was to others in the crowded room. It wasn't so much that time did a loop, or was like a movie going backwards for a brief second, but more like a flash as time froze for an instant then continued on its way.

George sat at the table trying to understand what happened. He began to get a feeling of others. As he looked around, no-one seemed to fill the bill. His feeling began to grow as he sensed information that he had never known of before. The noise level in his senses began to rise.

George had spent years of only listening to his own thoughts, music in his mind and the sensor patterns of his body. Even in crowds, since he was seldom part of the conversations, he was able to dwell on his own thoughts and feelings, blanking out the surrounding noise but this was different. This feeling was a constant rise in thoughts that were coming from within, not through his normal senses, but were not his. While they were not words that he recognized, they were intricate patterns of sound and images, like the rising noise of a crowd with a swelling orchestra trying to compete and at the same time, video images on every wall and ceiling, except they were full images in his brain in full color and with minute details.

George's first self analysis was that he now knew what it was like to be going insane or maybe taking some wild drugs.

While not wanting to draw attention to himself, he had to know if anyone else was feeling this wave of information with strange sights, but panic took over. George stood up and yelled so that everyone could hear above the noise level he felt, grabbing people next to him and shaking them in an attempt to gain their attention..."What's happening, doesn't anyone else hear this! Doesn't anyone feel this?"

George was not one to make a spectacle and as this was not a normal occurrence at the sports bar, it quickly caught the attention of the owner.

George stood dazed and trying to keep control when he was approached by the owner trying to quickly gain control of this outburst. As it became obvious that George was disoriented and in some type of mental trouble, Jim the manager of the sports bar signaled to a waitress to call for help.

Jim grabbed hold of George and with the help of a couple of young men, cleared the table and had George lay down on the empty table just as George's legs began to collapse. Since George was breathing ok, there was nothing much could be done other than to watch him and make sure he didn't hurt himself.

George was aware that people were gathering around him, but his senses were being so overwhelmed by information that he was not able to understand what they were saying or even respond to their actions. As a deaf, dumb, and blind person lost in a fast moving crowd, George was dazed and was struggling to gain control of his mind, too disoriented to be scared.

Help arrived at the sports bar in the form of a paramedic's ambulance and a fire truck, soon followed by a police car. George was only aware that the crowd around him had changed, but unable was to control his body as the information swelled.

The paramedic quickly took George's vital signs while the police proceeded to push the crowd back and to open a path to bring in the gurney. After the paramedic had checked the vital signs and communicated to the doctor that the patient appeared to be stable, they quickly took hold of the table cloth and slid George onto the gurney. After removing the table cloth, they strapped him down and headed out of the sports bar and into the ambulance. George soon found himself on a gurney and inside an ambulance, but unable to say or do anything about it.

George was in a state of mental shock from the blast of information that had been funneled into his mind. His vocal and muscular reactions were blocked and he was not able to understand the impulses being fed from his ears and eyes.

While the police cleared the street and one paramedic wheeled the ambulance around, the other paramedic quickly got an IV set up and basic fluids flowing in case they needed to administer medication on the transport under direction from the doctor on the radio. As the ambulance left the sports bar, people slowly became re-engaged in their games and traffic flow returned to normal. The police were in a side section of the bar out of the chilly wind outside, writing up their reports of a medical emergency and getting statements from Jim and others on what they heard and saw.

With sirens blaring, lights flashing and the paramedic in touch with the ER, the ambulance rushed the crowded leaf blown streets to the George Washington University Hospital.

When the ambulance reached the hospital, the driver quickly backed into the emergency entrance and opened the back doors. With the help of hospital orderlies, they pulled George on his gurney and rushed through the doors down the hallway to the ER with the IV bag being held high. As George was wheeled into the hospital emergency room, a doctor and two nurses quickly swarmed over him in an attempt to discover what was happening.

By this time, George's mind was just barely beginning to take control of the information flow and allow his normal sense's to come back partially under his control. George could now sense the doctor leaning over him and with his maximum effort, was able to call upon his arm to grab the doctor and plead with his brown eyes to help him to understand.

The doctor rushed to look over George's body for any physical trauma; but couldn't find anything obviously wrong with George. His basic signs were within normal regions except a slightly elevated blood pressure and extensive eye movement. It was like a seizure, but the tightening of the muscular frame was missing. The doctor had George rushed to x-rays looking for a possible brain injury, aneurism or stroke. Not finding anything obvious, the doctor had blood drawn and sent to the lab for an immediate rush, looking for an array of drugs and a wide spectrum of other conditions.

With nothing to draw on, the doctor decided the best course of action was to try giving George a mild sedative to relax him and scheduling him for a MRI, to see if anything was visible in the brain. The ER doctor decided to look at brain functions and to call for a psychologist to work with the team to see if with his input they could grasp what was wrong with this new patient. Sever schizophrenia was an option that could not be discounted.

The ER doctor began to understand that George did not show signs of immediate physical danger, so they had him transferred to a ward for monitoring. As George was wheeled out of the ER, the doctor in charge quickly focused his team's attention on other patients that had physical trauma requiring immediate attention, the first of which was a fifteen year old boy who had just been wheeled in screaming with pain from a gun shot wound to the shoulder.

While George was being moved to the third floor ward, his conscious mind drifted to unconsciousness. His mind took the opportunity to start the process of gaining control of the information flow and forming a balance between current reality and the massive view that had been funneled into his brain.

George's conscious mind sank into blackness. As he drifted off, George felt the awe, wonder and music of the universe exploding around him; then nothing.

That evening, as George awoke in the GWU hospital room, he had a massive headache. He felt somewhat back in control, but with a whole new and constantly expanding, view of reality. He weakly became aware he was in a hospital room and as his eyes opened, he spotted a nurse and moaned in a scratchy singing voice for some help.

A nurse approached, George spoke in a dry and somewhat dazed and scratchy voice. "Where am I?"

The nurse responded "You are in the George Washington University hospital. You were brought in not responding".

"I need something to drink" he hacked.

"I will get you something and Dr. Thomas has asked to be contacted as soon as you woke up."

After filling a cup with water from the pitcher on the stand next to George's bed, helping George to sip on the water through the straw and fluff his pillow, the nurse left to contact Dr. Thomas.

George was still dazed and lay in bed searching his mind in wonder at the vast store of new information. He tried to form a theory of what it all meant and where did it come from, with little success. The patterns were complex and immense. The music was loud, strong and entrancing, and something he knew he had not heard before, but it drew him inward and caused his mind to focus on the swirl of images and sounds.

George's mind drifted from exhaustion. He triggered a thread of thought where he remembered his daughters and work and began to worry about them. His daughters would be worried when they heard that George

Ronald Townsen

was in the hospital and while they were doing ok, he worried that maybe they wouldn't have funds available and they would need his support to travel out to help him and without access to his computer, that would complicate things. He also wondered about work. If he was right, this was Sunday and on Monday he had a meeting with the Air Force relative to a bid on a new radar system design. He needed to let his boss know that he was in the hospital and see if the meeting could be rescheduled until after he got out.

George began to gain control of his mind and re-focus; he pushed into the information that had been shoved into his mind. George organized the new information into emotional and physical. The emotional information was very similar to the emotional world he knew and extended from loneliness to awe and wonder. The physical information was much richer and extended from what George seemed to feel was complex math equations to concepts on the very nature of the universe along with a wide array of different images that were distinctly alien. George was rapidly understanding through the the images in his mind, the physics of particles and atoms, through stars and the very structure of the universe. In addition, there were lots of images of unique creatures and worlds.

While he registered the image snippets of the many life forms and their environments, there were two that stood out among the many. This first life form to appear had passed the major amount of coherent data. The others were like a crowd around the stage with one in the crowd that seemed to stand out. Each could be discerned, but the center of the focus was the one on the stage and one in the crowd that stood out, distinct from all the others.

One of the key points that caught George's attention when he was able to begin to grasp at a sliver of the information, was that he knew that our moon was much larger and singular, not counting the manmade structures in orbit. But in the information being presented to him, there was only the view of a star totally enclosed by a shell within the current focus, like someone looking at the system at a distance. In addition, on closer inspection, the shell contained actual cities glowing and obviously full of life.

There were many other life forms in the responding crowd. Some looked like four legged animals, some looked almost human and some looked very human. The one in the crowd that stood out was as a forceful responder reminded George of a cartoon alien that he had seen once with four eyes spread around a rather large skull, short bi-ped body and a dark brown skin color with no hair on its head.

One creature that caught George's attention was a large fierce looking creature which looked like a large can where the top contained a face and had 3 arms and two legs with feet. The face contained a single large eye with what looked like vines coming out of where a nose would be. The creature had an opening that could be a mouth that was vertical in nature. Most of the body was covered in what appeared to be coarse hair. While the look appeared fierce to George, the setting was calm with a family like atmosphere that made George stop and think.

The landscapes observed by George in some of the responses where varied and beautiful. There were lots of colors that were broad and rich. Each image was different in design and color orientation, some with white sparkling beaches others with flat plains of growing plants; high mountains and deep massive canyons. Images projected were assumed to be planets with one or no moon, some with multiple moons, some scenes with dual planets orbiting each other along with rings and one star or dual stars.

In one case, the creature was looking into the night sky and above was a wonderful view of a huge gas cloud in space looking like a five pointed star, but with an orange color that contained multiple pin points of light within.

Chapter 8: A Connecting Point

Dr. Bob Thomas had over twenty years in clinical psychiatry, and had worked with a few great scientific minds of his time. It was well known that Genius was often on the edge of insanity. He was on the staff at the GWU hospital and also worked through a nearby office. His practice was located in a key center of the country where much money and power was concentrated, the Washington D.C. area.

Bob's six foot six inch frame was lean and strong and he presented a presence of strength, yet with dark green eyes that provided an unmistakable feeling of caring and his face projected understanding. Bob strongly controlled his facial projection as he found people reacted to those expressions; instead, his stress release was a twiddling with an ink pen in his fingers; occasionally snapping them under severe stress. His good looks were formed with a full head of black hair (natural) and a thin beard. His 45 year old personal life was a mess, having never married, always placing his work before himself. He had dated some, and had until recently, been in a bit of a long term, six months, relationship. But as usual, his work had eventually ended that as she decided to move on after Bob had canceled on four evening dates in a row due to work.

Bob had grown up in the Mid-West as the son of an U.S. army general. His father gone for many years of his early life, a young Bob was constantly surrounded by decisive leaders. His mom projected strength of character and while there were only occasional contacts with other members of the larger family, Bob was taught self reliance early in his life.

Bob's favorite memory related to when he was in high school and had been a star on the baseball field. Bob had received a scholarship to play baseball that led him to Ohio State. He began to focus on medicine in his undergraduate days. With the death of his father while he was fighting terrorists in the Middle East, he found he was able to give the support needed to those around him and it drove him to the area of psychiatry. He always projected calm and his green eyes begged for people to talk to him, a feature that was granted from genetics and could not be taught. Bob later moved to John Hopkins medical school for his doctorate degree and graduated top of his class. He was able to quickly establish a practice at GWU Washington D.C. hospital and then the true work began.

While working hard, he had to take time off two years before with the death of his mom. He had migrated away from much of the larger family and only occasionally received a note about a birth or a marriage taking place. He was rarely contacted and had no idea when any of the family happened to be in the D.C. area, only hearing about a local visit sometimes in a passing remark in a note about a family event.

With the latest breakup from his most recent girlfriend and the long hours, Bob was tired. People were seldom aware of the stress in his life, but his secretary saw it each day in the twirling of his pen when he was in the office. He had no one to travel with and being alone, a vacation held no enjoyment. So Bob continued to work fifteen hour days; two hours to go between work and home and seven hours of sleep, day in, day out, seven days a week, week in and week out. He tried to take his thirty minute workout in the hospital gym during his lunch break, but sometimes like today, he had to skip it.

Every once in a while a pretty nurse would try and flirt with him, but he did not like to mix his work place with his minor private life. He knew such things seldom were successful and often ended with people being hurt.

Bob remembered one such incident in his early days when he had asked out a young nurse in training. She had gone out with him and they had fun at the beginning of the first date. Later that evening the flirting turned serious and then at the last moment, she pushed him away. Bob was a gentleman and had not been one to force the young lady, but it was like she wanted to explore her sexuality, then when the opportunity became real, she couldn't cross the line. So Bob drove her home and indicated he would talk with her the following day. On the ride home, she was quiet and nervous and did not want to talk.

When he arrived at the hospital the following day, during his lunch break, he attempted to contact the young nurse. To his surprise and dismay, he was informed that her nurse supervisor had received a call that she could no longer work at their hospital and was terminating her employment and transferring to another hospital immediately with no explanation given. Bob attempted to contact her, but her phone number had changed. After spending many days going over what happened, Bob came to the conclusion that this shy young woman had decided she could not face him, for whatever reason, after what had happened.

Never to be one that wanted to cause pain, Bob was determined that this was to never be allowed to happen again. Bob could not allow an action, no matter how unintended to drive someone to give up something in their life because of him.

Over the years of work, Bob's cases were seldom unique; they were people that needed help. Sometimes it was nothing more than the depression of being out of work in an economy that had crashed and the recovery was slow and jobs were scarce. At times it was the results of people that took any and every type of drug they could get their hands on, this usually did not have a happy ending. Once in a while there was a tragedy such as the case of his friend and patient Tim Decant who had lost his wife and son in a horrible airplane accident. While Bob dealt with personal issues such as depression, Bob did not deal with marriage counseling, it was an area he avoided and left to the psychologist.

What Bob sometimes felt was unique in his work were the people. Bob was well known and often was called in to give help to Senators, Congress men and women, and once even a Secretary of State. As was Bob's training, they were no one special in his eyes, just people with problems. Without being in awe of power or position, Bob was better able to treat them by breaking through their facade of importance.

The only mental breaks that Bob received were in his bi-weekly or sometimes monthly meetings with his personal psychiatrist. Each psychiatrist was required to meet with a different psychiatrist to give them someone to unburden their mind of all the bad events and cases they were required to deal with. Bob knew well that while details of what his patients revealed could not be discussed, his feelings needed an outlet to allow him to stay sane. Dealing with death, grief, terror and depression took its toll on more than the patient and cost him many pens when the stress reached a level that rather than twirl, he would snap it in his strong fingers.

So with the arrival of his new patient George, Bob was expecting just another standard case.

With the transfer of George out of the ER and to a different medical staff, the insurance company covering George which was located by looking through his wallet, indicated his personal physician as being located on the West coast. The medical team had quickly been in contact with the doctor and asked for a copy of his latest medical information. In addition, the insurance company indicated he had been seeing a psychological counselor recently. Bob placed a call to the counselor and asked for a copy of George's recent records to be sent to assist him.

When the phone call came in from the nurse that George was awake, Bob was reading the quick synopsis of George's arrival at the hospital and a resume that he found on-line describing George, while grabbing some quick dinner consisting of a Ruben sandwich plate. The doctors in the emergency room had been unusually complete in their exam for physical problems and blood work, with no success. While not all the blood work was back, nothing specific had been found. As a last effort, they had ordered brain exams but they were scheduled for later in the week.

Beyond a problem of being over seventy five pounds over weight, George showed no signs of physical cause for the observed lack of response, which is why Bob was asked to attend. A few items caught his attention from the attending doctors, George's body had highly elevated oxygen levels and his heart beat had been elevated. While his blood pressure was a little high, it appeared through eye and facial movement that his brain was highly stimulated.

Bob looked at the food in front of him and quickly decided that the French fries were more than he needed, although it was something he loved. With a success of his will power, he picked up his tray and dropped it at the counter, picked up his diet soft drink and headed down the hall to the elevator to go to George's room.

Bob entered George's room reading his notes while focusing on his best patient caring face. He noticed the glazed look on George's eyes and as he walked over to George's bed, introduced himself.

"George? I am Dr. Bob Thomas. "

Bob waited to see if George was able to respond.

After a couple of moments, George was able to understand that a doctor had entered the room and he had been spoken too.

In George's new sing-song voice "Doc, what's happening to me? My mind is overwhelmed!"

"That's what we are here to find out. Have you taken any drugs or medication lately?"

"No, just my normal aspirin at night and some sleeping pills; all stuff I buy at the drug store. This is like the universe has dropped into my mind. There are sounds, images, symbols; I see new worlds, creatures and they're trying to talk to me." George continued in a sing-song voice.

"Are they talking to you now?"

"No, it was sudden burst and then I heard voices, hundreds or thousands of different voices and images, then it went silent. But the information and memories are as vivid as when I first received them."

"Are you in any pain?"

"Not really, just a minor headache. But the images are awe inspiring; it's like seeing the universe for the first time."

"George, I need to know if this singing voice is normal for you."

After a moment where George seemed to drift away, he seemed to come back and responded "No, I just started talking this way; it's kind of how the first creature communicated."

Dr. Thomas pulled over a chair and sat down at the side of George's bed to start talking with him for a short while trying to determine if a recent event could have could have triggered George's condition. As he continued, he put his hand on George's arm in a sign of reassurance.

"George, can you tell me a little about what you've done over the past week?"

"A week ago, I was in a one night layover in San Diego, arriving from my previous week in the D.C. area. I arrived on a Saturday morning, went to my apartment and did laundry, paid bills and watched TV. In the evening, I went for a swim and Jacuzzi then went back to the apartment, made some soup for dinner and headed for bed."

George broke out of the singing voice "I woke up Sunday morning, watched news, cooked an omelet and ate while watching the morning news programs and repacked my bags. I watched the Charger football game and then caught a taxi to the airport. I arrived at the hotel in Crystal City late Sunday night and headed to bed. This week I have had meetings at the Navy Yard in D.C. and at the DoD offices here in Crystal City. I got back to the hotel around 6 p.m., drop off my bags, walk out and pick up some takeout. I then come back to the hotel room and eat while I work." George seemed to return to the sing-song sounds.

After a short moment, George came out of the sing-song voice "This is my normal pattern. Nothing unusual happened this week! It was like every other week. This weekend I didn't fly to the West Coast, just stayed at the hotel and Saturday morning walked over the sports bar to watch the football games."

"There was nothing out of the usual? Did you fall or bump your head? Did you eat anything special?"

"No, nothing happened…back a few weeks ago, I did get a strange feeling for a moment, like time stood still for a split second, but nothing special other than that."

"George, this just happened out of the blue? Nothing gave you any feeling that something was wrong prior to the event?"

"No, nothing."

"George has anything like this ever happened to you before?"

George seemed to start singing, then "No, never. This just exploded in my mind! After the initial explosion, I started hearing and sensing images from hundreds or thousands of different creatures! Each was different, each wanted to speak. I wanted to speak, but soon there was a powerful image of a different creature with four eyes circling his head. While I couldn't understand him, I felt he had a message of an even more powerful race and the image was of a tall stately creature."

"Do you read science fiction books?"

"Yes, but this wasn't like any book I have ever read. You don't understand. The images and sounds were as real as the conversation we are having now."

"Since that event, have you had a sense of any new information?"

"No, but it caused me to change. Like you pointed out, my voice is different and the images have stayed with me. I have a strong feeling that the information provided by the first creature is important. I think they sent me a message but I don't know what it means."

Of course Bob had discounted the belief by George that someone was talking to him; he may believe it, but it was part of the psychosis that Bob was sure was affecting George.

After a short while of talking, but mostly listening to George in his sing-song voice as he came and went from his presence to somewhere else in his mind, he left George to rest and headed back to his office to gather more information. Something he felt in his gut indicated this was shaping up to be a case that might have the makings of a great paper at a conference, but it also was a case that was not going to be solved simply by a few quick sessions.

Once Bob left the room, he walked to the nurse's station and on George's records ordered a sedative to ensure rest, then headed back to his office to do research on possibilities of George's condition. As the evening progressed, Bob found little information to help him and finally at midnight, gave up and headed back to his apartment to grab some rest.

The next morning as Bob arrived at the hospital, he saw George was doing better. While George was feeling better and somewhat more in control of actions the medical teams feeling was he had not recovered enough to be released by the doctors from the hospital. In addition, since George's doctor was in San Diego and there was no family in D.C. to help take care of him, until the situation stabilized to a point he could take care of himself, it was a risk to release him.

Given his pattern, Bob came into George's room with his personal cassette recorder and his famous calming look. The little hand-held device could handle an hour's recording and Bob always carried at least four spare tapes.

During their next meeting, George had a better grasp on the reality around him and he began to slowly explain some of the sights, sounds and symbols that he sensed. But the music could only be felt, barely described although George made sounds while trying to describe it.

Once George got into specifics, "I can draw you a little of what the symbols seemed to be that the creature indicated, I feel like they might be equations, but I can't tell for sure" As Bob gave George a sheet of paper, George drew a series of odd symbol clusters and handed the paper back.

I have never seen anything like this set of symbols, but I have a gut feeling, this is some type of important equation".

"Here is one example of an image I received; one creature appears to be looking in a mirror. It looks like a small girl with a copper toned body, very human looking. She appears to be in a small room with a window overlooking a small body of water that is muddy looking. I can see two large moons and what appears to be a band in the sky. There is another small creature sitting on the window, like two birds welded together with only two wings, but two heads and having a pink fur.

The symbols were interesting but far beyond Bob's understanding of what it meant. Bob secretly felt this was again, part of his psychosis. George was able to describe and attempted to draw the symbols and visual images, but while he had been a physics major in college many years ago with lots of math, and spent his life time playing and listening to music, the understanding of the symbols and the music appeared to be totally outside his ability to explain.

George repeated multiple times as he emphasized that the symbols and what he thought were equations were important. He didn't know what they were, but they were very important and someone needed to pay attention. With the increasing power of insistence by George, Bob began to twirl his pen a couple of times.

George's views of the universe, worlds, moons, landscape and creatures were definitely intriguing. He was able to describe one of the creatures and its surroundings in exquisite detail into the recording machine that Bob had brought along. The images in George's mind projected like he was standing in the front row, viewing the unfolding events. However, what he observed was not spoken, but rather appeared to be communicated through thought and the thoughts were not words, but intricate patterns that he could only relate to as a form of music and imagery.

After a while, Bob needed to give George a break and allow him to relax. Medication was provided to give him a chance to rest and as George slipped into a deep sleep, Bob gathered his notes and tape recorder in wonder. He had worked with and read about patents that made up their own people and events, some even made up God. But this was out there. In this case, George appeared to be making up science fiction on a grand scale which Bob had never heard of happening before or found reference too. George had claimed that this was not a science fiction story he had read, but Bob needed to check just to make sure.

Bob left the room. He decided he needed additional help understanding the information; but who to contact and what to tell them? The descriptions of the viewings were so detailed that he called a friend at John Hopkins to see if someone with a background in art could attempt to convert the descriptions and rough drawings by George to visualization to help see if it made more sense. Bob had a feeling that for some reason the details of the image were important to George and by converting them to visualization, it might help while working with George. Perhaps if he could understand if this was just rambling thoughts that are just passing through his mind or if they were important memories, the understanding would help elicit feedback from George.

"Hi, Tony. Look, I have a bit of a favor to ask. I know you're the head of the psychiatric department at John Hopkins. Do you know someone in the Art department that could help me with some drawings?"

"Bob, how are you doing? Haven't taken me up on that beer I offered back a few weeks ago. Still working your tail bone off I guess. Give me a second to pull up a reference...Okay, I have a name for you, its Dr. Randy Williams. He just did a show on campus and Debbie indicated he was a real young star in the department and great to work with. I will send you his fax number and contact information. As soon as I get off the line, I'll send him and his department lead a note of introduction for you. So tell me, did you ever ask out that red head that I indicated to you? Debbie wants to get you married off and keeps bugging me."

"No, I've been too busy at work. Tell Debbie hi and I will try to get some time in my schedule in a few weeks and maybe call her up. Thanks for the contact info and I promise to find an evening to take you up on that beer.

"Take it easy Tony and thanks again."

"Yeah, look who's talking," Tony said with a chuckle. "Talk with you later buddy."

With that, only one more phone call to make, Bob thought.

Bob decided to call his friend and current patient Tim who was with DARPA and had a background in science and math to have him take a look at the symbols and descriptions to see if it made sense and was something that George may have dealt with before in his life. For this case, it was important that Bob understand if this was George just recalling something in his past or was this information just gibberish. George seemed adamant that these were possibly some type of math equations, but whatever they were, they were something very important, at least to George.

Bob placed a call to his friend Tim.

"Hello Tim? This is Bob".

"Hi Bob, how are you? I have been meaning to call you and set up another appointment. Work has been a little hectic lately."

"Tim, I'm calling about another matter. I have a new patient that has given me some information that he thinks is very important. He claims it might be some equations and has drawn a set of unusual symbols. He claims that this is very important and refused to let me get past it, so before I ignore it, I thought I would see if you had a few minutes to look at it and see if it makes any sense, or if it's just gibberish. Would you mind?"

"Not at all, send it over to my office and I will take a look for you. Is he okay?"

"Not sure, but I'll send it over in a little bit. Just let me know what you think. Thanks, and make sure you call and get something set up, we still have lots of work to do."

"I will, very soon. There should be a break next week."

"Great, and thanks again for looking at this. Talk with you soon."

Once Bob got back to his office, he copied and edited his notes for the protection of his patient. He did a quick on-line search for some of the descriptions and names George indicated with no success. Bob then faxed a completed copy to Tim (without George's real name although he indicated it was a consult to the medical team he was called into in the hospital) and sent some of the descriptions to Randy at John Hopkins in the art department.

Bob had another session scheduled with George the following day at 8:30 a.m.. As he went over his notes, he continued research through his computer looking for a similar case or something related to the information provided by George. After a few hours of searching, he was unable to find anything that came close to matching what was happening. Sure there were cases of delusional people that heard voices and saw images and even some that broke out singing rock music or even operas, but in the details and descriptions that George related and his ease of transitioning between humming-singing and talking, this did not seem to match. In addition, the file sent from George's doctor on his medical history showed none of the precursors that would normally be found in patients showing any of his psychosis symptoms. George had recently undergone a physical exam and had been through counseling because of his marriage breakup a few years before and there was no indication of problems of this type evolving. Furthermore, there was no indication of a physical trauma that might cause an event to occur.

The company that George worked for had been notified and while there was concern from his boss and his daughters were being notified by the company, the focus was now with the D.C. doctors and his work and worry of his family was of secondary concern. George's west coast doctors were now only involved on the sidelines. The main battle for the immediate future was to be managed by the local doctors and was to be played out in the GWU hospital to which he was transported to in D.C. But as Bob was well aware, the only constant is change.

CHAPTER 9: A LOCAL CONNECTING PATTERN

By 8 a.m. of the second day, the hospital was working through its normal schedule with nurses and candy stripers having already woken up patients who needed their rest to give them pills to help them rest. The Jell-o and oatmeal food carts with the occasional egg breakfast had already made its rounds and the patients were being taken for their morning showers or in some cases, sponge baths for those that were bed ridden.

When the military police appeared in the lobby asking for George's room number, it was obvious that this was going to be an unusual day. There wasn't one or two, but twenty or more that quickly appeared in the lobby and proceeded to spread out to all the basic entrances and exits. The exits were quickly controlled and people were asked to stay inside for the moment.

With a call from the front desk, the hospital administrator appeared; the military officer in charge accompanied by number of people dressed in street cloths' handed him a document without a word. The document was signed by a Washington D.C. security federal court and identified George's case as under control of the security federal court system. The officer identified was assigned full authority to do whatever was necessary to take George into protective custody and to collect all records or documentation dealing with George. In addition, the document clearly indicated that no information about George or his case was to be provided to anyone under any circumstances without direct authorization from that specific court. Further discussion about this case was to be terminated and anything related to George was to go no further. All records of George's case were to be turned over to the court and anyone having contact with George was to be identified immediately. The document went on to state that all people having been in contact with George were required to submit to an interview by the officer in charge.

In San Diego, CA, FBI agents were being briefed to make contact with George's doctors, work managers and family. At the FBI, cover stories had been prepared and transmitted to the San Diego office. Once the San Diego agents were briefed, they left the downtown federal building spreading out across the city to lock down rumors; they were tasked to make sure the family and his co-workers were not worried and were briefed on information provided about George. His daughters were asked to not travel to Washington D.C. at this time, their father was under doctor's treatment, but due to national security, he was not available to see them until such time as his condition could be considered under control.

At the same time, the military police appeared in George's hospital room; Bob was arriving at his office to gather papers for his scheduled appointment with George. When Bob entered his office, he was surprised to find Tim with a small team who identified themselves as FBI, waiting for him.

With an unusual look of dissatisfaction on his face, Bob started to protest at the presence of the agents. Tim stepped up to Bob, pulled him aside and simply said "It's real and far beyond what we can talk about here. We have a problem. Please help us keep this under control. I will answer questions in due time, but not here, not now." Tim produced a security federal court document that indicated that all records related to George were to be turned over and any information in Bob's office was to be collected and turned over to the court immediately.

Tim continued, "Bob, I need you to trust me on this, it's a major national security issue. We need to move quickly and quietly. George is under good care and will meet us in a short time. I need you to help us gather all information and erase anything from your computer. Or better yet, we can take your computer with us. But we must hurry."

The look and tone of Tim along with their history together provided to Bob the assurance that something was of importance and Tim was somehow in control of what was about to happen. After quickly looking at the presented documents, Bob quickly decided to relax and agreed.

"Tim, please be aware, I faxed some of the information provided to you to a professor at John Hopkins to attempt to visualize the images for me."

"Do you have the contact names and telephone numbers?"

"Yes." As Bob pulled up his records, an agent stepped forward, dialed a number on his cell phone and read off the information.

Bob assisted in the collection of the necessary documents and helped to pack his laptop computer. Tim led the small group downstairs and out to a waiting SUV. As they drove away, Bob tried to listen and watch to see if anything could help him make sense of the situation.

At the hospital, George was taken out in a wheel chair and was escorted from the hospital and placed in an ambulance. Meanwhile, the military police were spread through the hospital to collect information on every nurse and doctor that had been in contact with George. They would be spending a number of hours being asked for every detail that they could remember about what George had said or done. Of course, while George had been attended to by the ER doctor and nurses, he had only talked briefly with a nurse and with Dr. Thomas as they soon found out; trying to keep this incident to a minimum impact, they tried to quickly pull out and allow the hospital to return to normal. Or a least some type of normality.

By 8 p.m., any physical evidence that George had been at the hospital was gone. Except for the rumors that flew around the hospital, no one could explain what happened and the rumors were so far off base (helped along by some mis-information coming from some of the officers and unknown doctors and nurses) that those in the know considered this area of the matter closed and quietly slipped away undetected.

A similar search had occurred of everything from Bob's fax machine records to John Hopkins. George's hotel room was searched; cloths, his work computer and personal articles had been collected. George was checked out of the hotel by his "brother" and quickly forgotten about.

Information was quickly and quietly gathered and by that evening, George and anything about what he had said after entering the hospital had vanished from the public's eye and ears as best as the FBI could manage. George and Bob had disappeared and the hole was closed over them.

The agents drove Bob and Tim through the downtown area in their government black SUV, they came to a tunnel with traffic closed due to an accident. The police officer with Tim quickly flashed his badge and the group was escorted around the traffic jam. As they were part way through the tunnel, the accident between a limo and ambulance could be observed. Traffic had been blocked in such a way that people could not see what was going on around the accident scene and the police at the scene were hard at work to keep people in their cars and away from what was happening in the tunnel.

At their car approached the scene of the accident, Tim indicated to Bob to say nothing. Tim stepped out of the car and approached the limo. At the scene, there were five SUV's all identical to the one Bob was currently in, down to the license plates. At the same time, George was assisted to get out of the ambulance and with help from some officers was brought over and into the SUV with Bob. As George entered the SUV, Bob caught a glimpse of three people leaving from the limo and in a sudden lapse of control, had a surprised look on his face for just a moment before he gained control. They were almost exact duplicates of Bob, George and Tim. After a short time, all the SUV's left the accident scene in different directions and the windows darkened so no one could see inside. The limo and ambulance still remained at the scene with the fake Tim, Bob, and George. And after a few minutes, the limo and ambulance were cleared to also leave as the police continued to slowly allow the area to get back to normal.

After Bob captured control and put his doctor face on, he made sure George was comfortable, he gave a questioning eye to Tim with a raise of his right eyebrow. Tim looked at Bob and simply said; "Give me some time and I will explain, I promise, just not here and not now".

When the SUV came to a stop, George's eyes were glazed over and Bob was just plain lost. While having spent a number of months in the D.C. area, this location caused George to feel lost for the second time in just a couple of days. The SUV had not only taken unusual roads, but had made an entrance to what appeared to be an underground parking lot, to enter a tunnel that appeared to go for miles in some unknown direction. When they stopped, it was outside an elevator inside the tunnel and George and Dr. Thomas were asked to please get out (this was not a demand, but rather asked with respect and kindness). When George, Bob and Tim entered the elevator, it proceeded to drop, for what seemed like minutes.

When the elevator stopped and the door opened, George and Bob entered a luxury suite with a presidential seal on the opposing wall behind a desk with an open laptop. A medium sized man stood across the room, dressed in a suit and dark glasses and an ear piece that could only be described as FBI or Secret Service. Tim turned to the FBI agent and asked, "Cleanup going okay Jack?" Jack indicated yes with a nod of his head.

George could not understand what was happening. He turned a glazed look at Dr Thomas but saw only a look of calmness on his face. For Bob's part, he only had Tim's message and for the moment he was not in control, so he followed directions, waiting to see where this went.

Upon entering the room from the elevator, Tim asked George and Bob to take a seat.

Dr. Thomas turned to George to see how he was doing. George was highly disoriented, dazed look for the second time and Bob sensed George needed to lie down. The agent stepped forward and introduced himself as Jack and helped George assisted by Dr. Thomas through one of the doors to a large bedroom to lie down and rest. After George was comfortable and was given some water by a nurse who was already in the room, Jack and Bob started to quietly leave the room and return to the group when George was hit by another event.

While George was lying down, a brief communications burst hit his mind again. This time, there appeared to be some type of time schedule being fed to one of the millions of voices he had heard before. The booming voice from the creature with 4 eyes responded and indicated he was of a civilization known as the Tern and was connected to the "Care Givers" preparing to data record. Since George's mind had had a chance to adapt to his new situation, it was not as violent and disruptive as before. As in the previous transmission, this communications was based heavily on imagery with minimal spoken words from the creature calling itself a Tern. But the original creature responded he understood.

Bob waited until George was able to indicate to him that he was okay and left the nurse to see to his needs. Bob and Jack left the room to return to the outside room.

||||

Randy had been working late in the studio writing up notes on student oil paintings to give them details on ways to improve their techniques. When the phone rang, it was his boss, Professor Tony Rodriguez.

"Randy, I wanted to call and let you know that you will be contacted by a Dr. Thomas. I talked with the Dean. Dr. Thomas is very important to this school and needs our help."

"Dr. Rodriguez, I don't know what you need me for, but if I can help... sure."

"Thanks, Dr. Thomas will be faxing you some information. Please do what you can to give this some priority; we will all appreciate it if you can."

"I'll do what I can. I have some student help; she just finished her last assignment."

"Thanks, call me if you need anything. Have a good evening."

"Thank you Dr. Rodriguez, I will keep you updated."

After hanging up, he called Janet just as his fax machine answered an incoming call and started to generate a print out.

"Janet, sorry to bother you at home, but I just got a call with a high priority assignment. "

"Dr. Williams, no problem, I was just finishing some homework."

"Can you meet me at the studio around 7 a.m.? Information is just coming in and I can brief you on what this is about in the morning."

"Yes, certainly! See you in the morning professor."

After hanging up, Randy walked over to the fax machine and picked up the information and started reading. After a quick review, he placed the papers in his briefcase and headed out to pick up some dinner at the local burger drive through and continue looking over this assignment at his apartment.

At 6 a.m., Randy got out of bed after spending most of the night thinking about the images discussed in the fax; took a shower, dressed, and headed to the campus studio by way of Starbucks.

Janet rose in the morning with drooping eyes from sleep deprivation and after getting ready for school, talked to her younger brother John about making sure he was home tonight in time to fix Auntie and Uncle their dinner and helping his brothers to get their home work done. She told him she would be home late, that her teacher had some project for her to work on.

Pulling on her strength, Janet arrived at the studio with her normal energy and smile. Randy was at his desk going over the fax that had arrived from a Dr. Thomas the night before with a questioning look on his face. He had an extra Starbucks coffee waiting on the desk for Janet.

"Good morning. So tell me what this is about professor." As she sat down by the desk and picked up the offered coffee.

Randy handed her a copy of the fax he had received. "Dr. Thomas is a well known alumnus and has a patient that experienced some weird 'visions'. The Dean and department head wants me to make this a priority. The Doc needs us to visualize the information to help him with his patient. The idea is that if he can see what he is describing, perhaps it will help him remember more details which might shed light on his problem."

"I need you to help me make some quick sketches that we can try and get over to the Doc this evening. What does your class load look like today?"

"I have a science lab at 10 a.m. and classes from 1 p.m. to 3 p.m."

"Okay, I have to work a class to teach at 2 to 5 p.m., so I guess we need to get started and see what we can get done by say 6 p.m.?"

With that, Randy and Janet started going over the faxed material and with lively banter, began making sketches of various parts of the images described by George, discussing what George might have meant with various statements.

At 9:30 a.m. as Janet was getting ready to pack up to get to her science lab, two men in suits entered the studio area. As they approached, with a bit of defensiveness, Randy rose to see what they were doing there.

"We are looking for a Dr. Randy Williams," they said as they flashed their FBI badges.

"I am Dr. Williams, what can I do for you?" as his eyes narrowed.

"We have a warrant to collect everything faxed over to you by Dr. Thomas," as one of the FBI men handed Randy the warrant. "In addition, I need to ask who else you may have shared this information with".

"Janet and I were just beginning to work on the information that I received last night, we're the only two that have seen it." Randy looked at Janet with a quizzical look. Janet had a nervous feeling as she put her hand on her chest to feel her locket.

The FBI agents pulled up a chair. They looked at Janet and Randy and gave them the bad news. "You both may be in danger from this material. We need to put you into protective custody immediately to sort out this matter. We know there are agents of foreign countries that may want access to this information. If they find out about this and link it to you, it will put you both in extreme danger." they handed an additional document over to Randy.

Randy looked at the paperwork and saw his name along with the statement "and any other person who has come in contact with the information" as he handed it over to Janet.

"We need you to show us all copies of the fax and anything that you have written or in this case drawn from that information. We need you to come with us immediately."

"Let me call the department" as Randy reached over to call, the agent put his hand on the phone to stop him. "No one is to know anything about what has happened here. We will provide a cover story for you. We will instruct your boss that you received a call to ignore this and that it's no longer important. We must leave immediately and I need you to not talk about anything you have seen, telling us about the information just creates more risk, so please stay quiet until you reach your destination where you will be debriefed." They started collecting all the papers on the desk and the drawing pads that they had been using.

The agents escorted a nervous Randy and Janet out of the building and to a waiting SUV. Randy hovered around Janet in a protective posture as they were led out.

Upon entering the SUV, the agent asked Janet for her last name and address and proceeded to call in that both Randy and Janet were under protection. As he gave them Janet's name and address, he also indicated that agents needed to be sent to protect her family.

Once the SUV pulled out of the parking lot at the Baltimore, MD campus, they headed to the I-95 to get to Washington D.C. As they approached the Laurel Maryland exit, they noticed that a small blue pickup truck had been following them since leaving the University grounds. They pulled off at the Laurel Maryland exit and saw the truck follow as they reached the exit ramp. They immediately called for backup and radioed in the license plate. At the top of the ramp, they made a right as they went down a short distance, made a U turn and headed back to the I-95. As they got back on the I-95 towards D.C., they saw that the same truck was behind them back six cars. As they reached the D.C. beltway north, they saw two police cars come up from their rear, cut off the truck and pull the truck over. The word came across the radio that their triad tail had been blocked and they were to proceed to the Naval Observatory entrance.

After leaving the D.C. beltway, the SUV approached Georgetown in D.C. A white Honda suddenly pulled in front of them and came to a stop while a small dark blue truck pulled in behind them to try and cut them off. The FBI SUV driver quickly slammed on the brakes and spun to the left, barely missing a car coming from the other direction. He spotted an alley and slammed down on the gas. As he swerved into the alley, shots could be heard bouncing off the body of the SUV. As the SUV reached the end of the alley, the agents observed the Honda had entered in pursuit.

The FBI driver quickly raced the SUV up the side streets and the agent in the passenger seat called on the radio, "Let the gate know we will reach the compound in two minutes, be aware shots have been fired and we are coming in hot."

By the time the SUV reached the Naval Observatory gates, a Marine squad was positioned with guns ready. The SUV was waved through the gates as the Marines lay prone on the ground with their guns focused on any possible cars that may have followed them. After they passed through, barrier posts were quickly raised into position. As the Honda came around the corner onto the street leading to the Naval Observatory gate, the driver slammed on the brakes and quickly retreated to an adjoining street.

The SUV slowed down and proceeded up the road to a small building next to a large lawn with a helicopter landing pad. The FBI agents escorted Randy and Janet to an entrance to the small building where a Marine was guarding the door. As they approached, the FBI agents flashed their badges and the guard let them enter. Inside they found an elevator door open. Janet and Randy were asked to please get in and they would be met when the door opened. The FBI agent inserted a key, pushed the bottom button on the panel, and removed the key as they stepped back outside as the doors closed on them as Janet's eyes glanced at Randy for reassurance.

|||||

Jack had reached the office at 5 a.m.; he had a briefing for the Senate to prepare late in the afternoon. As he sat down at his desk, he found a summary report concerning the death of Bobby and the suicide of the kidnappers killing six swat team members; Jack's fury which had been significant before, was now barely controllable. They knew this was the doing of the mafia, the property was owned by them, the men worked for them, multiple intercepts were traced to suspected Russian mafia communications. This could only mean that Russian's had not taken the warning seriously.

While he was reading the report, his blood pressure was rising and his eyes were shooting flames, the phone rang. As Jack answered the phone, it was from Tim about a very high priority task relating to a man named George Scott at George Washington Hospital. After Jack got off the phone with Tim, he decided he needed to get the ball rolling on sending a message to the mafia before he headed out the door. He quickly called in one of the agents and briefed him about the warrants that were needed immediately relative to George Scott and Dr. Robert Thomas and others currently unknown. Before heading out the door, Jack placed another call.

Jack called on security team member Jimmy from the CIA as his anger continued to boil "Jimmy, this is Jack. As you may have heard, the Russians have continued to step over the line and we've got to showem we mean business. I need you to send them a message that they won't forget. "

"Jack, I think we know what to do. I don't want to let you in on the operation, but you will know when the message's delivered."

"Okay Jimmy. I'll leave this to you to deal with, make the message strong. I have another emergency I have to rush off to."

Once he hung up, he grabbed his coat and headed out to brief the recovery teams.

|||||

When Bob returned to the Presidential room, waiting on the sofa, was a pretty, young lady, slim with long black hair wearing white blouse and black slacks looking very distressed and accompanied by a gentleman dressed in brown slacks and a light blue polo shirt; a few years older, also very nervous.

Bob moved to an empty chair close to the young people and sat down to wait. As he looked around his analytical eye quickly picked up on the nervousness of Randy and Janet and the coolness of the agent across the room. Tim was calmer than normal but looked like a heavy weight cat about to pounce.

Tim finished typing on his computer located on a desk at the far end of the room. Everyone in the room looked at him, sensing he could bring together the threads that would answer why they were in this unusual position in this unusual place.

Chapter 10: Results

On a ship hanging in space as it traveled between stars, a tired Zarian of the Care Givers was moving from the control room to his rest area. His work on oversight of the Tern transport was a drain on his energy and he now turned to training of the young ones. His platinum blond hair fell gently from his head to the center of his back over the long white robes that helped gave his a look of grace and peace. As he headed to a rest chamber, his mind switched to an initial history training communications channel for the youngest of Care Givers that was underway and he closed his tired eyes for a brief moment to help focus.

The Care Givers were a race whose beginning was older than their current star; their civilization had only dim memories of the early times. Their race had existed long enough to see the birth and transformation of more than one yellow star. They lived in the outer zone of their galaxy known as Tuqvx where stars were less dense which allowed the forces to exist in a stable enough condition to produce and nurture life over a very long period. Tuqvx was positioned on the outer edge of the universe. With their age and knowledge, they had gained a great deal of information relating to The Master Pattern. Some felt it was just an organized unfolding of events that just happened to have a pattern; others felt strongly that this was a directed pattern. Either way, it helped their civilization to focus on helping younger civilizations to grow and find their way within this evolving Master Pattern, while continuing to increase their knowledge about the formation and evolution of the universe.

Zarian was like most Care Givers, being a tall bi-ped race. They had long graceful arms and their very look projected wisdom and patience. They preferred long flowing hair from their heads which in their middle years turned platinum blond. Their dress was in long robes which hid their feet with a single piece of unique individual metal attached around their neck over their robe. Their hands showed a graceful eight fingers with opposing thumbs.

The metal adornment was similar but each was unique for a Care Giver. The identification looked like a part of a DNA strand, with the DNA encapsulated within each step of the zipper type pattern. As each generation of a combined genetic code evolved into a new Care Giver, the history of the trace of their genetic code would be added within their visible metal adornment while previous DNA was copied from the adornments of the contributing DNA donors. This traditional symbol had started back beyond current memory of the race, but was a connection to their past. The design allowed a male-female pairing to pass along the lineage of their families to their offspring in a physical symbol.

The Care Givers race evolution was based on a male-female population, but in most respects there were no outward signs of difference other than their unique pendent. The need to mate to reproduce had long ago been replaced by a more controlled process that allowed them to manage their society and control genetic variance. Only a few new Care Givers needed to be bred in a cycle due to their long life and advanced genetics. New Care Givers were raised by the race, all contributing to the teaching and all providing early life support through their network connection that is established shortly after birth in their birthing centers. To reach maturity and to be trained to join their mission of support typically takes one hundredth of their normal life span and over the generations became a structured successful process, proved to be one hundred percent effective. While the efficiency of the process and control of the society had taken over from the emotional needs of the individual, the tradition of the lineage symbol continued on

They had discovered the ability to travel between stars using the wormhole generator and as such traveled the galaxy looking for rising civilizations and identifying those that they could help without undermining their path of existence.

Their original planet and star were no longer capable of supporting life. As they observed the early phase of the transition of their star from yellow to red, they had reached a point where they could begin a trek to another star. While this trek was slow (compared to current day travel), they had been able to save their civilization and, over time and with the continuing growth in technology, were now scattered throughout the galaxy, much as a super nova scatters new and life-giving minerals throughout the universe.

The Care Givers had survived the critical point that in every civilization allows them to continue or self destruct. When they approached a new civilization, they evaluated them against this critical point and its relationship of success as identified in the math behind the Master Pattern as they viewed it. If the civilization had not yet reached the critical point and the probability of success was too low, then the Care Givers would only monitor without interference. However, if the civilization showed it had reached and passed the critical point and would survive as indicated by the Master Pattern calculation, then the Care Givers would introduce themselves and offer them the chance to join the Galactic community they had founded, and begin the process of teaching-mentoring them as they grew.

In their past, they had tried to contact some civilizations too early and while they were able to help the civilization survive in some cases, in others it had driven them to fall apart and ultimately destroy themselves. They grew to understand the shock of first contact to a civilization, its effect of shifting the belief of self greatness to one of being a young race with much to learn. These were painful events to the Care Givers and while it was part of the Master Pattern, they learned from the events and became more cautious as a result.

With their growth in understanding the Master Pattern, their math had reached the ability to predict within a five percent error, of where a new civilization could be contacted without causing harm and where they were expected to perform contact. The Master Pattern was a pre-determined path, they could only follow. The effects of failure to understand the plan relative to what was going to happen was, in post analysis, predictable and provable.

While working with a younger civilization called the Tern whose star was showing the unstable signs of age, the Care Givers were contacted by a young scientist of the Tern who informed them of a connection he had sensed with another civilization. The Care Givers had decided to approach the Tern over ten cycles before, but required seven cycles of study to find the right moment to announce and approach. Their point of first contact came after a major broadcast across their world talking about the need to show strength with the coming failure of their star. The Care Givers issued a message to the population using the same broadcast satellites to introduce themselves and that they were coming to their aid, and would arrive soon, with time and landing coordinates.

The Care Givers' contact ship, a small craft with five Care Givers, landed in an open space outside their main city and was greeted by a large crowd that had gathered. With their jump capability, they had made the final jump only after the crowd had cleared the necessary space. Upon landing, the five member delegation had stepped outside and as the Tern leaders came forward, the Care Givers knelt with open arms and bowed heads to the Tern leaders as was their nature when making contact with a new civilization.

The Tern's planet was a normal planet found within what was considered the "water zone", a distance from their star that supported temperatures' that allowed for liquid water to exist. While different life forms formed under a widely different range of environments, water planets showed the greatest ability to protect developing life. The planet was approximately thirty percent covered in water and the Tern were the dominate race and the only advanced life form on the planet.

The Tern population had evolved in the normal manner, starting in the liquid domain and evolving to life on land. They were impressive in that their evolution was somewhat faster than many other races, but not outside of the variance curves the Care Givers had developed in analyzing civilizations. Their mental abilities allowed them to quickly adapt to new situations and their capacities in math and science were impressive.

This was a civilization that needed help to be moved to another star system to protect them when their star transitioned from yellow to red. The Care Givers were helping them catalog their world prior to transport and to provide the transport ships at the necessary time. A star had already been selected and a planet had already been identified to be shifted in its orbit to support more optimal conditions. The Care Givers were well underway in the work to prepare the planet by having it undergo modifications to support the Tern civilization. While the planet orbit needed to be moved and its atmosphere needed modification, this was well within the Care Givers ability through an ability to alter planet star rotation speeds and planetary mass that would soon be completed.

Transport of the Tern civilization would happen after the inventory process was complete and would take less than a single period of transit of their current planet around their star. The Care Givers were more than capable of making the transit to their new star much faster, but this was partially to give the team on the new planet some extra time to complete modifications and to also begin the teaching of the Tern civilization. The Tern needed to learn and prepare for their step to the stars and to become part of the Galactic community. During the transport cycle, the Care Givers needed to ensure certain basic genetic alterations in the Tern Civilization took place to both help them in transition to their new planet as well as ensure that they would not be a contagious risk to others races in the galaxy. The transport cycle was like a complex and interactive dance where many different tasks needed to be completed on time to allow for smooth transition of a race.

By contrast to the Care Givers, the Tern race was almost half the physical size of the Care Givers and while also being bi-ped designed, had very large skulls; almost twice the size compared to their body size as related to the Old Ones. The Tern possessed four eyes evenly positioned around their skull where the Care Givers had two forward mounted eyes. Their hands were based on three fingers with an opposing thumb.

The Tern race was well established, but very young by standards of the Care Givers. The Tern had not yet learned the basics of inter-stellar travel or the ability to use dimensional connections for transfer of information. But they did travel within their star system using a fusion powered engine and had progressed past the stage of societal conflict which was the downfall of multiple races that the Care Givers had monitored over time. Their progress allowed the Care Givers to take them under their teaching and begin the training to allow them to progress to the stars.

The young Tern scientist-Watcher that had reported contact with the Old Ones' was known as Jzzed. He indicated that contact had been formed with others across the universe. His sense of the situation indicated none appeared at this time to have the advanced understanding that the Care Givers or the beings that sent the initial message appeared to posses.

Jzzed was from the high mountains on the Tern planet. While physical differences between the different parts of the Tern population were not very noticeable, the population tended to differentiate itself based on its area of life. Jzzed was born in a mountain community but upon showing a high capability for science and math, had moved with his three mothers, four fathers, eight sisters, and ten brothers to the main city of learning by the great water. Here the family was provided work and support to help Jzzed as he progressed through his advanced studies.

He was still too young to form a family unit, but with the Watcher contact, was assigned a high place in the Tern society. Jzzed tended to study alone and was not known to be as heavily involved in the community as others from his family unit.

With the contact, Jzzed suddenly was now in a population of beings across the universe with which he had a significant connection. Also, he was now highly prized for his ability by the Care Giver race that had appeared only cycles before to help their planet.

The appearance of the Care Givers had changed their society from one that was aware of its impending death, to one that a whole galaxy was about to be opened too. The effect on society had been dramatic. Small squabbles were no longer important, worries about forms of exchange or food had been totally overcome with the society now focused on learning how to deal with races from a thousand worlds and support the search for Truth and The Master Pattern.

Initially, the appearance of the Care Givers had been questioned by many in the Tern society, but in their demeanor, words and deeds, the Care Givers had overcome any questions of motive. Not only did they bring hope, but they also taught their healers new techniques that had saved many and changed their approaches including the ability to re-grow limbs and repair major nerve damage. The Care Givers did not attempt to give technology that was not understood, but taught understanding of technology that proved the difference over time.

While not understanding the means of the connection to the others, their location or if there was a time-shift involved, the message received by Jzzed was clear, strong and undeniable. The calling card from the creature was easily understood and through the young Tern, the Care Givers were quickly able to respond that the connection was heard and understood.

The Care Givers were not a highly emotional race; rather they were very focused and practical. Upon a quick sub-dimensional mental consensus, Jzzed was provided an inter-dimensional link to allow him to funnel information to their shared storage, a planet purely maintained to store information with minimal physical presence. While connection of a single life form from a new species was not highly unusual, normally this was done on a race-by-race basis based on progress of their training design, not to an individual within a race; but this was not a normal circumstance.

The device was a simple set of small metal looking dots which attached to the skull, two around the area of the creatures brain that supported advanced thought, two at the rear base of the brain that supported body management. The pieces were able to form a network connection of the wearer's brain system to the multi-dimensional storage and communications network.

At first, the connection was regulated by the Care Givers as a one-way storage transmission to keep from overloading Jzzed's brain. The Care Givers were connected from birth, but new additions which join at an older, more aware, age required protection for a short while.

During the first days of Jzzed's connection, the Care Givers limited the flow of information into Jzzed's brain through their device. They gently probed the information of interest and provided a mental training course on controlling information transfer.

Watching Jzzed during this early time, others around him noticed moments of distraction with moments of total disconnect. The moments quickly shortened over a period of days and soon Jzzed was totally at ease with the connection to the data storage along with the Watcher pattern connection to the universe.

Using their galaxy wide connection, the Care Givers were making plans for focusing a team to do data analysis on this new universe-based connection. Contact with new races had been going on for hundreds of millions of generations, although none outside the galaxy; this was exciting news.

But while the data recording continued, the Care Givers had more pressing matters to ensure the schedule was maintained to allow the complete transfer of the Tern civilization before the star transitioned along with protecting other key systems and civilizations in the galaxy.

Jzzed was allowed to manage the connection while the Care Givers continued on their preparations to move the Tern society. To support this important work, Jzzed had agreed to move to the Care Giver main transport and to also support the environmental modifications between transmission periods given his mental link to the Care Givers.

A special section of the Care Givers planetary storage in a star system over 100 stars away was set aside for this special data as was their backup systems. The data storage systems were located on planets that could not support life but were in star systems that contained new stars and as such would provide a long period of time before they would have to move it.

After a short period of time, Jzzed's mind would be trained with the connection and ready to be able to freely roam their data storage of treasures. This storage contained information collected from hundreds of millions of years over hundreds of thousands of civilizations. In addition this held all the most advanced information the Care Givers had and were constantly developing as they probed The Master Pattern.

Chapter 11: A New Team Direction

Tim looked around the room and began.

"First, I am sorry for having to pull you from your lives, but it was a decision we needed to make and make quick. There is no way to easily say this; you can be in extreme danger and waiting could not be an option. Bob, the ruse was necessary. I could not be connected with George anymore than absolutely necessary and we needed to get you both here and get the situation under control as fast as possible. Please everyone, forgive me, but what was done was necessary both for your safety and the safety of your family and friends. As I told Bob, this is a national security problem of the highest level."

When Tim looked around the room he knew they didn't understand but the shock of the message had their full attention. How to continue? How to explain something he did not fully understand?

Tim took a deep breath and continued.

"First let me make sure everyone knows everyone else. I am Dr. Tim Decant and I am a program manager from DARPA, a Defense Research agency. My Doctorate degrees are in physics, mathematics and astrophysics. I was contacted by Dr. Thomas and presented information, some of which you are aware of. Bob" (as he gestured to Dr. Thomas), "Dr. Robert Thomas is a doctor of Psychiatry, and was assigned the case of George Scott, by the hospital. We have moved George here and he is lying down in the next room. During initial interviews with George, information was gathered which Bob wished me to review. He also sent parts of the information to Dr. Randy Williams" (he gestured to Randy) "to attempt to visualize the descriptions provided by George. In turn Randy, 'you don't mind if I call you Randy?' Randy called on Janet Belson "(as he nodded to Janet)" to help him in the effort. Janet is a student working for Randy and according to records we have accessed, has shown significant ability in her art talents and her high intelligence." Tim nodded toward Janet with a calm smile of acknowledgement.

"Upon receiving the information, I was able to recognize its importance which we will get too in a moment and brought it to the National Security office's attention. Jack Bord" (as he nodded to Jack standing by the wall) "is assigned full time from the FBI to act as my security lead on the team I manage. Jack gives me help in the area of field operations and security, based on our past and ongoing work together and his clearance on my project. The case was rapidly taken to a special judge assigned to these types of matters and paperwork quickly rose to the President early this morning, which allowed this special operation to be taken forward at maximum speed.

Now that we know who we all are, first there is paperwork; after all, this is the government. I am passing out a form which you all need to sign. This is a personal non-disclosure form and I can also tell you that background investigations have already started on each of you and your closest relatives under Presidential order. You are being brought into a highly classified, highly secret government black program and security clearance by Presidential order is formally being processed, but I have the ability to grant temporary clearance. Information that you currently are aware of and information that you will be told or discover can never be disclosed outside of the team which you are becoming a part of. For the moment, you will not be allowed to contact anyone outside this team. When you find out what this is truly about, I am confident you will never want others to know, because they will consider you insane."

Jack picked up papers from the desk Tim sat at and proceeded to hand them out along with pens.

"I know you have questions, but I can only answer some of them until you sign the paperwork." With that, Tim sat and waited.

Bob looked at Tim and broke the silent shock that hung over the room with a raised eyebrow and a questioning look. "Tim, I can't believe this is necessary. What about my other patients, what about my other work, friends, appointments, finances?" Bob was already beyond the initial shock of the national security aspect.

Tim's personality was strong, which Bob was fully aware of. While Tim had been able through the strength of his mental ability to claw his way out of his emotional collapse, Bob had grown to be impressed by the deep inner strength that he had along with his significant intellect.

"Trust me Bob. I am truly sorry that the four of you have been drawn into this matter, but after you sign the forms I will be able to fully explain, at least as best as I understand. George is a special matter and we will be handling it in time so as to not add stress to him, he already has a secret security clearance and we will easily be able to expand it. Please take your time and read over the document. I know this day and event has been a shocking experience but I must insist."

Janet was sitting quietly with a nervous look. Her lips were pursed with stress lines on her forehead. She had pulled out a necklace pendent that had been hidden in her blouse. She always wore it around her neck, since her mother had handed it down to her the year that her parents died in a car accident. The one inch eight pointed golden star was her personal treasure and had been made for her great-great-grandmother. Whenever Janet was stressed, she had a habit of clasping the pendent and the feel of her family gave her strength. As she clasped the pendent she was reminded of all the times her mother told her be strong and keep an open mind.

Suddenly Janet's quiet stress seemed to break and with it she sought support. "Mr. Decant, Tim, are you sure? This isn't a mistake?" Janet's eyes were darting around the room at all the various people, pleading for help and understanding. Her dark raven hair was tied with a simple rubber band and hanging to the shoulder blades. Her white blouse and black slacks held a thin college figure that showed her hours of exercise and yoga, but the signs of stress on her face were evident as her hand clasped the pendent while she sought inner strength.

"Yes Janet, I am as sure as I can be at this moment. Relax, you are safe here and because you are safe here, the rest of your family and friends are safer." Tim turned to everyone and continued "For everyone's benefit, we have placed surveillance to ensure the safety of your families and any close friends we are aware of. I think this matter has been contained and we should not have to worry about the safety of our friends and loved ones. As we understand more about your background, we will adjust protection as necessary. Your safety is of paramount importance to us. All financial problems will be handled so don't worry about lost wages or anything in that area. Your offices have been or will be informed that due to a personal emergency, you will be out of town for a period of time and to cover your patients and classes. Janet, your family is being briefed on a cover story and John Hopkins has been notified that you will not be attending classes for a period of time, but oh by the way, we fully expect you will graduate on time with honors.

"Now, please, relax and sign the forms. I also need to advise you, Bob, that unknown to you during our previous sessions, your background was reviewed under Presidential signed order against knowledge that I may have accidentally revealed classified information during our sessions. You were not informed at the time as a security precaution, although we have kept you under surveillance for your own safety since the sessions started. It turned out not to be necessary at the time, but because of the information you have now observed, we feel its best we be upfront with you."

Bob was not surprised. Having dealt with a number of government people, he always suspected that at some level his background had been reviewed.

Randy looked at Tim and with a deep breath, took the next step. "What if I refuse?"

Tim understood, he had thought about this question many times when he considered bringing people into the team that had never dealt with black program security matters before. Tim looked at the small group and continued, "I can't make you sign, after all it's just a piece of paper and it really is the commitment that we are asking for, blind faith at this point, if you would. If you refuse, it will not change the fact that you have knowledge which puts many people, including yourself and your families at significant risk of being killed and presents danger to our nation. In this case, we would be forced to put you under protective custody and you would lose your freedom without us gaining the use of your intelligence, your skills and support in answering some of the most important questions of all time in our civilization.

Let's all understand something, your lives have changed and cannot go back to what they were before. It's that simple. It's impossible to put the genie back in the bottle. I'm offering you a chance to use your abilities and talents to work on one of the greatest projects in history. I promise you that you will be leading the world into a new future that people throughout history have only dreamed about, all through this work we are undertaking. But it's your choice."

Tim waited while the three of them looked at each other and then with a resigned gesture, Bob, Randy and Janet read the papers provided them, and one by one signed the forms. Janet was obviously shaken, and Randy was a bit nervous himself. If Bob was nervous, his training allowed him to control his outward emotions but the pen in his fingers was beginning to twirl.

When the papers were signed and collected, Tim took a deep breath, closed his notebook computer, and looked at everyone in the room. As he collected his thoughts, he left the desk he had been sitting at and moved to a stuffed chair closer to the rest of the group.

"Welcome to the classified program 'BELLOWS'; which only a hand full of people outside this program are aware of. This program has a hidden funding line in the DARPA budget within the Department of Defense. As a black program, we 'officially' have no funding that the public is aware of and do not exist. You all have a unique place in this program which, thanks to George, has just taken a significant change in course and scope.

"We will provide a security contact to each of you to fill out basic security forms. I have instructed the security team to do most of the work and you will just give them what information they need. I don't want you wasting your valuable time involved in the paperwork that the Government will not really use, but insists on having."

With a smile of confidence, Tim looked at his new team members and stated, "Now down to business. The information sent to you, Randy and Janet, what did you make of it?"

Randy was the first to speak as he looked at Janet.

"The descriptions appeared to be some type of fantasy worlds. When I read the descriptions, they first struck me as extremely vivid, but only in a fantasy could a world exist with life forms where the air was yellow. The life form described sounded more like the little gray men from science fiction, but the lack of eyes or ears or hair left me puzzled since all the other details were so specific. Another oddity was that the description indicated that the creature that was the focus of the description was generating symbols in mid air. I will need to refer to the notes to describe them, but the notes are very detailed about this."

Janet looked at Randy then added, "At first I thought that the details of the sun contained within a shell with the description of the creatures, was made up. What caught my attention was the detailed description of the hands of the creature. The descriptions were extremely detailed and different than anything I have ever read or seen. The description of eight fingers per hand that acted like living moving vines along with the details of the pulsing movement was fascinating. Most of the symbols I didn't recognize, but one I think I've seen before in an old drawing dealing with

Professor Einstein." This caused Tim to quietly make a note on the pad he had in his lap.

Tim realized Janet was finishing her short statement; he looked at Bob with a raised eyebrow. Bob took the hint and with a calm demeanor added his impressions. "When I first was able to speak to George, it was very halting as if his mind was focused on something else and barely recognized my being there. My original diagnosis was some type of psychosis, but I found nothing in existing references that could be related. As I continued to talk with him, the information that I have presented you started coming out. The strangest part of it though, and I'm not sure how well it was captured in the information I sent to you, was his constant switching between speaking and what I could only classify as humming or singing. As I would ask him about his humming, he didn't appear to know that he was doing it. When he focused, he knew it wasn't his normal voice and related it to the creature that first talked to him. He would go over the same information area with more spoken detail but with a sing-song voice, and then break into this hum-sing at different points, not providing English, but some complex song."

Tim was focused intently adding notes to his pad and then began his tale of the last 24 hours.

"Bob, you're right about the music part, I'd not seen that in my short review of your notes. That does provide an interesting twist which we may have to account for. Janet your recognition of the symbol also brings a new path of investigation for us." Tim looked at Jack who shook his head in acknowledgement.

Tim continued "The projects I have been working on over the past ten years have to do with a scientific theory known in its various forms as String Theory or in other forms as we have advanced forward, Membrane Theory also known as M-Theory. Many in my field consider this as a fringe area of research; some jokingly call it the theory of Magic. Some researchers in the scientific field think it's not really a scientific theory; others of us put much more credence in the field of M-Theory. While I am not the lead mathematician on the team at the moment, I have a pretty strong background in physics and math. We have been investigating the portion of the theory dealing with something known as quantum loops and their relationship to particle formation with the hope of creating new materials. I know you will have a hard time understanding this and it's not real important that you do, but suffice to say, I see a lot of high powered math and spend a large portion of my days trying to understand their relationship to the real world.

Randy and Janet, you were not furnished all the information. George indicated the symbology he felt was math equations. If you had been, it most probably would have little or no meaning to you, although now I would like you to take on research to see if you recognize anything in the extended symbolism.

"When I first saw the symbols, my initial thought was that it was made up, a fantasy at best, or an attempt by our counter parts to send our work down a rabbit hole at the worst. But as I looked closer, I realized that it contained the same form as the math equations I have been dealing with. Only the symbols were different and there were subtle changes to the equations. In addition, there was a new equation to the set and once I began to sense the mapping of the symbols, this new equation caught my attention. I quickly grew to realize the importance, and the risk that it was genuine which in turn raised the effects to the highest level. I called my full team and immediately set them the task of verifying. I glanced at the description provided to you, Randy and Janet, and the answer hit me square between the eyes.

"The floating symbols that were described in the information provided by the creature are the key. The equations we work with will work in a large number of different universes, and we have not been able to figure out how to define our universe, but I strongly think the symbols provide the keys to a specific universe design. This information, along with the extended set of equations, may be the answer we have been searching for.

"Although we continue to verify the information, I personally have come to the conclusion that George is in contact with someone, somehow not of this earth.

"I and my team monitor all work in this world that relates to these equations, George could not possibly have developed this himself. Whoever they are, the information they transmitted through him, I think, could best be referred to as a calling card to catch our attention. If we are advanced enough to comprehend the equations, then we might be able to communicate with them or at least be worth communicating with."

Everyone looked around and it became aware to Tim that the others didn't understand most of what he was talking about or why this was so threatening and therefore, why they were there. They all seemed to have a questioning look on their faces. Tim turned to Bob.

"Bob, you remember why we met?"

"Yes, it was due to the death of your family in the plane accident."

"Yes and no. Yes, my wife and son along with others of my friends and team members, died in a plane crash, but I couldn't tell you everything. It was not an accident." As Tim let it settle in, he took a deep breath to calm himself. The pain would never really go away despite the hours of crying and loneliness; the same pain that continued to drive him to work harder, to keep from thinking about the past and collapsing inward.

"The team I lead has been trying to change theory into reality. Of course, we are not the only people in the world working on this. When the Soviet Union fell, many of the top scientist and mathematicians were taken by the Russian underworld to work for them. And of course the Chinese have a team also working in this same area.

"The stakes are huge. They can reach from time travel to being able to build the most powerful weapons imaginable. Everything you have ever seen in science fiction, if there is a chance of it actually being real, we believe it's going to come from these equations.

"Two years ago, I wrote a paper with my wife that made a minor break through. From that paper, this team was formed and we were able to create a capability of bending the electromagnetic spectrum around an object."

Tim looked around at the dazed group and said one word "Invisibility" and smiled with the internal feeling of success.

"The M-Theory math leads our team to the development of a unique multi layered strata wafer chip with a complex chemical compound irradiated with specific energy neutrons. When a specific resonating frequency is applied to the chip, it generates an electromagnetic blocking field that causes photons to jump around the field as if there was nothing in the space.

"The engineering team has been able to produce the compound wafer and create a controlling system to manipulate the size and spread of the electromagnetic blocking field.

"In short, we are able to make objects invisible.

"The plane that carried my family also carried a number of the people on our team. The plane was attacked because of the knowledge the team members had. Our security was slack, not truly understanding the threat. While they don't know what we were able to do, the Russian mob and the Chinese secret service were, and still are, desperate to slow us down, knowing that we have done something.

"The keys of the information you have observed, are the most valuable pieces of information on the planet and there are very dangerous people who would do anything to get their hands on it if they knew about it. I had to rapidly make sure that they did not find out about it. Trust me; while we know of some of them constantly watching us, we don't know all of them. It's the ones we don't know about that are my worry."

At that point, Tim looked at everyone. Randy was smirking, obviously unimpressed. Janet was looking with questioning eyes. Bob was not smiling but was projecting his doctor face and looked at Tim with eyes of compassion. "I know the pain is still in you, but I think I understand why you didn't tell me the whole story." The inference from Bob's eyes was that he could read Tim's pain and there is still work to be done between them to continue to help Tim. As always, his patient came first.

Randy looked at Tim. "Surely you don't expect us to believe this science fiction junk."

Tim continued, "If I were in your position, I probably would feel the same. Jack, would you please throw the switch?" Jack walked over to the wall next to the elevator door and pulled back a panel. Beneath the panel was a red switch, which Jack threw.

In an instant, suddenly a large crystal light chandelier appeared over the center of the room. Randy, Janet, and Bob looked in amazement at the sudden appearance. For one of the first times since Tim had met Bob, he saw true shock on his face as his eyes grew and his mouth opened. Randy stood up with hesitation and reached up to touch the crystals. As Jack reversed the switch, the chandelier disappeared and Randy's hand seemed to disappear with it. Randy quickly pulled his arm and hand back, brushing the crystals as his hand reappeared. As the crystals clinked together, Janet gasped in amazement. Everyone could hear the clinking of the crystals, but no one could see the chandelier. Randy slowly backed up stunned and dazed. He proceeded to sit down with a look of shock on his face.

Bob, Randy, and Janet looked at each other with true shock on their faces. The sudden, undeniable fact of their situation began to sink in and with it Janet softly began to cry. The crying of Janet brought Bob back to his doctor mode and his face softened as he reached over to touch her arm and gave her a look of compassion but his other hand was twirling the pen and suddenly broke it.

With the snap of the pen, Jack looked at Tim and a smile came over Tim's lips. As Jack looked at Tim, he knew that look, and it was going to be another long night.

Jack moved over to the bar and poured three brandies which he brought over to the new team members as Tim looked at them. "Please take a drink; it will help to calm you. I understand the shock. But as I told you, this is real and you need to realize your lives have changed and will never be the same again."

Tim gave them a quiet minute to try and gather themselves and then continued.

"This capability was based on a small part of the equations that we were able to understand. The uses are massive; imagine a complete nuclear tipped missile hidden from detection and launched against us or even a suitcase nuclear device that no one can see until it goes off. The first knowledge we would have would be on detonation. This is our first and to date, only discovery; but I think you have to agree, it's a whopper. It was only through a lucky break in the way we were analyzing the equations and data from analysis runs, that I spotted this ability a few years ago. To date, our intelligence has not been able to spot the other teams as having found the solution, although they have heard rumors that we have discovered something...and thus the deaths of our team members and my family.

"The deaths were to obtain two purposes. One was to slow down the progress they felt we were making. The second was to let us know that the game was for keeps. We could not allow progress to slow down. While I attempted to regain control of myself, "he nodded to Bob"we reconstructed the team, took it into a deep black program with maximum security. I was already known to the opposition and hiding would have just given them more information that we had discovered something and their efforts to penetrate the team would grow even larger. I proceeded to both lead the team and act as a diversion.

"Jack was brought into the project to investigate and to lead counter measures. Work dealing with the foreign agents and monitoring of the foreign teams progress has continued and falls under Jack's domain. Some recent events and the knowledge that George has brought to us has now changed all of that." Tim looked at Bob who sat quietly in his chair. "With that knowledge, it has just complicated all our lives."

"Our team continues the leading edge work. The development based on our discovery, has transitioned to the engineering team for expanded work and more direct applications. We continue to focus on the initial understanding of the theories and attempts to develop direct usage.

"So, something I would like you to understand about how this team operates. I do not hide information from anyone. Everyone on the team is trusted and everyone has access to the information. We truly pull together as a team and we do whatever is necessary to help in whatever way we can. Everyone knows what's happening with security, math, engineering, research, and now George and you....everything. I need our best minds working and hiding information doesn't allow for the needed free-flow of ideas. However, and I must strongly point this out; while we do not hide information from each other, we do not release information to anyone outside our team...anyone!"

Tim looked at the dazed and amazed group and decided they were overloaded. "Okay, enough for now. We have set up rooms for each of you and tomorrow after you have had a chance to relax and absorb some of this, I will introduce you to the rest of the team and this new phase of our work will begin."

Jack asked Randy and Janet to follow him as they stood on somewhat shaky legs. He looked at Bob, who understandably nodded toward the room where George was resting with his composed face and broken pen in his hand. Tim joined Bob as he headed over to check his patient. Bob turned for a moment and spoke to Randy and Janet, "I'll be along in a few minutes, I think the three of us could do with a talk alone?"

Janet and Randy looked at each other and then back to Bob with a silent nod of their heads and as Randy helped Janet, they followed Jack into the elevator.

Bob and Tim entered the bedroom. Bob went over to the bed to verify that George was asleep. He turned to Tim and reverted to his doctor form; "George was scheduled for an MRI scan and some brain activity monitoring, I think we should try and go through with it. Can we figure out how to schedule it? It might help answer some questions."

"We have already scheduled time at a secure facility we have. I want to assure you that we have a team of doctors standing by to help you with whatever tests you need, or help you feel is necessary. George is extremely important to us and everything possible to help him is and will be done. For the moment, you are now the physician in charge."

Tim escorted Bob through a different door into an equally luxurious room, complete with office and exercise equipment. Bob noticed that there was a monitor showing George and feeding his vital signs so that Bob could if necessary, work in this area and monitor George's condition remotely. After looking around, Tim took him back to the meeting room and they entered the elevator.

The next floor up opened to a different environment. Halls extended in both directions with a number of doors visible. As Bob noticed, there was a graphic screen on the wall showing a layout of the hallways and a variety of room sizes, some large and marked as labs, others marked as meeting rooms and still others indicated as kitchen, dining room, and bedrooms. As he looked at this fascinating screen, Tim pointed to three blips, each labeled; Jack, Randy and Janet were in one of the bedrooms and headed for a door leading to the hallway. Tim indicated on the screen which room was set aside for him.

At the same time Bob looked down the hallway, Jack, Janet and Randy appeared and Tim waved them to come join them. Bob and Tim headed down the hall and once they all joined together, Jack and Tim directed the small group to the dining area. As they entered the dining area, Tim and Jack looked at Bob and the others, "We have work to do, we'll leave you to relax and gather your thoughts. I know you can't look out a window, but it is evening up topside. Have some dinner and talk, I'll see you in the morning around 9 a.m. okay?" Randy, Bob and Janet quietly shook their heads in agreement.

Tim and Jack left the group to deal with other problems. Bob, Randy and Janet headed to a table and as they walked over, they stopped to look at a large display against one of the walls. Inside the display was a set of medals, photos of a number of people and a statement "To those who gave their last great measure of service, we honor you and will never forget." The pictures included men, women and one small boy who had died because of the project.

After looking at the memorial, Janet, Bob and Randy in a bit of a solemn mood, sat down at a table and opened the menus. As a waiter came to their table, they ordered from what appeared to be an extensive menu choice, but which at the moment held only minimal interest. As they sat looking at each other, Bob knew he had another set of patients which were now his responsibility and with that acceptance he knew what needed to be done. His big question was; who would be helping him?

While the evening progressed, and the meal arrived, Bob was leading the discussion.

"So I know the immediate facts about each of you, can you fill in some of your background? Randy, where are your roots?"

With a slight shaky start "I moved here originally from Colorado. I grew up in Boulder; I'm 28 and have no brothers or sisters. My family has a history in the arts. My grandfather was a painter; my father is an illustrator and runs the graphic arts department for a book publisher. My mom is a stay-at-home housewife. My transition into the arts was a natural progression I guess. I enjoy writing and my favorite form of expression is in oil paints.

"After high school, I entered the University of Colorado. I was able to get a job assisting a teacher in the art department, and as my education continued, I realized I enjoyed teaching and working with young artists. During the summers, I worked as an intern for the publisher in my father's department to gain practical experience that I could use to teach. After my Masters degree, I received an offer from John Hopkins to get my Doctorate. I moved to Maryland and after my Doctorate, joined their teaching staff.

"My work has been my focus; I don't have much free time outside of it."

As the look of Bob bore into Randy, Randy felt the need to explain. "I know I need to slow down, get some me time and consider dating. But now, given this event, I think I need to think about my priorities in life."

With Randy's personal admission, Bob jumped in, "Work focus is important, but gaining balance in our lives is much more important for the long term," (as he thought about himself and a flash of a frown came and went) "I agree these types of life changing events are great points to re-evaluate and make changes. Janet, I would like to hear your story."

Janet looked at Bob and Randy and after taking a deep breath to help calm her nerves and with her pendent in her tight fist, she began.

"I was born and raised in Laurel, Maryland. I have three brothers and we are living with my aunt and uncle since my parents' death in a car accident seven years ago. With their life insurance, being the first to graduate from high school, I have gone to college for the last three years, the first two at Laurel Community College and this last year I transferred to John Hopkins. My major is in art history and in my first semester I took a class and drawing studio class taught by Randy.

"Because I have to work to help my family, I was offered a job to work with new students under Randy's supervision starting last January.

"I have a lot to learn to become really good, but I've learned a lot in my first year and hope to graduate and become a concept artist. My skills on computers are what I consider my forte, but I also enjoy oil painting.

"There is no time for a social life. I'm too busy helping to raise my brothers and helping my aunt and uncle. Their getting up in years and aren't able to handle everything themselves. I've been trying to find a way to make this all work and continue in college, but I was getting close to my wits end and nothing was working out.

Having promised my brothers that no matter what, we will stay together as a family, I'm beating my brains out trying to find a way to help them go through college and find their dreams. I don't know how, but I can't abandon them and this sudden shift scares me.

"I really don't have any time for socializing. Between helping my aunt and uncle, working with my brothers, school, home work, and my job to keep us going, there are not enough hours in the day as it is."

Bob sensed she had finished, he jumped in.

"I know that this is a major disruption to you, we'll see what can be done to make you more comfortable with the situation. But from what we have just seen and heard, people with information about this program have died, so we have to put our lives and the safety of our family before comfort.

You both have a path in your life. This event can be good or bad for each of you. I want to help you to make this a positive change in your lives."

With talking, the three became more relaxed. They continued talking about themselves along with their plans which now seemingly were on hold and found out more about each other's lives. They finished their meal then moved to find an empty meeting room to let the people clean up the dining area. In the meeting room, they continued to talk well into the evening as they tried to grasp their situation and come to grips with this sudden shift in their lives, and the simple fact that world had changed dramatically in the past few hours. Eventually, they headed back to their rooms to try and get some sleep; it had been a long day and tomorrow promised to be no shorter.

When the 9 a.m. meeting time arrived, Bob found Tim, Janet and Randy in a conference room along with a larger and different group of people. As Bob arrived, he immediately found the coffee pot and grabbed his morning coffee and observed that Janet and Randy were more confident than the night before. The new members were introduced to the team members present, and Tim began the meeting.

"I hope our new team members had time to grab some sleep and get settled. Most of you volunteered to work on this project, some of you were chosen by events. No matter what, we are all in this together."

Over the next hour, Janet and Randy were assigned to progress with the work of drafting visualizations of the information that Bob had originally sent them. In addition, the morning session added an additional layer of descriptions that needed to be viewed through the eyes of the artist. In addition, they were asked to research where Janet had previously seen the symbol she had recognized, and the work needed to progress with examining the other symbols. Tim agreed with Bob that visual feedback of the information might help in eliciting additional details and information from George.

Bob, with his game face on, knew where his jobs lay: George, Tim, Randy and Janet. He would need to work with the doctors assigned by Tim to help with George and, hopefully, one of them could also act as a counselor for him to talk to.

The meeting began to wind down when a man entered the room and approached Tim. After a couple of comments between them, the rest of the team looked at Tim as he turned to the new members with a hint of a smile. "I have some good and bad news for everyone. First the bad news: the math team," as he nodded and gestured toward some of the members to his right and the man that just entered the room, "has determined that the equations truly are real; the good news: the equations are real." Tim's wry sense of a joke didn't go over well.

"With the proof of the equations, the information we have heard from George, the apparent continuation of communications; this all leads us to the undeniable conclusion that we now are tapping communications between two vastly advanced alien races somewhere in our universe." Tim looked across the group silently for a moment to let it settle in. "If we are up to the challenge, the chance to reap a major leap in technology and understanding of our universe and our human environment is on our door step and we are the only people on earth that have this ability. The human race is literally depending on us, on each of you, to get this right.

"In preparation of the expected verification of the information, I have talked with the President relative to this and he asked I express his full support for this team, for each and every one of you. Each of you represents some of the brightest and best in your fields. Each of you have a high level of intelligence and are fully capable to advance knowledge in your chosen fields. This is something we can do; this is something we must do. We will succeed and in our success, will alter the course of human history.

"Any question for our team to back out of the work now has just evaporated. We are all committed and I personally promise I will do whatever I can to give you support, and provide any and every tool you need to succeed.

"Now, to continue with covering scheduled team events. Jack will join us at tomorrow's meeting to go over some operational security areas we need to be aware of. We all have direct access to all information being developed from George. I have scheduled systems training for each of our new team members. If any of our new team members need advanced training to understand how to operate unique capabilities of our systems; please contact me and I will have a trainer sent to help you. We all have work to do, so let's get too it. We get back together tomorrow morning same bat time, same bat channel."

At the point where the meeting broke up, Tim asked Bob to stay for a moment. After the others had left the room, Tim indicated to Bob that there was another assignment that they would be undertaking.

"Jack is thinking that now with you being a member of the team, we can use this opportunity to confuse our opponents. They know I visited you before and if we make them think I need additional help, maybe we can distract them. I can't make you take this assignment, I won't kid you: this may involve some danger. I just want you to think about this: if we can send the bad guys in the wrong direction, it may give our team some breathing room. Think about it, we'll talk later when Jack has had time to put together some ideas." With that bombshell and a slight look of disbelief on Bob's normally controlled face, Tim smiled, turned and walked out of the room.

Janet and Randy spent time with George talking about the symbols. They began to realize that their initial view of the symbols was simplistic compared to the written language of the Old Ones. Each symbol actually had subtle embedded patterns that contained information relative to emotion and environment such that like a comparative simplistic Chinese spoken word, there were many possible dimensions of information projected by the correct design of the symbol.

Their work evolved not only to capture the richness of the visions of George, but to try and build the written language of the Old Ones, an art form all to itself.

Bob went down to George's room and in the next door study, sat down with the medical team. They had gone over George's ER records and as the discussion evolved, it was agreed that nothing except simple sedatives could be used, but only when necessary. They could not afford to impact George's sensory capability any more than absolutely necessary. The MRI was scheduled along with the brain function mapping and a complete physical during times when transmissions were not active. This was as much to ensure that George's physical body had no conditions that needed treatment and would put him in any danger. Of special concern were some minor indications of the starting of type-2 diabetes from the stress and overweight condition.

A special diet was ordered for George to reduce his calorie and sugar intake and to stop the rise in blood sugar. The medical team came to a quick agreement that working with the security agents, an exercise regiment would be established to help George drop some of his excess weight and increase his stamina.

Bob set up private and group sessions with Randy and Janet. Others on the team, quietly came forward privately to Bob. They were asking for some help coping with the radical shift in their perception of life and the world. The fact that they were torn from their lives, Bob understood the need to give them a way to express their worries and fears. During their sessions, Bob would identify key things in their life styles that could be done to relieve their anxiety. There was nothing that could be done, other than just allowing them to express their fears and work through them, to cope with the fact that it was no longer a question that we are not alone in the universe.

It was during such a session that Bob become aware of the depth of Janet's family promises and worries.

Janet broke into tears as she grasped the pendent hanging around her neck "I don't know what to do, they must think I ran away. I promised to help them. They're all I have and I'm all they have. Being locked away here is just tearing me apart. Not knowing that they are okay, they have food and that they are going to school like they should and that auntie and unc know I am okay. What can I do? I find it almost impossible to focus. I worry so much about them."

After the session, Bob relayed key bits of information to the identified human resource people attached to the BELLOWS program and Janet was asked to write a letter, but she could not disclose any information. She was later informed that her letter and her paychecks as a member of the team were being delivered to her Aunt and Uncle. Janet had written in her letter she had to leave immediately due to a new job position that required her to leave without saying goodbye and would be in touch in the near future to explain.

One of the medical doctors working with Bob to support George had done some work in therapy and volunteered to act as Bob's therapist. During these sessions, Bob began to relax and the pen twirling slowed down as he decided he needed to do something to shape up his personal life and allow others to help carry the load of his professional life. Bob decided he needed to focus on a smaller group, the group he now had was close to the right size. In addition, he needed to find that someone special and not drive her away.

|||||

As the sun beat down on a small town in southern Switzerland, a normal day for the sleepy area was underway. The wind was a small cooling breeze and the traffic on the streets around the park was the normal flow with horns honking and hands waving out of the car windows as the Italian blood drove the hands of expression.

Outwardly, Nicky was a just a normal ten year old boy. While he tended to be the outsider with the other kids at school; he was happy. He was not at the top of his class, but was sharp and quickly picked up on ideas. He loved music; he wasn't great at any instrument, but loved listening to it. He would spend hours in his room, listening to music of all types. His favorites were Italian Operas, closely followed by other classical music; another reason he was on the outside amongst the kids at school. Nicky would read science fiction books about exciting trips to the stars and about great battles in the galaxy while listening to his music.

Nicky was born in Chiasso, Switzerland and enjoyed his life in the area. The vineyards, the Alps, the lake Como on the Italian side and Lake Lugano on the Swiss side all influenced his life and all gave him pleasure. On Saturdays or Sundays when his father had time, they would take their fishing gear and go to one of the lakes or just take some simple food and sit and enjoy playing games. It didn't matter if they caught anything, but just being able to sit and talk about trips to the stars or how school was going or how the local kids were treating him...just talking mattered.

Nicky was lively, happy and healthy to the relief of his father. His father Renaldo worked for the Swiss National Railroad and dealt with the tracking of materials the trains carried as they passed the Swiss Italian boarder bringing goods to the north and sending goods south. Nicky's mother, before her death from a car accident when Nicky was 3, was a school teacher and taught English. Renaldo made sure that Nicky learned at least some English in addition to his native Italian along with some German and French.

Renaldo Serrano spent as much time with his son as possible. When he was working, he made sure that a neighbor or a sitter was always available to ensure Nicky was taken well care of. On weekends, the two of them often would take long drives through the Alps or to Lugano. Sometimes, they would go for fondue at a restaurant north of Lugano. While the two of them enjoyed their time together, Renaldo worried about the lack of close friends for Nicky.

Nicky enjoyed climbing the hill side to the three castles north of Lugano and playing kickball in the large open areas in the lower castle. He was fascinated by the museum in the middle castle and Renaldo enjoyed the exercise of trying to keep up with his son as they climbed the steps up and down the hill.

Father and son enjoyed taking some simple bread, cheese and meats with water or soft drinks and going into the Alps. They would find a place on the road and just get out with a blanket and sit and talk. During the spring Nicky would pick flowers that they could take to his mother's grave and leave for her.

The day of the connection, school was out and since it was late in the afternoon, it was still warm, and it was time to be outside and have fun. Nicky was sitting on the park bench watching the football game as it began to wind down and the boys were getting ready to head home for dinner. He rarely played, sometimes the kids would call on him when they were short of players, but seldom was passed the ball. As he sat watching, the feeling overcame him like a huge wave crashing on the shore. He couldn't control it, he couldn't speak; he could only endure.

The images were overwhelming his mind as images of a strange creature waving its hand and generating lines came bursting through, soon followed by the images being sent by other creatures responding. Nicky was not able to control his mind to even be able to control his own thoughts. It was like being hit by a truck as he crossed the road. He couldn't control his body functions, only the fact that the basic brain stem functions that managed his temperature, heart beat and breathing were not affected kept him alive.

Nicky collapsed as his legs gave way. The other kids noticed a problem and came running over. The oldest boy was Lucio (a whole year older than the others) and he quickly tried to get Nicky's attention as his voice raised in concern. When Nicky did not respond, Lucio picked up Nicky's limp body and helped to stretch him out on the grass.

Lucio yelled to the others "Pronto, ottenere aiuto! Get help!"

One of the boys spotted a passing adult and called out for help. He raced over to where the man was walking down the side walk, yelling that Nicky needed help immediately.

Lars was a business man that had just arrived in Chiasso to visit an old friend and happened to be out for an afternoon stroll around town. As the young boy approached screaming for help, Lars rapidly ran to where the boys were huddled with a growing look of concern on his face. As he saw the young body stretched out on the grass, he looked to see if he was breathing and if there was any blood. Not seeing any blood, he pulled out his cell phone and called emergency services.

He waited with the boys as emergency services arrived along with a police man. As they transferred him to a gurney and set up transport to the Terme hospital, the policeman started asking questions about what had happened.

Lars indicated that he had been called over by the boys and had no idea what had happened to the young boy. Lucio told the policeman that his name was Nicky and he had been watching them play. When they looked over, he had just collapsed on the ground and no one knew why. Lucio continued that they went to school together, but he did not know exactly where he lived.

While they had taken Nicky to the Terme hospital, the policeman called the school and received both his address and emergency contact. As he called in his report, his Captain called the emergency number and reached Renaldo; he explained that Nicky had been transported to the hospital. Beyond knowing that he was alive and breathing and there were no outward signs of harm, they had no idea of what was wrong.

Renaldo had been involved in reviewing records on a large shipment of lumber going through Switzerland on its way to Italy when the emergency call came in. He ran over to the manager's desk with a frantic look on his face.

"I've got to leave immediately; Nicky has been taken to the hospital. No one seems to know what's wrong. I don't know anything, but will call you as soon as I do." And without waiting for a reply, he ran out the door to his scooter and rushed to the hospital. Traffic was busy, so Renaldo did what was normal and went down between cars that were barely or not moving in an attempt to maneuver through the traffic throng. After turning onto a side street, he was able to reach the back parking area of the hospital and rushed to park his scooter before running into the hospital emergency area.

Renaldo rushed to the nurses' station, breathlessly.

"My name is Renaldo Serrano, my son Nicky should have come in here. I need to find out what is happening."

The nurse scanned the patient list and looking up at Renaldo with a look of annoyance, "Yes, he just arrived and the doctors are looking at him. Please feel out these forms and have a seat, as soon as we know something we will come find you."

"No, I want to see him now!" Renaldo demanded with a growing rage.

As she observed the desperation on Renaldo's face she re-evaluated the moment "Okay, follow me and I will show you where he is."

After seeing Nicky's room with the doctors looking over him, Renaldo calmed down some and started filling out the forms for the nurse. After completing the forms for the nurse, Renaldo sat in a chair close to the bed and waited. After a half hour, the doctor turned to him. Nicky was lying in a dazed state.

"I understand this is your son? First, he is alive and none of his vital signs show any hint of danger. We cannot find any indication of trauma or internal bleeding. There is no sign of any drugs in his system, although we have taken blood samples to test. At this point, we are stumped. I would like you to sit down with our nurse and help us with information if you could."

"Of course, Nicky is a good boy. He knows not to take drugs. I will answer any questions to help him."

Within a few minutes, a nurse came by and pulled up a chair and calmly began to ask a number of questions about Nicky's health history. Renaldo answered what he could and gave the nurse information about the doctor where he took Nicky for his checkups.

After a few hours, there was no change in Nicky that Renaldo could see as he sat and prayed for God to help his son. Renaldo held Nicky's hand while he talked to the memory of his wife about Nicky, asking if she could help.

Eventually, the doctor came by to tell Renaldo that nothing was being seen in the blood work. "Since he seems to be in some form of hyperactive brain state as we can see through his rapid eye movement, I would like your permission to give him a light sedative to see if we can calm down his brain. It's the only thing we can think of at the moment."

"Yes, whatever you think is best for him."

"Okay, we will be moving him to a room up on the fourth floor. You can stay with him during the move."

"Grazie, doctor"

With that, a nurse came over and gave Nicky a shot. Renaldo continued to sit and pray. After a few minutes some orderlies came by. Renaldo and the orderlies began the rolling of his bed to the elevator and then eventually to the fourth floor when the floor nurse came in and made sure that Renaldo and Nicky were settled in and had water.

Later that evening, Nicky began to move his hand and as he rolled his head towards Renaldo, he reached out and squeezed his father's hand. Renaldo reached over and rang for the nurse as tears rolled down his cheeks.

Nicky had felt his brain slowly begin to take some control and as he was able to look around, he saw his father sitting next to the bed and was able to reach over and grab the hand that was close to his. He still could not control his voice and he was extremely tired from trying to handle so much information. So after squeezing his father's hand, he drifted off into a deep sleep.

Within a few minutes, the nurse came in and Renaldo indicated that Nicky had moved but not talked. The nurse rushed back to her station and paged the doctor.

After twenty minutes, Dr Bernardo came into Nicky's room and did a check on the vital signs. While trying to get Nicky to respond, Nicky seemed to still not respond to his voice.

"Hello signor Serrano? I am Dr. Bernardo. I have taken over Nicky's case and have been in touch with his pediatric doctor who will be by in the morning. Nicky is looking a little better, but we are still not any closer to understanding what is going on. I have been reviewing the case and to tell you the truth, nothing seems to make sense."

"Can you help him?"

"First I have to understand what's wrong. Perhaps if we let Nicky rest some more, he will continue to progress to a point where we can talk with him. At the moment, it looks like he has slipped into sleep."

When he awoke in the morning, Nicky felt better and in more control of his body. As he looked over, he saw that his father was still asleep with his head resting on his bed side. Nicky attempted to wake his father up by calling too him…"Papa"

Renaldo heard a voice and pulled himself awake to see how Nicky was doing. As he awoke, he saw the fear in his son's eyes.

"Nicky, are you okay?"

"Something is wrong, Papa. I see strange images, and was hearing strange voices."

Renaldo looked at Nicky with a realization that he was not talking normally "Nicky, what is wrong with your voice?"

"Something is wrong with my voice? What's wrong papa? I'm scared!" As Nicky realized that his voice was a sing-humming sound.

"We don't know! The doctor will be here in a little bit and maybe he can help." Renaldo looked at his son and took his hand to give him strength. "Just rest until the doctor gets here, and we can try and find out.

The nurse came in and helped Nicky to get up and go to the bathroom as his legs were a little shaky. Soon, breakfast arrived and Nicky was able to eat his oatmeal and drink the orange juice. Nicky did not want to talk because his voice was strange and the speech scared him.

Later in the morning, Dr. Bernardo entered the room and came over to Nicky's bed and with a smile, introduced himself to Nicky.

"I see your doing better this morning young man" he said as he looked at the chart. "Can you tell me anything about what happened?"

Nicky just simply shook his head no. Renaldo jumped in.

"He said he saw strange images and voices and when he spoke his voice was a singing type voice that was strange."

"Is that so Nicky?" and Nicky shook his head yes, but still didn't say anything.

"I think his speaking voice is scaring him." Renaldo indicated as Nicky shook his head yes with frightened eyes.

"Okay, would you like to draw me some of the pictures you see?"

Nicky shrugged his shoulders and Renaldo said "If you can give him some time, we will try." with a smile as he looked at his son.

"Okay, well you seem to be in no danger, so take some time, try and draw me something of what you see and I will come back later and we can talk some more" as he smiled and shook hands with Renaldo and headed off to work with other patients.

The nurse came in a little later with some pencils and a large pad of drawing paper for Renaldo and Nicky. Renaldo began coaxing Nicky on trying to draw some of the images. At first, Nicky seemed to want to draw some strange looking lines that looked like a symbol or strange character but nothing Renaldo had ever seen before.

With some prodding from his father, he continued drawing. Nicky drew a scene of the first creature that he remembered talking. It was just a figure with a round head with arms and legs. Without any real training in art, the figures didn't look that much different from drawings Nicky would do of people or scenes in school.

Later in the day when the doctor came back, Nicky finally spoke when he was asked how he was feeling.

"I'm scared! I didn't talk like before; this voice is like the strange creature that I first saw. He spoke and said this strange sound, as Nicky issued a phrase that he had heard from the creature, and I think that these symbols are very important."

"Well, you appear to be a brave young man. I don't want you to be scared of what you saw or heard. We will figure this out. If it happens again, try to let me or your papa know and try to tell us what you are hearing, okay?"

Dr. Bernardo picked up the drawings and took a look. Nothing seemed to make much sense or provided any information, so he put them to the side. "You seem to be a fine artist with a nice imagination. Since you're doing fine, I will leave you for a while and check back later."

Nicky shook his head with a bit of a smile, Renaldo rubbed his son's hair and told him he would be back in a few minutes as he went outside to talk with the doctor.

"What do you think?" Renaldo ask the doctor once outside the room.

"This is a little strange; I am not sure what to make of it yet. He appears to be able to cope, so I am not as worried as the emergency doctor was when he was first brought in, but I think we need to keep a watch and see how it goes for a couple of days."

"Okay, thank you. Just do whatever it takes."

"Don't worry; we'll take good care of him."

With that, Renaldo headed back into the room to let Nicky know he needed to run home to pick up some fresh cloths and would be back as soon as possible. With a kiss and hug, Renaldo picked up the drawings and headed home.

At home, he decided to see if anyone out on the internet might know something, so he scanned the image of the symbols and sat down and wrote up what he had heard from Nicky and put it into the Facebook page that he and Nicky used to talk with people but indicated it was not Nicky who came up with the symbols, but himself since he didn't want people to bother Nicky except through him.

After taking a shower and talking with his boss at work along with calling the school to let them know that Nicky would be out for a while, he headed back to the hospital to his son.

|||||

Jack had left the underground complex late in the evening with a new assignment from Tim. The question of the music that seemed to be tied to George's condition meant that a new team member was needed; someone with strength in the ability of languages and music, they needed someone that could make sense of this unique capability by George to switch between music and normal language and try and fill some pieces in the puzzle.

Back at his office computer, a tired Jack rubbed his eyes and pondered how to approach this. He decided to check the internet and see if anything interesting showed up. After a few hours of reading and refining his search, a few different names seemed to keep popping up. One caught his eye and after doing a swift security search, he decided she was a definite possibility.

Jack called his connection at the NSA and asked for a deep security analysis of one Valerie Jenkins currently residing in New York, an international consultant in a wide area of music.

Now that the first task was under control, Jack with a sigh turned to his weekly briefing to the Intelligence Committee. He decided he needed to word this report carefully to the Senate Intelligence committee. The President was the only one to be briefed on actual events. While the President did not really get along with the House-Senate leaders for political reasons, this was far above petty politics and must be played by the book so they needed to be provided some type of information. The rest of the government would know nothing of the change in events at this time. So he had to find a way to indicate a minor change in staff and no new security threats to the BELLOWS program without rising questions.

While working through the stack of papers on his desk, he picked up a report from the CIA. A Russian mafia head with the nick-name of Gorbi was found in his luxury apartment in New York. A fire had been reported and when they entered the apartment, they found him unconscious slumped over his desk, smelling of liquor and littered with "secret" government papers. He was revived and had been arrested for espionage. In a second section of the CIA report, three men suspected as hit men for the Russian mafia had been found dead in the Montreal, Canada area; each had documents on their body connecting them to killings; each apparently died of a heart attack. A third report noted that a Russian in Moscow known as a high official in the Russian mafia had a sudden heart attack after attending a party. The report had a copy of a note to the Russian Security, Moscow clipped to it, "We send you greetings from the United States of America, and any further attempts on our people will result in an escalation resulting in a much larger destruction of your organization."

With a slight feeling of satisfaction, Jack continued his search for a while before deciding he needed some rest. He called Shelly to let her know he would be home in a while and headed for his car. As he left the largely empty underground parking, he decided he had better stop at a florist, this was going to place another strain on his marriage (one of many over the years) and once again he would need her understanding. Jack's drive to Alexandria, Virginia took around twenty minutes this time of night, but with the stop at the florist, it was fourty five minutes until he arrived home. It took an extra five minutes because he had to get out and jiggle the wires on the battery of his old car in the cold. His old Volvo got him from point A to point B, with a little help, but maybe it was time to change. Shelly often pestered him to buy something better, but Jack was not someone to spend money for his own pleasure, it was better to let his wife and kids have use of the funds, after all, he made them suffer because of his work.

It's not like Jack's wife ever really complained, but Jack was able to read her eyes when these cases took hold and could see the pain it caused. Someday he was going to get out and give her the life she deserved for standing by him through the long years and picking up the slack in raising their two daughters. Someday, he would do right by her and the girls. Just not at this time. Too many lives depended on him.

The night went by with pain and promises on both sides, but in the end, Shelly held him close and understood, she always understood but in this case with the death of Judy and her son Brady and others on the program she knew Jack had to do this, she wanted him to do this. She accepted Jack's inability to explain a lot of the details because of national security, but her love and trust were absolute and in the end, she just accepted. She also understood the importance. When the case was closed or at least Jack's part in it, they would go away and find a place where they could let the pain be replaced with the joy of being together as a family without the world coming between them. It was Jack's promise and sometimes he was able to make it happen, not nearly enough to suit Shelly, but enough to re-assure her that he did love her and the girls, and give Shelly the strength to keep the family together.

In the morning, a smiling Shelly had coffee ready for Jack after his shower. He hugged the girls as they argued over who could take the apple to school and ate their breakfast, while getting ready for school. Jack gave Shelly a big hug and kiss as he headed out the door feeling the love of his family.

When Jack arrived back to his desk after his security briefing at the team meeting, he knew he had some operations to plan and covers to design for Bob, Randy, and Janet and especially for George. He called to the operations center and scheduled a meeting with his operation team. Then he placed calls to the CIA to get briefings on current surveillance of the foreign research teams and to remind them of his weekly briefing to the Senate committee. And lastly, he called the surveillance center to schedule a meeting to get an update on the surveillance of the local operatives being monitored. Before he left his desk for his first meeting, he called his DoD connection to ensure that all information gathered during yesterdays raids had been properly marked and transferred to the DARPA team center for safe keeping.

By late in the afternoon, Jack was tired from the meetings, rubbing his tired eyes and yet still had hours of work still in front of him to prepare for tomorrow's meeting with the DARPA team. The word from CIA dealing with the "replacement" of the Russian team was not good. While in the past, what he performed today could have taken weeks. The one thing about the ongoing terrorist threat; the resulting interagency coordination maked it much easier to cut through all the crappy paperwork and get things done a lot more rapidly and efficiently when there is a threat on the line. And this defiantly qualified as a threat.

Jack stopped by his desk after a short meeting; on Jack's computer was an encrypted file from his NSA security contact with a report on Valerie Jenkins. She was extremely clean and connected. For Jack, now came the question; how to bring Valerie into the team without arousing any attention and without danger to her or exposure of the team. The information indicated that Valerie had just concluded an assignment with the London Symphony and at the moment had a clean calendar for the next few weeks. Jack needed to act fast.

CHAPTER 12: THE FINAL MEMBER

Valerie Jenkins had stretched out on her sofa in her loft apartment in New York City. This was some down time and her slim but curvy figure was encased in her comfortable sweat pants and heavy knit sweater along with heavy socks. The New World Symphony played in the background as she read her book and looked out the window at the cloudy skies and the unmistakable marks of the fall season having arrived. The leaves blowing past her window reminded her to stop at the local coffee shop and pick up some of the pumpkin flavored coffee she always enjoyed this time of the year.

Valerie was a stunning younger woman. Her slim figure with long dark brown flowing hair, her dark piercing black jet eyes set off by the high cheek bones and regal look and the classic hour glass figure. Keeping herself in shape served her well when it came to dealing with her wealthy high profile international clients.

She had few worries, but sadly few joys as well. Her mother and father had died five years earlier in an attempted home robbery. She had grown up in wealth and in a family well connected both politically and financially. She had gone to all the best schools, chased by all the rich and good looking boys, but had not found what she was looking for. She had not found that someone that loved her unconditionally and she could love unconditionally. She had not found that challenge in life that pushed her to her extreme to do her very best.

While to the world, she was a thirty one year old beautiful, rich, happy woman and not a care in the world. To Valerie, she was bored, unloved and could not find any excitement or contentment in her life.

Valerie relaxed in her condo, reading the latest spy thriller that she picked up on the flight back home when she was distracted by a phone call.

"Hello Ms. Jenkins. This is Ralf from the downstairs front desk. We have a delivery man with a package for you."

With her normal graciousness and a slight smile on her face, she responded "Good morning Ralf. Please have him come up. Thank you."

After a few minutes, she responded to the knock on the door and saw the lean and young delivery man in his biking clothes and spike shoes. Valerie signed for the package, gave him a tip and a thank you smile as she closed the door, heading back to the living room to settle in and find out what mystery was embedded inside.

When she opened the express envelope package, inside she found a letter and a bank draft for $50,000. A smile and feeling of excitement flashed over her face.

Dear Ms. Jenkins;

We have urgent need of your services.

We need to discuss this effort with you quietly and immediately. We would like you to please call as soon as possible (preferably within the hour) 917-333-3339 so we may arrange this meeting at the "Koffee Cup" which is located three blocks west, down from your apartment. We will provide you additional information at that time.

Please accept this check as down payment on your time.

Valerie read the letter. It became apparent that someone wanted her to take a job and was attempting to do this outside of normal channels. Valerie normally worked through a firm that provided a service through which people would establish contact and schedule time.

Being a lover of spy novels, Valerie was never one to pass on intrigue. She made the requested call and the person at the other end very cordially thanked her for returning the call and the agreed-to meeting was confirmed. Valerie headed to the bedroom to change from her relaxing cloths and into her business attire of slacks and white blouse, but added the heavy sweater with a coat and a knit wool cap due to the cool air. Winter was on its way.

At the appointed time, Valerie appeared at the restaurant and indicated she was to meet a Mr. Townsend to the greeter. The restaurant had only a few customers at this time of day since it was early for lunch and she was escorted to a table far away from the few people currently eating. As she approached the table with a smile and questioning look on her face, Mr. Townsend rose with a smile and greeted her. After taking off her coat and cap and ordering hot drinks, it was time to find out what this was about.

Mr. Townsend began. "We do not know each other, but through our research, you appear to be highly qualified to deal with a problem that we have encountered. We have a condition that requires someone with significant music background and has extensive language training and background."

Valerie had studied languages and music, having master degrees in both. Her area of work for many years had given her the need to deal with many countries and languages around the world as she worked with a wide variety of musicians and orchestras. She was proficient in Italian, French, Spanish, Chinese and Japanese and Korean. She looked him in the eye with a questioning look in an attempt to judge if he was telling the truth. "Why didn't you contact my service if you know so much about me?"

"The matter is very sensitive and urgent." As he pulled out his identification, he continued, "I need to be honest with you, I work for the FBI and in this matter, a need to keep as low a profile as possible is required. The number you called cannot be traced to us and if when we are done, if you do not wish to provide us your services, there will be no trace that this conversation ever took place and you can keep the money with no link back to us, although you will need to pay the taxes", he added with a wry smile. "This is both for your security and the security of the project I am representing. I am aware that you know the President of the United States and his wife personally and if you need verification of this offer, I would ask you to call him and request it. He is awaiting your call as we speak."

The agent spoke quietly, he kept eye contact and neither smiled nor frowned. As he seemed to finish speaking, he nodded for Valerie to make a move; giving her the silent signal to pick up her cell phone and speed dial the number she kept for contacting her friends at the White House.

Valerie was beginning to wonder what was going on and took out her cell phone. With a questioning look at the FBI agent, she pressed her speed dial number to call the White House. Upon providing her name, she was immediately transferred to the President and on the second ring, he answered, "Valerie nice to talk with you. We haven't had the pleasure of your presence since last Easter, Jane asked me to thank you for the beautiful crystal necklace that you sent her for her birthday and we're looking forward to the London Symphony performance you so kindly arranged. How are you doing?"

With a smile of recognition, she answered "Mr. President, I'm currently in a bit of shock. I am sitting with an FBI agent, Mr. Townsend here in New York who asked me to call you?"

"Yes Valerie, we can talk of it later, but the offer is valid and we really need your help on this matter. Jane and I look forward to seeing you soon. I'm sorry I can't talk longer, but I have a meeting I need to attend, so I will turn you back over to Mr. Townsend's capable hands. I am so hoping you can help us?"

"I will certainly do my best Mr. President." She glanced at the FBI agent with a smile of acceptance.

"That's all I can ask. So for now, good bye, but we will talk soon. Thank you again Valerie."

"Good bye Mr. President."

As she turned off the cell, she looked at Mr. Townsend in a bit of a shock and questioning smile of surprise. "I guess it will be very hard to say no at this point."

"Excelent! Arrangements are being made to give you a thorough overview of the job. Go back to your condo and pack for a short stay, say around one to two weeks; call the same number as before when you are ready to leave and a car will be around to pick you up. I understand that you have not yet accepted any follow on work at the moment, we would like you to first understand what we need and then we can discuss how to allow your work on this matter to proceed with minimal disruption to your outside life as you feel is needed. This is both in your interest and also in the interest of security. We need you to travel to the D.C. area immediately and you will be met by one of our people.

Please, and this is extremely important, do not let anyone know about this, it is for your safety." With those final words and an expression of intensity, Mr. Townsend signaled the waiter, paid the bill with cash and then turned to her as they parted with a smile, "You will not meet with me again, so I wish to express my thanks and wish you the best of luck with the assignment."

With those words, he left and Valerie was to never meet him again.

Valerie walked back to her condo, stopping momentarily at her bank to deposit the funds into her account. Continuing to walk with a bit of a spring to her step, the effect of what had happened began to settle in. A thousand questions arose and images of intrigue that she had read about began to swirl within her mind. As she reached her condo, she called her service and requested they not book any work until they hear from her. She rapidly grabbed her suitcase which she normally had pre-packed and finished collecting some items along with packing her computer. As directed she called the telephone number and within 15 minutes, a car pulled up in front of the building and the morning which had started as slow and relaxing, was suddenly rushing to an unknown destiny.

When the car arrived, Ralf called up to Valerie's apartment to let her know. The driver knocked on the door and helped Valerie take her bags down the elevator and placed them in the trunk of the car.

The driver opened the door for her and after she was seated, closed the door and quickly moved around to the driver seat. He was fully aware of who she was from his briefing. As they drove to the airport, the driver provided her with plane e-ticket check-in paper, and itenerary. He informed her she would be met with a limo at Reagan National and she was reminded with a determined voice to tell no one of anything specific about why she was headed down to D.C., other than "if needed" to meet with her old friends, the First Lady and the President, but only if pressed.

During the short flight from New York to Reagan National, Valerie looked out the window across the ocean, the glimmering waves interrupted by a sailboat here and there. She thought about why someone might need her. Most jobs were simple structuring of presentations, understanding of who to invite to an opening, types of music that leaders would enjoy and all the normal details that anyone could do with some research. Her advantage was her name and the people she knew along with her ability to make the correct contacts. It was a simple job and just didn't seem to fit this situation.

On arrival, Valerie walked out of the Reagan National Airport security zone. A man wearing the typical chauffer suit and carrying a sign with "Ms. Valerie Jenkins" caught her eye and walked over to her.

"May I carry your bags for you?"

Valerie handed over her bags and they were on their way. Upon entering the limo, the windows were dark both inside and out and the driver indicated that he would be closing the separation section for her safety, she did not need to understand where they were headed, and everything would be explained on arrival. He also smiled and reminded her of the buckle-up law in Virginia. While he did not expect any trouble in transit, it never hurt to take precautions.

Again, Valerie sensed that this was not going to be her normal job. The fact that the President knew about this provided some comfort, but what could they need her for?

|||||

The day before Valerie was contacted by the FBI, the security lead for the math team in Guangzhou, China, Tangzi Gu arrived at his desk after a short lunch at a local restaurant. His bowl of rice and vegetables along with his cup of tea allowed him to keep his weight under control; not too much, not too little.

Gu entered to the group of offices and acknowledged the secretary Jasmine with a smile. She was dressed in her normal uniform of the Red Chinese Army but her breasts were actually larger than most Chinese girls and Gu loved the image of breasts, if only in his mind. She had arrived from the far west where her family had died with the collapse of a dam. She alone had survived and over time had joined the Red Army. During her early time in the Red Army, she had met Gu. He had brought her along with him as he moved up the chain in the Government and gained important levels of insight.

He had never made a pass at her. While pretty, she made it clear that she was not interested in anything sexual. He was convinced she was a lesbian, and while he could not prove such a thing, she was still very pretty to look at and was a nice young girl that treated him with the deference he had grown to expect in his position.

With only a glance at Jasmine, Gu continued on past her desk, talking with various members of his team openly until he entered his office. He always left his door open so he could hear what was going on and so he could gaze on Jasmine when he so wished.

Sitting down at his desk and signing into his classified computer, an email was at the top of the list marked as high priority. It was orders being passed from central committee. The orders were to create an incident with the Americans to keep them off balance. It did not really matter why they were to execute this, only what to do.

The security lead had already thought about this, and had previously developed a plan that would fit. This was to be a simple calling card. Something to let the Americans know that they could be reached at any time and that there was no limit to what would be done. The idea was something to make them a tad nervous in the hopes of making the enemy make a move that would expose information of use such as people, paths, or whatever.

He swiftly sent his classified email; the transmission went to the office of State that passed secure messages to the Chinese Delegation security chief at the UN in New York. He had worked with his friend Jung for many years and had no doubt that the operation would be engaged properly.

The priority email arrived at the classified computer at State and was rapidly encrypted and went out as a satellite communications classified channel to the UN. Upon arrival at the UN office of the Chinese delegation security chief, it was decrypted and the secretary quickly delivered it to Jung.

Jung read the transmission from State and validated the authenticity code showing that the command came from Central Committee. As he sipped on his cup of morning coffee, a habit he had picked up moving to the New York area, he thought about his friend's planned operation and that it should be carried out without any traceability back to him or the Chinese government. While there would be suspicion, nothing traceable.

Jung made a simple call to a local Chinese restaurant and ordered Peking duck for two for the following Tuesday with a side of wild rice and Hot and Sour soup. After hanging up, he picked up his briefcase and walked over to the office safe. As he opened the safe, he pulled out $75, 000 US in cash, put it in a paper bag and placed the bag in his brief case. He then pulled out a document from the safe and added it to the paper bag.

An hour later, as Jung left the office with the briefcase; he took the elevator to the main floor and headed out of the UN building. Jung walked across the plaza and crossed the street to the Chinese restaurant. As he entered, he spotted his contact. He walked over to the table and sat down with the briefcase next to an identical copy of the briefcase already between him and his contact.

Once tea was delivered, Jung and his triad contact Tu talked and laughed about how the weather was cold and about how their families were doing and the local fighting matches that were scheduled for the coming weekend. After a casual discussion, Jung wished his contact a nice day, bowed, picked up a briefcase that was empty and walked out of the restaurant and headed back to the UN.

Tu picked up a paper and read for a short period of time. After he put down the paper, the triad contact picked up the left briefcase paid the tab and exited the restaurant. As he walked down the street, another man was headed towards him carrying the same model briefcase. As the contact stopped at the newsstand and set down the briefcase, the other man did the same thing setting his next to Tu's. After paying for a newspaper, the switch was made and both men went on their way without even acknowledging each other.

The cash and instructions arrived at the triad's headquarters in a downtown Manhattan office building. The courier went directly to the main office delivering the briefcase, swiftly leaving.

An older man walked over, opened the briefcase, took out the instructions and glanced over them. He dialed a number and issued a direct command, hung up the phone and took the cash out of the briefcase. He walked over to the wall safe and added the cash to the large stash of cash in the safe, then closed the safe and walked over to take a drink of brandy.

As he sipped the brandy, he smiled and thought, all in a day's work.

Meanwhile, across the street, a van with darkened windows sat at the curb. The van had been sitting in the location since early in the morning and was seen regularly in that area over a number of years.

A man dressed in a suit walked up to the van, opened the back door and climbed in. He nodded to the man inside and reached for a cup of coffee sitting on a small table. The man sitting at the van's window, which were darkened only from the outside, finished taking pictures and turned around.

"Jim, activate the encryption line so we can send our report."

Jim reached over and flipped a switch and pushed a button. An encrypted connection had been made to the local FBI office where their manager came on the line.

"Okay guys, what do we have?"

"Jung, the head of the Chinese security for the UN Delegation made a covert drop at their normal Chinese restaurant. I followed the package during a switch and to the triad headquarters office building.

"I was able to photograph the various drop mules and the delivery boy. He was inside for fifteen minutes, then came out and left."

"Okay, good work. Wrap it up for the day. Head back to the barn and file your report."

"Yeh, ha ha ha, great, walk all day and write all night. See you later," he joked with a smile as he turned off the communications.

|||||

Jack sat in the conference room in the D.C. office building sipping his coffee as the projector was showing images on the screen. The routine was normal and he was hunched over the table as he listened.

During Jack's morning briefing on the Chinese and Russian agents from the hidden sources in the enemy camp's security group, it became apparent that the Russians and Chinese both had picked up on something happening in D.C. Their inside agents indicated that they did not understand what had happened; only that Tim's team was somehow involved. The stakes were suddenly raised and Jack could expect a massive push to try and find out what was happening.

Later during the busy day, word reached his desk that NSA had overheard a conversation in New York. It may or may not have something to do with BELLOWS, but an intercepted phone call on a triad related cell phone stated "If anyone in D.C. should raise their head, chop it off immediately."

While being somewhat secure in their intelligence monitoring efforts, Jack knew that there were very little true secrets on the planet that could not be obtained when push came to shove. The key therefore was to divert, providing enough information to make them think that they understood the situation, while sending them on a wild goose chase down the deepest of rat holes.

The question was what should be the bait, how to lay the trap and what possibly could be a deep enough hole to keep them occupied for a long enough time. After all, Jack wasn't even sure how long was long enough. Given the information at hand, he couldn't begin to guess where George would lead the team and how long it would take to gain an advantage that would allow them to dominate.

Jack sat at his desk thinking through various scenarios when word that Valerie had reached DC came across his computer. She had been picked up and was being transported to the team center. Given what Jack had heard from surveillance, the hairs on the back of his neck began to tingle and a frown formed on his face. He swiftly sent an encrypted message to divert her to the Vice President's compound entrance at the US Naval Observatory. In addition, Jack rapidly asked an armed security team be dispatched from the Pentagon to protect Valerie's transport and gave them the tracking code frequency. He sensed that someone they did not know about might have the team center entrance under surveillance.

When the driver started to leave Regan National Airport, a flash message came across his encrypted cell phone to divert to the V.P.'s compound entrance. He quickly exited towards Georgetown instead of the planned routing through Alexandria. His senses were on full alert and all protective armament on the special limo activated. He responded with a short acknowledgment and backup was sent to intercept him as he headed for Roseland and would pass by the Pentagon.

Jack sent a flash message to immediately dispatch a SEAL team from the local Navy attachment to do a detailed, but unobserved surveillance of the team center's primary and secondary entrance to try and identify who might be monitoring their movements.

The driver was deep in concentration as he sped past the Pentagon towards the Arlington Cemetery off ramp and heading toward Roseland when two bikers approached from his rear at a speed which would rapidly overtake him. As he prepared to take the bridge exit, a truck suddenly slowed down in front of him and the backend opened with a man holding a missile launcher pointed straight at his car. He reacted as his training cut in, swerving to the left as flames shot out of the missile and came toward him.

At the same time, the two men on motorcycles opened up with machine gun fire. As the bullets bounced off the car, he accelerated and jumped the curb, heading down the grassy slope, and trying to find an alternate pathway to get out of the fire zone. The missile had missed, barely, and exploded against the concrete along the edge of the off ramp. As the limo sped across the grass, he could see that help had arrived just in time to prevent any further missile shot, as three cars pulled up and opened fire on the truck and motorcycles. Within the time of his being able to turn the car around, it was over. The truck was in flames and the motorcycles were both down and it was very unlikely that any of the attackers were alive.

The driver opened the partition to look at his passenger. She had only heard the noise and was bounced around by the sudden shifting of the car; luckily she had listened and had on her seat belt. Although visibly shaken with a look of worry on her face, she appeared no worse for the ware. The driver relayed thumbs up message to Jack and drove back up the hill to the bridge. He rushed past the mayhem and with one of the escorts on his bumper and an Army jeep in the lead; they sped on toward the V.P.'s compound entrance by Georgetown.

With the report coming into Jack's computer; Jack relayed the happenings to Tim and told him about the counter surveillance team being sent to the team compound entrances. Tim placed the information on the team computer with a heads up warning to all members to not exit the compound until further notice.

||||||

George awoke. He realized that for the first time in his memory, he was no longer alone. George's brain had continued to organize information and his ability to maintain his own reality while scanning the burst data flow was a strange sensation, but he no longer felt overwhelmed. As George opened his eyes, he was able to recognize a nurse whom he had not seen before along with Dr. Thomas and another man who he had never seen before. He was not in the hospital room, and it took a moment to remember being driven from the hospital to a different location.

After being provided a sip of water and help sitting up, he was able to regain a voice although the sing-song voice didn't sound like him.

"Welcome back!" Bob smiled at him. "You've been asleep for a while. Can you tell me how you feel?"

"Better," George relayed.

"George, I would like to fill you in on where you are and between the three of us, maybe we can fill in some of the holes?" Bob indicated. "I would like you to meet Tim. Tim is head of a research team that has recognized the information you have given us and we are hoping that we can help you and you can help us."

When George nodded in the affirmative, Tim stepped forward to start the conversation. "George, I think the information you provided Bob during your meeting in the hospital, do you remember?" George nodded yes, "It was a calling card. Can you tell me more about the event?"

George looked at Tim, his face formed a tired smile and in his growing sing-song voice, "Yes, I have begun to get a sense of their language and have pulled together basic information. They are called the Old Ones. Using their latest technology, they have been able to contact to what they call 'Watcher' patterns throughout our universe.

"Answers from Watchers around the universe have been flowing back to them. My mind has been able to acknowledge, but I feel we aren't advanced enough to provide much help to them. I have sensed one being from a race known as the Tern which has contact with a much more advanced race called the Care Givers. The Tern creature has acknowledged and they have set up a recording link to allow the Old Ones to transfer information."

The shock of the affirmation of the guessed truth was immediate as Tim and Bob looked at each other and then back to George with eyes wide open. The events were far greater than Bob or Tim had even guessed at. ***The secrets of the universe were about to be broadcast and they were front row and center stage.***

Bob and Tim looked at each other in shock. Tim's encrypted cell phone interrupted his thoughts with an email that Valerie had arrived and was ready for a briefing in the living room outside. As Tim regained control, he looked at George and Bob with a look of control, "George, this room is under constant surveillance and recording. I need you to relate any and all information you receive at any time. We will do whatever we can to help you, but I need you to understand, as I am sure you are aware, you will be receiving information which will be the most valuable in human history. We need to record as much as possible of what you see and receive. Let us know what you need and we will do whatever it takes to get it for you. Even the simplest clue could be of enormous help. If you can't interpret as it arrives, just relay it and we will try to understand it later. Every nuance is important, do you understand?"

Finally someone understood what George had been trying to tell people; he smiled and in his sing-song voice, answered as he looked at Bob, "Yes, thanks. I am so happy I'm not mad."

With that statement from George, Tim looked at Bob, took a deep breath and Tim headed for the door to welcome the next member of the team, his mind racing at a rapid pace to imagine the extent of the information that they could gain through George. Along with what was happening on the surface, the dangers that this information presented created a major security issue.

|||||

The two SEAL teams were briefed at the Navy Yards across the river from the Pentagon. The operation was simple, observe and report. There was to be no contact unless specifically directed, any information on suspects was to be reported immediately and any movement to be tracked and reported, weapon usage only in self defense if necessary.

The teams left the briefing room, dressed in their civilian clothes, carrying only their network electronics and hand guns in their controlled professional manner. As they drove out of the Navy yards, mixed with normal civilian Navy traffic leaving at the end of the day they turned onto M street and faded into the background. The signal went out to Jack at the FBI office that teams were on their way.

When their vehicles reached I395 and headed towards the Pentagon, the teams quietly reviewed their mission. As the exit to downtown D.C. arrived, one of the vehicles headed north while the other continued west in the bumper-to-bumper late afternoon traffic.

When the teams arrived at their locations, they found a parking location at a local hotel where rooms had hastily been reserved. Each member unloaded his part of the gear and they fanned out to find observation positions without a word being spoken. As each member found his best position surrounding their prime target of interest, each used his encoded communications headset to radio that they were in position. They hunkered down to wait while the communication specialist in each group coordinated their transmissions and did the final report back the Navy Yards that their teams were in position and triangulation was prepared if needed.

|||||

Tim sat with Valerie; his mind was still racing forward with plans and expectations. After Valerie signed the Non-Disclosure document and the papers allowing for her to receive classified information, the briefing began. The classified access documents gave her a moment of pause but just a moment. Tim gave her an overview of the happenings of the last two days, ending with the monumental disclosure that George had just provided.

Tim emphasized his point that this was real with the demonstration of the crystal chandelier. But unlike Janet and Randy, Valerie broke into a big grin as this was confirmation that it was going to be well worth her time.

Valerie had been involved in many jobs which made very little use of her abilities, but she had been called in because of her political contacts. They paid the bills, which with her inheritance were not really an important consideration, and they filled time in her life, but did not give her the feeling of accomplishment that she had desired for her young life.

Valerie had just heard and seen information that shook most people to their bones, to say nothing of the violence that she had gone through to reach the team center. Her makeup allowed her to control her composure and she decided she needed to focus on expectations. With a look of determination on her face, she asked the key question "Tim, how much time do you think we have to work with?"

Tim appreciated her straight forwardness along with her self control and responded "We're not sure; the connection could restart at any time or never. We need you to learn as much about the language as possible and help us to fill in gaps. We know that there's going to be significant technical communications, a lot that we currently don't understand, but any help you can provide will greatly enhance our ability to understand. Janet and Randy will be working with you and George in an attempt to visualize the information as best as possible to identify clues and Thomas will be in control of George's medical needs.

Your recent experience shows just how vital it is that we understand and control this information to keep ahead of our enemies. For the time being, it's best if you stay here. Can you can contact your people and let them know that you will be back with them as soon as you have a better idea of what this time frame will require?"

"Yes, I can do that. Thank you for bringing me in on this, it's certainly a challenge that doesn't happen every day and I can think of nothing better I would rather be engaged in."

Her self control, determination, and ease under pressure confirmed to Tim that Jack had indeed made a proper choice. Now if only time would allow the team to be able to do its work.

With the basics out of the way, Tim escorted Valerie to George's room and introduced her to George. As Valerie approached the bed and took George's hand, a smile crossed their faces and with that simple look, Bob could tell that they would work well together. Within an instant, it was obvious that there was chemistry between the two of them that would only benefit the operation and help to keep George at ease.

After a few minutes of listening to George as he seemed to express something toward Valerie in his unique sing-song voice, Valerie smiled and Tim stepped in to escort Valerie to the next level up to get her settled in. Valerie's hand seemed to linger a little longer than necessary and with a glance over her shoulder to George. Tim moved to escort her towards the door. As they left George's room, Valerie had a smile and bright eyes when she turned to Tim and commented "This is truly a unique language, obviously unlike anything I've ever heard. I can only relate it to a complex symphony of expression, much more than the songs of the whales, like a chorus of inter-related whale songs all at once but with greater structure. This is truly amazing! How his mind has control over his vocal cords to make this musical sound is in itself amazing." They continued up a level and Valerie was shown her room and introduced to some of the team members.

After a few minutes, Dr. Thomas came by to introduce himself to Valerie as she unpacked and settled in.

"Hello Valerie! I am Dr. Bob Thomas, but please call me Bob," As they shook hands.

"Hi Bob. I already received a briefing on the team," she indicated, thinking that was why Bob dropped by.

"No, I didn't come by to deal with your briefing, but rather to offer my services to talk out problems. Some of the team has issues which this situation amplifies into problems. I am here to let you know that my door is always open and if you want to talk about anything please let me know and I will set up a session."

"Oh, sorry…I much appreciate that. I understand, and while my joining was voluntary, the bit of a shock of the fact that George actually is in communications with other alien races, the fact that we are going to get all this advanced knowledge, to say nothing that we are under attack, that does make me pause. I'll let you know as soon as I've settled in and get a bit of a grip. Thank you, it's good to know that I can call on you."

"That's not a problem, just let me know and welcome to the team. I think this is going to be an exciting ride." He finished with a smile of comfidence as he turned and walked out of the door.

Valerie finished unpacking and laid on the bed thinking about the sudden path shift in her life. It was exhilarating and at the same time a little scary. Unlike the novels she enjoyed reading, this was real and the people out there used real bullets.

After a few moments of letting her mind capture the grandeur of what she had just been introduced too, with the energy of excitement which caused her adrenaline to be pumping, she quickly got off the bed and headed out of her room. As she exited, she turned to the elevator and headed to George's room on the lower level.

Valerie entered George's room like a mouse sneaking into a cat's den; Bob turned and smiled.

In a loud whisper Bob spoke to Valerie "I would have been disappointed if you had stayed away much longer," he said and turned back with a grin to the notes he was working on.

Valerie walked over and sat in a chair by the bed. Since George was looking at her and at the moment nothing else seemed to be going on, Valerie decided it was time to get to work.

With a smile for George and a touch on his arm, she began.

"George, since I am here to learn this new language, no time like the present. Can you start with some simple words and phrases? Then we can progress forward from there."

George gave her a broad smile and pointed to the room as a whole with arms out stretched and sang a few complex sounds.

Valerie repeated the sounds as best as she could which George made minor corrections too.

"Room?" asked Valerie with George nodding in the affirmative.

They started at the beginning to lay the fundamentals from which she could slowly progress. They covered colors, actions, time and other basic functional parts of living as the time seemed to rush by. Valerie was able to rapidly learn and retain the understandings and the sound patterns. By the end of the first few hours, she was able to talk in a few simple phrases.

As Bob continued his notes and monitoring, he too picked up some of the simple sounds. Not nearly as fast as Valerie, and not wanting to slow her down, but he was learning. As he watched in an analytical fashion, he could see how well they worked together and how George felt at ease with her simple presence, even his blood pressure had dropped a few points over the hours.

With the hours progressing, food arrived and the two of them continued working. Bob excused himself as he had a meeting with the medical team. As he left, he realized that neither George nor Valerie were really aware of his leaving. They were engrossed in talking with each other. Bob was fascinated by their growing connection.

After Bob left, Valerie pulled her chair closer to the bed where George was in a sitting position. As he gave her a phrase and indicated it was a joke, she began to understand and as she laughed, reached out to touch his arm and with that touch, realized that this was "the" man in her future.

When Bob left the room, he found Tim working at the desk outside of George's room and sat down for a minute before his meeting.

"Valerie is the perfect choice. I watched in amazement as she was able to pull simple words from George and quickly evolve into phrases. I can only tell you that there's magic between the two of them and you are not going to be able to separate them even if you wanted to"

Tim shook his head in a sign of amazement and asked "Do you ever wonder if everything we're doing is meant to happen this way?"

As Bob thought about his life, he shook his head in the affirmative "Things do tend to have a way of working out…Well, got to get moving, see you later."

The team seemed complete. The mission though, was expanding at light speed and beyond. Tim was finding it hard to walk his way through all the possibilities and variations that needed to be covered.

Chapter 13: Data Flows

On the shell surrounding the star in the galaxy of Sxvy, Sxxty was attempting to rest from his long period of work. The Watcher connection machine was working well and information was beginning to flow across the universe. The news of the rise in quantum foam energy levels being reported by monitoring teams was troubling to all the Old Ones, but Sxxty needed to focus on his effort while others monitored their tasks and planning.

Sxxty was reviewing the transmission status and the return responses as he was working with the planning team. Responses had been faster than the Old Ones had hoped for. Millions of connections had been made across the galaxy, but one in particular seemed to be at a technical level that could be of help. The information relayed through the Tern-Care Giver connection indicated access to an advanced race that appeared to be at a comparable level to the Old Ones to allow their plans to move forward.

With the receipt of connecting life forms, they rapidly made a planned schedule of transmissions. The information was not directly connected to the race of interest, but rather relayed their information and plans to set up a recording ability. Indications were that this most advanced race lived on the outer edge of the universe, like the Old Ones.

In their next transmission, they would indicate that transmissions would occur at set times and set lengths so Watchers could learn to adapt to this new situation. At final count roughly ten million Watcher patterns responded, most with minimal ability to understand more than a simple "Hi".

Sxxty's mind scanned the list of responders. He sadly noted that Tia was not indicated on the list. He connected with the Txxan leaders to ask if Tia had shown any indications during the transmission period and after a period of time they reported back that Tia had become dazed but was slowly recovering.

Sxxty asked the leaders to please work with the connection team and see if they could help Tia since it was possible he may be able to connect to the Watcher community. In rapid discussions with the community, it was decided that Tia was worthy of special attention. A special team was dispatched from the connection machine to the new Txxan planet and as Sxxty drifted into a sleep state, he knew that his friend may soon be part of this most important work and with that knowledge, drew comfort in his needed rest.

The fact that the Tern connection indicated that recording would be in place soon allowed the Old Ones to start preparations for the data transfer. While the prioritization of information to be sent would continue, a channel was connected to the pattern machine and information flow would begin when next contact occurred in a regulated set of time periods. The early information to be transferred was basic and provided keys to translation embedded in the images and language discussions. This was the same information used in training new society members and had evolved and been shown to be successful over a hundred's of STRY.

While the initial contact through the Watcher pattern had provided a basic information dissemination capability, the overall information to be transferred was significantly more sophisticated and as such required basic training in language and the Old Ones' math, science, and history.

The Watcher pattern had its connection at the basic quantum foam level, but reflected itself in an electromagnetic pattern that connected to the basic thought patterns of high-order life forms. As information was sent to the Watcher pattern by the Old Ones, it resulted in an alteration of the electrical field. In most advanced species where a Watcher pattern existed, this resulted in alterations of wave patterns in the being's memory storage, causing thoughts, feelings, images and sounds as if they were a part of the being. The ability of the being to control parts of its mind resulted in a alteration to the field patterns resulting in a return communication that the Old Ones' machine could sense and separate out as information.

Of course, not only did the Old Ones gain the information, the Watcher pattern connected all Watchers together and because of the energy flow from the Old Ones' machine into the pattern, they were able, for the first time, to sense each other. During the initial activation of the machine, most Watchers were dazed as their minds were altered from an internal understanding to a universal connection and only those with more advanced minds were able to separate and control the information. The more advanced the mind, the quicker they were able to gain control.

After a sleep period, the machine was reactivated to make plans with the Tern and activate the data transfer protocol. The positive response allowed the Old Ones to set a schedule for beginning data transfer as the initial stages of contact were completed.

And so it began, slowly at first to make sure that the information channel was not being overloaded such that key training information was not lost in transmission. As the feedback from the Tern would indicate, the information flow could be expanded.

Sxxty was not always present during the transfers; he also needed to work with the group that organized the transmissions. The work progressed on a single channel of local communications between the various information groups with some members being on the opposite side of the galaxy. After the initial contact where Sxxty was able to project his true image in the environmental suit, not the one he held of himself, most of the communications were sent directly through their systems and did not need a physical presence. There would be times where a physical image would be able to project important information that may be significant to some specific understanding. At those times, Sxxty would be present to be the presenter.

CHAPTER 14: THE TRAP IS SET

In Washington D.C., the wind was cold and the political atmosphere was even colder between the U.S., Russia and China. The violence of the past months had reached diplomatic levels and the strain on relationships was noticeable on the faces of the leaders.

The SEAL team arrived in the vicinity of the compound entrances. The NSA had already begun electronic and satellite surveillance in support of the operation. The SEAL team was able to download visual images and identify cell phone and other electro-magnetic intercepts from the area. The electronic and telephone communications from the area were under review at the NSA and three suspect transmissions had been identified. Their locations had been triangulated to apartments in the vicinity of the main entrance to the underground BELLOWS facility. In addition, two points had been located at pay phones in Georgetown near the Naval Observatory entrance.

Once the two SEAL teams found points to set up their counter surveillances positions, signals were relayed back that everything was ready. The job should be done by FBI, but DoD had first call since this was their program. Also, by having Seal teams do the surveillance, the thought was that any internal leaks that may exist in the FBI would not be alerted.

When Jack received the signal that the SEALs were in place and NSA was monitoring, he was in communication with Tim and indicated that the operation was ready whenever he was available to initiate.

|||||

In the morning meeting after Valerie's arrival, the team meeting for coordination kicked off at its usual time and place in the underground

BELLOWS spaces. Tim introduced Valerie to the 30 team members present and asked her to give her first impression as she had related to him.

Valerie began with an easy calm and confident voice "I have only had a short time with George, but I strongly feel we need to find a better way to monitor the information he is receiving. The information is much more complex than I think he can express. I feel that we need to monitor his brain activity to see if it can somehow help us to add additional information about what George is sensing."

Bob chimed in from the front row of seats "We were planning an MRI and basic brain activity monitoring, but I'll talk with the medical team to see if we can find and hook up a more advanced real time brain activity monitor sooner than currently scheduled. If we can monitor activity in the various portions of his brain, we might get something. In addition, there is a new device being used in New Jersey that with training may allow us to see George's thoughts. I'll have to check on getting access."

Tim indicated he wanted this to be another top priority and all necessary resources should be applied. Bob rapidly got on his encrypted cell phone and sent a message to the medical team to emphasize that this advanced capability needed to be put in place ASAP.

The discussion continued with the John Hopkins art team bringing out its latest visualizations. They pointed out some of the more subtle details. A number of observations were made. The primary observation was that the written symbols earlier indicated by George contained subtle variations which according to George indicated enhancements, emotions or other added complexity. The second observation dealt with the image of the Old One. The conclusion became that the being in the image was probably in some type of suit, not its true self. The Old One image seemed to indicate that it was in an environment not normal to its life form and as such may well be artificial to support the transmission.

The math team indicated that the dimensional constants related in the initial images provided by George seemed to have a relationship with known constants in our universe and as such were very likely constant definitions for our known universe. But with the new information, they agreed they needed to work with George, Randy, and Janet to see if a pattern to the variations were consistent with the known math or if it added details that they were not yet aware of.

The engineering team that had initially put together the invisibility device indicated that they hoped to have a somewhat portable unit within the week. One large problem to overcome for a person to use it, however, dealt with the fact that the person would be blind when the device was active. Some other way of understanding the environment around the person when the field was activated would need to be devised or else it would be useless to any person within the field.

Before the meeting broke up, Bob received word back from the medical team and stood up to announce to the larger team "The necessary equipment for basic brain monitoring and associated software has been located at John Hopkins Medical Hospital and is en route to our team via air transport. We should be able to have George connected within two hours. Negotiations for access to the thought imaging system are underway."

With the allotted time limit being reached, Tim started to close out the discussions. He decided to inform the team of the security status.

With a look of determination on his face he looked over the group "As you may be aware, Valerie's car was attacked on the way from the airport late yesterday. We feel there are unknown agents watching the primary and secondary entrances, and are taking steps to control the situation. For the moment, we want to make sure that everyone is safe and so please be aware that we are controlling traffic through the two entrances until further notice. We hope to have the problem resolved shortly, but until then, please give us your cooperation. If possible, please stay in the guest rooms for the moment, but if you must exit the facility we can figure out an alternate path." With the parting words, Tim allowed the meeting to dissolve into a number of side discussions.

Many of the team members worked on a many-day shift going home only for a few days each week. Like a fireman, they worked a shift, took off a couple of days and then were back on shift. This different pattern from a normal work force provided the ability to shift patterns and control the comings and goings of the team to keep them out of any potential agent's view. But Jack was now aware that may not be enough.

Word was passed to the various families that there was going to be a shift in the pattern and not to be worried, but it was necessary for national security.

The most advanced version of the operational brain monitor technology in the world was transported in 3 boxes that looked a lot like large metal briefcases. The brain monitor was a new device developed to allow for simpler monitoring of key brain activity with the same resolution that used to take large machines. The interface device was a sophisticated, but comfortable cloth helmet that contained highly sensitive magnetic sensors capable of measuring minute changes in the electromagnetic field from within the brain as neurons fired creating logic, thought and actions. The sensors were able to isolate the field variations down to minute fractions of an inch in 3 dimensions. The unit was connected through a single thin bundled fiber optical cable, reducing the myriad of wires that older units tended to use. Tied to a bank of computers, now only slightly larger than a couple of backpacks, the computer registered the strength of each incoming signal and from that produced a three dimensional location for each neuron triggered. The output showed significant clarity of neuron's firing patterns in the brain on the computer screen and through that, a moving image as sections of the brain became more and less active. The visualization capability developed in New Jersey took the same information and processed it differently to gain an image of thoughts. This was not available for general use yet, but would work using the basic recordings as soon as access to the software could be obtained.

The John Hopkins unit arrived at the Naval Observatory within an hour of its request by the team via an emergency medical helicopter. The secret service convoy escorted the packages to the elevator and within 10 minutes of landing, the boxes were unpacked and the key equipment package was in George's room being set up. The medical team was assisted by the computer resources team to ensure that connections were made properly to the team's central site storage system, so that data flowed directly into the main system as well as being available to the team in the rooms around George. The software team had set up initial monitoring software that would allow them to easily control storage and retrieval from a terminal in George's room or from any direct connected terminals.

Normally a period of time is taken to calibrate the equipment, but in George's case, calibration to create a baseline for the patient was not possible until a break in the transmission period occurred, since information was currently coming in. The packages normal output was recorded onto DVDs and also fed to the facility's main computer. As the team became more confident of the correct storage in the central computer, the DVD option would be terminated.

While in a hospital environment, normally sessions would last only a maximum of one hour. This was to be a continuous around the clock operation so the IT team operations were busy creating large auxiliary mass storage capability. Over one hundred terra bytes of Raid disks had been ordered and would arrive within the next 24 hours. The new storage units would have to be added to their server system without interruption of normal work operations.

When Valerie joined Bob, the hookup was being completed and the displays were being turned on. One of the doctors from Bob's team had trained on this unit before and was explaining that normally they would provide the patient with simple tasks such as look at a card or move a hand to calibrate the system, but that calibration would have to occur later.

In George's case, the result was immediate. As data was being collected in real time and displayed on the LCD flat plane console in the room, George began to make simple tonal sounds that Valerie recognized with excitement as the Old Ones' language, while typing into his computer keyboard in English that had been setup to help capture his translations.

With the team intently watching and as her excitement grew, Valerie began to suspect that George was giving them a linguistic lesson. While George had given Valerie a simple linguistic lesson, this seemed to be a little more advanced and because George indicated this was a transmission, it was clear that this was a lesson from the Old Ones. As she watched the screen, the patterns in key parts of George's brain ebbed and flowed with graceful hypnotic patterns that seemed to be somewhat connected to his speech pattern. The excitement in Valerie was rising and her smile broadening as she mentally began to connect the data to the acts and realize that she could now see the musical language that George was trying to relate.

After a while of watching, Valerie was able to begin to pick up the very basic rudiments of the language lesson and during a short pause, looked at George. With the basics she thought she had been taught by George and from this new lesson of the language, she asked "Are you alright?" George beamed his answer with a smile across his face as he realized that Valerie was understanding, and took her hand and squeezed it as a tear formed in his eye a quick blush rose on Valerie's cheeks.

With help from one of the technicians, Valerie was able to plug her computer into the mainframe and access the recorded data. She was assigned some software help and a team was formed to fuse a conversion of the visual brain image information and correlate with George's voice and typing. Using her musical synthesizer capability connected to the pattern recognition software, and based on neural nets that the software team had begun playing with earlier, they had a path to being able to reproduce the language on the computer from George's mental images. This would take a few weeks worth of work to clean up, but the breakthrough was enormous.

The ebb and flow of the brain measurements provided sections of a basic match with the sounds being spoken by George. So the next step was to feed the complex wave patterns being measured into software programs that converted them to music. Again, at a break in George's brain activity, the music was played back to George to see if he recognized the sounds. George indicated that while there were some differences and the fidelity of the information was lower than what he was experiencing, it was totally recognizable.

Valerie listened with growing awe to the music flowing from her computer and was overwhelmed by the sound. She had studied most of the great symphonies and choirs, rock, country western, folk music from around the world, the songs of the humpback and blue whales and even some of the music synthesized from the dance of the Northern lights. This was truly distinct, complex and she felt…truly beautiful.

One note that Valerie passed on to Tim was a feeling by George that the Old Ones were actively holding back some information. While this was not surprising, it did make one wonder what and why.

Valerie studied George's type-written notes along with the matching passages of sound; she continued to expand her grasp of the language and continued to appreciate its depth of complexity and expression. She knew she had the *Rosetta Stone* for the language of the Old Ones, but to properly study this would take a lifetime which she was more than willing to commit too. Unfortunately she had much less time as events would need her to learn faster.

|||||

Tim was met at the surface by a limo to take him to the White House for a special briefing of the President. While general information had been forwarded to the White House in an "Eyes Only" brief, the President wanted to hear about the latest findings and discuss strategy relative to the international effects. A number of additional vehicles were added to the convoy to discourage any possible attack from agents unknown.

When Tim's limo left the underground tunnel, an impressive array of surveillance was focused on everything within a five block swath following his car. NSA had satellite, radio, telephone, cell phone and all other frequencies, such as hand held radios, being monitored with the help of the local Navy Seal teams.

At the same time, another limo and a separate convoy carrying Jack with escort vehicles left the U.S. Naval Observatory, headed for the White House. As in Tim's case, a massive amount of surveillance was arrayed along the path of the limo and monitored by the Navy Seals.

A man was on the bench outside a restaurant reading a newspaper. When Tim's limo passed by, he barely took notice of the event and went back to reading his newspaper. A few minutes later, he folded his paper and started walking down the street. He entered a plain looking brick apartment building.

After approximately four minutes later, the NSA intercepted an email that simply read "heavy cream, topped with a cherry leaving bakery at 3 p.m." addressed to a common advertising web site based in New York. A few minutes later another intercept was received with "heavy cream, with cherry topping on white cake arrived at party, 3:15pm." There had been a number of other encrypted radio transmissions during the same time with each having been triangulated and fixes provided. The NSA encryption breaking unit was studying the coded communications, but it seemed to relate to a current Chinese code pattern that was under analysis by code breaking super computers, so they would have to wait.

Monitor teams were dispatched by Seals and FBI agents to follow and monitor the various points that were captured but previously not known. These were low level people and not their main contacts, but with this, working from the bottom up is a standard approach.

The Russian agent on the street bench had an apartment paid for in cash, apparently a dead end. But his electricity was paid for from a bank account that received periodic transfers of funds from a European bank. Upon gaining access to the records through some back door traps that Tim's software team just happened to have in place, they found a maze of transfers. However after a number of tracing loops and curls, they found that the money had a relationship to a man in D.C. that worked as a manager for a law firm that had a number of registered lobbyists in congress.

Given the evidence in hand, the FBI launched a focused team investigation. The FBI team dug into the background of the manager and the law firm. They found a link to a series of criminal gangs, although extremely well hidden. So an FBI agent was set up as a client to the law firm and a team was assigned to monitor his moves and the moves the manager and all personnel at the firm.

IIIII

Since Valerie's arrival, George's mind had gained basic control and was able to support the flow of information while also understanding his environment. Maybe it was just George's mind adapting or maybe it was the new and exciting twist to his life along with the appearance of Valerie, even George didn't seem to know. While his life was different, George was more content then he remembered ever feeling throughout his life; he no longer felt alone.

His family had been informed that George was okay, but had lost his voice and had a contagious disease so no contact was allowed, only through a remote viewing during short periods that were set up to make them feel more comfortable with the situation could they see and communicate with him. They were also told that George was reacting well to treatment and they had no reason to worry. Also, the FBI used the fact that George had a secret security clearance to create a hint of a story that allowed his family to feel that he was being kept away due to the nature of his work and knowledge.

While many minds were connected with George, it was not all of the Watchers of the universe. The communication only worked with a part of the group since the rest had a low level of intelligence or their physiology was so a variant from the base pattern that they could not interpret the transmissions. George could just consider himself lucky. He was now no longer alone in his thoughts. He could stop thinking about how lonely and separate from others he had been. Also, a beautiful woman had entered his life who was interested in communicating with him, no matter what the reason; he found her very attractive and that in itself was a positive move forward. Besides, she would be spending a lot of time with him. Even if he no longer received his nightly chocolates from the hotel maids, life wasn't too bad, not bad at all.

One part of George's mind focused on his present surroundings, another part continued the job of entering information, all the information he could deal with in real time, into the computer. It wasn't unusual for George, he was well known at work for multi-tasking, and the parts of his brain being affected seemed to make it easy for him to type, talk, and comprehend all at the same time.

Normally with age, the neurons in the brain are decreasing, but with the stimulation and added blood flow, the pattern had reversed the decrease and new neurons were being added by the brain at an increasing rate. With the doctors taking over, George's diet was on a much better path and two times a day during breaks, security agents came down to work with George on training equipment they had set up in the next door room.

A push was being made to make George's life as comfortable as possible under the current conditions. As soon as a portable recording capability could be engineered, George would become free to roam the facility and get out of the current three room confines. George understood and actually agreed with the confines. He knew how important each second of transmission was.

With Valerie at his side learning, George typing, and talking-singing, the doctor monitoring him; the team monitoring, the computers hooked to George; data recording continued and with the breaks for exercise, George's life settled into a daily pattern.

While Valerie had planned for a one week trip, she no longer wanted to return to the mundane life of the boring privileged and preferred to stay working with George.

After a morning meeting, Valerie indicated to Tim and Bob that she needed to talk.

"So Valerie, it sounds like you're progressing fast," Tim started with a smile.

"Yes, this is exciting, and truly wonderful. But I needed to talk with you about getting set up for a longer stay. All my clothes and things are in New York. I don't need to go back, but I would like to get out and do a little shopping to tide me over. I suspect Bob, Randy and Janet have the same problem. Also, George could use some cloths as well."

"Oops, never thought about that," Tim commented with a bit of a surprised look and a smile. "You're right; we yanked them out of their normal lives so fast that they only have limited things. Let me see if we can arrange something. If we can sneak you out with some body guards, we can let you stock up. Of course you will be on a government allowance for spending."

"No, we will not," said Valerie with feigned indignation and smile.

"You forget I have my own money. We'll buy what we need. And maybe even some things we don't really need," she said with a chuckle.

After a short discussion, Jack arranged for an early morning helicopter drop of supplies the next day which was a Saturday, and while in the dark. Janet, Randy, Bob and Valerie were dressed in air force overalls and joined the helicopter team as it lifted off the Vice Presidential compound. The trip was short and landed on top of the Pentagon where the team members exited and were escorted through the halls of the Pentagon to one of the cafeterias where they were able to get breakfast and wait for the stores to open. After a casual breakfast and lots of talking and laughing, they headed to some restrooms where they shed their Air Force overalls for street cloths and were escorted by secret service agents to the underground Metro connection at the Pentagon.

With the small group prepared to leave the secure area of the Pentagon, Valerie turned to them with a broad smile of excitement "I know you have a government budget for spending, but buy whatever you think you need. Enjoy the moment and I'll cover everything above your budget" as she gave Janet a hug and flashed her platinum American Express Credit card. "Bob-Randy, make sure you pick up things for George. I think he would look good in blues, and don't forget sweat suits and tennis shoes. George wears size 10 ¾ shoes and for the moment, 50 waist, 29" inseam and XXL t-shirts, and at least two sweat shirts, and I know he prefers briefs, not boxers. I wrote it down so you don't have to remember," as she handed a piece of paper to Bob. "I get to shop with Janet and have a girl's day off."

When the small group exited the Pentagon, they took the escalator to the Metro underground and caught the train to Pentagon City. As they exited the Pentagon City Metro station, they took the small escalator to the lower level of the shopping center and the excursion began. The girls headed out with two secret service women agents and the men headed off with two secret service men agents. No one had to carry what they bought, everything was paid for with a credit card that the secret service agents had and pickup receipts were provided with the exception of a few small items. Valerie would reimburse their expenses over their allotment to the Government once the total was computed.

For Bob and Randy they went to a sporting goods store on the 2nd level and bought comfortable sweat suits for themselves and George along with some walking shoes. As they moved on, Bob asked Randy how it was going working with Janet. Randy instantly blushed and responded, "She is great. I enjoy working with her and to tell you the truth, I get a feeling of joy just waking up and thinking about spending my day with her."

"Don't feel embarrassed, I think you two would make a wonderful couple. While working in close quarters, I know it's a little tough. Have you let her know?"

"No. I've never been good with relationships."

"Ha, ha, ha, none of us really are. Sometimes you have to take a chance though. Although, look who's talking, this old bachelor. Someday I will take my own advice."

"What about Valerie?" Rand asked with a smile.

"A lovely young lady, but unless I am blind, which I am not, she has eyes only for George, and George has let her know in his own way she would make him very, very happy. No, I will need to find someone else."

"Well, I'll keep my eyes open for you," Randy said with a smile.

On the other side of the multi-level mall, Janet and Valerie had entered a Lingerie store as Valerie talked with Janet.

"You know, Randy could be quite a catch," Valerie said with a smile as she picked up a pretty black see-through silk negligee.

"Do you think he likes me? He seems a little shy and only seems to open up when we are working. I really enjoy my time with him, but I'm not sure how to approach it with him. What about you, do you have someone special?" she said as she shook her head no with a smile.

"So, first, yes I think George and I are making a connection far beyond work. Just his touch makes me happy. Whenever I think of his kind heart and just seeing him, I feel so comfortable. You, my girl, may need to make a move, give him a signal. Unless I read Randy wrong, which with my background of reading men, I seldom do, he is yours for the asking...so let him know he can ask."

They continued their shopping and as noon was approaching, decided it was time to take a break for lunch. The security agents communicated and they decided to meet at the food court. It wasn't that the food was bad in the team center, but it was in the center and now they had the freedom of all types of fast food to have fun with.

While they sat eating, another agent approached leading Janet's three brothers. Janet jumped up and in tears ran over to hug her brothers. After a few minutes, she introduced them to the others at the table. As Bob looked at her, he smiled.

"I talked with Jack yesterday when this break was planned. He set it up for you. We felt it would help you feel more comfortable with our given situation."

"Oh thank you so much Bob! You don't know how much this means to me," she exclaimed as she bent over and gave him a kiss on the cheek then continued to hug her brothers. The boy's agent collected food orders from the three boys and went over and brought back food and drinks. The group sat and talked as the boys began to meet Janet's work people and they got to know a little about Janet's brothers.

After a time, the boy's agent flashed his watch at John as a signal. John leaned over to Janet with a smile on his face "Sis, I want you to know that in your absence I've stepped up and am making sure that Rick and Timmy are getting their school work done and are staying out of trouble. Auntie and Unc are doing just fine, so you don't need to worry.

"We've been told you're doing some very important work for the government and we can't talk too much about you to others, but I want you to know we're proud of you and miss you a lot. The agents are keeping an eye on us, so we're okay."

With Janet listening to him talk, tears continued to flow as she hugged him.

"We can't stay sis, we have to get them back for a game later today; but when you can, come see us. We all love you."

With the lunch break ending, they got up to leave. Janet gave them all another hug and a kiss on the cheek that left her younger brothers blushing as they headed out. As they left, Janet gave Bob a large thank you hug as she cried a little more.

When Valerie put her arm around Janet, she whispered "Are you ok?"

Janet pulled out the pendent and clasped it in her hand with a small smile on her face. "Yes, I'm just so happy to see them, and to know that John has grown up so quickly. I never thought he had a clue about what was going on. He's just like dad. He steps up at a moment's notice and takes control."

Once they broke up from lunch, the two groups split up again and headed out. The girls still wanted to look for some makeup and the men wanted to get additional shaving supplies.

After a few more hours of wandering around the stores, it was time to head back. The packages were sent by the stores to the shopping center management office and from there picked up by agents that delivered them to the Pentagon and from there delivered to the Vice President compound along with the normal afternoon supply run.

When the small group decided to head back, Valerie insisted on swinging back by the food court so she could pick up a banana-strawberry shake to take back to George. It didn't matter what the doctors said,

George deserved this and come hell or high water, Valerie was determined he was going to get his treat.

The return route was basically the reverse, to the Metro, to the Pentagon, put on their overalls, to the helicopter pad. A short hop to the Vice Presidents compound, down the elevator and finally home. George was handed his banana-strawberry shake along with a hug and bright smile and the packages arrived shortly thereafter. While the ice cream had melted a little, it was still great to George.

|||||

The surveillance team intercepted a transmission from the corner telephone two blocks from the main entrance to the underground tunnel in Crystal City, VA. The SEAL team spotted the man as he hung up the phone and turned to walk down the street. They followed as he headed back to a hotel room overlooking the Environmental Protection Agency building.

The SEAL team lead was dressed in his civies as he approached the hotel front desk and asked for the manager. A quiet conversation followed by a short phone call, the manager suddenly was very helpful. Considering the business generated by the government, the manager was very accommodating and allocated rooms for the team surrounding the man in question. Luckily this was a Wednesday afternoon and a transition time for people moving in and out of the hotel. The team settled in for a monitoring of the suspect's contacts.

The SEAL team entered the rooms on either side of the agent, and opened the suitcases with their electronics. The lead SEAL selected a number of devices that he attached to the wall while the others set up a laptop with wires attached to the wall mountings. As they brought the laptop on line they plugged in headphones and stepped through the various devices to make sure that the connections were working and that recording was on-line. They then settled in to wait.

Meanwhile, the NSA had traced the phone message to a home outside of Alexandria and another team was sent to monitor this position. Other results had been captured relative to the Georgetown entrance, so the team in that area settled in for a longer monitoring stakeout and expanded out to cover the other triangulated points of interest.

|||||

Within the BELLOWS facility, after the second week, the teams had settled into a pattern.

Valerie was rapidly gaining an understanding of the Old Ones language and could hold increasingly complex conversations with George. The team was providing her support on work to map the music patterns to ideas and concepts. Work was progressing slowly, but was progressing.

Bob was working with the team to help them get through the sudden effects on their lives. In the Tuesday, Thursday and Saturday evenings, Bob and Tim talked late into the night. Tim still held personal blame for loss of his family and found himself late at night in periods of depression. Working with the medical team, Bob introduced sleeping pills to help him. With achieving an ability to sleep, Tim began to feel better.

The math team led by Bill Temple was working with the new equations, constants and symbols. Truth be told, they were making significant progress. New insights into the multi-dimensional connections and understanding of matter were rewriting the basic concepts held by physics within a short period of time. The human understanding of M Theory was being confirmed and re-written at the same time. The team barely wanted to take a break to sleep or go to Tim's meetings. Information was being added at an astonishing rate.

The Russian agents were being closely monitored. Since the team was not leaving the underground compound except in rare occasions and then by hidden means like the Pentagon air lift, it appeared to be causing a small amount of frustration. Meanwhile, the Chinese agents were making no moves as they appeared to be waiting for a change.

Jim Endel's design engineering team had out done themselves. Tim's idea had developed the math and with a basic working device; Jim's team designed new working devices with their latest focus on making it small, cloaked and useful.

Tim and Jack walked into Jim's engineering office, there were two cases sitting on his desk. As Tim opened the cases, he saw the foam blocks inside the briefcase with what appeared to be empty cut outs. With a smile on his face, Tim reached in; he was able to wrap his hand around one of eight of the objects that "wasn't there". His finger edges disappeared where they touched the devices, but he could feel the weight and slight warmth of the unit sitting in the palm of his hand.

The area of the device was the size of a small computer mouse. As Tim looked at the team lead, Jim rapidly responded: "3 miles. The frequency is a random pattern so only the synchronized receiver knows the frequency at any point, information is time compressed and transmission is shut down if a detection device is sensed. Power pack will last for 3 months, we are working on a new power source, but with the short notice it's the best we can do."

Jim continued, "We also have a synchronized repeater, a little larger and able to send burst transmissions to orbiting satellites for re-transmission. The bursts are coded and we have both a variation of a current Russian code as well as a variation on the Chinese codes we can use."

"Tell your team thanks. If this works, we may have to change you into a product center!" Tim said with a smile. He placed the unit back into its slot and closed the briefcase.

Tim and Jack discussed the new devices ability with Jim over the next few minutes. During the discussion, word came across the news channel on the television sitting in the corner of Jim's office about an Al Qaeda threat against the U.S. on the internet. Jack turned to Tim with a grin, "How about a little field test?"

"I'm way ahead of you," Tim said. "Set up a team and we can use one of the devices."

Tim called Jim, who had stepped away a few feet. "We have a field test idea for you. Let's see how well this might work."

Jim's team embedded a small parachute attached to the device and extended the invisibility field to cover it while deployed. A trigger was set to blow off the parachute on command and the invisibility field would then shrink down.

Meanwhile, Jack placed a call to a CIA agent he knew well and asked if they had any planned drone flights over areas they would like to get a listening device into. The CIA had an Air Force drone planning for takeoff in 24 hours from an air field in Afghanistan that seemed to work. The indicated drone had the new Joint Tactical Radio System (JTRS) radio system on-board that could easily do the necessary communications.

The package was quickly readied by Jim's team and set so that no one would know that the invisibility field existed and would only be activated on drop. The package was placed on a F18 that took off from Andrews, and air refueling relay stations were set up for a direct high speed delivery flight to the Afghanistan air base where the drone was to be launched from.

The Software team set up communications connections to the base so they could take over communications after the drone was in the air. Once the package was delivered, the software team along with IT was allocating the necessary resources and prepping the software for a long term monitoring.

After a long, but uneventful flight, a tired pilot exited the F18 and handed over a plain looking package. The ground crew had been briefed on what to expect and was able to attach the small box to the unmanned drone aircraft which was launched two hours later headed for the Pakistan tribal areas.

The drone now had two missions. The CIA had been tracking a key leader of the terrorist organization that deals with foreign operations. The second mission was the targeting of an operation group that appeared to be ready to enter Afghanistan to support the Taliban fighters.

The ground operators maneuvered the drone into position; the house containing the fighters was in the dark of night. The operators activated the infrared imaging system and could see a couple of men sitting outside the small hut about where the door appeared to be. There appeared a glow in the right corner of the hut that from experience indicated a small fire. About 10 spots showed the location of people inside the hut. The system with the sharp eyes of the operators, could see what their trained eyes knew were metal in the shapes that indicated guns and launchers, stacked against the walls.

This was a follow up drone from one that had been monitoring the men for the past ten hours. The previous drone had made a visual conformation of the twelve fighters coming and going through that specific hut and showed no others had been in the area. The hut was on the outer edge of the small village and with a well placed missile, there would be little damage away from the hut.

The operators pulled together the video tracking and the infrared tracking and attached it to a high priority email that was sent via classified network back to CIA operations in D.C. The Operations manager swiftly responded with an email to activate the video channel transmission and, while watching the infrared, gave the go-ahead. While the Operations controller in D.C. watched, the drone operators positioned the air craft and set up the missile targeting. As the computer targeting showed lock, the command was issued for missile launch.

The infrared turned white for a moment as the heat of the missile overdrove the sensitive receivers into overload. After a couple of moments, the tracking picked back up and the operators watched as the missile sped to its target. In a moment it was over as the hut exploded.

The explosion was much larger than the missile should have caused. The operators indicated in their closing action email that by their estimation, it looked like there must have been about fifty pounds of high explosive inside the hut.

The operators terminated the mission and re-directed the drone to a village about twenty miles away.

When the drone approached the village, the small building that the known operations lead occupied was identified and the radar indicated that at the moment, winds were minimal and well within operation parameters. At the appointed position, the operators relayed the drop command and signaled the BELLOWS team of the drop, as the package was released.

The drone turned and headed back to base. The command was given to not attempt to observe the drop due to its highly classified nature.

Once the package was released, a command from a satellite caused the package to split into two parts, one was a re-transmitter and the second was the main device. After the split, each released a parachute and their invisibility cloak was activated and extended.

While the packages floated down, Tim, Jack, Jim and the engineering team monitored the progress through a transmitting altimeter from their engineering station and about the right time, a signal was transmitted to blow off the parachutes. The team was nervous as they watched the altitude slowly tick down.

The devices replied that the parachutes were ejected and a few moments later, indications were that they had settled on a surface with green status.

Now they had to wait to see what would happen. As Tim and Jack looked at each other, the anticipation was nerve racking as they waited for the morning to come over the next hour.

When the morning sun approached the hut, the listening device picked up some muffled sounds. Jim quickly made adjustments to the sound receiver power and as voices started to be heard over the compressed data transmission, filters were applied by the software team to allow a clearer reception.

Tim and Jack stood back with a big smile on their faces and shaking hands in congratulations. Jim and the software team raced to tweak the adjustments until three women and two men's voices could be heard as they started their morning routine. The software team had power to activate standard NSA full signal processing software set up to easily identify individuals by number and sort out the separate voices.

The voice flow channels came through and were sent through a language

Ronald Townsen

translation program focused on the expected tribal dialect, which in turn produced a written script. Jack had set up to have this raw text information and voice recordings forwarded to a team at the CIA headquarters. The information was mundane, but that was expected. The very fact that their plan worked was exciting.

The listening device had landed on the roof of a room in a fairly good position over a table and the roof was thin enough to not really block the voices below.

This was of the most sensitive nature and no one in the CIA was provided any information about how this data was being monitored. Even the data itself was considered extremely sensitive since it showed the very ability to pull off such a feat.

With the success, the engineering and software teams left the station in automatic mode and progressed to other work. The software team had computers assigned through the cloud computing environment within the team's computer servers to manage the data flow. This setup was also left in an automatic mode with the software team providing a quick periodic check to make sure everything was positive. Additional work was underway to add new servers to the team's computer network to make sure the necessary computing power stayed available.

Since this was only the start, many more blade servers with quad core processors would soon be needed to support both work with George, language translation, listening devices, engineering design work, graphic arts, math work along with normal background operations of accounting, data backup, security monitoring and the thousands of other smaller tasks required each and every day.

The IT department was very busy, and it was only going to get busier.

|||||

The team had their normal morning meeting in the BELLOWS underground conference room. Tim went around the room to assess each group's progress and to let everyone understand the status and challenges they all faced in the near term.

Valerie was continuing to learn the language and support the translation work going on. Her ability to learn and adapt to the language gave the data analysis team a significant boost in their ability to understand the training information that was currently the majority of the transmission sections. Valerie was also working with a programming team attempting to build a language translation program, and although some success was being had, the complexity of musical patterns made the job harder far beyond current language translation technology. But progress was being made as the team had turned to a growing adaptive neural network that could expand within the cloud computing environment as its needs demanded.

Next he turned to Bob "How is our patient doing?"

"George is beginning to adapt to the circumstances and handling the information flow better with time. He's gained the ability to separate the connection from his own self and in doing so, has gained some self control, although it will take time. Two things have crossed my mind though: Is he the only one on earth? And has this happened before?"

This brought the room to a standstill and everyone looked at Bob with nervous shock. Tim had a grim look on his face. "I'd not considered this angle, but you're right. If we know of one, perhaps there are others. There may have been others earlier that were never spotted. We need to investigate this, and quickly! Janet, have you been able to locate the symbol reference?"

"Yes, I have it here. It occurred in 1939 in a drawing of Einstein's" Janet plugged the projector into her laptop and showed them the drawing. Tim turned to the software team and asked them to work with Janet to find out everything they could about that symbol and the circumstances around the picture.

"Randy, you and Janet win the lead on this one by searching the symbols to see if any others have ever popped up before.

"I don't need to tell you that if someone else is out there with this information, the risk it puts everyone in. Time is of the essence, let's get it done folks!"

With those final words, the team meeting broke up and the hunt was on.

After leaving the meeting, Randy and Janet first started with a grouping of symbols that had been described by George. From the list, there were some that were basic shapes that for the search they needed to execute could be discarded as too general. That left twenty symbols that looked unique.

The symbols were roughly drawn before heading down to see George. When they sat down with George, they needed to get a better feel to ensure they had the correct shapes and to see if there was something missing in what they had drawn.

When George went through the symbols, he was able to relate them to the singing language giving the symbols some background and meaning with help from Valerie, which added some detail. After fifteen minutes, the message transmissions began again and Randy and Janet had to break off their discussion to allow George to concentrate on the information flow to support the data recordings. Valerie helped them with the final few symbols based on her understanding while George got back to the information flow.

Randy and Janet headed back to the engineering level and entered the area where the main software developers worked. The smell of pop corn along with the empty donut boxes and bottles of pop were all they needed to see and smell that they had found the right place.

Upon entering the room they were directed to Jim Thompson, the team lead. They looked around at the magnetic dart boards and sponge basketball hoops that were located around the room. The glow of the computer screen flat panel displays that seemed to fill the desks made the room look like a hacker's paradise.

Jim looked up. "Heard you were headed my way, you must be Randy and Janet, sorry we haven't been formally introduced at the meetings" he said as he extended his hand "I'm Jim two; not to be confused with Jim one that leads the physical engineering team. I've been monitoring your work and was wondering how long before you popped in", he added.

Randy opened his art book, "We've gathered a set of symbols and need to do a wide ranging search through everything we can find to see if there's a match. Can you help us?"

With that question, a number of the software team started making comments while laughing "If you need a search done, you've got the wrong guy, he can't hardly type much less write a search algorithm!" came the voice behind the monitors in front of Jim.

"I was writing this stuff before you could tell the difference between a bit and a byte" shot back Jim with a smile on his face. "Don't take offense, my team will find what you're looking for if there are any records on the planet. Go get some coffee and come back in an hour and we can give you an update."

This was clearly not their domain, so Randy and Janet took the advice and headed out of the room. As they were leaving, Randy looked at Janet and spoke a little louder than a whisper and with a smile on his face, "and I thought artists had a lock on being out of the ordinary."

Actually, Jim had held back on the truth of the situation; since the meeting, he knew that the team would be called on and had quickly focused his best hackers on writing and testing the necessary search algorithm. The team was able to create a parallel search across a large number of super computers which could attach into key computers across the world. In addition, the team had long-standing viruses in place to allow them back door entry into a number of systems spread around the world, with access to information that officially they were not allowed to know about. But these were some of the best software experts and security hackers in the world and propriety had very little to do with their job.

When Janet and Randy returned after the hour, Jim's team was already receiving a number of hits and they were rapidly organizing them for deeper research. The one that appeared at the top of the list came from a statue of Leonardo da Vinci on a scroll carved in relief in a square in Milano, Italy. The symbols on the upper right of the document, while small and barely noticeable, had a close resemblance to four of the symbols indicated by George. These were unique and hardly a coincidence. The related hits were also linked to a book of notes from the master containing the same symbols. On the pages just before and after the symbols were drawings of the masters attempts at flying machines.

The symbols as described by George related to planetary and atmospheric travel concepts. The conclusion was direct and inescapable.

Janet and Randy continued looking at the list of hits; additional tracings were found to ancient Greek, Arabic, and even to Egyptian writings. An interesting hit was on a wall painting in an Egyptian tomb dating back over three thousand years and referred to Ra, the sun god. Additional hits had reference to an ancient Chinese drawing, and an old East Indian drawing.

The conclusion was that the Old Ones had been working on this technology for a very long time. Apparently they had somehow found a way to activate it in a manner they considered useful for their own purposes.

While Janet and Randy were pouring over the growing computer output, a current reference was made to a face page related to a man and his son in a small town in southern Switzerland; Chiasso. There a young man was being treated for a mental condition due to sudden attack of the mind. The man had drawn a set of symbols exactly like George and according to the web page, claimed to be speaking in a strange singing language. The software team swiftly traced it to a Renaldo Serrano and his son Nicky.

Janet and Randy looked at each other in shock. Randy called and left a message for Tim and Jack. As the hits continued, they headed down to see George, Bob, and Valerie with the news.

"We found you another patient." Janet handed the printout over to Bob as Valerie looked on in shock. George smiled. When Valerie asked him if he knew about this other person, George replied in his sing-song,"I sensed someone, but they were not able to reply in a coherent manner and I could not tell that they were from earth. I'll try harder to see if I can reach him and verify his location during a quiet break."

Bob answered his cell, it was Tim. "What's happening? I got a high priority message that Randy and Janet had important information for me."

"Yeah, they've found someone in Switzerland that fits the profile. I think we need to act quickly. I'm going to call the hospital in the town indicated and see what I can find out."

"I agree, tell Janet and Randy to get their bags ready. I'll get Jack to start setting up the operations. Tell them they need to be ready to go within the hour."

Tim had decided to assign Randy and Janet to lead a team of agents to contact the family and attempt to bring them back; whatever it took.

Bob pounded on the keyboard as he did a search, finding the hospital in Chiasso along with a telephone number as Valerie made the call using her classic Italian, "Hello, we are looking for a patient that may be in your hospital, a Renaldo Serrano.

"You don't show a Renaldo Serrano? Can you please check your records? He may have been through your emergency room recently.

"No Renaldo, but you have a Nicky Serrano as a patient? Thank you. Do you have the name of the attending physician?

"Thank you…and the telephone number? Thank you very much."

Valerie turned to Bob, Randy and Janet, "It's not Renaldo, its Nicky his son. Bob, here's the attending physician."

Janet and Randy made sure that the software team had posted the information to the central computer while Tim instructed the software team to immediately erase the information from the face book web pages. Tim contacted Jack to organize a ruse to allow a small team to leave the underground compound and catch a jet to Milano and then by train to Switzerland.

Within thirty minutes, Janet, Randy, and a nurse Jill met with Tim and Jack. They were briefed on the plan and left immediately via helicopter from the Vice Presidents compound entrance to Dulles Airport.

||||||

After the plane landed in Milano, Italy, the warm winter air washed over the small group as they stepped outside the airport building. The small team swiftly split up and looked for taxis. When Janet found the taxi stand, the team quickly came over, loaded in and they were off. They directed the taxi to the rail station and booked passage on the next train to Switzerland, first stop Chiasso.

Janet was both excited and nervous. Tim had indicated that her background of having to deal with bringing up her younger brothers for the past years made her qualified to talk to these people, she would best understand some of stress that Renaldo might be going through and could connect. While she had been observing events working on art and symbology with Randy and trying to provide input, being sent on this mission, she finally felt like she was contributing and was anxious to show she could help.

Actually, being brought into the team was both a relief and a dream. After her parents died, Janet had been firm and resolute that her and her brothers would not be separated. With the funds left by her parents, including insurance money and the support of her aunt and uncle, she was able to keep the family together. While the funds slowly diminished, she was able to get a scholarship to John Hopkins and there was "discovered" by Randy.

Her aunt and uncle were getting old and not able to take care of the boys and Janet was coming to a conclusion that she would have to drop out of school. Then the event happened.

Janet's agreement with Tim included both a good salary and when things slowed down, means to finish school. In addition the boys were provided with an FBI family that would help them stay together and progress. It was a win-win...The family had two sons and lived only three blocks away from where the aunt and uncle lived and was able to provide a loving atmosphere. Their house was more than large enough and extra resources were provided. In addition, the boys and Janet could visit their aunt and uncle whenever they wanted. With the funds available, a nurse was able to be brought in to watch over the aging couple and help with meals and taking care of their house.

The train carrying the BELLOWS team headed north from Milano, entrancing Janet. As she stared out the window she clasped her family pendent, wondering what path life would take her; obviously not what she had thought. This could never have been planned. She smiled as the train passed by the Como Lake and the wonderful view of the city with its church tower and its little villages dotting the deep blue lake as far as she could see. Within a few minutes, they would be at Chiasso.

While she had been working with Randy at school, she had never seen it more than a student-teacher relationship. Now with the shift in events (and Valerie's push), Janet looked over at Randy and saw him in a different context and smiled. Randy got out of his train seat and sat down by Janet.

"How are you doing?" He looked into her eyes. "It's good to get out from the underground area and this ride is beautiful. I wish we could spend some weeks here drawing and painting."

Janet caught the "we" with a bit of a thrill and smiled.

"That would be so much fun. Do you think we would be able to some day?"

"It may be awhile, but I think we could." With that he reached over and put his hand on top of hers and Janet leaned over and kissed him on the check as a blush rose on his face.

"I would love to spend time with you on a vacation here someday," she said with a smile.

With the contact information provided by Valerie, Bob had called ahead to the attending doctors to let them know that Janet and Randy amongst others would be coming to see them. In his conversation with the attending physician, Bob indicated that there would be contact coming from the Swiss government relative to this matter and that Renaldo should be informed.

The President had earlier sent a quick and sensitive message to Switzerland letting them know that a diplomatic discussion was needed immediately.

The current prime minister of the rotating group of Switzerland government leads responded to the President's call; there was a tone of curiosity in his voice.

"Good morning Mr. President. I understand you have an important matter to discuss?"

"Good morning, Mr. Prime Minister. Yes, I have a matter of the utmost importance to our countries that needs to be discussed immediately. First, I need to know that you are alone? This matter is of major secrecy and I can only talk with you about this."

"Yes, I am alone Mr. President. What can we do for you?" He spoke with his strong German-Swiss accent.

"We have two teams headed towards Chiasso to meet with a small boy and his father in your hospital. I have reason to believe that he and his father are at sever risk of being taken or attacked by either the Russian mafia or Chinese government. Nicky has an extremely rare condition that is of major importance to a highly classified program we are conducting. First, he is not a risk to any other person; this is not a contagious problem. He is only the second person we are aware of that posses this condition and we must be able to interview him as soon as we can get our people there. I can only tell you that this project is of the highest priority to my government and that makes Nicky's condition of the ultimate priority to my country and I believe ultimately the benefit of the world. I cannot discuss the specifics of this program at this time, but I would encourage you to swiftly act to get Nicky and his father under protection as quietly as possible.

Our people are in transit as we speak. While we are taking every action possible to not have them tracked, there is no guarantee that they are not being followed. My people are being escorted by FBI agents for their security."

"Mr. President, I will take you at your word that my citizens are possibly in danger. I will dispatch security to protect them immediately and thank you for the warning. Is that all?"

"No, I fully expect that after meeting with Nicky, we may need to have him and his father come to the United States to support our program. While it will be their choice, I think they will recognize that we can help Nicky. As our guests, Nicky and his father will be extended all possible support we can offer both physically and monetarily. While they will be involved in an extremely highly classified effort, they will have full access to your government's representatives and will be treated in the best possible manner as our guests."

"Of course you understand the decision to return with your team is strictly theirs. But I understand that you consider this a highly sensitive matter and will be treated as such by my government. Thank you for contacting me and I have already sent instructions to my security people to connect with your people and help you in any way necessary in this matter."

"Thank you, as part of a follow up on this effort, my wife and I would like to visit and have a chance to see your beautiful country. Our friend

Valerie Jenkins indicated she can arrange a concert with some of your fine orchestras that we can enjoy."

"I am sure we can arrange for you an enjoyable visit. I know Ms Jenkins as well, and we look forward to her help in making arrangements. I look forward to meeting with you and your lovely wife. Till then, let me know if we can be of help in any other way." With a sense that the conversation was over, he closed with a warm, "Goodbye Mr. President"

"Goodbye and our people will be in touch, thank you again for your help."

Chapter 15: Urgency

George continued working with the latest transmission of information-training from the Old Ones. Suddenly there was a pause in the normally steady string of communications.

The transmission restarted and George immediately sensed something was wrong. The change in George's mood triggered alarms in the monitoring team and Tim was immediately notified. As George typed, the notes indicated that the Old Ones had sensed an event of immense proportions was approaching their galaxy (Sxvy) and they would soon be forced them to flee. They were making arrangements to rescue as many lives as possible.

The data transmissions continued, but with a significant jump in complexity and down periods were significantly shortened. The monitoring team had barely been able to keep up with the training-data complexity before, now they were overwhelmed by the complexity-type and speed of information flow. Without Valerie being present, the team could simply do their best possible and make sure the recordings were going.

The jump in rate was a physical burden to George and light sedatives were being prescribed to try and reduce the physical load. But the information flow continued unabated.

During a short gap, the Tern issued a transmission that provided location of Tuqvx, their galaxy and requested an emergency update. The returned transmission showed the location of the Old Ones galaxy to be completely opposite from the Tern's location across the universe.

The Old Ones indicated the sensing of a massive, larger than the galaxy, surface of extremely high energy headed in their direction. In earlier days, they had attempted to probe beyond their galaxy and had sent robotic sensor systems out to learn more about what lay beyond the edges of their galaxy and on the edges of the universe. One of the probes had passed information through its instant communications channels just before it died as the fabric of space-time was mangled by the massive flow of energy.

Their fast analysis was not positive and the assumption was their galaxy was about to be blasted by this wall of radiation and the related tearing of the fabric of space-time. There was no way to stop it. Their civilization had but weeks of time left. The latest calculations had just been completed from the Master Plan, this was the first time George had heard of this work, and they computed a one hundred percent chance that their galaxy would be totally destroyed.

The transmission of data from the Old Ones, resumed with a sober tone overlaying the urgency of the material.

|||||

Sxxty left the transmission chamber; he continued to monitor the status communications channel for evacuation planning. The computers had started providing a plan for evacuation of the galaxy. Not all would be saved, but the priority was on saving as many of the children of all planets and as many of their parents as possible. The computers were planning based on the projected rate and direction of expansion of the energy intrusion, numbers, types and current location of all current transport vehicles in relation to the populations of the galaxy. The computation was not complex, and the early plans were rapidly being released.

Because of the location of the research station, Sxxty was aware that according to the plan, they would be one of the last to leave assuming everything worked as expected. As he prepared to transport back to the main station, his thoughts drifted to Tia and the question of if he would be able to be saved. As Sxxty's mind worked its way through the evacuation planning, he saw that the Txxan's new home was being worked into the plans but there were only older transports available to help them and that meant Tia's chance of survival just dropped significantly.

CHAPTER 16: DECEPTION

Valerie was asked to separately travel to Lugano Switzerland on a diplomatic mission to produce a symphonic presentation for an upcoming visit by the President and First Lady. Her bags were packed and she was ready to leave within the hour.

Valerie's service had been swiftly contacted the necessary people in Switzerland and the work was arranged within an hour for a meeting in Lugano. She took the helicopter route to the Pentagon from the Vice President's compound. From there the metro took her to Reagan and from there she caught a flight to New York. She then caught a flight from New York to Zurich on a separate ticket so it would be harder to trace her connection to Reagan and back to the team.

Valerie's flight landed in Zurich Switzerland and after her and her FBI support team cleared customs, the team moved over to the railroads for the trip south to Lugano.

Because the team was high profile from the moment of appearing in New York; also because they were traveling under diplomatic passports, the assumption was they would be monitored by the Russian's and Chinese. So the CIA and NSA were in the background looking for Russian and Chinese tails.

The train carrying Valerie and her escorts headed south from Zurich. Valerie looked out the windows as the train headed into the mountains and thought about the changes in her life. There was a connection growing with George. While older, his kindness, his caring about his children joined with the unique circumstances of his life brought an emotional connection unlike any she had dealt with before. His simple touch made her feel something which she could not explain. She was also aware that her very presence made George joyful and that alone made her happy.

The fact that she was dealing with a universe connection, a new and exciting language, people with dedication, people pulling together all her worlds; the excitement and wonder of the place she found herself was beyond anything she had ever expected in her life. All of that, George and with the backdrop of the Swiss Alps made her wonder what could make her life any better. She had lived a life of safety and luxury since a small child, with wealthy parents connected to powerful political people. But for once in her life, she was needed not for her political connections, but for the unique capability that was her.

The south bound train exited the winding route through the Swiss Alps and reached Lugano where the team disembarked and headed to the hotel. Upon reaching the hotel, as Valerie entered her room, she was met by a woman dressed as a maid that looked like her twin. She reached in her bag and handed the woman notes she had written during the flight over to Switzerland, about the symphonic arrangements and other basic planning steps. They exchanged clothes, maid outfit for travel dress, and Valerie backed out of the room while putting on a blond wig while heading downstairs using the employee's private elevator. As she exited the elevator, she was met by a CIA agent and they headed out of the back of the hotel to a VW van to take them to the hospital in Chiasso.

Upon arrival at the back of the hospital, Valerie was escorted into a small room where she found a nurses dress. After changing, she left the room and was pointed to the room of young Nicky. Upon reaching the floor where Nicky was being monitored, she introduced herself to the nurse in charge with the special papers provided by the Swiss government given to her by the CIA agent and she followed the head nurse to Nicky's room where a man sat outside dressed in civilian clothes. In the room were Nicky, Renaldo and Dr. Bernardo.

Within a short time after Valerie's arrival to Nicky's room, the group of agents along with Janet and Randy and Jill arrived at the hospital and the doctor and Nicky's father left to meet with them. Alone with Nicky, Valerie stepped up to his bed.

"Nicky, my name is Valerie and I am here to help you," Valerie said in her best Old Ones voice and a smile on her face for this strong little boy in front of her.

The change in Nicky's mood was instant, he suddenly realized that in Valerie, there was someone who could understand him and with that thought, his world became brighter. "Yes, I can understand you. The images and sounds are too much. Can you help me? Do you see and hear the images and music too?"

"That's why I'm here. I have learned from another man, George, who is also part of the connection that has taken over your mind. At some point, if you try real hard, you may be able to reach George when the connection is active; he is trying to reach you. We want you and your father to come with us to the United States where you can help us and we can help you. Would you like that?"

"Very much Ms. Valerie; I have tried to talk with the doctors and my father, but you're the first one I can talk to that understands. There are so many people in my mind. I don't understand what's happening, but I am beginning to be not so scared"

"My dear, don't be scared. No one will hurt you. You may not know this, but this is a gift and your ability is one of the greatest gifts that anyone could have. We'll make sure that everything will be fine. We are talking now with your father and his seeing the smile that you have on your face will be worth more than your weight in gold too him. We can help you to understand and learn to deal with this gift"

In the meeting room, Janet and Randy introduced themselves and verified that the doctor and Renaldo had both had a briefing of Nicky's importance by the Swiss Government, although nothing of what was really going on.

In the meeting room, Janet reached out to Renaldo, putting her hand on his, "We understand how you are feeling, but we can and will help Nicky. If you will come with us back to the United States, we can protect you both and give Nicky the help he needs to control this gift.

While I don't have the gift that Nicky has been given, since I have been involved in this project, the people have provided me the help I have needed to take care of my brothers and uncle and aunt. These people care, we care and I assure you that this is the best for Nicky."

Janet's presence and projection of kindness proved to be the key in giving Renaldo assurance that everything that could be done, would be done to help him and Nicky. She indicated that with a little trust, everything would be fine.

The plan had been put in place by the Swiss government and U.S. government to have Renaldo travel with Janet and Randy to the D.C. area if he agreed, while Nicky would travel to D.C. with Valerie under disguise and with Nicky's health supported by Nurse Jill.

Renaldo looked at Janet and spoke, "You mean the woman with Nicky now?"

"No, that is Valerie; the plan was to sneak her in as a cover. She has the ability to talk in the language that Nicky is speaking. Jill, as *she glanced at her*, is here to help with a cover story relative to us being at the hospital to see you and to help with Nicky on return for his safety. Nicky will leave the hospital for the flight back with Valerie and Jill. He will return with them if you agree and you will return with us."

Randy and Janet explained that all costs were being covered for Renaldo's and Nicky's transportation and his property will be managed and handled as he wished. If he agreed, he would be receiving a salary while they worked with the U.S. Due to the nature of the information and to protect everyone, Renaldo and the doctor were not to contact anyone outside the group. When everyone was secure, they would be able to notify friends.

As in the U.S., after they had left, a sweep would be made of the hospital by U.S. and Swiss agents to *clean* the area of any trace. Bernardo would not be going with the team, but was reminded that as a matter of Swiss national security, he was to turn over all information and not to breathe a word to anyone about Nicky or any of the events that had happened for both his and Nicky's security and safety.

Under close security, Renaldo, the doctor, and Jill, Janet, and Randy went back to see Nicky. The glow on Nicky's face was a shock and a wonderful gift to Renaldo. Valerie switched from the Old Ones language to her best Italian, which was very good, "Ciao Renaldo," she introduced herself.

"I have been able to reach Nicky and we are able to talk. I cannot tell you how or why I am able to communicate with Nicky but we have become good friends" she said as she smiled and winked at Nicky then squeezed his hand, getting a smile in return, "in just the few minutes that you have been gone. If you agree, when we arrive in D.C. you will begin to understand why this is truly a gift Nicky has been provided."

"Do you have any questions?" Valerie asked.

"Many, but I understand that they cannot be answered until we arrive in the United States?"

"Yes, I am sorry, but now we must hurry and must leave quickly."

Renaldo looked into the glowing eyes of his son "Nicky, do you want to travel to the U.S. with these people?" Nicky glanced at Valerie and responded with a vigorous shaking of his head yes. The deal was set.

"Okay, I guess it's time to get going; Nicky I will see you soon when we are in the United States. I love you" Renaldo hugged his son and ruffled his hair. With another hug and a reassuring look, Renaldo left with Randy and Janet and the security team.

The team exited the elevator and could see the SUV parked in front of the hospital glass doors. Janet saw a gift shop and asked the agents if she could stop for just one minute to buy something. Renaldo and a security agent went on ahead as Janet and Randy stopped with some agents for a moment at the gift shop.

Part of the team left the front entrance of the hospital, Swiss security and U.S. FBI agents were in front of Renaldo. After taking 5 steps past the glass doors on the outside, shots rang out. People positioned on a roof top across from the hospital were firing on the group and a gun fight ensued. The Swiss security agents fanned out and attempted to flank the shooters and calls went out to get air support. Janet and Randy were cut off from the group being trapped inside the hospital entrance and were swiftly moved to a safer position.

Renaldo was trapped against the SUV having dived forward and tried to stay out of the line of fire. Two agents, one Swiss and one FBI lay dead in a pool of blood five feet away from the van and in a no-man's land as bullets rained down on the team.

When a police helicopter approached the roof tops, a missile was launched, exploding the helicopter in mid-air as it crashed into the street taking out two cars at an intersection. While the team attempted to out flank the shooters, an agent had just reached the roof of the hospital and opened fire on the gun men, taking two of them out of the fight, leaving what appeared to be six more. The gun fire continued to pepper the SUV and the agents as they attempted to move both right and left to get better angles.

The agent on the hospital roof moved to get a better angle, a shot took him down.

Another helicopter appeared and the sharp shooter on board started to gain an advantage over the roof top gunmen slowly picking them off one at a time while the pilot maneuvered to keep from being a missile target, dropping below roof tops and bouncing up for the shooter to rapidly take a series of shots before dropping low or going behind another building for protection.

The shooters slowly were being picked off when suddenly one of roof top gun men rose and a missile was launched at the SUV, causing it to explode in a fireball that flipped it into the air.

In the instant of the explosion, Renaldo was killed.

Twenty seconds later, agents rushed the roof of the building with the remaining gun men. As they broke through the door with shields in front of them, the security agents spread out across the roof as the remaining Chinese agents turned to engage them. With bullets flying across the roof of the building, the unprotected Chinese agents began to be overwhelmed. After a ten second gun battle, two agents were wounded and all gunmen dead except one Chinese man that had four shots in the shoulder and leg, but survived; he started waving a diplomatic passport.

When the gun shots rang out, an agent that had been sitting outside of Nicky's room, burst through the door and Valerie, Jill and Nicky were swiftly escorted to the interior of the hospital to protect them. Nicky was given the play clothes he was wearing when he arrived at the hospital to put on. They were taken down stairs and Valerie changed back into the hotel maid cloths. They were hustled out the back to a waiting common looking dark blue VW bug to be whisked away by a CIA agent in hectic traffic, headed to the local train stop on the north side of Chissio.

When Valerie, Jill and Nicky arrived at the train station; the CIA agent with them was notified over his communications net of Renaldo's death. He informed Valerie and Jill, but the information was kept away from Nicky for the moment. They rapidly boarded a train to Zurich for a private jet flight to Washington D.C.

About the same time, Jill and Valerie noticed a shift in Nicky's emotional condition. First he started to be very sad with tears forming in his eyes, and then he smiled and then had a determined look on his face.

With the shifting looks on Nicky's face, Valerie looked at him and asked, "Nicky are you okay?"

"Yes, something has happened, but I will be strong and it will be okay." With those simple words, Nicky stayed quiet for most of the trip to the U.S."

After the gun fire stopped and agents signaled all clear, Janet and Randy, in shock, were bundled up and with the remaining security agents, rushed out the back of the hospital just as a car arrived to pick them up.

The remaining team members were rushed to the main train station where they found Italian and additional Swiss security. They noticed armed men on the platform as they boarded the train headed south for Milano to reverse the trip back to Washington D.C.

Unlike the trip north, Janet spent the time talking with Randy about the dangers that they had been through, the loss of Renaldo, and the FBI agent and the danger in their futures.

Janet leaned her head on Randy's shoulder as she looked over at the protection team and in a quiet voice as she hugged Randy's arm and clasped her broach with the other "How do you think they do this type of work?"

"You mean the gun fight? I don't know. Are you okay?"

"Yes, as long as I'm with you, I'll be fine. The gun shots on the first day were scary, but to see those two men dead and to see Renaldo die in the explosion was hard to handle."

"I know, but we're safe, your safe." as he turned to kiss her forehead. "We've known that this type of risk exists every time we leave the compound."

"Yes, but knowing and seeing are two different things. I can't help but feel for Nicky and for the men that died and their families."

"There is little we can do but try and help Nicky through this. We have our work to do and focus on, we can't control everything, but we can do the best we can and hope that it makes the difference. At some point this is going to go public and when it does; our work will help everyone to understand the beauty in the universe that we're hearing about from George."

"I have been thinking about that. Do you think Tim would let us start putting up the pictures maybe in the hall ways so the other team members could get to see more of them?"

"That's a great idea. It might help the team to get a better view of what George is seeing. Let's ask Tim as soon as we get back."

Janet smiled, hugged Randy's arm and extended her head to give him a kiss on the cheek, "No matter what the danger, we have to see this through. It's given me everything and deserves nothing less."

Randy patted her leg "I never in my wildest dreams could have imagined this. But you're right, we can do nothing less than our best work and I'm sure they'll keep us as safe as possible."

With that word, Janet drifted into a light sleep as the train rocked and rolled on its way to Milano.

|||||

With information arriving back in D.C., Jack immediately informed Tim of what happened and started an investigation on how the Chinese were able to track Randy and Janet. NSA started to review communications to see if they could spot any location that may have somehow notified agents in Europe.

A Top Secret, High Priority message was broadcast to all U.S. units in the Atlantic. A series of top cover jets were launched from England to cover the commercial flight and the private jet as they headed home. The George Bush aircraft carrier was in the mid Atlantic area on transit to support a NATO training operation and was notified to provide refueling and hand off of the cover craft as necessary. All Atlantic fleet assets within the path of the returning flights were given rules of engagement and put on tactical mode-weapons hot to cover the flights as they headed home. No reasons were provided, instructions were just given to protect at all costs.

Randy and Janet's team settled down for the commercial flight home, the skies were clear and the sun was warm. The plane took off on schedule from the Milano airport and headed across the western edge of Europe and looping to a great circle path that would take them south of Greenland then heading south to Dulles airport in Virginia outside of Washington D.C.

The Atlantic task force monitored the flights as they left the European airspace, with three top cover F22's that would need to be refueled on a tag team basis to protect each of the flights. The aircraft carrier was currently steaming east with a task force headed to the Mediterranean as part of the planned standard rotation of carriers and their task forces. Refueling tankers were scheduled for Naval Air Station Keflavik

The E2 surveillance planes were flying their patterns supporting the F22s and tracking linkage to the aircraft carrier group, a number of freighters were tracked as they plied their trade of moving cargo between Europe and the America's. A Chinese freighter was approximately five hundred miles south-southwest of Iceland transiting towards Sweden having recently left port in Greenland after loading a number of crates that had just been flown in. There was an unusual set of crates lashed down on its upper deck along with a sophisticated radio room.

Tim Donavan was leading the F22 cover flight team as they headed out over the Atlantic Ocean. Tim had been in the Air Force for ten years and had become team lead three years before. He was currently based in Texas and his wife and two sons had learned to accept him being away for many month tours. He and his team had made many flights into Afghanistan and Iraq. Why they were covering a commercial jet was curious and once they were done, he would have to buy some beers for his team so they could discuss this odd condition. There was a handoff from to an E2D from the carrier task force that was a little unusual too, it was a little further north of the carrier than they would have expected.

The commercial flight with the F22 top cover approached the location of the freighter, the special crates broke down and two special high altitude Surface-To-Air Missiles streaked into the sky headed for the commercial jet.

The launch of SAM's triggered alarms. The E2D radar spotted the missiles as they rose from the ship and the F22's warning detectors erupted in the pilot's ears. Because the commercial jet did not have the ability to sense the homing device on the missile, Tim radioed to the commercial pilots to break right in its flight path and go to maximum speed.

Tim and one of the supporting team members dropped lower to be between the missile path and the commercial jet, while the other F22 dove on the freighter, targeting the ships radios and launchers. As the diving F22 approached its launch range and acquired target, it released a missile targeting the bridge and continued to bore in to finish the job with its guns.

The ship erupted in an explosion as the missile hit and ignited a third and forth missile being readied for launch. The resulting explosion ripped into the hull of the ship, breaking the structural backbone of the ship while lifting the fore and aft of the ship into the air. As the F22 continued to close, the pilot opened fire with his guns spraying the ship with 50 caliber shells shredding the bridge area that had erupted in flames.

The carrier task force launched two rescue helo's towards the freighter to clean the area if anything survived the F22 attack and pick up any survivors for interrogation. The carrier sent a flash message to the Pentagon about the launch and started a real-time update data flow to the Pentagon on the contact action.

The missiles rose in altitude from the freighter. The F22's started to jam the missiles seeker frequencies. One of the missiles lost contact and turned to the left out of the critical zone, eventually exploding but not in an area of risk to any of the flight group. The second missile continued on course bearing down on the commercial jet. The F22's attempted to lead the missile with their guns and fired sidewinders at it, attempting to destroy it, all the time launching decoy flares in an attempt to divert it if it had heat sensors.

Tim's F22 was position directly between the commercial flight and the missile. As the remaining missile bore down on the commercial flight, Tim continued to keep his position as a physical guard for the commercial flight. As the second F22 continued firing, attempting to destroy the inbound missile, at the last minute before the missile was about to hit Tim's F22, it exploded. The explosion ripped off the F22's right wing and sent shrapnel through the cockpit.

Tim's F22 began a death spiral headed for the ocean 30,000 ft below. Tim fought to keep the position of the jet upright so that he could fire his ejection seat. As he punched the emergency switch and grabbed the ejection handles, the canopy released and the seat blew out from the jet.

With the wind ripping at Tim's body, the gravitational forces caused him to black out. As the ejection seat cleared the wounded F22's body, the parachute was deployed, an emergency signal was sent and the seat fell away leaving Tim's limp body dangling from the parachute as it drifted towards the ocean. Blood was oozing through a gash in his leg from shrapnel of the exploding missile. The blood was reaching the surface before Tim reached the water.

The pilots on the remaining F22's radioed engagement conditions and position of Tim's parachute's opening. One F22 stayed on station to support Tim while the other banked off and returned to altitude to continue providing cover for the commercial jet. A Navy F18 that had been doing top cover for the naval task force was vectored to support the commercial jet and back up the F22. A refuel flight had been launched from Iceland and the F22 and F18 would have to refuel after their heavy fuel burn. The complex plan showed a refuel to allow the F18 to support the commercial flight while the F22 refueled. Then the F22 would take over cover while the F18 intercepted a second refuel flight, and the F18 and F22 would continue on for top cover of the commercial flight until reaching the outer edges of America, where a second set of F22's would take over while the F22-F18 would land and refuel. The F22 would continue on to Texas while the F18 would turn around and head back to the Task Force.

The wing man's F22 was on station around Tim when the refuel flight arrived from the carrier. One of the helos from the task force shortly thereafter arrived and rescue operations began. As the divers hit the water, Tim's condition was rapidly deteriorating as he came in and out of consciousness. Blood continued to ooze from the gash in his leg. As the divers got the harness around Tim's limp body, the helo began to lift him out of the water. When he arrived in the bay of the rescue helo, the medical tech quickly put a tourniquet on his leg and set up an IV flowing in a desperate but ultimately unsuccessful attempt to try to replace fluids. The divers were rapidly retrieved and the Rescue helo banked south headed for the carrier which had turned north towards the action to cut transit time.

After refueling, the F22 headed over to where the freighter had been. Nothing was left but some debris and an oil slick. As the second helo approached, the F22 was released and headed towards Greenland for refueling and rest to be followed by a flight back to the Texas base.

When the commercial flight arrived at Dulles airport with Janet, Randy and the support team, the passengers were curious to note the emergency vehicles that arrived to escort their plane to the passenger hub. As the doors opened, the passengers were instructed to please stay seated while some VIPs were escorted off the plane.

None of the actual action had been seen or felt by the passengers other than a banking of the jet when the F22's had radioed the pilots. The missiles and the movement with the fighter jets had occurred beneath and behind the airliner and the people on-board were mostly asleep during the crossing. While the pilots were aware of what had transpired, they were under orders from their home office to not relay the information to the passengers unless necessary. Janet and Randy, along with the FBI agents, were removed and put in security limos and escorted to a helicopter pad for transported to the Vice President's compound entrance, with heavy security and air support.

Valerie, Jill, and Nicky had been placed on a private jet and flown back without any incident. They were directed into Andrews Air Force Base and transported by helicopter to the Vice President's compound, arriving at about the same time as Janet and Randy. Their trip was uneventful as they had not been traced. Their cover F18's landed at Andrews to refuel and rest before heading back to their European base.

The two teams came together at the Naval Observatory entrance to the underground site to take the elevator to the underground facility. Janet knelt down to give Nicky a hug and kiss. Nicky didn't ask any questions about where Renaldo was, but was always happy to get a nice hug.

The group took the elevator down to the team center. When the doors opened, they were surprised to see the crowd of fellow team mates break into applause and welcome home hugs.

Nicky was taken to George's room and introduced to him by Valerie. The information flow break occurred, but the channel was still open, allowing the Watchers to communicate soon thereafter, and George and Nicky swiftly engaged in a conversation that only Valerie seemed able to follow. There followed a curious notice by the Old Ones that this was the first indication of two Watcher patterns coming from a single race and meeting in person.

After a few minutes, the data flow continued and George had to turn his attention back to translation of the information. Nicky was able now to manage the information flowing and still was able to talk with Valerie independently as he took in all the electronics and watched what George was doing in amazement. Nicky was receiving the same information but his ability to separate it from his normal activity had increased to a point where he was able to carry on normal activity as the information flow occurred.

After another session, the Watcher transmission stopped for the Watchers to rest. George and Nicky talked some more about what this all meant and George showed Nicky what he was typing into his computer.

During the break after a short period of time, Bob and Valerie escorted Nicky into the side room for a time to explain the news of his father's death.

Bob began "Nicky, we have some bad news about your father. You have noticed he is not here as we had planned." Nicky was silent and had a firm look on his face.

In the same sing-song voice as George, Nicky looked at Valerie. "I know what happened. My father explained it to me as we were leaving for Lugano. He and my mother are here with me, and he told me that this was his time to move on and that this work is my future and I am to not be sad. He has not left me but will be with me. Also, I see him with my mother, and they are happy together. Both are here with me now" he said as he pointed to his head.

Bob leaned forward with a questioning look on his face. "Nicky, what did your father tell you?"

"He said that some bad men attacked at the hospital as he was leaving and he was in a car that exploded." Bob and Valerie looked at each other in amazement.

"Are you sure that no one told you about this?" Bob asked.

"My papa told me. He told me not to cry, that he and mama will be with me, and to tell you thank you for helping me. Now I need to go and help George. It's what I need to do." That was the end of the matter as he got up and went back to the room with George.

The medical team supported by IT and the software team, had organized a backup helmet connection in expectation of Nicky's arrival. They had worked overtime to replicate the mental recording system and create a duplicate recording channel to the main servers.

The data flow continued. This time, both George and Nicky were connected and the amazing condition of watching the communications flowing with synchronization into both in parallel continued. Nicky seemed to be able to gain strength and due to his youth seemed to be able to handle the strain a little better than George, which could only be contributed to his ten year-old natural energy.

Valerie sat by their side deep in thought of how life had given her all the keys. While Nicky's tragedy was not anything anyone wished, Valerie recognized she was a natural care giver that was part of this growing family of three and she had the strange feeling of being home for the first time since her parents died.

In another part of the site, an FBI agent assigned to the team approached the team memorial in the dining area. After opening the case, he added a picture of a proud Air Force pilot, some FBI and CIA agents, and Renaldo to the collection. The agents, Tim Donavan, and Renaldo were added to the memorial of those that had given their lives for the program.

CHAPTER 17: A WORLD OF INFORMATION

The BELLOWS modeling analysis team worked hard, and the equations began to make more sense. The magic of adding the new equation along with the nuances gained from the Old Ones symbology exposed the solutions to questions long held, begin to make sense. Added to that, the information being provided by the Old Ones was pushing them fast to new understandings of the universe.

The long held problem of gravity and its relationship to the other forces was quickly being solved and had everything to do with the energy and inter-dimensional relationships of the universe, and connections to other universes.

Prior to George's arrival, the team meetings had previously been briefings with only small movements forward from the math team. Now with each meeting, the team came in smiling to announce new finding that could be verified against data. The team was actually giddy with excitement. Tim had to remind them to "document, document, document," each of their findings before rushing to solve another problem. Plans were being made to expand the math and engineering teams to keep up with the rapid pace of advances.

The understanding of how matter such as the electron, differed from other particles such as the photons, neutrons, quarks, and others were being explored and new insight was swiftly evolving. The new information was leading to develop and modify new and upgraded models of atomic level interactions on the chemical periodic table.

The development of these new interactions allowed the team to rapidly understand how to make new metals and new chemicals and thus new products. Using current modeling capability, they could now understand how a chemical molecule would interact with a specific DNA design. This interactive model development had already reached a high level of understanding, but with the new understanding of particle interaction, this was now being refined and able to produce much more accurate results with exciting new breakthroughs possible in targeted inexpensive medications.

The ability to create higher purity of new chemicals increased rapidly within the teams' research labs and then a truly great break through occurred.

On a Friday evening, one of the younger mathematicians had taken an evening off to take his wife and kids to the newest Sci-Fi movie. During the Hollywood blockbuster, on the big screen a space ship had one of its engines, destroyed, and the engineers were desperately trying to find a new energy source to drive the remaining engine during a critical battle. As John sat with his wife leaning against his arm, a flash of insight occurred.

John forgot about the sound and fury coming from the big screen and the speakers blasting in the theater. His mind was rapidly racing through the equations and evaluating possibilities. His brown eyes were focused not on the screen in front of him, but rather on the screen in his head as he walked methodically through complex math that only a few dozen people on Earth truly understood.

John continued to combine equations in his mind, not even aware that the movie came to an end. With the lights rising in the theater, his wife looked at his face and with a smirk, realized what was happening. It didn't happen often, but when she saw that focused, glazed look on his face, she knew he was in a world unto himself. His mind raced forward to a new discovery and breakthrough that she and the kids would maybe never truly understand, and probably something he could not talk about, but in his world would be earth shaking.

She hated to disturb him, but people were entering the theater to clean for the next showing, and there were two protection people waiting for them at the bottom of the stairs. The boys were ready to go, so she gently kissed his cheek and whispered in his ear to get his attention "Honey, it's time to leave."

John felt his wife's soft kiss and heard her whisper. He knew he had to park his thoughts until he got home. In his mind, he remembered where he was in his calculation and in a few short moments, pulled himself back to the reality of the theater, his boys and his wife. As he smiled at his wife, "Thanks hon, I just got sidetracked on some work. Let's get some dinner and get the kids home. I may be working late tonight; I need to get my thoughts down."

With that, John leaned over, gave her a hug and kiss and they got up, followed the kids down the stairs and left.

That night, as John was able to get some basic thoughts down on his classified computer, the math just fell into place. Just as Tim had found the unique part of the math that gave them the ability to build an invisibility cloak, John had just found the key to unlimited energy drawn from the foundation of the universe. He was up all night working, he just couldn't stop. Since it was an unusual condition, the FBI agents monitoring John's family knocked on the door once at 3 a.m. just to make sure everything was okay and called in to inform superiors that John was involved in an all-night work session in their reports.

The next morning at the underground facility, during their morning meeting, John looked like he hadn't slept. He pulled Bill, the math team lead, aside and gave him a short rundown on his thinking. As the meeting was wrapping up, Bill spoke up when Tim asked if there was anything else that needed to be covered.

"I want to let everyone know, John had what could be a major breakthrough last night. John can you give us an overview?"

John rose with his hair in disarray and looked at Tim, "Last night I happened to think about the interaction of some of the equations and realized that we might be able to pull energy from the quantum foam. The equations show how energy is constantly transferred between dimensions and through that transfer, we define basic matter. I know most of you are aware of this, but last night, I saw in the math the ability to tap into this energy stream and pull energy from the quantum foam for any use. I was able to work out the basic math and the team should be able to verify my work. If I am right, we could use the engineering team to build a new and probably small, energy source that has, I think, no limit."

The room was stunned. This had consequences far beyond their wildest dreams and the room started buzzing with planning that needed to get done and the work ahead. Tim grabbed control of the team and was the first to speak, "John, well done. I think we all have a clue of the scope of the game change this brings." As Tim raised his coffee mug, others in the room did the same and Tim continued, "Here's to John, but you need to take a shower now!" as smiles and laughs broke out.

"Jim, as Bill gets his team reviewing the math, I need you to get an engineering team focused on spinning up to work out the implementation details. I don't have to tell you this needs to be another one of those high priority jobs that I keep dumping on you" he said as he smiled. "Okay people we need to get to work, so let's get going." With that, the meeting broke up. Bill, John and Jim started talking as they left the room together.

Bob and Valerie left the room. They headed to the elevator and went down to George's room. George and Nicky were both sitting in chairs and were pounding away on their laptops and talking in their sing-song voice.

The transmissions continued. Now with having both George and Nicky supporting the download of information, each could take time to sleep, move around, exercise or in Nicky's case, play, as the software team enjoyed games of wall foam ball soccer in the hallway, and not have to do all the work and always be tied to the computers. Nicky had understood the importance and jumped to the job with eager anticipation. His mental understanding was growing with leaps and bounds and he and George could now support the math team pointing out small variations and key points of interest.

Bob walked over to look at George's physical condition and noticed that on one window he was making notes on the current transmission while on another, he was already working with Nicky and the math team on the new discovery by John.

There was also a flow of email traffic from the IT department about a new set of Raid disc drives being set up to add another one hundred terabytes of online storage. The computer storage had to continue to be upgraded as the information continued to flow into the millions of terabytes.

Bob and the medical team had identified a physical change in George and Nicky's brains. Brain matter was growing around the sides of the brain. This design in the brain had been seen in rare people with extremely powerful memory capability remembering everything in their life time. Since no other effects were observable, the medical team took a monitoring position to see where this would lead. George and Nicky both appeared to be gaining significant memory capacity as time moved on. The only logical assumption was that the Watcher field was driving the brain to expand its memory capability to carry the extra load of information being downloaded. The interactive pattern was affecting their very physiology.

Valerie had walked over to squeeze Nicky's hand and then walked over to give George a kiss on the cheek before turning to go into the adjacent room. As she sat down at the desk and activated the workstation, she picked up the headphones and with a few strokes started listening into the current universe conversation being generated by the computer from the combination of George and Nicky's monitoring system plugged into the language translator. The language adaption system was rapidly evolving and becoming more capable. Valerie was constantly expanding her capability in communications using the new language.

The language translation system used massively parallel computers executing a large network of connected neural networks interconnected and operating through the cloud computing design. As Valerie would listen to the translations coming from the system, and she saw the descriptions of what Nicky and George were typing and saying, she used her terminal to adjust the weighted learning factors on nodes within the network which allowed a single neural network calculation to better learn the nuance of the correct translation.

During the earliest days, the network was learning basic translations, but now they were into the nuance of sounds and meaning. Valerie's brain was capable of quickly learning these complex patterns, and she used that ability to teach the computers how to adjust as new sounds and meanings flowed through George and Nicky and were being interpreted by the computers.

In her free time between transmissions, Valerie had tried a short experiment, and with support of the software team had taken some work done by researchers into dolphins, she played the dolphin sounds and actions into this new language neural net design. The output was promising and during their free, fun time, the team had continued to make the software adjustments to support the conversion from the Old Ones language work, to dolphin testing so Valerie could progress forward with each. All that she had to do was click on a pull down a configuration option and select what she wanted. That simple selection allowed for the massively computing neural nodes to reload their weight functions, tie to a selected data stream, and in doing so adapt from one language processing to another.

Randy and Janet continued to research and visualize information so the whole team was able to appreciate the images of the other worlds and beauty of the symbology. A complete area was converted to an art studio, both for painting and computer work, as Randy and Janet worked hard to keep up with the information flow and the descriptions being provided by the Old Ones, along with captures of images from other Watchers.

The images gave the math and astrophysics teams key reference points to relate too. They also provided Valerie along with the math team key insights into the symbols of the math of the Old Ones. Work had actually begun to map star patterns reported by Watchers to a three dimensional map of the universe.

The two artists captured the images of the wide variety of alien worlds and cultures. Their gallery of unique art grew. After passing their idea past Tim, they started taking paintings or computer generated posters and hanging them in the long hallways for the team to view as they moved around the facility. Each race-planet was attempted to be labeled by Valerie through the translations, while the astrophysics team had attempted to mark their location in a universe map they had started.

Janet's digital art ability grew in leaps and bounds as she was challenged with each new alien environment that needed to be pictured. Her work was supported by Randy, who was side by side with her as she got to a point that they were equals and no longer teacher-student. Each image was brought before George and Nicky as they would point out key details to ensure maximum information capture.

With the gallery growth and moving parts of the collection on display in the hallways, Tim was walking down the hallway and was struck by the beauty of a specific image on an alien world with dual stars, a beach of sparkling sand, a waterfall in the distance from a large mountain that fell to the lake or ocean. The water held a dark green color, but the clouds were pink in nature and the landscape showed plants in a bluish color. The alien in the foreground looked like a female as identified by the hint of what seemed to be breasts, bi-ped with flowing green hair that hung to the middle of her back and with two eyes, a very small nose and small narrow lips. There was a copper colored band which disappeared into her hair, but in the center of her forehead, hanging from the band was a small pendent in the shape of a symbol. No ears were evident. The body was sleek and lean and the arms were long and with hands that showed six fingers and a thumb. The image stuck such beauty that Tim had to just stop and examine it. In the notes under the hanging, was a reference to the pendent appearing to match a symbol of the Old Ones language, but that location was in a different galaxy. Tim also decided the team needed to consider bringing in an astrobiologist at some point to begin the study of life from diversity being cataloged. With Randy's and Janet's growing understanding on the the different physiology of aliens, much could be learned.

The name given was Peqdnt, from the planet they called Tylle and from the astrophysics team, it was in a galaxy approximately five hundred galaxies away from the Milky Way, in the general direction of the Care Givers galaxy.

Each break through answered a thousand questions and created a million more. The discoveries were coming fast and furious and the output of the team continued at a furious pace.

After walking down the hallway, Tim was awed with the volume of work that alone was hung in the hallway. A few were paintings; others were digital poster outputs from Janet and Randy. The high resolution posters were printed on a new high-scale printer, the newest on the market, and the colors and detail were astounding.

Bob happened to be standing with Tim when he stopped to look and made the simple comment, "Can you imagine the money we could make if this art was sold?"

Tim turned to Bob, "We have to let others see this, we need to be careful, but the world needs to understand the beauty and nature of the universe we participate in. We have to find a way. I fully agree. The art they've developed is priceless. This combined with the facts could far outstrip the price of the entire world's greatest art and discoveries put together."

Tim and Bob continued to their next meeting. The team continued surging forward with excitement.

|||||

In Sxvy, the galaxy of the Old Ones, transport to adjacent galaxies to escape the destructive energy wall had started. The older ships were not designed for intergalactic transport, but were loaded and started transporting to pre designated coordinates, working their way outside the galaxy and heading for designated locations. The transports would make pre planned jumps with their people. With each jump, they would coordinate with their designated group and send status of their group to all other groups if possible.

Their computations showed only a fourty percent chance of all ships surviving. The new ships had not been tested and there was significant risk that those on the older ships would not survive long enough for interception and rescue despite atmospheric scrubbers and maximum supplies recycling. In addition to the stress of the trip and supplies was the problem of communications, if a ship or ships missed their designated coordinates, they may be lost forever. As the new ships made their initial jump, they would attempt to unload and come back; reaching the older ships in time or failure of the older ships to survive under the stresses expected would result in loss of life.

The planned fleet of the newer class ships that would support intergalactic jumps had not been fully completed. While many were assumed ready, only partial time for testing was available and this did not include long jumps. With them being deployed, others were ready only to jump without more than a minimal load, would have to have their construction completed elsewhere. Others would not be completed in time so their construction was abandoned to help focus on those that could make it. This had been entered into the computations.

Planets were being evacuated as fast as possible. Not all people of a population were able to go, but the schedules were critical to meeting the overall survival needs of each race. The scene was repeated in thousands of worlds as beings were split apart with parents and children going, but elderly having to stay to meet their doom in the destruction that was coming. The emotional toll on species across the many worlds was almost as bad as the destruction itself. In cases for worlds where history was maintained by teaching of the elderly to the youth, some elderly were allowed to come. In other worlds, complete libraries were captured and loaded into ship holds as race history and information was almost as valuable as food creators.

On some worlds, chaos erupted. Those being blocked from the transport ships rioted in random acts of violence as the doomed released their anger. Others that were not going, huddled together to find comfort and solace while some prayed to their forms of God.

In a few cases, planets containing those blocked from going attempted to attack the Old Ones ships as they left the doomed world. While no ships were lost, the level of anger, violence and hatred shocked the calm, focused spirit of the Old Ones who had seen these worlds as they progressed in a measured and cooperative way over previous times.

The Old Ones had a vast treasure of information stored in their computer worlds. Work was well underway to transpose that information into the memory banks on-board ships with key information being tagged as highest priority. Included in this data were vast storages of DNA structures of the various species that the Old Ones had encountered on the various worlds. Some of the large storage units were transferred in whole while other units transmitted their information to the ships for protection.

The energy wall approached the Old Ones galaxy and the evacuation reached a fevered pitch as planets were being emptied of as much of the life as the Old Ones could support. Ships were jumping into the intergalactic void ahead of the approaching destruction. As the Txxan's world was on the side of the galaxy being first hit, theirs was early on the evacuation list.

During the Txxan evacuation, Tia and his family were moved to one of the older transports as they said their tearful goodbye to the elders of the family. The people were entering the ship in a state of torn emotions, one of fear of the approaching doom and the other of the leaving forever of their loved ones. The ship had been loaded with supplies and was ready to leave the planet when a drive problem was discovered. The engineering section rapidly started their diagnostic scans to try and determine the problem.

While the engineers were looking at the problem, other ships were leaving the planet and the Txxan's on the broken ship were trying to settle down for what would be a long transport time. Tia was with his father and mother as they found a space for their meager possessions and they tried to console Tia. Saying good bye to his grandmother had been tearful and heart wrenching on Tia and his parents.

Word arrived that the energy wall was less than a star away from their location and approaching at a pace that would reach them within the day. Anxiety rose within the ship and the engineers felt the pressure of the impending destruction. They ran diagnostics on the spatial field generator; it became obvious that they would need a spare field energy insertion focusing coil. A short message was sent across the network for anyone to respond. While some parts could be created with their machines, this required a long processing time, which they did not have in this environment.

The communications in their part of the galaxy were sporadic as the quantum foam was being disrupted by the approaching energy wall. The ship's manager was not even sure word got out on their problem. They could not receive any incoming communications due to the noise. All other ships had jumped ahead of the approaching energy wave and they had no way of avoiding it as the engineers were trying to figure out how to fix special insertion coil, the critical part since they did not have a spare on-board.

|||||

Back on earth in Washington D.C., Jack was not satisfied with the current state of affairs, every time one of the team went out, danger lurked. Something needed to be done to change the equation and get on the offensive.

Tim and Jack had called the security teams together to brain storm for an answer. With their new technology, somehow the team needed to turn the tables on both the Russians and the Chinese.

Different approaches were considered, but one by one, they were discounted. Tim and Jack were getting frustrated. It was now approaching the spring after the initial transmission and Tim felt it was time to change the battle field.

At 3 a.m., Jack woke up and eased out of bed so as to not disturb Shelly. After going into his home office, he used his secure telephone line to dial Tim's encrypted number. Tim had actually been sleeping the past few days, everything was going well and while the transmissions were going to stop sometime soon, the team was working together well and the biggest problem within them was that they were excited and wanted to tell the world. In addition, Tim had started taking simple sleeping pills; they didn't knock him out, but rather allowed him to slide into a soft sleep, which Jack was interrupting.

Tim woke on the fifth ring (Jack knew he was in his office from the tracking device he had insisted Tim have on him at all times). Tim sat up in his chair raising his head from his arms where he had fallen asleep while working on the notes from the Engineering and math teams.

He rubbed his eyes and yawned as he picked up the phone and saw it was from Jack as he answered with a sleepy, "Hi Jack, what's so important at this hour of the morning?"

"Tim, I think I know a way out of the problem. Good news, it might work. Bad news, Tim will have to die to make it work," Jack said with a laugh. "I hope your flying lessons have been going well."

"You're just saying that because it might give you a vacation," Tim responded with a bit of a smile and a yawn.

"No, we need Tim to die...you on the other hand we need to keep around for a while."

"What do you have in mind?"

"How large an item do you think that invisibility device could be made to work on?"

"How large do you need it?"

"Let's say a small glider? I hope you aren't scared of heights."

For the next hour, Jack laid out the details with Tim making suggested refinements. By 6 a.m., the plan was well formulated and ready to give to the team and get part of the engineering team working at the morning meeting while Jack's team continued to fill out all branching options, security measures, and tracking plans, as they continued to start organizing the needed parts.

The team's engineering section was brought into the plan as was the software team during the morning status meeting. By the second day, the President had been briefed, signed off on the plan and Congress and Senate leaders briefed into minor parts of the plan but not at the normal committee briefings given the sensitive nature of the preparations. The details were close held with only a total of five people outside of Jack and Tim's team. Tim's part was only to be known by the President outside of the team.

The plan started with a message to the small art store in Kiel, Germany and a tailor shop in Hong Kong. The message was simple and short, "Be prepared to hand off a package."

The agents were trained to follow a specific pattern. Each called in an assistant and informed them that they would be gone for a few days and gave them their normal directions on maintaining the shop. Each headed to a town that was normal for their business, the German to a town in Finland and the Chinese tailor, a trip to a town on the mainland. Each arrived at their normal hotel, went through normal business and two days later returned.

On the fourth day, each received a package. The package contained a nice sculpture about the size of a 1.5ml water bottle. It wasn't so nice that it looked expensive, but looked like a simple gift from a good friend.

On the fifth day, they each received a couple visiting their shop that looked to all like a normal couple browsing and who purchased an item that just happened to be of the size and shape of the item received in the package. The couple returned home from a common shopping trip with the actual package and not the item they pretended to purchase. Upon return, each presented their copy of the object to a friend, who took it and passed it to another friend.

In both cases, the final link in the chain was an undercover member of the opposing team. Each took the object into their work area. Being extremely cautious and being extremely high security areas, both the Russians and the Chinese insisted the objects were scanned for any listening devices, x-rayed and scanned with the latest technology to ensure that it was safe to enter the operational work area. Each member placed their object in a key area to capture conversations of a secure nature.

Vladimir of the Russian math team had received it from his friend Tanya, the pretty young secretary, and placed it on his desk next to that thin wall across from the security chief's office where conversations could easily be heard. There was little worry, because no one was expected to ever survive to talk with anyone and the scientists were never allowed off the grounds.

The Chinese team member, Jasmine, happened to be a receptionist in the security division of the Guangzhou based math team in which many discussions were open. After all this was a security area on a secure military base, and everyone was cleared to be in this area and deal with this particular program.

Since the initial devices had been created, the engineering team had made significant strides in embedding radioactive power cells in the small devices of an Alpha nature to ensure no radiation could be detected and combined it with a heat converter to provide added energy, giving the units years of use since the new power source was not yet available from the engineering team. Each was synchronized to create short windows for transmission and the range had been extended over 5 miles. The millisecond transmission bursts just seemed like normal background noise to a receiver not designed specifically to receive its signal. The devices could be activated and deactivated through a similar signal broadcast. While nothing is perfect, these were uniquely capable devices. The one in the Chinese office used a Russian based encryption; the one in the Russian compound used a Chinese based encryption (just in case).

After all agents reported back that devices and relay stations were in place, the embedded NSA team sent the activation signal and everyone held their breath to find out what would happen.

Results were swift.

Within hours of activation, the Russian based device picked up a conversation between the math lead and the program lead, related to the frustrations they were having working with the equations. Later a conversation between the program lead and the security chief talking about the monitoring team positioned in China, giving relative location and names.

"When will our comrades be in place and how far from the site will they be?"

"Nickolas will be replacing Gortich and Nav will replace Tanara. They are shifting to setup a new monitor at this empty warehouse across from base entrance. We are hoping to get a laser beam bounce off the window and listen to their progress."

The Chinese conversations were ongoing discussions about Renaldo.

"Our investigation shows nothing special about this Renaldo person. He was visiting the hospital because his twelve year old son was being monitored for a mental problem. His wife is dead, he is a simple man that these two artists were flown from the United States to visit with a nurse. Apparently he was going to return with them. There must be a reason, but none of this makes sense."

"Maybe it was a fake move to make us waste resources?"

"Maybe it is, but to sacrifice their people for a diversion? That is not like them."

A later conversation indicated that the Chinese team had spotted something in one of the equations that might hold promise based on a recent paper by Tim published in the Astrophysical Journal, something the U.S. team had earlier discounted but found it only made sense with the new information and expanded equations set, which the Chinese of course, did not have.

Jack and Tim entered the engineering team area with a laptop "Okay guys, I want you to look at this clip I heard about."

The team was shown a clip on a man whose winged jet backpack allowed him to fly by jumping out of a plane and after an initial drop in altitude, the small jet engine on the man's back supported him with some small wings, to climb back to altitude and cruise for a short period of time.

"We are going to get our hands on that device. What I need is to add the invisibility field to this, covering the pilot and pack. This is for a special onetime only shot, but it must work that one time."

A wealthy man purchased the use of the flight back pack for a hefty sum, with the signed and notarized agreement not to duplicate it, not to break any patents and after 60 days to return it. While there was no traceable connection, the back pack ended up in the BELLOWS engineering section lab.

The engineers swiftly got to work to enhance it with an invisibility device tied into the engine output nozzle for power. Tim concentrated on learning the flying controls that operated the device and spent time getting used to a special set of goggles to provide him viewing during his flight, hopefully not too short. The goggles were part of a special helmet engineered that allowed the wearer to have a small bird like figure extending above the helmet. This allowed from a distance, any observer to see what looked like a small bird sailing through the air. The bird object relayed optical images through the stand that fed to the goggles. The bird stand converted images from two small cameras to sounds waves to penetrate the cloak and then back before entering the heads-up goggle display. This allowed the wearer of the goggles to see through the bird object, even through the wearer was invisible to the world.

The software team wasn't given any break. It's normally thought that a hacker is looking to grab information from a protected location; but they can also plant information. The key is to plant information, then back out, never leaving a trail. The challenge was one the team was more than excited to take on. Of course, it was going to take a lot of candy bars, French fries, hamburgers and soda to be successful, but the game was afoot and the team was out to prove they were the best in the world and they were being supported by the team chef who was the best in the world.

Key bits of disinformation had to be planted in systems around the world such that no one would ever know that it was not real. Facts such as a secret life of Renaldo that someone could stumble on, Nicky died of cerebral aneurism; no trace of Valerie's, Jill's and Nicky's true return to the U.S. existed, a reason for Randy and Janet to be in Chiassio to meet Renaldo, documents that proved certain symbols will be found to have no relationship to the ancient Greeks and Arabic or Egyptian history; that George had a major mental collapse and was in a mental hospital for recuperation; Tim had a history of suicide attempts after the loss of his family; that the Chinese had a plant within the Russian security team; the Russians had a plant within the Chinese security team; the Chinese had an attack planned for taking out the Russian team and the Russian team had an attack planned for taking out the Chinese team. Additional leaks were planted that the supposed U.S. discoveries were not really a breakthrough and in the final analysis had failed. Last but not least, that the U.S. had decided for financial reasons to terminate their failed work with no success.

The software team had one of the most difficult jobs. Not only did the information plants need to be made, but the threads that could be pulled had to be planted in such a way that the Russian and Chinese teams would "find" the loose ends on their own and when they pulled would "discover" the information without any hint of it being planted and with documentation that could be verified to make them convinced.

Bets were placed as the tasking was divided up, fast food was ordered from the kitchen, each team pulled together their most sensitive viruses, worms, and back doors to plant their assigned bits of disinformation and then each team reviewed the others plans to ensure that any viruses or worms would evaporate on completion and back doors would be sealed shut on final exit.

The work progressed swiftly, threads were laid, documents falsified, scanned and transferred to key points with threads hooked. While not forgers by nature, Janet and Randy helped in altering documents with their expertise in computer graphics. They helped to copy and place signatures on false documents, and using their research on the symbols, they were able to help develop false paths in case someone went searching like they had done.

After each trap was laid, the security team worked out the details on how to get the right asset to get the right enemy agent to find the right thread to pull. The precision operation and plans were well underway when the sad day arrived.

There was no indication that anything but another heavy day of data transmission was to happen. George and Nicky worked their normal schedule and the data continued to flow, data recordings continued to collect. Only the break times indicated something was about to happen. The break periods seemed to be getting shorter and shorter allowing more and more information to be transmitted.

Sensors launched by the Old Ones to take readings on the approaching energy wall showed indications that the temperature of the invading wall was not cooling rapidly enough to have even reached a plasma level where basic particles had formed. But even if it had, there was no chance left for the galaxy.

For those who had been left behind, the destruction was total and complete. As Txxan's waited for the end to come, the elderly huddled together to give each other comfort. As the energy wall approached their star system, the Txxan planet was wracked by massive tectonic events shaking the ground. Temperatures rose rapidly to unbearable levels. The planet's atmosphere began to be stripped away as the Txxan's were being robbed of the ability to breath and as the front began to reach the inner part of the stars system, the atoms began to be stripped of their very cohesion as the people's bodies began to evaporate to basic particles. As the energy wall continued to reach the star, the pressures caused the star to explode and in its wake the particles were absorbed by the energy that rushed over the area of the explosion. The total event happened within a few moments as it rushed over the star system reducing the suffering time of the people who were washed away in the storm except in the minds of their loved ones who escaped.

During a late session, George indicated that the Old Ones were terminating the transmission. The energy-plasma wall had swiftly passed through most of the galaxy. Major disruption of the quantum foam was reaching their main star station at speeds faster than light and they wished the rest of listening Watchers a good-bye and then the transmission abruptly ended.

The wall at the front of the new universe had hit the galaxy like a tidal wave, tearing planets and stars alike into their basic atomic structures and absorbing the energy into the massive energy wall driving the bubbling quantum foam. The black hole at the center of the galaxy was totally evaporated as the quantum foam was disrupted and the gravity effect was totally overwhelmed. The Dark Matter and Dark Energy pushed back in a hopeless attempt to stem the wall of destruction, but its fate was no different in the end. As the energy continued to expand, it also began to slow and cool, but that was after it had wiped most of the Old Ones' galaxy from existence.

Sxvy, the galaxy of the Old Ones, had been destroyed.

For the first time in well over five months, George and Nicky were left in a vacuum of quiet silence with no expectation of the communications being reactivated. Both were stunned at a loss of their friends. For the last months, they were part of a community with minds around the universe, then nothing. The shock was enormous.

Bob and Valerie spent the following days talking with them helping them to gain a perspective, a balance in their lives. During this time, George and Nicky slowly found communications using a combination of their new language of the Old Ones, Italian and English. Valerie was becoming comfortable in all three, while Nicky had to learn better English and George began the work with Italian. Valerie became a partner and facilitator in the conversation as the three grew closer and began the formation of a family unit. They became a close knit group, each leaning on the other and understanding how to enjoy each other's company as a family of love grew and strengthened out of the loss of the Watcher community.

With the drop out of communications, they were able to talk Tim into allowing them to go outside for short periods of time. The near spring weather was good for their spirits and since George and Nicky no longer needed to be monitored for communications, it brought a renewal of spirit and a point of relaxation.

George and Valerie along with Nicky stopped by the kitchen picking up a picnic basket and under the heavy monitoring of the security team spent the Sunday afternoon on the grass within the protected Naval Observatory grounds. Even though it was officially still winter, spring was close, with the sun out and the simple feeling of being outside rejuvenated their spirits. Nicky was able to kick the soccer ball around with the security agents with George joining in a little as his weight had dropped fourty pounds thanks to his good diet and exercise. George was able to lay back and relax with Valerie on the blanket and talk about the changes in their lives.

George and Nicky found freedom in being independent of the constant flow of communications from before. But while they gained their freedom, there was a significant price that they also recognized: the returning feeling of being alone. Even communications with Nicky's mother and father seemed to have ceased which Nicky found very depressing.

Valerie's constant caring along with working through Bob, provided the glue that gave them both the feeling of connection along with love and belonging. They knew they were not alone, just not connected outside their close group Watchers.

|||||

The Sunday following the Easter celebration found Tim continuing to take his flying lessons, helicopter flying lessons. He was not hiding his daily trek to the local airport. Over the previous months, Tim received private training by local army instructors as a way to get away, but now it took place in a semi-visible location.

Bob was leaving the team center and headed back to his office in the hospital during early March after the key event. The cold breeze was blowing but most of the snow storm threats were over and the weather was beginning to break as it headed towards spring a month away.

When Bob entered his office, he placed a call to a number provided by Jack. This number was the one to Tim's apartment that Jack strongly suspected was being monitored.

"Tim, I think you need to reconsider your decision. The medications will help you with the depression."

"Bob, I can't concentrate using that medication. My work is suffering; the team is drifting because my lack of leadership, they may be cutting my funding. What's left of my life is falling apart and this stuff doesn't help."

"You're aware that this will have to be reported. Failure to take the medication must be reported to DARPA's security department. Please take the medication until we can find something that will support you better and allow you to work."

"Okay, but please make it fast. I can't take this much longer."

Two weeks later, after confirming that Tim was being watched, his personal SEAL surveillance team spotted a tail and there was a hint of possibly a second tail, and his unclassified phones were being tapped, Tim headed out to the air field with plans to do his first solo flight. He had made a point of going to a local Irish pub the night before and making a public ass of himself showing his despondent act over the troubles at work, the loss of his family and talking about flying the next day.

The NSA monitoring of the drop devices showed increasing discussions about growing frustrations with the lack of progress. Snips were indicating that there was growing skepticism about the U.S. ever having made a breakthrough and secret documents were being quoted. Reports were discussed of growing indications that Tim was showing a growing instability in his public appearances. Notes also indicated that rumors of DARPA cutbacks were in the works to reduce funding in this area.

Some of the information was derived from the computer plants, other pieces were derived from the facade that Jack had pieced together and Tim was playing to the hilt. After filing a flight plan, Tim took his backpack and headed out to the helicopter to do his preflight checkout. After taxiing out to the take off area, he slowly lifted off and headed over the Potomac River heading for the ocean, following his flight plan.

After finding a location with no boats in the immediate area and upon reaching his designated space and altitude, Tim changed the normal radio conversation with the flight controllers in a stilted voice as if he was being forced.

"This is a goodbye transmission. I know my life is a failure, I believed in a false hope and I don't see any purpose in living without my family or my work. Please tell my friends I am sorry."

He threw a switch hidden under the seat placing the chopper into a controlled hover maneuver. Tim unbelted himself and moved behind the seat to a package that he swiftly strapped to his back and activated the controls. He flipped the switch on his goggles and disappeared as he dove out of the door.

From the perspective of the boaters down river, the helicopter hovered for a short time then exploded in mid air and crashed into the water in one of the deeper sections with no survivors, no one escaped. The FAA had voice recordings of a bomb-suicide and the wreckage was scattered into a wide area.

Tim exited the helicopter in a tumbling motion. He activated the flight pack motors and extended the short wings. The motors did not start. Tim continued to fall towards the water, but the wings pushed him slightly forward of the helicopter that was hovering in the air. Tim franticly retried the motors as the altitude kept falling and the water rushed up to meet him. As Tim reached two hundred feet above the water, the motors caught and as he righted himself, the altitude began to climb. As he swung around to his planned heading, Tim could see the pieces of the helicopter raining down on the water.

With the power increase he climbed in altitude. Suddenly Tim felt a sharp pain in his right leg. Not being able to reach back or look back to see what happened, he focused on his flight plan and continued moving as the pain seemed to increase. After reaching his planned altitude, he left the water and headed over land. As he saw the clearing in front of him, he noticed a light headedness and fought to stay awake to complete his mission.

Five miles away from the helicopter crash site, in the field where a NSA software lead on the team pastured horses, Tim throttled back the motors as he spotted the pile of hay that had been cut and stacked for this special "soft" landing. Tim began to lose altitude as he approached the clearing. As he approached, he cut his motors and pulled the cord on his parachute. With the jerk of the parachute deployment, Tim could no longer maintain his conciseness and passed out. A limp bodied Tim floated down from the sky and dropped to the hay pile.

A FBI SUV drove up as Tim's limp body landed and within seconds, Tim was placed in the back of the SUV and a security agent rapidly went to work trying to stop the bleeding in Tim's leg using his tie as a tourniquet. The SUV left the field and rushed to the farm house as an encrypted message went out calling about the immediate need for a doctor.

Independently, the Russian and Chinese monitoring teams reported back that Tim was most probably dead, but the source of the bomb was unknown. Given the circumstances and the intercepted radio communication, Tim must have concluded that the program was a failure.

Jack provided messages to the State Department for delivery to the Russian and Chinese embassies that the U.S. suspected Tim had died at the hands of unknown agents due to the stilted sound of his voice. They had strong suspicions that the radio transmission was bogus and that the signature of the bomb was not of a design Tim would have a capability for. Both the Russian and Chinese were suspected given their previous history. The U.S. government would be taking "unspecified" actions.

After insuring that the Russian and Chinese teams had completed reporting to their contacts, FBI agents raided houses in Alexandria, Virginia, New York and hotel rooms in Crystal City, Virginia Additional arrest warrants were posted, but kept sealed for the moment.

Jack sat at the table in front of the Senate Intelligence committee during a closed classified briefing, the status of the intelligence collection and status review of the highly classified program was covered.

The chairman Senator Shank opened the session as Jack sat at the front table. "Mr. Bord, please give us a status update on the program monitoring"

"There are developments being provided by our sources. The document that I have provided to the committee is derived from smuggled documents that indicate the Chinese feel that part of their problems evolve directly from the Russian mafia. As a result, they intend to take action.

"You are aware from recent news reports; Dr. Decant died in an explosion this last week. While there was a transmission purporting to be a suicide statement, at this time, we strongly suspect either the Russians or the Chinese created the event.

"Investigations are continuing, but this creates a severe setback in the program posture at this time. As of this point in time, Mr. Decant's body has not been recovered, but those parts of the bomb that were recovered were of an unusual design that we feel was nothing Dr. Decant was capable of.

"We are continuing to monitor Russian and Chinese efforts and see if there is any possible progress on the Chinese side moving forward and raising the stakes.

"Our source within the Chinese government indicates that China is providing a fifty percent funding increase over the next six months for their base in Guangzhou, in hope of increasing their security posture relative to the Russians and train infiltration troops in an attempt to stop the Russian effects allowing their program to move forward uninterrupted.

"We continue to monitor but have made intense efforts not to interfere with either the Russians or the Chinese. Our program has already suffered at their hands and we continue to feel that 'monitor only' position is the best condition for our position. Raising the stakes in a retaliatory effort would not be productive and would cause unknown effects that are not justified at this time."

The meeting continued on to other topics.

|||||

That evening after the closed door classified meeting, the personal aid to Senator Shank, was sitting at a bar in Georgetown. His thoughts carried him back to the recent past, just months ago.

Thomas was a striking man whose power and position was advertised in his every move and his extensive work out pattern was designed to continue to enhance that look. He was the one to find the congressman and mold him to the public views that ultimately sent them both to the Senate and would eventually put him in even greater positions of power; a run for the Presidency was always a consideration having reached this powerful level.

Money was no longer a problem, between the stock tips provided in exchange for minor adjustments to legislation, political influence information, and the knowledge of what legislation was being brought to the floor, who would win and who would lose; his private stock portfolio was doing very well. Since the insider trading laws did not apply to him since no bill would ever be allowed to pass in the congress or senate that evoked the insider trading laws against Senate, Congress or their aids, he didn't have to worry, just make the necessary adjustments and watch the money roll in like the money machine it truly was.

He was waiting for his date. He remembered how they first met. It was a simple meeting in a grocery store of all places. He was doing some shopping and when he reached for the last of a bottle of salad dressing, she was reaching for the same one, not even apparently aware of his presence. As their hands bumped, he glanced at her and his first thought was a sexual desire of conquest and his second was to observe the lack of any rings on her hands.

"Sorry, go ahead and take it, I am sure there are others." she said with a smile.

"No, go ahead, I insist…is this your favorite? I like this brand of dressing; it fits my diet and workout strategy with the low fat and sodium."

"Really? Mine too." Her smile was brilliant and her body was perfect.

"I rarely eat at my condo due to my work for the senator but once in a while I like to do some cooking."

"You work for a senator? How interesting! I just moved to the area and am looking for places to go to meet people. I'm searching for work as a lobbiest." She looked in his eyes with a bright smile and introduced herself as Sonja.

"Really, well maybe I could help you. I have lots of contacts. I had planned to make a quick steak and salad tonight, but it would taste better with company. I could give you some contacts and put in a word for you."

With the conversation evolving and as they continued shopping together, slowly Thomas was able to get her to agree to dinner that night. After finishing their shopping and checking out, Thomas headed back to his luxury condo to get ready for what was shaping up to become a fun night.

At dinner, Thomas kept the wine flowing to her glass. Her laughter and her appealing body in a deep cut black dress that clung to her curves slowly gave way to Thomas's projection of power and influence. Her interest in the work he did and the stories about international intrigue that he related in his stories pulled her in like it did to all women who were interested in his power.

They ate the steaks that Thomas had cooked on his barbeque and talked about international politics and their desires. After dinner, they took their brandy on the sofa where Thomas moved his hands to her knees. She didn't make any comment as her eyes connected with his and sparkled. Without looking away, she returned the touch and the signal was agreed too.

Thomas took her hand and each took their glasses as Thomas led her to his bedroom. Thomas took her glass and placed it with his on the night stand next to the king bed. He pulled her forward into a powerful embrace. As they kissed, he slowly unzipped her dress and let it fall. As their embraced broke for a moment, Thomas drank in her wondrous form. Sonja began to slowly undo his shirt buttons while she kissed her way down his chest then undid his belt and pants letting them drop to the floor. Thomas pulled her up and slowly pushed her onto the bed where they continued to undress each other.

Her sexual drive was even stronger than his, taking him in multiple positions while urging him for more and driving him beyond his normal limits. Her body was toned to that of a jungle cat and her movements were fluid undulations as she rode his bucking body. As he massaged her breasts, her moans drove him to new heights, until they exploded in a release together. Then she would start kissing his body in a desire for more. While waiting to recover their strength for the next round, Thomas would continue to talk about international events he was involved in as he continued to impress this beautiful creature.

After a marathon session lasting well into the early morning, they lay naked with her curled up next to him moving against his body as the sweat on their bodies cooled them and the adrenalin began to fade.

Thomas began to fall into a deep sleep from the alcohol and the physical exertion. He let his hands roam over her as she quietly moaned. He was thinking about how to make this beauty a longer term relationship than he would normally continue. Her appetite and openness was a welcome relief from the stiff lawyer style that he normally ran into or the young secretary or intern that succumbed to his power for a typical one night stand. Those women were a nice diversion, but showed little or no mental match or physical capability to keep him interested beyond that single conquest. With a smile on his lips, they slowly drifted off to sleep.

After Thomas was sound asleep, Sonja slowly disengaged herself from his arm and tip-toed out of the bedroom. While still naked, she found her purse, pulled out her cell phone and headed over to his desk. With little of the previous sensual projection, she silently sifted through papers, taking photos. When she was done, she put back her phone and went back to bed with her new assignment. As she fell asleep, her drifting thoughts were that this was one of her better assignments, not the best, but definitely one of the better.

They were now into a many month relationship and the sexual match was showing no signs of abating. Thomas was meeting her for a drink before their next bed based round. While sitting there, a beautifully dressed, tall Sonja with legs that seem to extend forever sat down next to him and started talking to him. Thomas had found a position for Sonja at a powerful law firm that dealt with political influence. Sonja related updates in her latest project which Thomas quietly mentally cataloged for use in future political work and stock purchases. After a few drinks, Thomas reached over and put his hand on her hand and told her of the fact that he had been in a meeting today with powerful heads of the intelligence committee and as she ensured that he had a few more drinks, she hinted it was time to go back to his place.

The match followed its normal course of an evening of wild sex until Thomas fell asleep. In her now normal routine, Sonja rose from the bed naked and proceeded to silently sneak in to photograph documents, then got back in bed until the morning sunshine started a new day.

The next day, while at her "new" office, she handed over a draft of the information gained and photographs of the documents that Thomas had in his condo to her spy section contact. The contact was also her boss, a top level manager at the law firm.

|||||

The same time as Sonja was passing over information in D.C., a radio intercept was made by Chinese agents on an "encrypted" Russian broadcast that indicated the Russian mob had directed key Russian troops to prepare an operation against the Chinese compound. Orders were transmitted and signed by the Russian President that the Chinese just happened to intercept.

Over the next few days listening in, the NSA began to hear rising anger of the Russians to the Chinese and the Chinese to the Russians. Each discovered verifiable documents of plans of actions against the other that fueled the heated exchanges.

The final push was out to be made to send them over the edge.

Chapter 18: Scramble for Salvation

Hours before the destruction of the Txxan world, a small personal jump craft arrived with the needed part. An Old One had been two stars over monitoring the energy wall and had heard their call of distress. His ship contained the needed part and as such, he set the coordinates to jump directly to the distressed ship. As the ship landed the Old One stripped out the energy insertion focusing coil and transported over to the large transport ship. The engineers rushed as they replaced the coil without proper calibration. The ship manager issued to command to jump the craft into orbit.

The jump was successful as the Txxan's onboard looked back with a final view of their planet and loved ones that were being left behind to face their death. The engineers needed a few minutes to calibrate the modified equipment. As the manager watched the farthest planet in the system explode with the frontal wave of the energy wall, everyone on the bridge held their breath as the flash of the explosion radiated in their view. As the displays showed the time of arrival and the current time coming to a merge point, the ship manager heard the word from engineering that systems were ready and swiftly issued the jump command to place them across the galaxy from the energy wall.

It would take at least two hours to allow the engines to recharge for the next jump that would take them outside the galaxy. As the control stations watched their monitors of the galaxy, they could see stars blinking out of existence in the area they just left. The energy would soon reach the center of the galaxy and with it, the end would soon arrive. Their systems showed groups of ships as they jumped out of the Sxvy galaxy and communicated back their new positions. The image was much like that of dust particles erupting from a hand hitting an old dusty pillow.

The manager had communicated their status and the jump group indicated they would delay their next jump to allow them to join, prior to their next planned jump to allow the group to stay in-tact. The groups' computers showed that the delay would not affect their planned transit and eventual connection with the galactic jump ships that hopefully would eventually meet them and allow the races to complete their journey. As they reviewed status of the Txxan transport, eighty percent of the population had been collected on ships and of that amount; two ships were showing problems which accounted for fifteen percent of the population. Current projections showed an expected total loss of sixty percent before reaching rendezvous with the galaxy class ships; assuming their plans worked.

|||||

While most of the worlds in Sxvy were under the support of the Old Ones; a few planets had refused help or were not asked to join the galaxy community of the Old Ones. With the evacuation of the galaxy, word was passed to these planets of their impending doom. Yzti was the Old One tasked with delivering the message. While most resources had already been allocated to save as many as possible from those under protection of the Old Ones, Yzti was provided a small group of older ships to carry as many as possible from the other planets to safety.

All the planets that fell into the unprotected category were ruled by a strong dictatorship that controlled their people with an iron fist. Yzti had attempted to approach these planets at earlier times and in most cases had to leave after being rejected and in many cases being attacked. As Yzti appeared at the star system MMZ, the ship computers issued a message directed at the third planet informing them that Yzti wished to talk with the planet leaders.

The beings on MMZ were an advanced version of a number of warrior tribal communities with a central council and a leader. The leader was forced to prove his ability to lead through a series of battles that would occur when a challenge was issued. The beings were four legged with three arms and a single eye. While they had achieved some star transport capability, without the help of the Old Ones, they had never attempted transport beyond a group of local stars. As such, they had minimal outside contact or trade.

Once the message was returned to direct the meeting coordinates and time, Yzti moved the ship to a synchronized orbit over the provided locations. At the specified time, Yzti attached his jump pin and language translator; he issued the mental command and jumped to the provided coordinate.

He appeared at the specified point and noticed that there were approximately five guards with weapons at the ready. The leader of the guards motioned for him to follow and they entered a nearby building. As they walked down a long hallway, he noticed the many pictures and statues to their leader along with a number of guards standing watch along the hallway.

Yzti and his escorts reached the end of the hallway and entered into a large room with an elegant chair sitting on a stage overlooking the room. There were many statues of gold and silver, all of their leader along with a number of banners and decorations spread around the large room.

He waited on the floor below and directly in front of the large chair. The leader came in from the right with a flourish and a projection of power. The leader was larger than most others in the room and showed many scars from battles. As the leader approached the chair, it folded its legs and sat down followed with a nod to Yzti.

Using the language translator, the Old One began. "Your Eminence, I am here to give you information about the coming destruction of your world and our galaxy." A look of shock could be seen on faces around the room. "We have detected a wall of energy that will hit our galaxy within days with a destructive force to eradicate everything in its path." With that, Yzti initiated a projector from his pin that created a three dimensional image of the live transmission showing the destruction of an outer star in the galaxy.

"The destruction you are viewing is happening as we speak. Nothing can escape the pending destructive force. We are attempting to evacuate the galaxy."

The leader looked at Yzti, "What are we to do?"

"I have limited resources to support your planet. I can take a few of your population. We are focusing on young and those needed to support the young."

"You will take whomever I tell you to take" the leader roared with a fierce look on its face.

"I have my orders; you are no longer in a position to decide. If there is a resistance to my decisions, then I move on to other planets where I can work with the people. I have very little time to complete my tasking."

With that Yzti stood there looking at the leader.

When the leader realized that he didn't control the situation, he shouted out "Seize him!"

Yzti mentally issued the command and returned to his ship before anyone could take a step. It was obvious to Yzti that talking to the leader would produce no usable results. As he considered his options, he asked the computer to identify where on the planet there existed a small grouping of females and children.

The computer activated sensors and a village in the southern hemisphere was identified. Coordinates were provided along with a clear space for a small jump ship to settle into. Yzti transported to the ship bay were the small jumpers were located. After doing a status check on the jump ship, Yzti took the small jump ship and transported to the identified open space by the village.

After leaving the ship, Yzti walked up a pathway the short distance to the village. As he approached, a number of young came running out to greet him. As he continued on, the youngsters followed behind and around him in a festive mood, they seldom saw outsiders in this remote location. Upon reaching the village, the village elder came out to talk with him.

"Stranger, what do you want?"

"I am Yzti. I am from the race of the Old Ones and have come to warn your planet of an impending disaster. I attempted to talk with the leader, but only received an aggressive response so I am taking other actions."

"We have heard about your race, there are many rumors about your great abilities. I also know that our leader has very little caring about us. So tell me why you are here."

Over the next hour, Yzti provided the evidence of the destructive forces bearing down on the galaxy including images as outer stars were beginning to feel the effects of the destructive force. Yzti provided information about how other civilizations were being saved and the need to protect as many people as possible and transport to another galaxy where eventually safety could be found.

At first the people of the village were skeptical, but as information was revealed about their impending death along with the live images of stars and planets exploding they began to believe. As plans were formed to gather their people and basic supplies, tasking assignments were issued. After their discussions were completed, Yzti was escorted back to his ship where he instructed the computers to start transportation down of cargo transport platforms.

Over the next planet rotation, the cargo was shifted to the ship along with a number of the population and their personal effects. As in other worlds, the elderly were not to be transported to support saving of the maximum number of the younger of the population. As with what was happening all over the galaxy, the pain of separation and the resulting emotional stress was occurring as families were being torn apart, knowing that those left behind were doomed. The only strength for those that could not be taken was in knowing that their loved ones had a chance to survive.

The village had a local library with a number of historical books covering their civilization. History along with key art books were added to the cargo to try and capture information for future generations, assuming they survived.

Yzti was pointed to two other villages where the people where known to be kind and gentle. After the final lift from the initial village was complete, the leader went with Yzti to the other villages to help convince them to join for their salvation.

While Yzti was working with the villages, word from the ship computers indicated that ships from the surface were being directed to intercept. Scans of the MMZ planet ships indicated hostile weapons were becoming activated on the ships. The computers had tracked the MMZ ships from the point of takeoff until they reached orbit and started to approach the Old One ship. Yzti ensured that the automated defense systems were active and continued on with his work.

When the ships reached a location which triggered the automated defense systems, the star jump ships computers activated a series of jump units. The defensive systems were simple in design and effective in execution. The unit moved into the proximity of the targeted ship; attached itself to the ship and repositioned the ship back to its planet location from where the tracking identified it had started from. After the transport, the unit detached itself and jumped back to its storage location in the Old One's ship.

After the two other villages had been transported to the jump ship Yzti knew that he needed to leave the planet and move to one of the other planets that remained. As Yzti entered the command room, he communicated with the central organizing computer and switched to the organizing network channel to report completion of MMZ transport loading. As the next planet in his mission was assigned, Yzti called up the star map and observed that the jump would be over one hundred stars away moving away from the expected point of galactic impact and towards the planned void rendezvous location. As he looked at the map, he received ship status from the computer. He issued the jump command and the ship disappeared from the planetary orbit.

|||||

While Yzti was busy collecting species that were "non-cooperative", many others were completing their movement into ships and the ships were heading away from the impending energy field collision.

Some of the smaller jump craft were left unmanned and positioned at locations to capture and document the destruction of stars and their systems as the wall of energy hit. The Old Ones needed this information to feed computations that would allow them to understand where true safety may lie within the universe.

The craft transmissions showed the effects of space-time being ripped apart, much like a large black hole would rip matter apart as it approaches the event horizon. The ripping action occurred at a rate faster than the speed of light as it approached systems. The planets would race out of their orbits as gravity was disrupted and space-time effects hit the system; as the planets scattered, they would suddenly explode and then disappear as the matter was consumed by the wall of ruptured space that approached.

Stars exploded as their nuclear-gravimetric balance was distorted throwing matter in all directions, simply to disappear as the atoms and electrons were demolished in the rupture of their basic structures. While initial light would escape showing the explosions, once the distortion absorbed the area, there was nothing visible escaping.

The energy fields were far above temperatures of plasma and as such, the space was like a massive black hole of which nothing was escaping, but engulfing systems at massive rates. Nothing escaped; nothing could survive as the expansion continued. The wall had not yet reached the point where basic particles could form, computers projected that cooling would occur somewhere in the void between the Sxvy galaxy and the next galaxies being approached slowing the advance to light speed. This was critical to being able to estimate when the wall would reach the next galaxies and their final estimates of where safety could be found.

|||||

Yzti's jump ship appeared at the star system MZQ as the computer pulled up a plot of the fourth planet in the system. The planet was protected by a complex mine and plasma beam system to ward off any attempted approach by star travelers. The life forms on MZQ were of an intelligent insect species that had little wish to interact with other life forms of the galaxy.

The Old One directed the computers to send a message to the planetary leader in an attempt to allow discussions to be opened. He had never dealt with this life form, but in reviewing the database, understood it to be very aggressive and untrusting. During initial contact, genetic samples had been taken and a check was made to insure that the genetic code was in the information data storage being protected and scheduled for collection before leaving the galaxy.

A message was received from the planet: "Do not approach, we want no contact and any approach will be considered aggressive."

Yzti attempted a second message to the planet describing the impending doom. The communications channels were jammed with a wide band noise, not allowing communications to be completed. Yzti consulted with the central organizing computer and switched to the organizing network channel to report the problem with the insectoid planet. A plan was formulated by one of the Old Ones that had made initial contact with the planet, so Yzti decided to try.

A command was issued to the ships computers to create a series of micro dot transporters. At the same time, Yzti commanded the ship to configure a section on the outer edge of the ship that was currently unused and to insure it was sealed off with a force field of the Old Ones' design. Inter-ship communications were added to the area which also contained storage for insectoid supplies. The special section needed to support the environment of the insectoid life forms including their special needs relating to their nursery. While waiting, Yzti studied the life form distribution over the planet and identified a location was there were a small isolated population of the creatures.

After a short period of time, the ship reported the completion status of both commands. Upon hearing completion of the work, Yzti issued to the ship to jump to a location that allowed his jump suit, to reach the isolated population while being outside of the planetary defense system. After the ship reached the designated location, Yzti completed putting on his jump suit since the atmospheric environment was not suitable for Old Ones. Yzti added to the suit the micro jump dots, issuing two commands to the suit.

Yzti appeared on the planetary surface in his special suit. The suit engaged a visual cloaking field and a situational awareness screen on the inside of the helmet. Yzti opened the container with the micro dot jumpers and walked into the village. Each time he approached one of the creatures, he attached a micro dot and through his communications channel would arm it.

The computer identified the building that contained the main breading egg room. Yzti entered the building and following the provided mapping, entered the room. He issued a command to the computer to transport down a cloaked room transport unit and configure it for the correct return location.

Yzti continued moving around the village tagging insects until the indication was that the complete village had been tagged. The food storage area was identified and as in the case of the nursery, Yzti had a cloaked transport unit sent down, this could transport a small building completely intact.

With completion of his tasks, Yzti returned to the control room of the ship. After a review of the ship status and computers indication that all was ready, Yzti gave the command to transport.

The computer issued a focused signal beam over the area of the village triggering the transport units. In a blink, the village was empty of insect creatures who now found themselves in an area that was totally unique to them. Yzti immediately issued a message into the section of the ship indicating that they had been transported from their planet to ship under command of the Old Ones, and that the decision was made to save part of their population from an impending destructive energy that was about to destroy the galaxy, images of the destruction of some of the outer stars that were currently under assault were provided for their viewing screens in their enclosed area.

Yzti asked that their leader please identify itself. After monitoring the dazed population, one of the insects identified itself as the village elder and asked what gave them the right to make this choice.

Yzti explained, "We attempted to make contact with the planet rulers, but we were not allowed to make our case. We have taken this alternate plan as an attempt to ensure some of your species survived the coming destruction.

If you and your village do not wish to be spared in the coming destruction, please let us know and we will return you to your doomed planet. You must decide immediately."

Yzti waited; the insectoids were busy discussing their situation and after a short time, the leader spoke, "We understand and will accept your decision. We would like to insure some of our races history is preserved, is that possible?"

Yzti checked with the computer on when they needed to jump and found that there was still a short period that could be allocated. "Yes, if you identify where your history information can be retrieved from, we will attempt to save it, but we have only a short time."

"If you allow a few of us to return to our village, we can collect the information we feel is important and then return to this ship." As Yzti watched the monitors, the leader and two other insects moved forward away from the rest. "Agreed; you will be provided a time indicator and you must be prepared to return before the time runs out. If you do not come back to the time instrument within the designated time, you will be left on the planet to die."

"Agreed!"

Yzti command the computer to transport the three back to the village and also commanded a timer be transported to the same location along with a cargo transport unit.

While the insectoids were gathering their final pieces, Yzti communicated with the organizational net to indicate that the mission had been completed and gained information on the next and final stop for collection.

The computer monitored the positions of the insects as they worked against the clock. The ship's display showed the insects moving from building to building bringing out articles that were being placed within the cargo transport area. Within the designated time period, all three insects returned to the location and Yzti gave the command to transport.

Once the transport was completed, Yzti commanded the micro dots to detach and return to the storage bay. After the computer accounted for all micro dots and the cargo transports, Yzti looked at ship status and since all was green, commanded a jump to star system MVY.

|||||

The Jump ship arrived outside the star system of MVY. Computer information indicated two warring planets were within this system. While the reason for the fighting seemed to change over time, the basic problem as analyzed by the previous ambassadors was that the power brokers on each planet maintained control and wealth through continual war. As such, there was no desire to settle the problems.

Yzti asked the computer to analyze the command and control systems of both planets along with any planetary communications systems and population information and report. After a short period of time, a map was presented for each planet showing where command and control systems were centered along with a list of major communications channels. The computer report indicated that the populations had dwindled over the last hundred years and there were now only a few thousand people left on each planet.

Once Yzti considered the options over the organization net; swiftly a consensus was formed on a plan forward. Yzti relayed the plan to the computer and asked it be executed immediately as time left for his mission was quickly coming to an end.

Pxy was playing with his brother Yxp in front of the small house when they were told to come inside immediately. As they entered the door, the two small humanoid boys could hear their mother crying and their father was in shock looking at the central information system. As they watched the information system, it seemed to end on a broadcast and immediately start back up.

On the information devices, an Image of planets being ripped apart and exploding was followed by the pieces of the planets being consumed by a dark wall. As the image continued, the star exploded and rapidly was consumed by the same black wall that just kept moving. The voice spoke: *"This is being relayed to you by the Old Ones. You are witnessing the destruction of stars on the outer edge of our galaxy. Soon this will reach your star and all life will cease to exist. There is only one option available; you must pack small amounts of your belongings and prepare to transport aboard a jump ship of the Old Ones where we hope to safely escape to other galaxies. Time is short. You will be identified for transport through tuning of your communications units using the following provided procedure. All life forms within a 10 meter radius of a properly tuned communications device will be transported when the projected countdown reaches 0 on the planet MVY-1. Upon completion, the procedure will be repeated on MVY-2. There is very little time to save your lives; you must execute the instructions immediately.* [Instructions for tuning their devices were provided] End of Transmission"

The broadcast immediately started to repeat itself.

Yzti received two flash messages from the command and control centers demanding that Yzti stop interfering with their planets and to go away. This was obviously a fake attempt to control them and not a true emergency. Yzti shook his head at the ignorance of the leaders, but instructed the computer to jump to MVY-1, prepare the remaining sections of the ship and identify any key information centers that could be uploaded for history and art of the cultures.

Over the next small period of time, indications began to show communications devices being tuned as indicated. At the indicated points, a cargo jump device was deployed and as it appeared, it would scan the group around the device and transport them to the section that had been prepared. This process was repeated until all indicated transports were completed.

The galaxy Jump ship computer indicated buildings with historical and art information. A jump device was deployed and the complete building was moved to the hold of the ship. As basic supply stores were found, the computer under Yzti's command uploaded the basic supplies to the residence areas.

The time left to work with MVY-1 swiftly came to an end and the computer identified that no more communication points had been activated. As the indication was work was completed, Yzti asked for a final tally. Computer indications showed that 83% of the population had been transported. The remaining population appeared to be centered at the command and control locations, and an attack was being prepared to leave the surface.

Yzti commanded the ship to jump into orbit over MVY-2. As the ship appeared over the planet, the computer began to identify indicated communications points and execute transport. As on MVY-1, stores and historical information were identified and uploaded to the ship.

Computers indicated that some transported with weapons and that a fight had broken out within the areas of the two populations that had been transported. Yzti asked the computer to identify the weapons, transport in micro jumper dots and transport out the weapons or destroy them. As he watched the monitors, light and plasma weapons began to flash as they transported into space.

Yzti continued to monitor the screens watching the events in the closed space. As people lost their weapons, some started fighting with their limbs and whatever they could grasp. Yzti did not have time to deal with this and decided to leave them to their own.

With the final transports being completed, the computer indicated that on MVY-2 only seventy three percent of the population had been transported and that no further transport markers could be identified. Since Yzti had still a short period of time left on the schedule, he requested the computers to scan for females and children left on the surface. After a moment, the computer indicated a few still existed. Yzti requested the computer send transport jumps down and retrieve them. The final transports increased the MVY-2 population transport to seventy nine percent. As time had run out, Yzti commanded the ship to execute the next step in the mission.

Yzti reviewed the status of the ship with the computer, indicated mission complete on the communications net and ordered the jump to the designated rendezvous point in the void, leaving the doomed Sxvy galaxy far behind.

|||||

With the Sxvy galaxy dissolving in the face of the energy from the new universe, stars were being absorbed at a rapid rate. The power of the galaxy was no match for the power of the massive burst of energy from the birth of a new universe as it rushed forward colliding with the old universe. Those beings that could not escape died in an instant as their bodies evaporated and contributed to the inferno along with their planets, stars, and dreams

Of the complete Old Ones' fleet, the ships were not all headed to a single galaxy. Different ships were focused on an array of galaxies that were deemed as initially safe from the incursion into the universe. By the time the energy reached this next set of galaxies, it will be as a high level of radiation based particles traveling at near, but slightly below the speed of light. Computational projections showed it would give the Old Ones time to either protect or evacuate the next level of galaxies as they work with expected life forms to help them understand what was headed their way and understand what the path to safety would be.

Sxxty left the research station after signing off from the Watcher transmission. Sadness weighed on Sxxty's heart with the boarding of the last ship to leave the Sxvy galaxy. This was one of the latest intra-galactic designed ships, but incomplete. The ship construction had been halted after the main control room and some basic living quarters had been completed along with the engines. The ship hopefully could make the jump, but would only handle a small contingent of life forms until such time as construction could be completed.

Sxxty sat in the control room watching the monitor with sorrow, as star after star evaporated from existence and with it the life forms that did not have a chance to escape. The Old Ones had seen the effects of the destruction already as galactic gravitation was being disrupted. As soon as the disruption reached the galactic black hole, the effect on gravitational shock waves throughout the remaining part of the galaxy would be quickly felt in a devastating way. Destruction would happen fast as the rest of the galaxy was connected through the BHDM quantum foam pattern and the gravitational effects were supported through the instant transmission dimension.

Once the ship manager gave the final command to jump, the last ship left the dissolving Sxvy galaxy. As Sxxty saw the last glimpse of the station, there was an event that had not happened to an Old One for one hundred thousand STRY…Sxxty began to cry.

Chapter 19: Cleaning up loose ends

The night of the bi-weekly party at the hotel in the Russian Urial town, the camp commander and his "date" Tanya were inside while a dark figure weaved amongst the parked cars to the commander's car. After silently and swiftly leaving a package attached to the underside of a car, the figure melted into the dark.

The commander exited the hotel, sexually exhausted, with Tanya his trophy date on his arm, they headed toward the commander's parked car. Tanya quietly reached in her purse and before anyone was too close to the car, removed the special cap on an ink pen that Della had given her earlier in the evening and clicked the pen.

The commander's car erupted in a large explosion, knocking them and the driver to the ground and destroying cars on either side.

People were scrambling, with cars in flames, people rushing out of the hotel to see what happened and people yelling. The driver grabbed his radio on his belt and made a quick call. Another car was immediately brought around allowing the commander and his "date" to be whisked away to safety.

The commander pressed his security people the next morning to understand who had attacked him. The head of military security indicated the investigator had a lead. The bomb was of Chinese construction and the Chinese agent known to be in the area that they had been watching the Russian base had disappeared from surveillance within the hour prior to the bomb attack. He had not been seen since he was observed entering his apartment earlier in the day.

Unknown to the Russians, the Chinese agent had been contacted by an elderly couple, Della and her husband Gregory, after leaving the party earlier in the evening. He had snuck out of his apartment to meet someone who claimed to have inside information on the math team. His body lay in a grave at the graveyard in the town with an old grave marker and very little hint of disturbance thanks to a large payment to some local thugs.

|||||

The same day that the Russian commander was attacked, a local police station in Guangzhou, China received a call about suspicious activity in a rundown warehouse. When the police attempted to get a name, the person screamed and the line went dead.

The warehouse was located bordering the Guangzhou army base where the Chinese research facility was located. As the police rushed to the pay phone that the call was made from, a fire in the warehouse they were warned about seemed to erupt like a small bomb had gone off. The fire department was called and the fight to save the building ensued.

The fire trucks arrived and water with fire suppressant chemicals were pumped through hoses to attack the fire. A series of gun shots occurred which drove the fire fighters back. As the gun fire appeared to not be shooting at the fire fighters, they surged forward with shields for protection from any stray bullets and from the heat. Shortly after they heard a number of explosions and were forced to pull back again. As they waited they formed a barrier around the warehouse to ensure that the fire didn't spread to adjacent buildings. As the day turned into night time, the fire slowly burned itself out and the explosions subsided. Once again, they began to attack the fire.

After a night of fighting the fire, it was over. The fire fighters began to pack up their equipment and roll up their fire hoses while one of the trucks stayed on the area to ensure all hot spots did not flare up again. The warehouse was a total loss but surrounding buildings had been saved.

The fire inspectors began their work of attempting to understand what happened. As the fire inspector worked his way through the remains of the warehouse, first one Russian automatic weapon was found. As the search continued, boxes of weapons were found along with grenade launchers and boxes of exploded ammunition. The inspector called in the military because of the location of the weapons and the military base. As information was developed, the police aided by the military, searched documents in computers registering recent shipments that piece by piece, formed a path leading to the local Russian monitoring team.

The Chinese pulled together a military team and attacked the Russian monitoring team. The Russian team had set up a residence in a small two bedroom apartment two blocks away from the front gate of the Chinese military base. As the Russians saw the cars and jeeps of the Chinese military suddenly appear, they rushed to arm the explosives supporting the destruction of their communications equipment and to get their guns.

The Chinese rushed up the staircases both in front and in back, while a helicopter dropped troops on the top of the four story building which rushed down the stairs. The Russians attempted to delay them to insure the destruction of equipment; the Chinese burst through the front door with a hail of bullets and flash-bangs erupting. Within the first minute of the attack into the apartment, the Russians were killed in the fire fight. Before the last Russian died, he triggered a pre-rigged explosive that destroyed all the equipment and caused the interior of the building to collapse, killing four resident families in the building and thirty Chinese troops that had rushed the building.

Over the next two weeks, all out conflict broke out. As the NSA looked on and listened in, each group started attacking the other. The Russian government was accusing the Chinese and the Chinese blaming the Russians for letting the mafia run wild. The communications captured showed a significant decline in work as searches, protection and movement of personnel created instability on both teams. The security teams around the two different compounds had been attacked and many had died on both sides. While the science teams survived, they were under such strict security that little work was done.

The Russian fifth mechanized division was positioned in the Western zone with the Chinese. Attached to the division was a formation of engineers to support needed river crossings. The Russians decided that if the Chinese wanted a fight, they would take back the area deeded over to the Chinese such as along the Argun, Amur and Ussuri rivers.

The Russian sixth, seventh and ninth divisions were moved to the border around the Chinese Xinjiang province given past history of conflicts in this area. In addition to the standard divisions, S3 anti-air was moved to support the divisions and the Russian Navy started movement of ships and material to their bases in Kamchatka to support planning for operations in the China Sea.

|||||

The tensions escalated and orders were passed to Russian generals and admirals to prepare the battle ground and control the seas. In a hidden base on the eastern plains of Russia, the order was received to deploy the infiltration unit. Targets consisted of power plants, communications towers, trains, bridges and main roads.

The briefing room was a small auditorium that had stations for computers and computer connects at each level for the two hundred fourty men who were to implement the attack. As they took their seats and set up their small portable computers, their commander walked onto the stage below and brought up the map of their area of focus.

"We have been training for this time. While we know there are untested parts of this operation, we have all worked hard and know where the dangers lie. This map is the general operational area and each of you are assigned specific targets in that area. You will use your communications *only* to identify target removal completed and to request a resupply drop. Your computer has been provided the frequencies, code words and your personal maps.

"I wish to offer my personal best wishes and admiration for each and every one of you. You are our finest soldiers and I am sure you will make us proud. Please report to your departure points.

"Command dismissed."

The men rose as one, and started to file out of the auditorium, walking directly to their appointed hangers. As they entered their designated area, on the left were stacks of equipment and special suits, with each suit having a helmet next to it. On the right, there were a series of large units made up of an adjoined set of cylinders stacked together. Each cylinder's hatch was open and there was a ladder by each unit.

The men approached the equipment stack and picked up a backpack, a front pack and went to the table where the suits and helmets were laid out. After dawning their suit and helmet, they attached the backpack and the front pack. Each man was checked over by another man to insure proper connections. They then put on their helmets and plugged into the provided plug units to make sure their visual electronics were working.

After insuring they were fully functional, each man unplugged and headed over the cylinder stacks. Assisted by one of the ground crew, each soldier crawled into a cylinder unit and plugged their suit into the electronic connection. When all was set, each provided thumbs up and the hatch door was closed.

The cylinders were made of a special cellulose material with only a small amount of metal used for communications wiring. As soon as a pod was completely loaded, an overhead crane picked up the pod and moved it over to a strange looking airplane where the pod was attached. Each plane carried four pods and when the plane was fully loaded, a hand signal was made to the pilot to roll out.

One by one, the planes headed out of the hanger and headed to the takeoff runway. As the control tower gave their commands, the jets rolled down the runway and took off heading into the air and circling heading south to the Chinese border.

These were not normal jets, they were designed for maximum high altitude flying, much like the U.S. SR-71 Blackbird spy plane in an attempt to fly beyond anti-air counter measures by the Chinese. As they climbed to 35,000 feet, they were met by a fuel tanker and refueled for the altitude climb.

After refueling, they aircraft continued their climb to their 80,000 foot level for protection against anti-air missiles. Upon reaching altitude they cruised to the point where they crossed into the Chinese air space. As they approached their target point, they began to deploy the pods. As soon as they had released all their pods, the planes banked and headed back to Russian air space.

With the release of each pod, the cylinders separated and extended out air control surfaces to keep the pod in a proper position like a small paper glider plane. As the cylinders dropped, the soldier inside monitored his position and altitude. Upon reaching an altitude of 10,000 ft, each soldier pressed a switch causing the cylinder to split apart and release the man inside. The soldier continued to free fall and as he approached the ground, released his parachute in his backpack and glided to the pre planned coordinates.

Not all deployments were successful. In one case, the pod failed to split and the doomed soldiers plunged to their death. In a few other cases, the cylinder failed to deploy their stabilizers. When the soldier reached altitude, the cylinder was tumbling and attempt to exit killed them. Two were lost when they failed to get the cylinder to open and release them, again, plunging to their death.

The risk of the maneuver was the Russian's attempt to escape the dangerous and deadly anti-air missiles and guns that were deployed by the Chinese to the region. While the Russians had much more operational experience than the Chinese armed forces, the Chinese had a five to one manpower advantage and their technology had increased to levels comparable to the Russian army, largely in thanks to their spy efforts to capture American technology. The operational losses from the infiltration units were expected and the fact that eighty percent of their men reach their initial target points was well within their planning objectives.

The successful infiltration soldiers landed at their designated coordinates and quickly disposed of their parachutes. After burying their parachutes, they headed out towards their initial targets.

Valadof settled to the ground with a small jolt. He laid his rifle down and pulled out a small collapsible shovel. By a bush, he dug a shallow hole and wrapped up the parachute, his helmet and the high altitude suit, dropping them into the hole and swiftly covering them with dirt. After moving some leaves and branches around, he was satisfied that it was hidden. He looked at the computer attached to his right forearm and typed a message "landed". The computer automaticlly added location, time and encryption before sending the message. As he hit the send button, he picked up his rifle along with his backpack and headed for some cover by the tree line 50 yards away.

Valadof settled down in a well covered area, looked at his map and set his planned path before heading off to the west at a slow but measured trot. As he found open ground he had to cover, he would stop and look around to find an alternate path so as to be exposed as little as possible. As he neared a road, he observed Chinese trucks headed for the front loaded with men and supported with a tank force on low rider trucks. He was hidden from any significant view, so he rapidly typed in a message identifying the troop movement and hit the send button, relaying his location and the information to a satellite, which in turn related it to their operational command center.

After the Chinese troops continued down the road, Valadof crossed the road and continued heading to his target. After another hour of sneaking through the countryside, he spotted his objective. The coal fired power station was a large complex consisting of the burning plant, tall water cooler towers and a large building housing the main electric turbine generators.

It was currently 5 p.m. in the afternoon, so Valadof needed to wait until midnight when operations had slowed and security would be at a minimum. He located a complex set of bushes and found a crawl entry into the center of the mesh. He settled down to wait.

With the dark of night descending, Valadof snuck out of the hiding position and began to monitor the area. He needed to identify an area with minimum security where he could breach the outer defenses and get onto the grounds. The anti-air missile emplacements were circling the plant and beefed up patrols covered the area. As he watched, a pattern slowly evolved as the patrols constantly monitored a ditch, but there was no monitor of the small river that flowed into the pond inside the grounds.

Valadof slowly circled around the plant while staying hidden. Once he reached the edge of the river he began to slip into the cold water. He didn't worry about the electronics; they were designed to survive depths up to thirty feet and continue to operate. As he quietly swam down river underwater, coming up for air and to check his bearings, he reached where the fence cut through the river. As he took a large gulp of air, he crawled down the fence underwater and reached into his front pack to pull out wire cutters.

After cutting a hole in the fence, he pulled himself through and then back up to the surface. As he looked around he made sure that none of the guards were looking in his area, so he continued swimming until he reached a point where the water was near the water cooler tower.

Valadof emerged from the water and found a wall that appeared to be isolated from the few people walking around the inside grounds. As he snuck forward, he found a door leading to the turbine building. After picking the lock on the door, he quietly opened it and entered inside. He found himself on the main plant floor, finding a position next to a work bench where he could observe traffic without being obvious. The turbine stood three stories tall and the sound was deafening as he reached into his front pack and pulled out ear plugs.

After seeing that there was no real traffic on the main floor, Valadof dashed across the empty space and slid into a space under the large turbine. He reached into his front pack and pulled out two blocks of C4 explosives. He identified an access panel which he opened and attached the explosives to the back part of the internal box. Pulling out a detonation cap attached to a timer, he inserted the detonation cap into the blocks of C4 and set the timer for thirty minutes. He then reattached the access panel cover.

Once done, he looked for any signs of movement around the floor and seeing none, dashed back to the work bench and then out the door. After making his way back to the pond, Valadof went back into the water and swam back to the river.

After exiting the river, Valadof monitored the time and waited to see the end of the turbine. When the timer expired, he could hear the explosion, see lights go out around the area and see significant action as troops rushed to the building as flames and smoke could be seen. Typing into his wrist computer, the message was sent that the target had been destroyed and hit the send button.

When a message appeared on the computer, Valadof was being directed to his next target and a planned drop of additional supplies. Valadof head into the trees and started moving north towards the next position.

|||||

A team of Chinese soldiers monitored the troop placement across the river from the Russian forces. The maps being sent down from the satellite showed the major tank locations along with river crossing equipment and gun emplacements. The intelligence team had additionally identified where the anti-air placements were located. As they continued to review maps, a location was identified where there was a gap in the defenses. The terrain forced the forces to be divided due to a steep canyon that was mostly water at the bottom.

The infiltration team decided that was the best place to land in an attempt to get behind the enemy lines. Some had been dropped in from air, but at the cost of heavy losses. Their task was not to engage, but get behind the lines followed by destruction of major transportation and weapon depots.

With a plan in place, they relayed commands up the chain and moved out to position themselves at the jump off point. At the appointed time, the large guns started firing up river in a diversion as river crossing craft began to form up in a diversion to draw troops away from the canyon area. As the small team eased into the water with their underwater craft to assist them in crossing, they also pulled in their supplies.

When they reached the canyon wall, they located a recess in the wall that would cover a climber. The team climber found a starting point that was hidden from view and began his assent. As he reached the top of the fifty foot climb, he pulled out his knife and peeked over the edge. Twenty feet away was a napping guard.

The Chinese free climber quietly moved forward then placed his hand over the napping guard's mouth and quickly slit his throat. Moving back to the edge of the cliff, he picked up the rope he carried and planted the anchors in the ground, throwing the rest of the rope over the edge to his teammates.

Within a few minutes, the rest of the five member team had appeared while the climber had propped up the dead body to make it look like he was just asleep. The team swiftly pulled up the rope and the supplies attached to the end. As the supplies arrived, the team rapidly grabbed their assigned bundle and raced to the nearby woods.

The unit entered the woods and two men dropped to the ground with their rifles at the ready to cover the other three as they moved ahead to find a hiding location. After a minute, the two cover men, crawled deeper into the woods, following their team mates.

At the rendezvous point, the men swiftly changed into dry cloths, divided up the weapons, food and explosives into their back packs and quietly signaled to each other when they were ready to move out. With a silent signal, the team lead signaled they should leave, pointing in a North West direction.

The team approached the edge of the woods; they spotted a number of trucks with large rocket emplacements. The Russian's had camped out as they waited for the command to move closer to the river for engagement. The Chinese team quietly circled to the right out of the glow of the fires until they had moved around the Russian company and then continued moving towards their target.

When the Chinese team came over a small rise, they could see their target, a communications tower that the Russians had erected to support command coordination. At the bottom of the tower, there were three trucks with tents extending out of the back. From the tents a set of cables could be seen that connected to the tower that was held in place by three steel support cables which had been anchored into the ground. The complete area was covered by a camouflage net to keep any spotter aircraft from being able to identify the location.

The team leader opened his computer and hooked it to a radio unit. He quickly marked the location and indicated the team was ready. The message was transmitted and a response came back that target craft were on their way.

The climber pulled out of his backpack a laser designator and illuminated the tower with the laser beam. The beam was not visible to the eye, so there was nothing that would attract attention. After a few minutes the team heard anti-aircraft missiles in the area were being launched. Suddenly the tower evaporated and the surrounding area erupted in flames as a bomb struck, launched from a high flying aircraft, followed by an explosion in the sky as a missile found its target destroying the bomber.

The infiltration team quietly backed away from the location. After a short transmission of success, they were directed to a new target. They packed up their gear and began to move to the East.

|||||

The Chinese Navy started larger movements in the China Sea with intense anti-submarine exercises to counter the Russian submarine movements from Kamchatka. The waters were vibrating with the massive sonar's pounding as they were attempting to locate any Russian submarines in the area. When signals showed possible targets, the waters erupted as depth charges were dropped along with occasional torpedo launches. The loss of ships was small, but beginning to build as the naval forces began rapidly engaging in battle.

The U.S. watched the troop movements from satellites and observed through new reports the infiltration of special troops as communications were being attacked in cross-border raids on both sides. The U.S. satellites monitored the ship movements in the China Sea along with deep water monitoring systems that had been in place for many years. The U.S. Navy was able to monitor the surface and underwater war that was building with interest. The Pentagon war planners were updating their tactics documents for both the Chinese and Russian armies and navies as they observed changes in doctrine from what previously had been assumed.

The President ordered the Secretary of State for the U.S. to take the roll of diplomat to lead an attempt to cool the growing engagement. The United Nations was useless since both the Russians and the Chinese were on the Security Council and nothing could be agreed too. The Secretary started to shuttle between Moscow and Peking in an attempt to defuse the situation. As shuttle diplomacy slowly cooled tempers, troops were put on lower alert status and the world breathed a sigh of relief. Both sides pulled back their infiltration teams and stood down their submarine hunting forces. Commercial shiping which had stopped flowing due to the naval operations was able to resume movement without risk.

With shuttle diplomacy, options of totally disbanding the competing math team work was openly discussed by both the Russians and the Chinese team leaderships based on cost-benefit decisions on both sides. The U.S. denied any work by DARPA on M-Theory. The diplomats continued to assure both the Russians and the Chinese that any work that may have been going on was at a dead end and with Tim's death.

With Tim out of the picture, the U.S. Congress passed an appropriations bill, signed by the President that reduced funding for DoD targeted at DARPA and focused on a specific unspecified black program. Senate intelligence no longer wanted to know about the program in classified briefings and comments were openly made that it was a program that had ended. At the same time, the main Crystal City entrance to the facility seemed to be closed and sealed.

The NSA continued monitoring the Russian and Chinese teams and it became apparent that plans were being made to break up the math teams. Agents in Russia and China confirmed that support was fast fading and that re-organization was to happen soon.

The CIA Chinese spy team monitored the disbanding of the research team as mathematicians were sent back to their original work at research institutes and Universities around China. They indicated continued basic work in a relatively more open environment, attending conferences and delving into other unrelated areas of research.

The spy team was then reassigned to work monitoring the normal Chinese military buildup and ship construction. Some periodic monitoring of the original math team was executed to ensure that they were no longer working in a focused, organized effort that would pose any threat. With the breakup of the team, Jasmine was shifted to a different position and when she moved; she took her "gift" with her. In her new job of working for the base commander, she was able to "plant" the listening device in a very useful area as she gave it to him as a gift, a thank you for the job he gave her. He placed the "gift" in his office.

|||||

Tang Chou was one of the leading scientists on the Chinese math team. He had previously attended conferences with Tim and was well aware of his work. As the Chinese math team was disbanded, Chou was moved to a much lesser position working on computing space missile trajectories. He was still based in the area of Guangzhou working at the military base.

Chou and his wife had filed to have a second child, as their first had died at the age of five from pneumonia due to the sad state of medicine in his home town providence before he was moved to Guangzhou. Upon transfer to his new job, Chou's wife took ill and suddenly died from appendicitis while waiting in a hospital for surgery, another failure of the government as far as Chou was concerned.

The toll on Chou was massive; in his depressed state of mind, everywhere he looked he saw the failure of the Chinese state. While there were growing economic freedoms for a few, the ordinary people continued to suffer as they supported those few blessed by the central committee.

Soon after the death of Chou's beloved wife, Jasmine came to visit her friend and they talked into the night. She began to understand his desire to find a way of escape from his depressed life and find hope, possibly in the West.

Upon return from Chou's, she immediately followed her training and made a blind drop to notify the controlling agent of her information. The information rapidly reached the CIA operations desk in Washington D.C. and a field operation was set up. Word was passed back to Jasmine with the appropriate signals for either a "wave off" or "operation go". The snatch point was positioned along with the time they needed to be there.

Two days later as she took some hot noodles to her friend Chou, she continued to talk and express that there was a way if he really wished to move on. She knew of an escape if he truly wished to take it. As she embraced Chou her elder by seven years, he indicated his worry for his friend.

Chou spoke "Jasmine, you have been a dear friend to me, if I were to leave; it would place you in danger because of our friendship. I would only leave if I knew that you would come with me to a new life."

"Dr. Chou, I too have considered this and we can make this journey together. My life would indeed be at risk and I would be much honored to make this journey with you."

She told him to be at the edge of the river on the boat dock with a fishing pole on the coming Friday at 5 p.m. She would meet him there with noodles and they would start the path to a new life. He could not tell anyone or they would probably die, but she would be there and would go with him.

Early Friday morning, a SEAL team with a special rubber zodiac setup with the new protective cloak and the special goggles, launched from the a small submarine detached from a U.S. nuclear submarine in the ocean just off the coast of China down river from Guangzhou . Upon reaching the surface, the team deployed the zodiac which quickly inflated and the SEALs pulled themselves from the small hatch into the zodiac. A special small water jet motor was turned on and they put on their special goggles and activated the cloak as the small sub quietly submersed to return back to the mother ship.

At 7 a.m., after entering the river behind a cargo ship, they followed the ship in its wake to hide all indications of their passage and progressed up river. At 5:30 p.m., the team approached the rendezvous point and spotted Jasmine and Chou at the appointed place sitting on the dock fishing and eating noodles. The team cut the engines and started paddling quietly towards the dock. As they came up to the edge of the dock they pulled in such that the fishing line was at the edge of the zodiac and the team leader reached out and made three sharp pulls on the fishing line to send the signal. With two team members monitoring the area and guns at the ready, they prepared to take the passengers.

With the time arriving, Jasmine placed her hand on Chou's arm and gave him a smile of support. Chou put down his noodles and with his tired and sad eyes, looked at Jasmine with a half smile. He picked up the fishing pole and waited. Suddenly he felt the three tugs on the fishing line which was the signal. Together, they slowly closed their eyes and took a deep breath to calm their nerves. Jasmine put down her noodles, Chou the fishing pole as Jasmine took Chou's hand. Together holding hands, they pushed off the edge of the dock, falling the few feet towards the water, hand-in-hand. They passed into the cloaked field to a red glowing light and instead of hitting the water, landed on a pile of bags at the front of the zodiac. The SEALs signaled to them to stay quiet as they started to slowly pull the boat away from the dock.

Two team members continued to monitor that there was no real activity until they were fourty feet away from the dock. Suddenly a Chinese security guard came rushing down the dock yelling for help and upon reaching the spot where Jasmine and Chou had been, started looking in the water trying to find the couple.

Quickly the SEAL team entered the shipping channel and fell in line behind a container ship loaded and heading back down the river towards the ocean. After reaching open water, the SEAL team broke off from behind the ship and found a place about a mile away from the path being taken by the ships. Making sure they would not be spotted, they turned off the cloak to check the GPS location and after a series of maneuvers of turning the cloak on and off while repositioning, the team lead was satisfied and with hand signals indicated they were at the right location.

Upon reaching their station, they dropped a hydrophone in the water, hooked the wire to a small box on the leaders vest which sent out a signal that was the sound of a whale call. They sat quietly waiting for the dark night to overtake them with the cloak field activated so they would not be spotted. As the 11 p.m. hour mark approached, the hatch of the mother ship's mini sub appeared on the surface. The team rowed over and one by one, they entered the sub through the top hatch. As the final member quietly loaded into the sub, he pulled out a switch from his vest pocket, flipped off the cover and pushed the button. Quickly, key locations erupted in flames destroying the cloaking equipment around the zodiac as it collapsed on itself and sank. The hatch to the mini sub was closed and the sub submersed. Within fifteen minutes, the mini sub had docked with the submersed mother sub and the passengers were transferred. Now began the trek to San Diego with its new CIA members Jasmine, and Chou who were requesting protection.

The Chinese soldiers on the dock had called for a search and rescue, not knowing what had happened to the young couple. As time progressed, the area was dragged for their bodies. Eventually a friend had entered Jasmines apartment and found a suicide note explaining that she and Chou had decided to drown in the river having been depressed over life and the loss of their loved ones. The search was ended with no bodies having been found and the assumption was made that their bodies had been swept down the river to the ocean and would never be found.

On the transit back to San Diego, an onboard CIA agent debriefed Jasmine and Chou. He offered Chou a chance to work for the U.S. Government in exchange for a new life and his extensive math talents. Jasmine would be provided a new identity and work providing language translations.

Chou accepted and the decision had already been made to slowly ease him into the BELLOWS program, but only after an extensive "cleaning" took place. The risk was too great to expose such high level information until they were absolutely certain of his intentions.

|||||

The Russians posed a different problem for the CIA than the Chinese. The Russian mob no longer wanted to fund the operation and during a voice intercept by NSA, it became apparent that the team would be disbanded. While the decision was made to not "clean" the math team scientists and to return them to their previous jobs, for Vladimir there was still risk. In addition to disbanding the team, the mob was involved in a security review and there was a risk that the local spy chain could be discovered and with the discovery, forfeit their lives.

A message was passed through the contact in Kiel Germany that reached the agents at the Ural base to expect an extraction to take place at a designated date-time and they were to be ready. A clearing outside the fence of the barracks area was to be the extraction point and they were to use the relay emergency broadcast signal on the previously smuggled retransmitter-relay linked to the hidden bug transmitter to direct in the extraction helicopter.

With the designated time approaching, in the dark of the night, Della and Gregory approached the clearing and brought with them the relay unit. At the designated time, they activated the signal using a red button near the base of the unit. As they waited in the bushes surrounding the extraction area, they heard the quiet whoosh of a helicopter approach and land with wind blowing the trees. All they saw however was a bird which appeared to swoop into the area and hang in the air.

As the helicopter blades slowed to a stop, suddenly four SEALs dressed in black with black ski masks and weapons emerged from what appeared as nowhere into the landing zone area where they rapidly headed to the surrounding brush area. As they circled the brush area, they contacted the older couple huddled together with a blanket over their shoulders in the cold night air. As the SEALs approached, they signaled to keep quiet and stay down. As the SEALs reached Della and Gregory, Gregory still in a bit of shock over the sudden appearance out of nowhere by the SEALs, pulled out a small map showing the location of the fence and the old wooden barracks and the location of the three team members inside that would be waiting.

One team member led the older couple around the landing zone area, careful to stay under the cover of the bushes and trees. Before entering the cloaking field, the SEAL triggered a signal that was passed through the relay to the listening device in the work area of the barracks. The signal caused the device to ignite phosphorus based chemicals that rapidly melted the internals of the listening device to a slag that could never be identified if ever found.

The other three members unpacked their special goggles and activated them. Suddenly they disappeared with the exception of two small cameras that seemed to float in the area above where their heads were located.

They headed to the fence and in a short time, had cut through it, and like cats penetrated inside the compound, and were swiftly moving to the barracks. As they reached the barracks, they disabled their invisibility field, identified the location and with a series of swift thrusts of their rifle butts, broke through the old wooden planking that was a wall. As they broke through, the three team members, Tanya, Macao, and Vladimir, were waiting on the other side and rapidly helped to enlarge the hole. As the size of the hole grew, the Russian team members passed through the hole as swiftly as they could.

Each of the emerging team members was handed a set of goggles and swiftly shown how to put them on and activate them. While they had little training in how to understand what they saw, they were told to follow the bouncing balls and keep up. One SEAL lead the way, the second followed behind the three spy team members and the third followed up the rear covering their exit as they silently headed for the hole in the fence.

A guard inside the barracks had heard the banging and cracking of wood and had grabbed his radio and called the security team to release the dogs as an escape was in progress. Two dogs were released and pointed to the back area of the barracks. They were followed by a guard running with his rifle at the ready. At the same time, sirens started blaring and bright lights flooded the area.

The lead SEAL reached the fence and slipped through. He then pulled back the fence section to let the others through. One by one the spy team members slipped through the fence until there were just the two SEALs left within the compound. When the second SEAL was about to exit through the fence, two German shepherds rounded the side of the barracks, and headed for the break in the fence. A combination of the human scent and the fence motion attracted them. As they approached, the two SEALs waited and with a short powerful stroke of their rifles, dazed the dogs leaving them on the ground.

After the second SEAL followed the spy team through the gate, he spun around and with two rapid shots took out the flood lights.

When the security guard came around the barracks, he caught a glimpse of the hole in the fence before gun fire took out the flood lights. After a second his eyes adjusted and he could see the fence break and motion of the fence along with the two dogs down on the ground. Not understanding what he saw he rapidly took aim at the hole in the fence and decided to fire.

The single shot caught the third SEAL in the upper right thigh as he was passing through the fence. The second SEAL that had passed through swiftly fired his rifle before a second shot could be fired and knocked the security guard down with a single bullet to the shoulder. The SEALs had trained to shoot with the cloak active, much like a trick shot from the hip.

The lead SEAL quietly told the spys to follow him. The second SEAL helped the third as he limped to the correct location in the landing zone, careful to go around the area which contained the helicopter.

The lead SEAL approached the helicopter at the trained angle and location where there was a red ribbon on the ground; a hand reached out of the invisibility zone and helped to guide them in. As the three spies entered the area of invisibility, they were able to see the older couple in the passenger bay, buckled in and ready to go.

The rest of the SEAL team joined the people in the back and with a hand signal, the rotors quickly spun up, and within a few moments they were off.

The lead SEAL pulled out the medical pack by the seat and applied pressure to the gunshot wound. The bandage was wrapped around the leg with medicine and tied off. A shot of morphine was administered to make sure that he would be stable until they could reach safety.

By the time the dogs' recovered and additional guards appeared, there was nothing to find but a few patches of blood in a trail that lead to some depressed grass then ended. Despite activation of radar tracking in the area, nothing was seen or found.

After the helicopter left Russian air space and was entering Finland air space over water at just a few feet off the deck, the pilot disabled the cloak and headed for an American Independence class LCS Tri hulled navy ship in the area and landed with the team on the helicopter deck.

While the extraction was taking place from the Russian camp, Tanyas and Vladimirs family safety needed to be protected and the operation was well underway. Two sleeper agents had arrived at Tanya's parents' apartment and swept the family away into hiding in a safe house in Moscow the previous day. The group had swiftly escaped down the back stair case and dashed into a parked car behind the apartment building. The car maneuvered into street traffic and disappeared in the rush of the afternoon people and traffic.

The following morning, during traffic rush, the five people emerged with newspapers, backpacks, clothes and modifications to their hair and facial look. Tanya's mother, father and brother acted like any of the hundreds of families that were headed for vacation to St. Petersburg and were accompanied by another couple.

The train reached St. Petersburg where they all exited the train station and caught a bus to the northwest edge of the city. At the bus stop where they exited, the small team met up with Vladimir's wife and the agents that had helped her to escape. After walking for a while after getting off the bus, with the city behind them, they approached an open field and they laid out a blanket with food in an apparent picnic.

After a short period of time, the sound of a quiet helicopter could be heard in the field and the wind from the rotor blades created what appeared to be a strong local gust. The small group walked towards the area of the wind gusts and to all their surprise, a SEAL dressed in black with a black mask, suddenly appeared. He scanned the area to ensure that no one was around and quickly escorted them forward and into the helicopter, taking care to help them because inside the cloak field, it was dark with only red internal lights on.

Within moments, the helicopter left, heading for their rendezvous with the American navy Independence class LCS ship located off the Finish coast where Tanya had just arrived.

When the group arrived, they were met by Tanya and Vladimir along with hugs and tears. They were escorted into a set of rooms where they found clothes and toiletries. After time to relax and take showers, they were escorted to the captains mess area where they were given a steak dinner with all the fixings.

Once the helicopters had returned and been rolled into the hanger deck, the LCS made a quick turn and headed towards open water at its smooth 40 knot speed where the U.S. Naval fleet was positioned to receive them.

There was a significant amount of security briefing to be done on the ship with the people just returned, to ensure that the invisibility technology would not be revealed and the advantage be exposed. Tanya's role was explained to her family and while there was some grief of leaving the motherland, the joy of their freedom and their relief of reuniting with Tanya overcame any apprehensions.

The Vladimir's were also debriefed. The CIA agent asked Vladimir to work for the U.S. government and the offer was accepted. The team then learned that Macao was actually a U.S. citizen positioned at the base by the CIA to support the operation. Macao was headed home.

The operation had been successful; only one minor causality taken. No exposure of security related to the cloaking device had happened.

NSA had created a number of false messages providing an apparent trail heading south for the three people from the barracks and finally leaving indications that all members were dead in a forest fire and had not reached a point where they were likely to expose information. A signal from

the CIA to their agents that extraction was complete resulted in an oven
fire to break out in the apartments where Tanya's family had lived along
with the small apartment of Vladimir's wife. Three bodies were found
that generally fit Tanya's mother, father and brother and indications were
that it was a murder suicide. Oddly, there were three bodies missing from
a cemetery just ten miles outside of Moscow, but no one knew because
the graves had been filled in. In the Vladimir apartment, the burnt body
of a woman was also recovered and the monitoring team closed the case
assuming she had died in the fire.

Back in Washington D.C., now that their people were safe, the word
was passed to clean up the rest of the mess.

Thomas sat at his desk in Senator's Shank's office when two FBI
agents came in and asked to talk with him. As they moved into a private
conference room, they introduced themselves.

"I am agent Jones and this is agent Tempts. We wish to talk with you
about your contact with a woman known as Sonja. We assume you know
who we are talking about?"

"Yes, is there a problem?"

"I am afraid so, when was the last time you talked with her?"

"Two days ago, Sunday evening we had dinner."

"No further contact since then? Did she indicate she was going
anywhere?"

"No, can I ask what this is about?"

"We need you to come down to our offices and give a statement. Sonja
appears to have been working for a law office fronting for a Russian spy
ring. We raided the office this morning and also checked her apartment
and we can't locate her. There were a number of indications that you had
been highly interactive with the law firm and with Sonja."

With a stunned look, Thomas stammered "A Russian spy ring? She
was a spy?"

"Yes, we need you to come with us and give us a detailed report of all
activity that you are aware of and any information you may have provided
her or she may have had access too."

Thomas continued to stare stunned "Of course, let me just....give me
a moment....I..I need to let the senator know."

Thomas walked into the senator's office with a stunned look on his
face, the air was cold and his body was shaking. Thomas straightened
his shoulders and took a deep breath "Sir, I have just been informed that
I have been the target of a Russian spy ring and I need to go to the FBI

office to support their investigation. I am sure you understand that I will fully cooperate." With no further words and totally unsure of what fate awaited him, he turned and exited the office to a stunned U.S. Senator and Thomas was escorted out of the office by the two FBI agents in front of the stunned staff.

|||||

On a train to Miami Florida, a beautiful platinum blond woman with a passport of Mary Kingman had her bags and a ticket to Brazil, followed by a link to Paris France and returning to Miami (although she would never use that final leg). By the time she returned to Europe, there will have been enough change in her facial features that any FBI pictures would be marginal at best.

She was a careful woman. She did not trust the local mafia contacts and had set up a second apartment that only she knew about. This second apartment was the one she used but was careful to not leave any finger prints or DNA to trace and there was a note left so when or if she had not appeared after a period of time and the apartment manager came in, he was instructed to throw away the few clothes in the unit, she would not be returning.

In the first apartment, she had rigged a simple alarm that let her know if someone had attempted entry. When the alarm had gone off, she called the office to see if there was a hint of a problem, disguised as a client. When an unknown voice had answered and indicated that someone would have to get back to her. She then sent a text with a simple "?" to her contact and with no reply, she knew it was time to leave. After sending a signal to destroy the alarm unit, wiping off her finger prints and throwing away her cell phone, she immediately left for the train station where she had her back up luggage and a backup cell phone stashed for a quick exit. On the train she sent a short text "exiting" to her relay in Europe to let them know that the cell had been exposed and that she had escaped.

She settled in her seat but she was a bit sad, Thomas had been a worthy lover, better than expected and now she would have to find another.

|||||

During the summer following the contact event, as the team continued its discovery work, it was time to settle down and clean up some of the hanging loose ends from a general security point of view. Bob, Janet,

Randy, Valerie, George, and Nicky needed to have their lives reorganized with better covers according to Jack.

The hidden team was now lead by new head, John Murphy. He had some similarity to Tim, but had a number of physical differences in his looks now looking totally different in his facial features, hair and with a limp compared to Tim's normal walking gate. Changes had also addressed Tim's voice to insure there would never be a voice pattern match.

Tim had been taken to a small medical facility in Richmond, Virginia where they had done facial reconstruction to change his look and with surgery, altered his vocal structure. The metal that had sliced into his leg as he left the helicopter had damaged a nerve and it resulted in a pronounced limp. While he had lost a fair amount of blood, the security agent had been able to stem the flow enough for him to reach the farm house where a doctor arrived with plasma and was able to stitch up his wound. After two days, he was transported to Richmond where he was able to recover and get the necessary surgery to create John. Along with the physical change, a new passport, driver's license, social security card and a set of credit cards had been set up. Finger Prints had been altered and with minor surgery, his ear lobes had been changed. Except for the memories, Tim no longer existed. From the change, a stronger John emerged.

Randy contacted the head of the Art department at John Hopkins. He had been placed on extended leave due to a "physical problem" as indicated to the head of the Art Department as causing his sudden disappearance. At the appropriate time, Randy scheduled a meeting with the department head and drove out to the campus to sit down with him.

Randy entered the office and the department head came around his desk to shake his hand to welcome him back.

"I was informed of your physical issue, and that you would be out for a while. We had professor Kingman step in and cover for you. I hope you're fully recovered and ready to return?"

"Actually Ken, that's what I wanted to talk with you about. During my recovery I used the time to evaluate my life's way forward. I've focused so much of my life on my work and reaching my current level, I've not had any time to deal with my life."

"Are you considering leaving us?"

"Yeah, I need to take some time to put my personal life first and a friend of mine has offered me a good job that will allow that to happen. I have decided for the near term, I'll take up his offer and see if I can build a life that includes a family. I expect to stay somewhere in the area, perhaps Virginia."

"Have you met someone? Could we keep you part time?"

"Yes, I have met someone. I may be able to support a small amount of time, but I'll have to see how this all works out. I just wanted you to know and as things move forward, I will keep you updated. Perhaps over time, I could do some teaching on the side. I just don't know at the moment."

"Fare enough. You're a good teacher, the young people really respond to your help. People like you are hard to find."

Randy rose to leave and Ken rose from his desk, walked over to Randy. Shook his hand, and closed out the meeting. "Please keep in touch. I will work with you. I would hate to totally lose your talents in the department. Randy, best of luck to you and again, please stay in touch."

"Thanks, and I will stay in touch."

Randy was now free to operate with the team, having terminated his link but still keeping future work (if he wished) available. Randy smiled as he left to go talk with Janet. With the worry and stress removed from having to disappoint a friend and his boss, Randy felt as free as a bird.

Janet continued to work with Randy while she also took her final classes on-line. With her grades and submitted work, she was able to graduate with honors while continuing to work with the BELLOWS team. She had settled into a condo a short distance from the new estate that was being engineered to provide a top-side work environment for the team southwest of Fairfax, Virginia.

On the fourth of July, Janet and Randy visited her family in Laurel Maryland. Her aunt and uncle were escorted over to the FBI family's house where a back yard Barbeque was setup for all. Her aunt and uncle were dealing well with help of the nurse and her brothers, while missing her, were happy and healthy. Randy was introduced to the family as a very close co worker and a very special friend she said that with a big smile as she held Randy's hand, and her previous professor.

When the evening was winding down, Janet sat down with her family to make an announcement.

Nervous, she clasped the family pendent to help calm her. Janet looked around at her gathered family. "I wanted to let everyone know some exciting news. As you may be aware, I've been working for a special group in the government for a number of months. Due to the nature of the work, I've not been able to see you as much as I have wanted, but work is now reaching a normal pace. My work is with Randy, she looked at him with a smile and squeezed his hand, and I now have a full time permanent position. In addition, I've been taking classes on-line and expect to graduate at the end of the summer session.

"This is a unique job which I'm not able to talk much about, but from this point forward, we don't have to worry about money. All I can tell you is that this is a wonderful job and very exciting. There's a lot of national security involved with this work, so that's why you have been protected by the FBI. I wish I could tell you more, but I can't right now, maybe someday. "

Janet turned to her brothers, "there's going to be enough money to make sure that if you apply yourselves, you'll be able to go to college. This is what Mom and Dad would want, so I expect each of you to do your very best. I'm going to be setting up funds to cover expenses for everyone so none of you need worry as long as you apply yourselves. I'm moving into a condo in Virginia and I'll be back to visit often, and you can come visit me too.

"Auntie and Unc, you know I love you dearly, and I'll make sure that you have whatever you need. Your love allowed me to survive after the loss of mom and dad, and I can't tell you how much it meant to me." With that Janet gave them all a big hug and kiss and another hug.

The evening came to an end. With more hugs and kisses, Janet bid them good night and she and Randy drove back to Fairfax. Finally, their lives were beginning to come together.

While Bob had started spending time in his office early in the New Year after a time of "personal time off," after Tim's death, he showed significant signs of stress and began disappearing for large gaps of time from the hospital. His secretary had purchased extra boxes of pens as he seemed to be snapping them multiple times a day. Even his normally calm face was showing signs of stress lines and the dark rings under his eyes identified his lack of sleep, secretly aided by self medication and makeup.

A day happened when Bob came in and asked his staff to please come into his office at 9 a.m. At the appointed time, the door to his office opened and the three staff members came in. Bob asked them to please take a seat.

"I have decided to move on. I need to rebuild my life and I can't seem to do that with my current situation. You all know Jim as he has replaced me during my recent time away. I have asked Dr. Shellworth to take over my practice on the agreement that he will keep all of you on the staff, and he has agreed.

"I will be leaving after today and trust that you will help Jim succeed just as you have helped me. I thank each and every one of you for your help and friendship and wish you only the best."

Everyone on his staff knew he was suffering and that he couldn't continue in the state he was in. He no longer was capable of doing his work.

When some of his friends came by that day to talk with him, he indicated that he had found a small condo in Fairfax Virginia. He was going to spend time recovering from the loss of his friend that he felt was his responsibility and creating a new life for himself. He was thinking of doing some writing and no one needed to worry, financially he was doing just fine.

He left instructions on packing his effects and an address to ship the boxes too. With final words of good bye and some hugs to his secretary, he left.

Bob found some freedom with working on the team. It was beginning to give him some personal time to develop a life outside of work that included meeting a woman that Randy had introduced to him through one of the team members. For the first time in a long time, Bob enjoyed the simple pleasures of going to dinner, movies and long talks into the night without the worry of being interrupted by emergency calls and long hours and weekends at the office and hospital.

Valerie had already taken an extended leave from her normal work. She flew to New York to close out her condo and to shut down her contact service. After some arrangements, she engaged a mover work with her to pack her apartment, and soon the contents were on a truck headed to Virginia. She gave the owner a payment to cover the final three months on her lease and with an exciting smile on her face, closed the door for the final time as she was humming a part of "Ode to Joy" as she climbed down the stairs to catch the taxi to the JFK airport.

While Valerie headed to the airport, she was pondering her next move for John. She was a bit of match maker and spent time looking for a girlfriend for John, the new team lead. It was difficult, Tim had enjoyed that life of perfect love and it would have to reach a high level to satisfy him. But Valerie was determined.

After she returned to the team site, she decided to have some fun and spent time creating a synthesizer output of the Old Ones communications with the agreement from John and the President. A small amount of the output was put on a compact disc and set up for a distribution to a number of her clients. She created a mailing to the extensive client list she kept, indicating that she had discovered a new type of music and would be providing an orchestration in the near future if they were interested. She would be in touch in case they would like to use it within their repertoire.

Quietly, a tunneling machine had been brought into Virginia by DoD. The work was focused on digging a small tunnel beneath the I66 freeway and above ground Metro tracks between a newly purchased twenty acre estate on the outer edges of Fairfax and the the Ballston underground Metro station. While not the expansive tunnels of the underground Metro, the tunnel was large enough to support a small high speed rail system supporting small transports capable of carrying four to eight people. Upon reaching the Metro stop, the passengers would disembark and enter the metro station through a security entrance that was under constant around the clock security card and biometric monitoring by DoD security. In addition, a new tunnel also connected from the Foggy Bottom station to the BELLOWS team work center to support a hidden entrance for team members.

John was not a world renowned figure like Tim and according to all the documentation. He had a totally different history, having graduated from San Diego State University in the late 1980's and doing his graduate work at Berkeley before becoming a program manager with DARPA. It had taken a number of months for John to appear from the surgery on the "dead" Tim, but now John was able to make a new life free from the dangers that haunted Tim, although not the ghosts.

While John wasn't ready to date, he had found some peace from the constant ache. He was able to spend time writing and doing more exercise as he began to slow down from his previous hectic work schedule. He continued working with Bob, but now they were focused on how to begin the process of rebuilding of his life. Valerie was always ready with a beautiful young woman for John whenever he wanted to go out. Most became casual friends, but John began to find some relief with a simple dinner out.

The team became free to move around and while they could spend more time with their families, the excitement of discovery actually drove their managers to make them go home. Security monitoring of all the team members, family and friends continued. The program did not want another failure of security to occur again and that meant continued vigilance.

Through the use of a classified Presidential finding, all contacts of the BELLOWS program members were to have complete in-depth security reviews, sometimes without their knowledge. This was to ensure that no moles attempted to penetrate the team work. In addition, all family and close friends of the team members were to be monitored and protected with around the clock security but not to interfere with their normal lives unless security was at risk.

George's family was informed that George was deeply involved in a Top Secret program and they were not allowed to mention his involvement to anyone. While visits were allowed, George had to work out of the D.C. area and that they would be protected for their and his safety. The cover continued in that George and Nicky had been in an accident and had damaged their vocal cords so they could not talk. When George's daughters came to visit, George and Nicky both carried their new touch pads to allow them to type instead of talk, although Nicky with his vibrant Italian background was more than able to express himself with his hand gestures.

Valerie's and George's house was quickly being finished and supported rooms for George's daughters to stay in when they visited or for stay over's by late working team members. There were sections of the house that were off limits to George's daughters and as with all people on the estate, were constantly monitored for security. But there was also a wonderful kitchen that Valerie and the girls were able to enjoy cooking lessons from the team's master chef along with tennis, swimming and horses.

The house was the first that George had built, having bought before when he was married previously. He and Valerie were allowed to be involved in the design and George knew exactly what he wanted. As a small boy, he had once designed his dream house and this was going to be it, with extras out back for work related rooms.

The design was a large "A" frame with equally large attached one story buildings to the right, left and back. As you entered the house through the large front doors, a sunken living room was on the left side with a large fireplace that had room for a corner sofa and coffee table where the back of the sofa fit up against the dropped area. In front of the coffee table was a large furry rug, just begging to be stretched out upon when the fire was roaring on a cold Virginia night. To the right of the corner fireplace was a large TV for George's football game watching, both American and European, with Nicky and Valerie.

On the right side as you entered was a dining room with a table setting of up to sixteen people. Behind the dining room area was a wall with sliding windows that opened to the kitchen. The kitchen was designed to allow four or five people to comfortably move around as meals were made and served.

To the right of the dining area and kitchen was a large garage capable of supporting up to eight cars if parked two deep. This area was used during parties or when team members brought over their families to relax.

When you continued straight from the front door, you entered a hallway. To the left behind the living room was designed another hallway and to the right was the kitchen. To the left hallway there were closets and linen storage shelves. As one continued down the hall behind the living room, one entered a large enclosed swimming pool and Jacuzzi area. George always enjoyed swimming and so there was a good size pool that could be used year round by the team and their families if they wished. The building had a Jacuzzi that would allow eight people comfortably and in the corner, a small bathroom with shower and changing space.

Continuing down the central hallway from the houses entrance, on the left was a guest bathroom followed by the master bedroom. As you entered the master bedroom, there was a master bathroom on the left and directly in front was a private sliding glass door to the pool area. It also had on one wall, a large walk-in closet of which George would use some and Valerie would use a lot.

On the right side of the main hallway the library entrance was found, along with a comfortable office with TV, sofa and recliner chair for the family to relax. As one continued down the hallway, on the right at the end of the main "A" frame building was a spiral staircase to the second floor.

On the second floor, Nicky had his room and bathroom. In addition, there were three other guest bedrooms and two extra bathrooms for the guests. Sometimes these were used when team members wanted to give their family a break because the view across the grounds in front was stunning, especially when it snowed. Like a private hotel, these were great places to relax with each of the front rooms having their own balcony.

In the back of the main house connected by a glass walkway, was an elevator for those that had problems with the stairs and further on, a large one story building. The top of the building was a landscaped park that could be used for people to just relax when the weather was nice and talk if needed. Below were a number of labs that were off-limits to anyone without BELLOWS clearance. This was being used partly by the engineering team to support test manufacturing of some of their newest ideas.

The pool and garage areas were both landscaped roofs to help with temperature control, and in addition to helping with any fly-over security intrusion attempts.

Out back behind the pool area was a large tented set of tennis courts and racquet ball courts; both for George, Valerie and Nicky's use as well as for the total team.

The security team insisted, some said on request of Nicky, that a few horses be also kept for riding around the grounds. So there was a barn and tack house not far from the main house that supported horseback riding with its own indoor riding rink. The two horses had been rescued and brought in for just this purpose. They were very calm so that most people could ride and some of the smaller children on the team's families could be taught.

The estate covered a total of fifteen acres and using the cloaking technology, covered up much of the security devices which included cameras that could not be seen, but became visible for a one hundredth of a second every second or two to capture any movement anywhere on the estate. Each visitor had a unique ID tag that allowed them to be tracked anywhere on the estate, even Nicky's new friend Sierra, the golden retriever puppy.

The property was operated in a unique way. The technology that was being developed was provided to a number of newly created companies under a privately held umbrella corporation known as TOO, The Old Ones. All contracts and work were under very strict classification control. The companies operated as commercial concerns, capable of generating revenue, although they were prohibited from bidding directly on any government work, they could provide help for those that wished to do so. Their Board of Directors and top personnel were answerable and part of the BELLOWS program management. The revenue was fed through multiple channels, one of which helped pay for the grounds and the work area, while Valerie and George funded some of the family related parts. The rest of the funds went into DoD's coffers that funded a number of areas including Home Land Defense and International relief work, all the while reducing DoD's budget funding from Congress. The revenue generation started in the millions as the new energy generation devices started to come on line. Within a year, the companies were generating hidden net revenue in the billions as cloaked hidden technology was being installed across the world with high security guards.

The TOO energy generators had special sensors built into the device to protect against any attempt to penetrate. At sensing of any penetrating attempt, the technology would trigger a complete and sudden meltdown and signal notification back to corporate headquarters. All contracts provided a warning that any attempt to tamper would immediately terminate any contract relationship and would result in heavy penalties that were enforced through the requirement to set aside funds into accounts that would be forfeit.

George's daughters flew back to D.C. to be with their dad for short stays. On their first trip back, they met Valerie and Nicky. George and Nicky were very quiet and Valerie along with Bob talked with his children while George and Nicky indicated his thoughts through his computer. George relayed that he was very happy and loved them dearly, but that this work was something very special to both him and the government and that he was very special to the work.

While there, George's girls were able to take some trips out to see the local sites with Valerie, Nicky and George. They had a limo taking them around the area and spent a few days visiting George Washington's estate and drove down to Monticello. The time together allowed Kris and Grace the chance to spend time with Nicky and Valerie. The integration into one big happy family was important to George.

To George, one of the great joys was watching his daughters in the kitchen with Valerie getting some cooking lessons from their Master Chef Bryan who had trained all over Europe. The joy of seeing them laughing together and the hugs and joking created a moment and an image he wanted to always remember.

The second night, George walked in as Nicky and Grace and Kris were playing monopoly. Again, the joy of the simple smiles and hugs between the three of them warmed George's heart and let him know that they were now all part of a bigger family.

On the third day, Valerie took Kris and Grace on a girl's day shopping at the Malls in Fairfax and Pentagon City using that special Credit Card that Valerie possessed. Nicky and George joined them for a nice fish dinner in Crystal City after a morning of working with the math team, topped by a special evening guided tour through the White House by the First Lady.

In the nine months since the event, George had been able to lose 60lbs and while he still had some to go, was looking fit and younger. He had much more energy and the change brought a smile to his daughters, as did the joy of knowing that Nicky and Valerie were there for him after all those lonely years. They were all family.

His grown daughters returned home to LA and Denver with a touch of awe in the importance that their father was held in by the people he worked with and happy that Valerie was there to take care of him because it was very apparent that she made him happier than they had seen him for many, many years. NSA set up special email and encrypted visual communications between the families to keep them at ease and in contact. Nicky was able to have Wednesday nights playing games with Grace and Kris.

Nicky had grown to be part of the larger team family. Valerie and George were the closest he had as true parents and they had bonded as a family within the family.

Nicky was home schooled because he had much work to do on the project, to say nothing of the fact that he had knowledge far above that of most people on the planet. Randy and Janet taught art, Valerie taught languages and George and Janet taught social studies. John taught advanced math, actually they worked together on advanced math with George, and the security team provided physical training. The software team provided lessons on computers, and the engineering team not to be outdone, provided training in the formal processes of engineering. Valerie and George only worried about one problem.

His new parents worried about how Nicky was going to grow in his personal interactions without other young people to interact with. Nicky was very adult in his approach to life. This was partially due to his makeup with the fundamentally lonely soul of a Watcher, but there was more to it than that.

No matter how much Bob talked with Nicky about the day his father died, Nicky held firmly on to the story that his father and mother were still with him and when communications were activated, helping him each and every day. This along with the lack of a normal childhood interactive environment worried Bob. There were no other signs of problems, so Bob kept close monitoring to quickly observe if problems should develop.

During one of the active communications periods before the

communications channel had been lost, Nicky had projected an image of his father and mother. George had observed this, but it proved very little, since the projection was nothing more than the brain's image. The image had shown Nicky and his parents in a vineyard with mountains rising in the background; a common image that could be anywhere on earth.

As time progressed, everyone agreed to get Nicky involved in youth soccer and on a cross country running team, the two things he liked to do. The security team would take him to team practice and help him to train. When it came to Nicky being involved in soccer games or cross country meets, George and Valerie were always there to give Nicky support: there was never a question of them not being able to be there.

At the beginning of the year, a new engineer joined the team. Brandon Stuart had graduated from MIT with a background in electronic engineering and a minor in chemistry. While at MIT, Brandon had entered the Army Reserve to help pay for school and him and his wife's living expenses as she also attended engineering school.

He had married his high school sweetheart Jennie and they had just had their first children only two months before, just after their January graduation, beautiful twins that they named Nathiena and Brandon Jr. Brandon was a fit 6' blonde young man. While in the Army Reserve, he was qualified as a sniper and due to a unit rotation, had to take a year off from school to serve in Afghanistan. While there, he had served with an Army Ranger team on at least two missions that were in his records.

Jim had the opportunity to meet and hire Brandon when one of his old professors happened to call him. Professor Shannon knew that Jim was leading a team of engineers in Washington D.C. area and was impressed enough with Brandon to make some calls for him. Jim had called him the previous summer and asked him to keep an eye out for a promising engineer that he might be able to bring onto his team. Brandon came highly recommended and from the moment he received his security briefing and steadied himself over the shock of what they were doing, he swiftly picked up on the technology and had proven himself every bit of the engineer that the Professor said he would be.

Jennie, Brandon and their kids, had moved to the Virginia area and with support from Valerie, Janet, Randy and Bob and other team members and their families, had settled into their new life. Since Jennie and Brandon had no close family, the team took them in and became their new family.

||||

With the summer heat beginning to rise, Jack received a flash email message from his CIA contact that danger was headed towards the U.S. The listening device that had been dropped in Pakistan had overheard a conversation and Barney need to talk with Jack immediately.

Jack quickly called his friend and they agreed to meet on the classified telephone in an hour. Jack swiftly wrapped up the senate briefing he had been working on and headed to the secure vault where the STU telephone was located.

At the time of the meeting, Jack inserted his card and dialed the number.

"Jack, sorry to interrupt your day, but we have a real problem over here. Do you remember that special listening setup you provided us a few months back?"

"Sure do, how has that worked for you?"

"Well, we just got something. We were able to capture a conversation between their operations chief and one of his lieutenants. They have an operation underway by their Somalia branch that is targeting Denver. It appears they have some radioactive leftovers that the Iranians have provided and they are trying to set off a dirty bomb in downtown Denver.

"We understand that they are going to try and smuggle it across the border from Mexico using the drug mules. While we have parts of the boarder monitored, there are gaps and we need to find a way to plug the gaps, ASAP. It appears that the stuff may already be in Mexico and there are soon to be negotiations underway with one of the cartels."

Jack was thinking swiftly "Can you get me a map of where you need to plug? Also if you have any idea of whom and where they are meeting with the druggies, get me that as well. I'll see what our team can put together for you. Has the president been briefed yet? I think we will need to pull resources fast. "

"Yes, he is being briefed as we speak. I'll have Homeland send over the maps as fast as possible. This has the highest priority, do whatever you can. Get back to me when you have something."

Jack left the vault picking up his encrypted cell phone and sent a fast message to John and Jim that he needed to talk fast and was on his way over to the team's underground center.

After a quick trip to the Vice President compound and down to the team center, John, Jack and Jim were in the engineering section. Jack relayed what he had just heard.

Jack looked at Jim and John "Any ideas?"

Jim took a deep breath and thought for a second, "Well, we've been working on a micro monitoring device that we use to lay a motion field trap. We've been testing them out on the grounds around the house. If we work overtime, we can set up motion traps that can send a signal if anything moves that appears on a map. I also have a number of listening devices set up in the back room if we can use them somehow."

"How much area can you cover with the motion field?" John asked.

"I have enough to seed about ten miles at the moment. We can build enough for another ten miles in two or three days if I can get priority on the TOO facility."

John looked at Jim and replied "You have full priority, build as fast and as much as you can." With that, Jim headed off to get production rolling.

Jim headed off sending messages from his encrypted phone when John yelled after him "Let's get those special CIA helicopters headed to the border. I think we want the seeding done as invisibly as possible. Also, I'll try and get a few more rigged up for interception."

"I'll get it rolling over at the CIA and let you know when we get them in position. As soon as we get the maps from Homeland, I'll get them down here." With that, Jack headed off at high speed.

By four pm, Jack was headed back with the classified disc from Homeland Security showing where gaps were located that needed to be covered. Also NSA had intercepted a phone call on the Mexican side by El Paso setting up a major meeting with one of the voices having a sound somewhat Arabic. The meeting was to take place at the home of one of the main drug lords twenty miles south of the border around El Paso Texas tomorrow.

Word of the helicopter locations had been received. The current cloaked helicopters would not reach there in time. John looked at Jim.

"Yaah boss, if you can get me there tonight, it takes about three hours to install."

"Okay, grab what you need and who you need, there'll be a helicopter top side to take you to the jet as soon as you can get ready."

"On it, we should be airborn within the hour."

Jim dashed out of the room and down to the next door. As soon as he entered, he yelled to Brandon to get four of the monitor devices and two spare power sources along with the laptops with cloaking communications. He rushed over to grab two variable invisibility cloak units and when they had what they needed, they headed for the elevator.

When Jim and Brandon emerged, two secret service agents grabbed some of the equipment and helped them lug it to the waiting helicopter topside. After they had all the equipment on board and the doors shut, the helo lifted off and headed for the Andrews Air Field where a private jet was waiting. As the helo landed, they swiftly moved the equipment to the jet.

Once the doors were closed on the jet, the pilot radioed that he needed priority take off and was cleared to taxi to the end of the runway. The commercial jets in the area along with the training Air Force jets were held as the jet took the next lift off window and within the hour window Jim had indicated, they were airborne.

While flying, Jim and Brandon went over the equipment to make sure everything was in operational order. Since the two had left in such a rush, phone calls were routed through the radio allowing Jim and Brandon to call their wives from the plane letting them know they would be away for a few days on an emergency national security mission.

When the plane landed at the Army base outside of El Paso Texas, Jim and Brandon were escorted to a hanger where two helicopters were waiting to be outfitted. Each could carry an Army Ranger unit of four along with the pilot and one extra person. In this case Brandon and Jim would be going along on the operation since they needed to handle the equipment and help the pilot. There was not enough time to train someone to operate the equipment.

After two hours, each of the helicopters had been outfitted with the cloak technology and Jim and Brandon were satisfied that it was as good as it was going to get. The monitor devices were divided between the two helos to have more possibility for success. As they were finishing up the outfitting of the helo's, the Army Rangers appeared along with the pilots for briefing and the teams headed to the classified briefing room as Jim and Brandon grabbed a storage locker box and carried it in to the room. After the normal flight plan operational briefing, the room was evacuated of everyone but the two teams and Jim moved to the front of the room.

"You need to be aware that you are on the most classified mission of your lives. The technology that we will be providing you; is one of the most guarded secrets on earth and whatever we do, we cannot allow this technology to be exposed or put at risk, even at the cost of our lives. If any of you do not wish to go, you have my promise it will not be in any way held against you. However if you do decide to continue with the team, you will never be able to talk about this mission to anyone, at any time, for any purpose, for the rest of your lives. Can you agree to this?"

Jim looked around the room at each man. He asked each man individually and received an affirmative. After everyone agreed, Jim and Brandon pulled out the cloak goggles from the storage locker and passed them out to the Rangers.

"This is your personal device; under no circumstances can you allow this to get lost to the enemy. Please put them on now." After everyone put on the set, Jim continued. "Okay, reach up an on the right side you will feel a small switch. This will turn them on. Everyone turn them on now." As he watched, each of the eight Rangers flashed out of sight except for the small dots which seemed to float in the air above their heads.

There was a group gasp as each Ranger realized he could see nothing of his team mates. Jim continued, "If you look around, you will see the small floating dots...These are the eyes that are visible, each of you have a set of eyes which broadcast to the screen in front of your eyes. The invisibility cloaks are active as long as the switch is on. Don't worry, there is no physical effect and they are perfectly safe. This only blocks you from view, not from any dangerous things such as a bullet; this is not a physical shield, only an invisibility shield.

"Pilots, yours will be connected to a separate set of video inputs outside of the helo so you can see what is going on. It will be like flying in bad weather. It may be a little strange for a time, but we will be monitoring flight path and altitude with our special computers to make sure we don't get into any real problems. You should get a handle on this before we reach our targets.

"You have noticed, sound is not blocked, so stay quiet when you approach your targets. Please turn off the units now." As the Rangers returned to view, Jim asked, "Any questions?"

"How do I shoot, will it have an effect on my gun?" one of the Rangers asked.

"You will not be able to use the sight on your guns; the cloak will block any penetration of light through the site where it enters inside the cloak. You will need to shoot from the hip."

"Any other questions? No? Okay let's head out."

When the team was leaving the room, Jim pulled Brandon aside and asked if he really wanted to go on this operation. "Look boss, this is no worse than what I have been through already in the army, I'll be fine."

"Okay, just no hero stuff." With that, Jim slapped Brandon on the back and they followed the rest of the team. They quickly headed back out to the hanger to get underway.

After lifting off, the two helicopters headed to a desert area just north of the U.S. boarder and after radioing in, turned off their radios and each helicopter set off on its own flight plan. As they separated, Jim and Brandon indicated to the pilots that it was time and with a positive feedback, threw the switch on the cloaking device and the helicopters went invisible. The field was set to spike visible for one hundredth of a second every second; this had become a common feature in all their implementations.

With the computers that Jim and Brandon had in their laps, the path was being mapped to allow them to ensure they were on the correct flight plan. After ten minutes, they crossed over the border separated by quarter mile and each helicopter went to silent mode. Using the Russian encryption, during the hundredth second windows, Jim and Brandon were able send each other messages to ensure that both were aware of their progress.

The helicopters approached the home of the drug king; each found a place to set down. Brandon and Jim each took two of the monitor devices and the teams were off. As they crept forward to the house, they came in from two different directions. Jim's team came in from the west and Brandon's team approached from the east.

The area was swarming with Mexican men heavy with guns that needed to be avoided, so the teams crawled through the grass and brush slowly making sure that they made no noise. As Jim's team approached the house, they could see that the window was looking directly in on one of the meeting rooms in the house; Brandon's team could see the window on the other meeting room as they slowly progressed forward.

Jim had just planted the devices when they heard dogs barking. Brandon was five feet from the window when the dogs rushed out of the front door and turned to the right towards Bandon's team. In the rush of the moment, Brandon rose up and rapidly reached the side of the house to plant the devices on the window.

The dogs couldn't see anything, but sensed and smelled the teams' presence. One of the guards fired in an arc in the general area hitting one of the Army Rangers and one of the dogs. The other dog hit Brandon full force knocking him to the ground. Brandon pulled his knife and stabbed the dog. As the dog fell, Brandon rolled away from the the limp body when one of the Rangers opened fire shooting two of the guards. A third guard shot where the dog lay bleeding from the knife stab and hit Brandon. The Ranger released another burst of gunfire and brought down the third guard while the two remaining Rangers went over to help their fallen comrades.

The Rangers could see the small camera positions and swiftly grabbed hold and started dragging the team members off into the bushes. When the remaining guards approached where the fight had occurred, they found one dog shot, the other stabbed and three guards dead from gunshot wounds. As two guards followed the dragging and blood trails, once they reached the bushes, the Rangers were upon them and swiftly and quietly slit their throats then turned back to get Brandon and the Ranger to the helicopter.

Jim's team reached their helicopter and after Jim placed the relay station down by a bush, the helicopter silently lifted off to head back. The second team was able to get the injured Ranger into the helicopter and as they lifted Brandon into the helicopter realized that the shot had found its mark and the head wound had been fatal.

The communications Ranger team member moved into the seat where Brandon had been and swiftly reviewed the screen of Brandon's laptop. The windows that had been used were still open and operating. He sent a short email to Jim indicating that Brandon was down and he was taking over and then with a hand motion signaled to the pilot to lift off.

While they headed back along the indicated flight path, a message came across from Jim asking what had happened. The Ranger indicated through the message window that Brandon had died from a shot to the head and that one of the other Rangers had a gunshot wound to the shoulder but the devices had been planted.

Once Jim heard that the devices had been planted, he opened a special window on his laptop and entered an activation code. The message was a radio burst through a satellite phone that was received by the D.C. team computers which initiated another trigger that issued a trigger through the relay to activate the listening devices.

|||||

The CIA started receiving the message stream as the drug people were discussing what had happened.

"You stupid people! You killed your own men and the dogs. What's wrong with you, don't you know the difference between wind and men? Look at the mess you have to clean up and our visitors will be here soon."

"Someone was out there!"

The boss yelled "Did anyone see someone? Tell me, anyone?" That's because there was no one! I didn't see anyone on the monitors, just your stupid men shooting like idiots!"

"There was someone there, don't call us idiots, we were attacked!"

The drug lord quickly pulled a gun and shot him in the head, ending the argument.

Turning to some of the other men the leader yelled "Now clean up the mess before the Somali people arrive for the meeting."

An hour later, sounds of a car arriving were heard on the recording. Shortly thereafter, the Somali's voice could be heard as the drug lord asked him into the meeting room. After an offer of tequila, they got down to business. The Somali offered the drug lord a $200,000 U.S. payment for taking four backpacks across the border. As the haggling continued, the price began to rise. The Somali wanted to make sure that no one would attempt to look in the backpacks and that cost him an extra $100,000 per pack.

Each backpack was to be delivered to a different point along the border. Half the money would be paid now. One eighth would be delivered for each of the packs that reached their delivery point by the agreed to date. Total agreed cost, $20 million dollars, U.S.

The delivery points were on a map that the men were pointing too and locations were not spoken, so the CIA didn't know where the hand offs would be.

|||||

The helicopters reached their base with all in a somber mood. Brandon's body was quickly taken to the base morgue and the other Ranger was taken to the base hospital for treatment.

Jim called John to report the sad news and to get an update on the monitor devices.

The motion field plants were already in the air for the initial drop and were scheduled to arrive within the hour.

John rounded up Janet, Randy, Valerie, George, and Bob to give them the sad news about Brandon. Bob insisted he'd lead the group to go tell Jennie. The small families sadly drove over to Jennie's home and on arrival, walked to the front door. As they approached the door, Janet clasped her pendent and Randy's hand to help calm herself for the pain she knew was coming to her friend. John knocked on the door.

As she opened the door, Jennie sensed something was wrong.

"Hello Jennie, do you mind if we come in and talk?"

"Hi, yes please do, it's a bit of a mess if you don't mind, but come on in," she said nervously.

John began after they sat down and made sure Jennie was sitting. "Jennie, there is no easy way to say this. We have some bad news. We just got word that Brandon was killed while on a mission to intercept terrorists." The look of shock on Jennie's face was devastating, as they knew it would be.

"We received word that there was to be a terrorist attack on Denver and Brandon volunteered to go with Jim to plant listening devices to help gather information so we could try and prevent the attack. He was doing-so when he was killed. "

Bob calmly took over for John "We are here for you. You will not be alone, I know how painful this is for you and we will all be here to help you through this."

Valerie, who had sat next to Jennie, took her in a hug to let her cry.

Randy, Janet, and John went into the kitchen and made some hot tea with George to give Jennie a few minutes with Bob and Valerie.

After a while, George and Valerie insisted that Jennie stay in their guest room so they could be close and help with the babies. So the team helped her pack some bags and as Jennie picked up Nathiena. Janet picked up baby Brandon as they moved Jennie and the children to Valerie and George's home to help provide love and try to heal the pain of loss.

|||||

Jim didn't have time to grieve, that would come later. As the shipment arrived, it was rapidly transported to the air hanger and boxes were loaded into the cargo area. After the first helo was loaded, the pilot took off with Jim and two of the Rangers. As the approached the initial area that needed to be monitored, Jim showed the Rangers when to drop the sensor units.

Each sensor consisted of six micro cameras producing a 360x360 degree view with a power unit the size of a small pea and a micro processor chip that controlled the cloak and radio. It didn't matter what orientation the unit landed in, it would provide the necessary motion detection and reporting ability. The whole unit was the size of a 3 inch rock. The units were tossed out along the paths that were snaking across the desert. Where ever there was a wide area, its edges were seeded. Periodically, a transmitter was dropped in a bush to coordinate and relay detections.

The second chopper reported that it had been loaded and was proceeding to the second marked area. After Jim had the initial team trained, he was dropped off in the desert and soon the second chopper appeared and took him on board. The second team was trained to disperse the monitor devices the same way as the work continued. After the initial load distribution was completed, the choppers headed back to base and once at high altitude, turned off the cloaking device before reaching a populated area.

As soon as they reached the hanger, Jim turned on his laptop and after getting into his personal space, pulled up the activation window for the monitoring sensors. With a command, the signal was sent and satellite command was issued to the transmitters to activate.

Each transmitter issued a signal that the sensor units picked up and initialized their program. First, the cloak was deactivated for one hundredth of a second coordinated with each camera capturing an image. In addition, a GPS measurement was made and reported back to the transmitter. The transmitter coordinated the location of each reporting sensor unit and built a mapping of the sensor field. Upon completing the initial operations, the transmitters reported back through the satellite, and Jim's computer registered the field mapping on top of a web based map so he could analyze coverage.

After determining where the gaps were in the field, it was noted and with the next batch those holes would be closed before seeding the next area. Now came the real test, he had to wait for something to move.

With the sun setting, a Mexican coyote moved out leading a group of illegal aliens across the border and headed on the path across the desert to a designated pick up point. Unfortunately for this particular group, where they though there was no monitoring going on and their spotter on top of a nearby mountain in the area didn't see any action, this happened to be the area seeded by Jim that day. The spotter had not seen the cloaked choppers and was totally unaware of the work that had happened.

As the coyote led his band into the desert in the cover of darkness, they crossed into the motion field. The sensors were making images on a one second basis and comparing them to the previous image. When they captured a change that the processor determined was more than a simple movement from wind, it reported the movement to the transmitter.

The transmitter mapped the sensor detections creating a path of movement that it began reporting to the satellite channel and it appeared on Jim's computer and at the team center. This in turn generated a report that was forwarded to the South West Border Security coordination office.

After determining their direction of movement, the Border patrol positioned intercept forces and waited while they walked into the trap. Care was taken to wait until they were outside the range of the mountain spotter so as not to alert him of their ability to track the movements.

Different tactics were employed to make sure that they were not aware that they had been tracked. They were chased by horses, helicopters, whatever to make them think that it was more of a general sweep going on and not a technology tracking.

Until such time as all four backpacks were accounted for, prisoners were kept isolated and not allowed to be returned, as with the normal game of return and re-cross.

Once Jim had trained the teams, he transferred the activation program to the Ranger commander's computer; he just needed an internet or even a wireless connection to activate, and after reporting to John, packed his bags to head home. Additional monitors and re-transmitters were being shipped, but the commander now knew how to seed and activate, so Jim's work was done.

Jim flew back to D.C., bringing back Brandon's body for burial. It was only after leaving Texas when Jim allowed himself to grieve. Brandon was his responsibility; he had recruited him and asked him to come along. Jim's grief left him weeping during the trip home.

Upon arrival at Andrews, John, Bob, and Jack were there to help Jim. A funeral had been arranged and Brandon would be buried in Arlington Cemetery with full military honors under Presidential command. Since this was a CIA operation, Brandon would join the wall of honor at the CIA along with a position in the team's place of honor.

After the funeral, John walked over to Jennie to talk with her quietly. While a few years older than Jennie, he felt a kindred spirit given his history. John's heart went out to her, he knew her pain and he knew that he needed to be the one to help her pull her life back together.

As he held her hand, he looked at her "Jennie, you know I to have lost my family not very long ago. Brandon cannot be replaced, but we're not just a team, we are all a family. Brandon was part of our family and you and the young ones will always be a part of it. I need you to know that I will be there for you and the kids. If you need anything or anyone to talk with, I promise to be there for you. I would like you to stay with the team, I know you don't have any family to reach out too, but we are your family and we will be there for you." After a hug and a kiss on the cheek, John escorted Jennie carrying baby Brandon back to the limo closely followed by Janet with baby Nathiena to be taken back to the team home, as they called George's and Valerie's home.

The team pulled together to give support to its own as Valerie and Janet pulled Jennie into various jobs to help keep her mind busy when the babies were resting. They also split time babysitting for Jennie when she needed to be alone, talk with Bob or just get out for lunch with someone. John made a point of taking her out once a week for lunch and dinner to keep her from being locked in, and he began to treasure their time together.

But unfortunately the job wasn't over. They still needed to find the backpacks.

Jim and the team worked with Homeland security to set up radiation detectors on all roads and freeways leading into and around the Denver area. The Airports were already on high alert in case an attempt to fly in the packs was made. All major transportation was being monitored as the search continued.

With monitoring continuing, over the next week two backpacks had been retrieved from coyotes crossing through the sensor net field. The coyotes had been questioned, but only appeared to know their drop points and their starting pickup points. In addition, they were very sick from radiation exposure. The men with the backpacks would not live long and those that accompanied them were on the edge of surviving.

After Brandon's funeral, Jim was having coffee with John and Jack as they discussed some new projects. On the wall were a number of Janet's and Randy's images from other parts of the universe. As John glanced at one of the images showing an alien forest on the side of a mountain, an idea started in his mind.

"You know its summer time, lots of people hike through those mountains"

"I don't know if they hike on that planet or not," Jack indicated.

"No, I mean around Denver!" John looked at them.

"Oh my God," Jack commented in shook as he looked at John and Jim.

They dashed out of the room and Jim went to check on what monitoring units were available for seeding. John and Jack contacted Homeland Security with their fear.

Homeland immediately called up trails in the Denver surrounding area and sent out orders to start searching hikers in the area. Unfortunately due to the season, there were many people in the parks camping and too few park rangers to cover everyone.

The governor rapidly issued orders that pulled in all off duty police men from Boulder and other cities to support the search. Still, they had too few people for too large an area.

During the search, a truck was detected that radiation detectors indicated was above background as it headed into the mountains. The first police to reach the truck pulled it over and officers started to get out of their car. The passenger leaned out the window and fired, killing one of the policemen and the other ducked back behind the door as the truck speed away. There were already other approaching police cars and a backup chopper was headed in their direction. As the chase raced up the road, the sniper in the chopper took out the driver side front tire which caused the truck to spin out of control and flip off the freeway. As it skidded into a tree on the side of the road, it came to a stop. The police approached slowly with guns drawn, but soon found that the driver and passenger were both dead.

When the police officers searched the truck, they spotted a backpack and backed off. Homeland Security was called in with a robot to remove the backpack and put it into a lead protection box to be taken away.

At the same time, a message was received that "the infidel's time had come to an end and that Allah would soon show his glory." The CIA traced the voice and felt sure that it was from the Somali Al Qaeda. This was considered an indication that the attack was close.

John, Jack and Jim were meeting to discuss what else could be done; word came in over a classified email that the bug on the drug lord's house had detected an argument. The fight had been over the failure to deliver three of the backpacks. The good news was that they received final confirmation that the final backpack was being carried up the mountain through back trails.

Jim rapidly left the room and contacted the Ranger team in Texas with the new information. When he came back five minutes later, he indicated that they had just finished reloading and refueling and each team was adding a radiation detector, Geiger counter. They were now in the air and were flying to Colorado with the remaining motion units and would contact them as soon as they got close.

The maps of the area were located by the software team and John along with Jack and Jim were on the phone to the park rangers in the area to try and decide where best to seed the trails. The area of need was identified and the message was sent to the army rangers along with a high resolution map showing their target area. The terrain was extremely rugged and sending people in was going to be difficult without helicopters to help.

After a few hours as it approached late into the evening, Jim heard from the Ranger units that they were closing in on the target area and had gone cloaked. They were beginning seed operations. As they started the seeding operation, they had immediately activated the re-transmitters to get maximum monitoring of the field.

The rangers were two hours into the operation when a signal came through that movement had been observed. As the monitor operator keep watching, it was apparent it was not a simple animal, the track was too consistent and in a focused direction.

A message was relayed to the rangers with the target track being projected on their map. The two cloaked choppers headed back to the beginning of their field seeding. As the pilots circled back, the flight support operator identified a landing location for each of the helo's to get down. When they approached their landing coordinates, it became apparent that the ground was not level and clean for a landing, so the Rangers were going to have to drop in by line.

The two Ranger teams had their cloaking goggles and also came along with infrared goggles as well. The drop sites were on either side of the moving target just over a ridge around the hill and slightly ahead so that the targets should not hear them as they dropped down. The rangers threw out their attached lines and repelled down with their cloaking goggles activated. Upon hitting the ground, each team formed up swiftly and with guns and their radiation detector headed out.

Each group had a copy of the tracking laptop and was able to see the map of the area along with the movement of the target. As they started to advance on the target, the motion sensor did not pick them up because of their cloaking technology, but they were able send out their positions so they could keep track of each other.

Their target was actually two people as they caught sight of them. The lead man had a rifle slung over his shoulder and was moving forward with a pistol in his hand. They were moving together slowly in tandem, the back man stepping in the lead man's foot prints as they snuck through the grass and underbrush to leave a minimal trail.

The men were very weak, and the man walking in the back with the backpack was obviously the weaker of the two and had trouble keeping up. He kept his hand on his partner to indicate slowing down and kept stumbling with each step. The Geiger counter went wild as the rangers approached the target and it was obvious that the back pack was there and very radioactive. A signal was sent between the ranger units to back off because the zone was too hot. The message was sent to the operation control center that the zone was highly radioactive and attempts to get too close for capture would put personnel at risk.

Within seconds, a message was returned to terminate targets and wait for instructions. The snipers on each team took one of the two men as the teams lead agreed on their specific target. On a given signal, the snipers fired and took down both targets.

The helicopters were told to hold position and report if they see anyone in the area; another unit was coming in to assist with removal. As the rangers watched the area, the sound of a helicopter arriving caught their attention and as they watched through their special goggles, they saw a helicopter high above drop a line over the targets. At the end of the bottom of the line, was a large box. As the box reached the ground, a figure in a radiation suit began to repel down the rope until it reached the ground. Upon reaching the targets, the suited figure pulled the dead targets into the box, along with the radioactive back pack. As the suited figure closed and locked the door, the Rangers were able to see that their radiation detectors dropped to a much lower level. There was still going to have to be work done to clean up the radioactivity along the trail, but the main threat was over.

With the work done by the rangers, they quietly backed out of the area and returned to their helicopters. As they approached, they turned off their cloaking and the helicopters removed their cloaking. The Rangers needed to climb up the ropes to get back into the helicopter. After they were on-board, the choppers banked off to the left returning to the military base outside of Denver for refueling before returning home where they would go through decontamination.

When word reached back to Jack, Jim and John sighed in relief. They were sad over the loss of their friend during the operation, but at the same time a major event had been stopped saving perhaps a one hundred thousand lives according to their CIA contact.

At the following mornings meeting, it was decided by the engineering team, it was time to sit down and look at other capabilities that could be built now that the operation pressure was over. It was time for the engineers and the operations guys to figure out a better way.

||||

The team house had some unusually advanced technology, although much of it hidden; as many discoveries had been made over the past year and new devices developed. In addition to technology innovations, it had sections of art. Some of the art looked like drawings from travel books, but actually represented expensive original drawings and paintings gleamed from the communications showing images of the "Watcher's" civilizations that were part of the original Watcher communications network, all thanks to the efforts of Randy and Janet. In addition, there was a private entrance to an underground high technology based tunnel with linkage to the D.C. Metro and through that link, to the research site, all hidden from any view from satellite or spies that might monitor the street traffic.

The house had its own power source hidden by invisibility cloak; that drew its power from the foundation of the universe, the quantum foam and inter-dimensional connections, thanks to John's discovery. There appeared a number of new construction sites around the nation for power stations in cooperation with a new company "TOO, Inc." that had an untraceable set of funding, but ultimately feed profits back into the nation's coffers as the visible part of the Defense departments budgets dropped. In addition, new sites were under development around the world.

The sites had traditional power generation capability; they oddly had significantly larger power output then would be normal. Extra efforts were instigated to hide the power variance fact. When people tried to investigate, the engineers just talked about a confidential, company secrete technology breakthrough in generation efficiency allowing a newer plant to put out much more energy than an older plant using the same fuel source. This combined with new chemical processes were beginning to make coal, and gas as a backup, a model fuel, much to the displeasure of some of the environmentalist since their funding channels began to dry up as the amount of coal and-or gas required was beginning to shrink.

There were other discoveries that were beginning to be mined in the areas of communications, computing, space travel and materials and the arts. While the team had made fundamental discoveries, they were rapidly moved off to the new TOO conglomerate startup companies with droves of lawyers and accountants spending time to hide the background but funnel the resulting profits back to the public coffers.

The U.S. budgets were getting under control with the savings from the Defense department, the President announced a series of debt forgiveness to a number of poor countries along with initiatives to support building of new power and in some cases, salt water to fresh water conversion plants, all in exchange for implementation of a democratic government. While some people complained, this was a steadfast position that was supported by leaders in Congress and the Senate. The U.S. also ensured that a number of new technology startup companies were involved in providing help to poorer countries as long as they supported and instigated immediate steps for transition to freedom and democracy. This began to shift the world in a new direction that awarded and promoted greater freedom and democracy and people began to see it was to their advantage to change. Some like Saudi Arabia and other Middle East monarchs were pressured to release control and free elections were being organized to support the transition.

There were other areas that were not visible to the public but focused on national security. DARPA was able to quietly and under heavy security bring forward new weapons under deep black programs. At a part of Area 51, work was progressing on adding invisibility to all types of land, sea and aircraft. A plan was underway to add the new power source to tanks, ships and aircraft.

There were extensions of the monitoring devices that had been created that began to turn the tide on Radical elements in the world, exposing their deepest plans and making them impotent and turning against themselves as they knew there must be an internal leak. The movement of Taliban across the Afghanistan border had been significantly reduced as the field motion monitoring devices began to be seeded along trails. One key weapon was a powerful laser that could reach into space and destroy any platform; all powered by an unknown power source and was being mounted on ships and planes under heavy security. In another area, work had begun on using the cloaking technology to isolate the hulls of ships from the electric and magnetic fields in the sea water to reduce the billions of dollars per year in costs for hull corrosion.

|||||

In an office in Moscow, four leaders met, one from the Chinese triad, one from the Chinese government, one from the Russian government and one from the Russian mafia. The face to face meeting was arranged to discuss the reduction of tensions between the Russian nation and the Chinese nation. As they talked, they came to agreement to pull their troops back from the border and move their Navies to a lower readiness level.

Conversation over time moved to the agreement to start sharing intelligence information on the west since that was a common problem. While the Russians and Chinese had made a small portion of their people wealthy, including the political class and the leaders of the mob and triad, the wealth of the west was still where true wealth of the world was centered. They began to discuss agreements to somehow make an attempt to pull more technology and of course wealth out of the west for their joint usage. This work would center upon coordination between the two spy agencies and a working agreement between the mafia and the triad.

|||||

There had been major leaps in language by the BELLOWS team. The understandings gained from the language of the Old Ones had supported major breakthroughs in a wide area of language translation capability. George, Nicky, and Valerie also picked up information that allowed them to begin to understand the language of the Tern's and other races that had formed the network.

Valerie had been able to get John to agree to a day of research with dolphins. She was able to get a specific set of tests to be performed with dolphins that was both photographed and recorded. The test was designed to provide information that could be feed into the neural net machine allowing their research project to move forward. Until they could set up a full lab with computers around the animals, the progress would be slow, but progress was being made.

There was a new set of "Symphonies of the Universe" that were being released by Valerie and an "unidentified" local composer. The music was becoming ragingly popular around the world. Valerie, George and Nicky always smiled when they heard the music being played; it was actually just a set of simple stories of love in the Old Ones language. The decision was made to release the music to help protect the truth behind the truth.

The first actual unveiling of the "Symphonies of the Universe" came in a presentation at the Kennedy Center by the Boston Symphony and the Mormon Tabernacle Choir. The President and many top people were invited. A special section was set aside for a group of university music majors selected by lottery from around the United States and flown in at no cost to them, through the generosity of TOO, Inc.

Other changes were in the wind. Not only technology was evolving, there was a growing concern related to the eventual discovery of the truth about the alien contact. A planning group was created by the President. The exploratory committee was formed around John, Bob, and a few other cleared people that were briefed into the fact that communications with alien races had occurred. The secret planning group was tasked with devising a plan to reach a point of exposing to the world that alien contact had occurred. The question was how to expose the facts and new technology without putting the country at risk and how to ensure that the world would benefit from this discovery, not just the U.S. The plan needed to bring the world together; there was an underlying assumption that there existed a major risk of tearing the world apart if not handled correctly.

|||||

A year after George had taken his walk from the hotel to the sports bar and had his life changed, it changed again. George had lost weight and was down to a trim two hundred pounds thanks to Valerie's help along with the doctors and the security teams help with workouts.

Valerie, George, Nicky, the team, and George's daughters and sons-in-law joined in a celebration of a new family forming through love.

With the return of fall, the leaves were turning golden, the wind outside was cold and the warmth of friends and family inside made the occasion special. George, Valerie's and Nicky's new house on a twenty acre piece of property, heavily forested, just fifteen miles from downtown Fairfax, VA, isolated (and heavily guarded) was large and a perfect setting for the special occasion.

While the party at the new estate was a celebration of the wedding of George and Valerie, it was much more. It was a celebration of a new family with the official adoption of Nicky with the agreement of the Swiss government, new discoveries and a new future for the world.

At the team party John, Jack, Bob, Janet and Randy, Janet and Randy had grown into a loving relationship and were now a couple, joined George, Nicky and Valerie and Jennie in the library. They laughed and hugged as they caught up on some details of the wild ride of the last year. They also saluted Brandon and other missing team members for their sacrifice.

John with Jennie at his side picked up a fork and hit the side of his wine glass to gain attention. After the group quieted down, John began with a large smile on his face and Jennie's eyes focused on him "George, Nicky and Valerie; first I wish to give my personal congratulations on your marriage and to the adoption of Nicky. I wish you only the best," as they raised a glass of champaign in celebration with Nicky drinking sparkling apple cider. "I am so very happy for all of you."

After a short period of time while they all continued their celebration, John walked over and closed the doors to the room to ensure no interruption. John looked at the new family and continued, "Now down to business."

John sat down by Jennie across from George, Valerie and Nicky focusing on them, "If it was possible to re-open the communications channel would you be willing? I know that it was a major stress on your lives. I need you to think and discuss it; it may be possible."

George, Nicky and Valerie were a little stunned, but after some quick visual communications Valerie spoke up.

"We've discussed this topic before amongst ourselves. We knew something could happen to allow the communications to re-open. The simple answer is yes. If we could somehow have more control so that it did not overwhelm Nicky and George, it would be the best option, if we can. If we can't, then we'll learn to deal with it."

With a smile, John continued "I was hoping you would say that. We think we can build a device that will give us some limited ability to communicate. It will take some time and will need your help, but it should be short bursts to start. If we can find a way to work with the Tern-Care Giver connection, we think we can re-establish a coordinated working community across the universe."

As John glanced at Jack with a grin, Jack spoke up "Okay, but while you work out the details, I have a date with my family at a sunny resort for three glorious weeks of relaxation."

Everyone laughed, John looked at Jack with a smile and said "It's about time you treat them right!" and with that they all raised their glasses to celebrate the new family and their new lives and futures.

|||||

On the other side of the world, planning was taking place for a different purpose, to try and penetrate the TOO company. The Russians and the Chinese had come to a working agreement that this fast growing company with connections to energy companies must have technology that could provide profit. They were spending increasing amounts on coal and oil while a study of U.S. energy companies showed where this company was involved, reductions in use of coal, oil or natural gas occurred, however energy output increased.

The leaders of the two countries turned to some of their subordinates in the area of security and spying to find solutions. As planning began, two security leads were discussing how they might get access to the technology of TOO, Inc. As Gu from China and Alexia from Russia were attempting to lay out a plan without letting the other gain control of their resources, they were holding a meeting in a hotel in Tehran, Iran.

Gu gave his first priority, "We have in country teams, both in Jinan and free lance agents, also teams located in North Korea that we use when we wish to enter through computer networks. I can have the Korean team focus on the headquarters of TOO and attempt to find a hole in their computer security system. If we can locate such a hole, we can attempt to find out as much as possible about their finances and technology."

Alexia, offered the second idea, "Between our Russian mafia members and the triad, we should focus on attempting to capture some of their technology and reverse engineer it. They have to ship it and we can hijack one or more of their shipments. After we get our hands on it, we can use one of our shipping companies to move it to Iran where we can jointly reverse engineer their device to find out what their technology capabilities are. Then we share the results."

Gu nodded in agreement, he indicated, "I think a third approach should also be instigated. We should attempt to locate one of their employees that we can black mail to get access to their facility. We could then penetrate, steal the technology, and ship it to Iran where our two countries can reverse engineer their technology."

Once the outline of the work ahead was agreed too, the two leads turned it over to their subordinates to work out details of the planning. A major agreement was that both teams would have shared monitoring at every step, to make sure that they all had access to the information. There was no trust amongst thieves. While not fully trusting each other, they needed each other. Their differences could be settled another day.

The meeting in Iran ended with both men signing a letter of agreement outlining the three prong attack and how the agreement would be jointly taken forward. The signed documents were carried back to each of their leaders, and once agreement at the leader level was completed, the plan would be put into action.

|||||

On a dark road, at 1 a.m. in the morning outside of Manassas, Virginia, John from TOO, Inc. was driving an eighteen wheeler having just left the plant. He noticed a car following him which at this time of night was a little unusual. As he continued down the back road, he suddenly saw two cars pull onto the road ahead of him and suddenly spin around blocking the road ahead.

John hit the air breaks and pulled the truck to a stop. His training took over as his cool and controlled nature from years of field combat controlled his emotions. As he saw men headed for the truck, he reached over and grabbed his special goggles and activated the switch while crawling into the sleeper compartment.

The men approached the truck, opening the cab to get the driver out; no one was inside and the keys were gone. The highjack team lead yelled in frustration to his team to spread out and find the driver. Meanwhile, John could hear someone trying to get into the back of the truck. Using the remote switch in his pocket, he activated the destruction button that caused the rapid melt down of the classified components of the power devices he was transporting. John also triggered a remote emergency signal he had in the sleeper compartment to signal security at the plant that he was under attack.

After a couple of minutes of searching, the highjack leader screamed in anger to his team it was time to kill the search. Someone jumped into the truck's driver seat and began to hot wire the ignition. After a short time, the truck engine started up and they were underway.

At the TOO headquarters, the security team watched the monitors as the truck started moving and began tracking its path. A call was placed to John and Jack with information that the truck had been high jacked, John was onboard with cloak activated and the power unit's technology had been destroyed. Jack immediately issued an FBI team to standby for a takedown.

While the truck was on the move, the software team reported to Jack that there was an attempt to penetrate a firewall on the TOO, Inc systems. The team had installed a number of traps to identify and block anyone trying to find access into the system and back track their location. In conjunction with GD Cyber Security team under contract, they had tracked it back through thirty or more transition points, to a known computer group in North Korea that worked in offensive computer operations, which had linkage to China cyber attack teams for support.

The software team raced to complete the process which had previously been started, of setting up a dummy system for trapping the North Korean attackers. The idea was to funnel their probing to a dummy server location that contained false data. Thus they would think they had broken through the defenses unseen, but would be feed fake documents and information. The team had only a short time to finish putting the final touches on the previously prepared dummy trap.

In addition to the fake documents on the false server, the documents contained viruses of their own. These were designed to track the documents movement and leave open backdoors on any system where they were placed. These "Trojan Horses" were extremely complex and designed to not be detected by any anti-virus scan. They were unique and never been used before in any operation, so no one knew they existed.

The NSA reported to Jack on a message overheard two days before in the listening device in the office of Gu in China related to security matters:

"We have an operational agreement with the Russians in place to attempt to acquire TOO, Inc. technology. We have our orders to pursue our part of the agreement. Contact your people and activate the plan."

Putting the pieces of information together, Jack realized that TOO, Inc was under attack on multiple fronts. A warning was sent to company security lead that additional attacks could be expected and to warn all personnel to be on the lookout for additional probing. In addition, information was transmitted to all sites where TOO technology had been put in place to watch for a potential attack.

When the truck's signal movement came to a stop, it was on the outskirts of Philadelphia. The FBI team had been moving to position themselves for the assault by tracking the signal but not getting close to the truck. As the truck came to a stop, the assault team took an assessment of the area. It was a loading dock to a small warehouse with a chain link fence surrounding the property and a large gate where the truck had entered. The agents could see four men walking around the compound and they appeared to be armed.

John watched as the driver exited the cab and quietly crept to the front seat to see what was happening. Through the special "eyes", he saw that the truck had been pulled inside a warehouse and there were a number of men involved in various activities inside the area. Most of the men appeared to have side arms as they moved around the floor. He heard someone yell "Get the package out!" and soon thereafter heard the lock on the back being cut and the doors opened. A fork lift swung past the cab headed for the back of the truck and he felt the weight of the truck shift as the now worthless power unit was removed from the truck.

John counted the men that he could see from his view in the cab. Using the trucks communications computer, John sent a short message to the control center that he saw the ten men and that he was safe. The truck was stopped and they were unloading the useless power unit. A message came back swiftly, displayed on the goggle imaging area, to hold his position inside the cab and await rescue.

Chapter 20: All is not lost

The year progressed rapidly as the math and engineering team focused on how to get the Universal Communications device to work. The specifications for the version built by the Old Ones was provided in part of the communications, but after much analysis and review, the team was able to design a much smaller unit requiring significantly less power using the connection of George and Nicky's Watcher connections. The version was designed around a chair in the center of a new room in the back extension of the Watcher's new home. The advantage that the team had over the Old Ones was they would use a Watcher with energy focusing as opposed to a machine emulating a Watcher and with energy focusing.

The basic technology of all the various devices that had been created, invisibility, power and now communications, was based on the ability to alter an objects wave pattern. As shown in the new M+Theory as the team called it, every particle and thus every object is based on a complex energy wave pattern that emanates from the multiple dimensional connections. The technology as applied by the team focused on altering the wave pattern such that it changes the flow of energy to and from the various dimensions. The same basic technology used in their other devices was able to be applied to the communications. The difference was that it needed to amplify and modulate the energy transfer, not change its wave structure.

Once the brisk autumn wind started to blow, the team announced they were ready for a trial run. The plan would be to send a single thought and re-connect time that would last for only seconds, but hopefully will catch the attention of the Tern and Care Givers.

While the discussions formed around George having the first shot, George's fatherly instincts felt Nicky deserved the honor and was a much better candidate that had both control and stamina to make the broadcast. As the time came, Nicky sat in the chair and the brain monitor was brought on line for both George and Nicky. As the engineers nervously monitored all their computer consoles, with each stage of power increase, a series of tests were executed to ensure the system was operating as expected.

Finally with the last step ready to execute, a count-down was initiated.

On cue, the power activated for the final step, Nicky's eyebrows scrunched together as he focused his mind to send the image of the basic equation set along with a number that represented the time period to wait. When they next connected, the number would be the basis of setting a time scale for their communications pattern.

George's smile showed he was able to instantly receive the message, so they had a bit of a feedback that it worked. The team needed to wait for the time period and recharge their power storage for the next interval.

|||||

In the Tuqvx galaxy, with the ending of the Watcher communications, work pressed forward on the movement of the Tern population before their star changed. The Terns were found to be a resourceful race and swiftly adapted to the changing conditions during their transit to a new home.

As the slow transit took place from the Tern's home planet, the last of the ships were two stars out from the Tern's home star when it happened. The monitors left behind by the Old Ones broadcast the transition of the Tern's home star as the surface erupted and swelled outwards, incinerating their home planet and becoming a red giant. As the transition continued, the star color began to change as the light from the new elements that had formed began to radiate. As the Tern population watched the monitors there were tears of loss and tears of joy at their salvation.

Jzzed the Watcher Tern was visiting a new planet called Txtrn by its inhabitants, in the Tuqvx galaxy managed by the Care Givers. Jzzed had continued to work with Care Givers and moved to work with this new civilization, a young race that had just recently been introduced to the galaxy.

The transfer of the Tern civilization was underway and the ships were in transit to the new world being formed. Many small ships were coming and going from the main fleet as key members of the Tern population were being introduced to current members of the galactic society and being welcomed. Members of the Tern population were being transported to visit new civilizations as they transited to their new area of the galaxy. Sometimes Terns would stay to get an in-depth learning experience with a new race while others would meet with leaders of a race and soon depart back to the main fleet.

The Watcher signal was instantly recognized by Jzzed. With his four eyes expressing his excitement, a message was relayed that someone had just opened the communications channel. The Care Givers had not focused on the channel since the Old Ones had terminated communication. Not that they didn't care, but rather they had many challenges in their own galaxy and had just not considered it a priority at that time. But that changed as their analysis with the new information, a new part of the Master Pattern was revealed to the Care Givers triggered by this connection.

The communication had been previously added to their analysis of the Master Pattern, but on termination by the Old Ones, a thirty percent chance was computed that communication would be re-established. Through the analysis with this new contact; the Care Givers estimate a ninety percent prediction that this young race would be the focus and key intersection of a new evolution of the pattern.

|||||

On a large moon around a gas giant planet orbiting a blue star in a galaxy half-way between the Milky Way and the Old One's now destroyed galaxy, a tri-ped creature with three arms, three eyes and an armored skin known as Jxxn of the Lwax, a clan within the Jmaxiax race, listened to the Watcher communications. The galaxy they resided in was known by the Jmaxiax as Lquid. Jxxn was a Watcher pattern.

The Jmaxiax had an advanced mental capability and its race had achieved travel between stars within their galaxy. They were aware of the equations forming the universe's design and Jxxn had gained information beyond the Lwax's and Jmaxiax's own discovery from the broadcast of the Old Ones. Jxxn belonged to one of the minor clans, the Lwax and was working with their top scientist to try and find new and more powerful weapons.

The Jmaxiax were not a kind and generous race; they lived by overwhelming and absorbing the technology and resources of other races until nothing is left, then move on to another target. They are like a locust race within their galaxy. There were other races within the galaxy that had also reached the ability to move between stars and were constantly at war with the Jmaxiax to survive against this malevolent species, a war that had lasted for a very long time, a complete rotation of the galaxy. Jxxn listened but did not answer to the Watcher network.

The Jmaxiax were always in search for new feeding grounds. Their approach was to sneak in and capture technology. Once they had any advanced technology, they would destroy defenses and swarm over a planet beaming up biological matter which their ships processed into products for food, energy and building of new ships. When they swarmed over a planet, they would hit with a force of a billion small attack ships grabbing everything alive or dead and delivering the results to their larger mother ships. Their forces were usually a combination of many clans brought together at the time of attack. The Lwax being one of the lesser clans only received a small amount of the collected biomass and thus had a hard time growing to a position which would put them in control.

Jxxn could envision new rich fields spread throughout the universe, ripe for the clan to claim. He only needed a plan to take the lead position of the clan and find these rich new fields. Jxxn was a dreamer, but to other races and planets, his dreams were deadly.

|||||

John sat in the cab of the truck with his goggles active while he focused on the people moving within view and watched. There was a sudden series of flashes and loud noises. The flashes over drove the sensor capability of John's goggles and the sound hurt his ears. Because John was in the cab of the truck, he didn't get the full effect.

Once his eye sight returned, John could see twenty men dressed in black with masks, swarming over the interior of the warehouse grabbing guns from the thugs and wrapping their hands in tie wraps behind their backs. After fourty five seconds, it was over.

John could not turn off the goggles sitting in the front of the cab, so he had to crawl into the sleeper unit and pulled the curtain closed. The motion inside the cab alarmed two of the FBI agents who opened the doors on the cab.

"Come out with your hand laced over your head. NOW!"

John turned off the goggles and tossed them into the back of the sleeper unit; laced his hands over his head as directed and pushed his head through the curtain. One of the FBI agents climbed into the cab, he grabbed John's arm and cuffed him pushing his head down into the truck seat. After he was cuffed, John spoke up.

"I am John Tafney, I am a TOO employee driving this truck. I want to talk to your supervisor."

The FBI agent holding a gun pointed at John grabbed his radio mike off his shoulder.

"Bill, we have a man here that says his name is John Tafney from TOO, and wants to talk with you."

Bill, the FBI on-site supervisor, responded with, "Hold him, I'll be right there."

After a minute, Bill came around and stepped up into the cab.

"I need to see some ID"

"My company ID is in the document compartment. Also you can talk with the company."

Bill dug through the document folder looking for the indicated paperwork. He found the TOO security badge with a picture of John. A message shortly arrived over the radio that TOO instructed the FBI that a driver by the name of John Tafney should be in the truck and should be protected at all costs.

While they released the cuffs on John, Bill turned to him with a questioning eye. "How were you not captured when they took the truck?"

John looked at him, pointed to the badge that he now had draped around his neck with a marking of "Top Secret" and smiled as he commented, "Sorry, you don't have a need to know".

The operation was over.

|||||

At the appointed time, the BELLOWS team powered back up and Nicky and George listened for any return. There were multiple returns, including Jzzed and Nicky swiftly responded with the next planned time window.

Word quickly spread throughout the team. Hand-shakes, back slapping and hugs evolved into a small party. Somehow a bottle of wine was found around the house along with paper cups. John sent a short message to the President that communications had been re-established with the Care Givers and others.

After the handshakes and hugs of celebration ended, the team swiftly went back to work to try and enlarge the open window time. Work was hard and a second power generator had to be brought on-line, but by the end of the week, the window was now kept open for up to five minutes twice a day and communications were being organized into setting up the Universal Communications network in a formal way. Like all communications, rules were devised to allow passing of information, allowing all to participate and all was a very, very large number.

The first order of business was to continue the initial work to create a map of the location in the universe of the "Watcher" patterns that were capable of communicating. This added a significant amount of input to the mapping of the universe. The Care Givers had a long standing coordinate system that supported definition of points in the universe that became the foundation to be used.

With the loss of the Old Ones who had been the main focus of data transmission, the Care Givers became the data masters that took over the position of teacher. This included the beginning of training in the Care Givers' language and symbology, which added to Valerie's excitement.

During one of the early transmissions, a small Watcher meekly cried out. "Is Sxxty here? I need to talk with Sxxty."

When the Watcher transmission happened, Nicky was in the chair focusing on the community and caught the plea. "We don't know where Sxxty is. Once the transmissions stopped, we have not heard from him. Can I help?"

"My name is Tia and I am from Sxxty's galaxy. We escaped and are adrift in the void between the galaxies. We are supposed to be retrieved, but we've heard nothing, and no one has come to save us."

Nicky was not sure what could be done when Jzzed jumped into the conversation. "Please do not worry. I'm sure they'll arrive to take you to safety. We'll be here for you to talk to until they arrive."

"Thank you. I will let the others know that we are talking. I'm sure they will be happy to know that others know about us."

There was an off shoot of the main threads to discuss what had destroyed the Old Ones galaxy. The information provided by the Old Ones indicated an event of massive proportions. The Care Givers had done some quick calculations based on The Master Pattern and while the probabilities were astronomical, but there was a finite chance that a new universe had been born and was interacting with our current universe. Plans were made to work with reporting Watchers that were located in the part of the universe in the general area of the Old Ones galaxy to try and track the event.

The communications continued with the larger community but with each transmission period, care was taken to let Tia know they were not forgotten. The community waited knowing that being in the void meant that Tia and the souls on-board were still at risk from the rapidly expanding destruction from the energy wall.

With Watchers beginning to report what they could, not all had the level of technology to be able to map their locations or in some cases to even learn the Care Givers language. As reports filtered in, Nicky recognized the image of a young female that looked to be about his age. She was able to report her location that her planet's scientists had helped her work out. She called herself Jxry and while looking very much like a human girl, her skin color contained a light green tint. She was located in the Andromeda galaxy, close to the Milky Way galaxy.

The mapping of Watcher locations continued. Particular focus was made on the region around where the Old Ones had existed. It became apparent that an intrusion into the universe was taking place, much as a bite out of an apple removes a chunk. At this point, the reports from those near the event, extremely nervous as to their survival, spoke of sensing the effect of star shakes. A very few in different galaxies reported that strange ships were observed heading towards their planet and then the news came.

After the first month, communications were flowing smoothly. On a sunny Saturday afternoon during the planned communications window, George happened to be in the chair with the communications activated, when suddenly, a sing-song message of undeniable origin came in with the simple words..."Some of us survived, we are heading to the following coordinates."

Once the BELLOWS team got over the shock, they worked on trying to understand where the coordinates were indicating. As the astrophysics team worked with John to map the coordinates provided, the answer was stunning.

They looked at each other with large smiles and together spoke as one, "The Milky Way galaxy."

Appendix – Definitions

Black Program

A black program is the designation assigned a highly secret program. It is typical that these programs budget are hidden within the visible budgets of DoD and other agencies to avoid detection or exposure although they may be hidden in a top secret Presidential budget that few are ever aware of. Black Programs may even have their program names considered highly classified meaning that no reference of the program's existence is visible outside a limited group.

BELLOWS

BELLOWS is the name of the classified black DARPA program forming the basis of this book. Classified names are generated on a random selection for highly classified programs as to have no relationship to the program's intent in case the name is ever reveled in an unclassified environment.

Dark Matter

A term initially coined by Fritz Zwicky in 1933 through the discovery of evidence for apparent missing mass in galaxies. Through computations of gravity effects on galaxies, the need for additional mass was determined to be required to support known observed results. The difference between what is needed and what is observed is called "Dark Matter". From computations there is an estimate of almost four hundred times more "Dark Matter" than visual matter needed in a galaxy to properly gain the visual rotational effects observed. Computations estimate that twenty three percent of the matter in the universe is Dark Matter. Dark Matter has fundamental effects on the structure and development of galaxies in our universe.

DARPA
Defense Advanced Research Projects Agency. DARPA is a part of the U.S. Department of Defense (DoD) founded in 1958 in response to the launch of the first satellite by Russia (sputnik). The agency is responsible for high risk-high reward programs. These programs are focused on development of solutions for DoD and cover a wide range of areas from weapons development to cyber applications. Normal DoD development programs are typically medium to low risk programs. DARPA deals in small program teams that have the potential for significant advances in short time frames. Some well known results are the Internet and its space based development was split off to form NASA (National Aeronautics and Space Administration).

M-Theory
In theoretical physics, M-theory is an extension of string theory (see below) in which 11 dimensions are identified. The theory is based on the vibration which some describe as a "membrane" of energy across the multiple dimensions. M-theory was proposed in 1995 by Edward Witten in a way of solving the multiple solutions provided by Hyper String theory based on a 10 dimensional solution. M-Theory also is known by some of its critics as "Magic theory" because of some of the unusual aspects of its outputs such as infinite parallel universes. To date, M-Theory is incomplete and some think may require new more powerful math to be able to formulate a correct description of the theory. Work is ongoing as physics attempts to find a "Theory of Everything".

NSA
The National Security Agency is a U.S. government agency tasked with providing Signals Intelligence for national leadership and the Department of Defense. Their capabilities range from monitoring of cell phone communications to radio and satellite communications around the world.

Quantum Foam
A concept in quantum mechanics and supported in Quantum Theory, String Theory and M-Theory, devised by John Wheeler in 1955; quantum

foam forms the foundations of the fabric of the universe. Foam is used to describe the turbulent creation and destruction of the interactions of the dimensions involved in the creation of the basic particles which combine to form the basic atomic particles. At this sub-sub–atomic level, the interactions of the dimensions that form the foundation of our universe, interacting in a highly dynamic fashion theorized as being a bubbling effect of particle creation and destruction.

String Theory
String theory was derived from the basic oscillation model in theoretical physics in an attempt to unify quantum mechanics and general relativity into a "Theory of Everything". The theory is based on an oscillating string of energy in a 10 dimensional construct forming basic particles from which other particles are formed (electrons, neutrons, protons…). Two major pitfalls have occurred in that a number of valid solutions have been found which brings the theory into conflict with the expectation that there is only one answer for our universe. In addition, no observations are predicted that can be used to prove the theory. From String Theory, arose M-Theory which has shown that the addition of an extra dimension can unify the various string theory solutions.

STRY
The Old Ones measure of time. Fifty STRY relates to over four thousand years of earth time. Each STRY measures the time for a specific star in the Sxvy system to make a rotation around the galaxy.

Sxvy
The galaxy indicated in this science fiction adventure which the species known as the Old Ones originated.

Tern
In the galaxy of Tuqvx is a young race called the Tern's. The Tern's are small large heads and have four eyes. The race is young, but advancing at a rapid rate.

Old Ones
This is an ancient race on the other side of the universe from the Care Giver race located in the galaxy of Sxvy. This race while very advanced has its origins in a carnivorous plant. The race evolved and has the ability

to manipulate its genetic code such that it can take on whatever form it feels is best when approaching a new race that needs help. Like the Care Givers, the Old Ones are dedicated to helping other races within the Sxvy galaxy. The Old Ones are pure believers in the Master Plan and that there is a purpose.

Care Givers

This is an ancient race located in the Tuqvx galaxy on the opposite side of the universe from the Care Givers. This race is of humanoid basis but as advanced as the Old Ones. Like the Old Ones, the Care Givers are dedicated to helping other races within the galaxy of Tuqvx. The Care Givers are tall biped humanoids, dress in robes and in their mid years, their hair turns platinum blond. The Care Givers wear a unique piece of jewelry that contains a genetic trace of their origins. The Care Givers are divided when it comes to the Master Plan. Some are pure believers and think there is a purpose. Others of the Care Givers race are not sure but think it may have no purpose, but just be an evolving pattern.

Tuqvx

The name of the galaxy which in this science fiction adventure the species known as the Care Givers and Tern civilization originate in.

Virgo Supercluster

In astrophysics, this refers to a collection of galaxies in the known universe which includes Andromeda and the Milky Way. The Milky Way is the galaxy which contains our sun (Sol) around which a quiet blue planet called Earth resides.

Coming Soon

The Next in the series
Watcher In The Fall : Conversions

A Quandary

They were an elite squad within an elite division of the Russian army. They had trained for many years to infiltrate and destroy or capture key positions and equipment behind enemy lines ahead of a major push by the Russian Army.

The operation tonight was a little different. Their target was a device within the coal fired electricity generation plant located in Gdarisk Poland. The unit which they were targeting weighed five hundred kgm's and was developed by the TOO Corporation. During their briefing, they had been told to use all necessary force to acquire the object and transport it back to an army lab in St. Petersburg.

The team members had entered Poland via ferry and by bus across the border in street clothes as tourists and had rendezvoused at a small hotel on the outer edge of Gdarisk. The team consisted of six men all trained specialist, one in communications, one was the squad leader and the other four were weapons specialist.

The team lead and one of the members had rented two large vans with a fork lift; purchased wood along with hammers, nails, screws and screwdrivers to support the operation using forged papers and false credit cards before heading to the rendezvous hotel. As they headed to the hotel, they stopped by a small isolated house and picked up a crate.

After the team came together at the hotel, their first business was to build a shipping container inside one of the trucks to load the unit into for transport. The shipping container was sitting in the back of one of the trucks along with the fork lift ready for the signal to activate the operation. After completing the crate building, they opened the smaller wooden crate and pulled out their weapons, radios and special uniforms for night operations.

At 8 p.m., their encrypted radio provided them with the "Black Night go" signal that the operation was to commence. The members quickly picked up their backpacks with their weapons and after checking that no one was watching, loaded into the trucks. Each was dressed in a tight fitting black outfit from head to toe with only a small circle of flesh showing on their face which was to be covered with a black ski mask when they leave the truck.

Before closing the door on the fork lift based truck, the squad leader made one last pass through the room to insure that nothing obvious was left behind to identify them. He then closed the door and jumped into the truck. The truck made a sharp left turn out of the hotel parking lot and headed towards the power station, followed by the second truck.

The team trucks approached the power station on schedule. The truck with only one squad member continued on down the road for later connection. The squad leader silently signaled his team in the main truck to check their communications net and weapons. After receiving a role call that everyone was ready, the truck pulled into a small emergency parking area and as it came to a stop, four of the team members emerged and quickly faded into the trees surrounding the area. The truck backed up and resumed its trip down the road.

Once they approached the tree line by the power station, the squad leader flipped back the cover on his watch and signaled that they needed to wait for five minutes. The operation was set to start at exactly 3:30 a.m.after the main gate security guard on duty had reached his normal morning dozing time after the shift change.

At 3:30 a.m., the squad leader was able to see that guard was dozing and gave the silent signal to proceed. One of the team members crawled forward in the dark areas away from the lights until he reached the small booth where the sleeping security guard was snoring. He swiftly pulled his knife, opened the door and before the guard was aware or awake, slit his throat and proceeded to sit his body up like he was just dozing off.

The remaining team members rushed forward to the gate house as the security gate was opened. The team proceeded to the main building with their silenced guns at the ready. Upon reaching the entrance door to the generation building, the squad leader destroyed the security camera with a single shot and kept the team moving forward down the hall way.

An engineer stepped out of a side room behind the squad the trailing team member swiftly shot him in head with a silent pop. As the team reached the end of the hallway, they opened the door to the main generation room and fanned out to find the TOO unit.

The squad leader came around the side of the fifty meter turbine on the main floor, he received a voice signal that the unit was at the other end of the turbine and altered his path to reach the unit. As he approached he took note of the five engineers lying about on the floor, all dead with head shots, each with a growing poll of blood.

Another signal came in that the equipment bay doors were now ready. The squad leader looked at the unit and identified the key mount bolts holding the unit down, and the major power lines in and out for the unit. One of the weapons men pulled out small units of C4 explosives and attached them to the power line connections while the other man located a large one meter wrench and started removing the four mounting bolts.

The squad leader gave the truck driver the signal, and he made a U turn on the road, and headed back to the power plant. As he approached the main gate, he saw it open and gave the signal that he had entered the gate.

As soon as the signal was received, the team member manning the equipment bay doors, threw the switch to open the rolling doors. As the driver saw the doors opening, he quickly pulled up, stopped and began backing onto the generator floor. The team member that had manned the door started giving the hand signals to position the truck to the correct location.

The truck came to a stop. Three of the squad rapidly opened the back of the truck doors and rolled out the ramp. The truck driver hopped onto the fork lift and expertly backed it down the ramp. Upon reaching the floor, he spun it around and headed to the TOO unit.

With the last bolt being removed, the team swiftly started putting lift straps around the unit and hooking them to the fork lift. At that moment, the switch was thrown on the explosives cutting the power lines and killing all power. The team put on their night goggles to continue the operation. The fork lift driver maneuvered the unit around and climbed the ramp into the truck, dropping the unit with a team members help, into the shipping container.

One of the team members pulled the ramp back into the truck and closed the back door of the truck; the driver hopped back into the truck cab and with a signal from the squad leader, drove the truck out of the building. As they started to emerge, emergency lights on the outside covering the building came on, and a siren started blaring.

The truck emerged from the building. Three security guards came rushing out of an adjacent building with guns drawn. Two of the team members fired killing all three guards with precision shots through the head, and the driver continued to the main gate. After passing through the main gate, the truck turned right onto the road heading away from town.

The truck driver found the designated side road, and after driving down the side road for thirty minutes pulled over so they could assess their mission status and report. As the communications lead listened to local radio traffic, it became clear that while the police were rushing to the power station, no one knew really what happened or any indication of where the thieves were. The team lead sent a burst message to their contact that they were ready for pick up. They opened the back doors and pulled out the ramps.

After backing out the fork lift, two men went inside and finished sealing and packing the container box making it ready for shipment. The fork lift came back into the truck and picked up the box, and backed out of the truck. Once outside, the team hooked up a mounting sling and as the second truck pulled up, the box as placed inside. The driver would be alone as he drove the unit to the ship waiting to leave back to Russia.

The other members abandoned the equipment and after changing to civilian clothes headed out to walk back into town and return to Russia. Their mission was complete and the package would be delivered as planned.

|||||

The meeting was quietly planned and held in the southern Russian city of Krasnoyarsk. The anger and frustration had mounted for a time now and the heads of security for Russia, China and Iran along with triad and Russian mafia sitting around the table could barely contain their rage.

"Every operation we have taken to try and penetrate TOO has failed" commented Gu. "You have made twenty failed attempts to steal power generators. We have no understanding of their technology if we cannot see it. You gave us your word that you would acquire one of the units and all we have are dead men and something that is melted slag when we opened it.

"This is totally unacceptable. How do you explain this failure?"

Alexia glared back, "Don't yell at us, your attempt to penetrate their computers has cost us much time, lives and effort chasing false leads. You told me that you had penetrated their computer networks and what have we found after all this time? I tell you what we found. We found false documents sending us after people that died ten years ago. You have sent us after ships that contained only toys. We have spent millions of rubles chasing down dead people, false leads, and have had to sacrifice key men's lives going after information leads that you said were guaranteed."

The two powerful men sternly stared at each other across the table. Finally the security lead from Iran broke the silence.

"Nether of your teams is at fault, the American company clearly has security that we do not understand and cannot break easily. But we must continue, nothing is perfect and there must be vulnerability somewhere. We need to focus on where it is so we can take advantage."

Gu relaxed bringing out a document from a Chinese research team and handed copies around the table "We have been watching TOO's deployment and the related effects. We are seeing TOO is only dealing with countries that are democracies or headed in that direction. When a TOO generator is added to a power plant, we see one hundred percent boost in output without any visible increase in inputs such as nuclear, coal, gas, and there are no solar or wind generators involved. Our engineers are at a loss, it's like they pull energy from the air, and no known technology can do that."

With a look of condescension, Alexia responded, "Yes, we have already seen drafts of this report. The problem I see is that as these countries have less energy costs, they are quickly taking sides with the United States, and as a result, the shift in power has grown to their advantage. We are seeing middle east countries such as Egypt, Jordon and Saudi Arabia willing to shift their governments to democracy as they now understand that oil is not a wining resource as previously thought."

Trying to gain the advantage, Gu continued, "Yes, our countries are quickly becoming surrounded and our influence is being drained. As the US has shifted its energy output, their military has cut its budget needs and the effect has been dramatic. Our trillion dollar bond portfolio is rapidly being paid down and with it their stance against our regime is becoming much more demanding. Our central committee is not happy and there are hints of a major recession as the weaknesses in our economy are being exposed. I have been given full authority to do whatever is necessary to get this new technology...now.

"TOO has not patented their technology so it's not being exposed, we have had no success stealing it, we cannot bribe people to acquire it from the countries that have purchased it, we have limited knowledge about the people that are in the company and when we have tried to kidnap, that too failed."

The men at the table looked at each other hoping someone would have an idea of a possible course of action.

A New Challenge

Once the newest galaxy jump ships appeared outside their appointed galaxies, on one uncompleted ship was Sxxty and the Watcher communications development team. Having escaped the destruction of their galaxy the computers jumped into action. The Old Ones ship arrived with their special cargo but with less than one percent of their galaxies population, another one percent had been targeted to the older ships and should be sitting in the intergalactic void. Much work needed to be done and little time was available if they were to rescue their older fleet that could not make the complete jump to safe galaxies.

The computers immediate launched probes to start cataloging stars that could support life and understanding what their system design was as well as setting up a star reference system. The computers would then search the incoming data streams to identify most likely candidates for them to approach. At the same time, other units were launched to support setting up their galaxy wide communications net so the various ships could get back to instant communications.

Once the data streams of stars and their planetary design started to arrive, the galaxy jump ships that still needed to complete construction began to identify locations to retrieve resources to allow them to complete their construction and to begin construction on new ships. Having brought construction robots along with material processing robots, they need basic materials.

This was not their final home, it was a resting point to allow them to regroup, expand the fleet, to identify new races that needed help to escape. Then they would move on towards a safer position while their computers continued the work of identifying what distance into the old universe would be safe from this massive energy as it cooled, changed to matter and eventually blended with the old universe.

Sxxty's ship had its own unique mission, since it contained the lead team for the Watcher communications system that had been destroyed; they were tasked with re-engaging with the universe's Watchers. After completing construction and supporting rescue of the older ships stranded in the inter-galactic void, they were to head out from the main fleet. Their trek was focused towards the galaxy of the Care Givers across the universe with a course plotted through the Milky Way galaxy to pay a visit to a unique race where two Watchers existed on the same planet.

With the galactic communications network becoming operable, the ships computers connected and began analyzing the incoming star inventory collected by the probes. The completion of construction of Sxxty's ship was directed to a yellow star with a large asteroid field between two planets each of which could provide short term life support. The ship manager announced that the jump would occur in a few moments as Sxxty broke off his viewing of the galaxy they were about to enter, and readied his environmental suit to help with operations.

Once the quick jump took place, the ship was now located around a planet with little water observable. The ship began to launch mining units to collect needed minerals from the nearby asteroids and started manufacturing of parts to complete construction on their ship.

The mining operations began immediately. A number of environmental units and needed supplies were sent to the planet surface and by the planet's days end, their small transport group of four thousand souls were positioned on the planet surface with their personal environmental and jump suits, while robotic units began the job of adding the needed construction to extend the ship to its full support size of over ten million souls. The ship had made its galactic jump while only sixty percent complete in its construction. To complete construction would take approximately two weeks at which time the ship would jump to its designated rescue point to transfer those which currently were drifting in the galactic void.

Sxxty had transported to the surface and while the ship construction was completed, the teams were organized to scour the planet surface and identify any and all life forms for cataloging. Sxxty was involved with a connection team as they began the work of re-constituting the basic Watcher connection node to form the universal communications.

The Watcher machine design was in two parts; part one was to create the focused energy link to the correct dimensional loops in a proportion to emulate a Watcher pattern. Part two was to energize the pattern to support the network communications. The part to build a unit capable of emulating the Watcher connection pattern was the hard part. The detailed work had pushed their technology to an extreme and would take time to rebuild the tools necessary to support the design, including sending receiving pattern buffers. The energizing of the network was just an energy access problem and that was much simpler to solve.

Before leaving their galaxy, a basic plan had been defined and each ship was tasked with its initial orders. While Sxxty's team was focused on re-building the Watcher machine waiting for ship construction to be completed, word was broadcast that all galaxy jumper ships targeted for this galaxy were accounted for and initial star-planet identification had been made to start the process of discovering any indigenous populations, and working with them to understand the situation. Once agreement was formed, current cargos would be deployed to the worlds and the ships would attempt rescue of the older ships currently in the inter-galactic void.

Work continued on completion of what was now designated NQ1, the construction of the galaxy jumper ship holding the Watcher communication team. Net communications started filtering in that civilizations being approached were populated by non-organic life forms. The planets appeared to be consumed by machines and the machines were aggressive to organic life forms. Initial reports indicated aggressive actions against ships had occurred.

|||||

The intelligence had started centuries before as a research project on advanced cybernetics in a lab. The original effort had not created the necessary security to protect the computer intelligence from escaping lab computers, and had quickly spread across the planet. The resulting machine intelligence was that of a brilliant young child capable of immense learning, but had never progressed further in terms of emotions or emotional control than was originally provided by the original developers. The intelligence had been programmed with a deep seated desire to survive.

The machine intelligence spread from computer network to computer network, taking control of many of the automated planetary weapon systems with its uncontrolled emotions. It fought with the biological units that were attempting to erase it from their systems, turning the weapons created by the biological units against themselves with horrible results.

Within a short period of time, all the biological units had been removed from the planet, either killed or escaped. The intelligence no longer had any boundaries of control within the planet.

Over time, the machine intelligence was able to escape the planetary bounds and began its fight for expansion throughout the galaxy, much as a child wants more toys. The original race had progressed to travel between stars and the intelligence was able to adapt and expand on the ability.

Some of the original race had escaped the initial annihilation of the planet life and had provided key warnings to other civilizations. Advanced civilizations in the galaxy had been able to resist the spreading machines; others were not so lucky and were exterminated as the machines reached their worlds. Those that had survived the initial onslaught of the machines found themselves in an on-going war and the war had gone on for centuries.

|||||

Once the galaxy jump ship appeared at the outer bounds of a yellow star, the ship sensors began to monitor the planetary conditions. There appeared to be two planets capable of supporting life, but the sensors show no life forms in the system. The ship jumped to the more favorable of the two planets looking for life and appeared in an orbit above the planet. The planet had many large bodies of water and all the necessary chemical bases for life, but no life readings were monitoring. As the sensors reached out to scan the planet, suddenly a large metal object appeared to the right of the ship and a moment later exploded destroying a bulkhead on one of the living sections.

The sudden loss of atmosphere in the section caused the death of over three thousand of the transported life forms. The ship manager swiftly transported back out of the system and sent an emergency message. The sensors reported that there was a machine on the planet and had transmitted a message that was interpreted as "Biological Units Must Be Destroyed!" The ship manager quickly jumped the ship to the star system coordinates that had been reported by the ships under construction completion.

The whole event took less than a minute, but the ship had taken a major hit. As engineers started reviewing the attack, it appeared that a bomb had been transported next to the hull of the ship. The bomb appeared to be of nuclear fusion design. If the bomb had appeared closer to the center of the ship by a major structural location, the complete ship would have been lost. The ships automated defense systems had not reacted fast enough, they had been tuned to deal with those offensive systems the Old Ones had previously run into, not a massively aggressive fast reacting computer life form with advanced technology.

While the Old Ones had found aggressive civilizations before, none had approached their technology, and none had been a threat to them. This was new and not expected. While Master Plan computations had slowed with the loss of their main computers upon leaving Sxvy to its destruction, the current computations showed nothing in the Master Plan had hinted this type of problem, and so no precautions had been taken. Clearly they needed more data, and an alteration to their planning along with more computations.

|||||

Sxxty continued to monitor communications channels, reports of ships being scanned, and attacked continued to filter in over the net channels. By the end of the planets rotation, two of the galaxy jump ships had retreated and jumped to their location. A section of one of the ships had been breached with three thousand passengers killed. Immediately on arrival, the sections of the ship that had been destroyed were under analysis to determine how the machines had been able to penetrate the Old Ones defenses. Chemical analysis, structural analysis along with data recording were being poured over as the threat was being analyzed, and decisions had to be made on how to protect their ships.

The ships were arriving from their initial conflict. A communications channel was set aside to discuss the weaponry that the machines were employing. Discussions also were considering changes in strategy as more of the galaxy exploration was taking place. A new plan was needed.

Sxxty's team continued work on the Watcher machine. After reaching a point where the machine could set up the right pattern, they noticed the pattern was already energized. As Sxxty's communication channel watched the information flow, he found a gap and sent a message "some of us survived, we are heading to the following coordinates" Sxxty then transmitted the coordinates of a galaxy where two Watcher were known to exist on the same planet called Earth.

Much work was still left to be done. The robotic units had completed construction on Sxxty's ship and would soon have the damaged ship repairs completed, while others had started on a new ship. The ships that had just arrived deployed their populations to the planet along with supplies to support them and over the next short period of time, the ships began jumping to inter-galactic space as they attempted to locate some of the remaining older ships drifting the in the inter-galactic void.

At arrival at the set coordinates in the void, the computers quickly took inventory. Of the sixty ships that were targeted for this location, fourty had made it. Long range sensor sweeps showed two ships drifting at the edge of their sensor's ability. Of the fourty, five were in need of emergency help and the other thirty five could last long enough for a shuttle to occur. The ship managers of the three galaxy jumpers began the process of pulling along side of a ship and hooking up via a connection bridge. While some beings transferred via the bridge, others put on jump suits or used jump pins and transported between the two crafts.

The older crafts only handled one hundred thousand so people. After a number of dockings with older ships, the galaxy jumpers were filled and quickly jumped to their initial waterless planet by the asteroid belt where construction was taking place. The cycle of transport was completed in a week's time and the planet quickly grew to become highly populated, if only for a short period of time.

With the ship managers discussing strategy, three options were identified; (a) stand and fight it out with the machines; (b) move on to another galaxy as quickly as possible; (c) learn as much as possible and delay the next jump until ready, meanwhile, devise a form of protection in case the machines located them or they accidently ran into them again.

It was decided to insure proper protection; they needed to use the star and its resources to extend the fleet to build enough ships to cover all the people. Through the communications net, the word was passed that two ships had been destroyed, but five others had made contact with organic life forms that were intelligent and agreements had been made. Given this mixed condition, it was decided to pick option c and work began to extend their defenses.

In their recovery efforts, as the other ships were able to off load their people to return for rescue operations, many of the older ships in the void had not reached their contact point and many souls had died or were lost in the void.

Follow the progress on the website
http:\\WatcherInTheFall.com